THE
HELLION BRIDE

G·K
Hall
&Co.

Also by Catherine Coulter
in Large Print:

The Wyndham Legacy
"The Bride Trilogy"
The Sherbrooke Bride

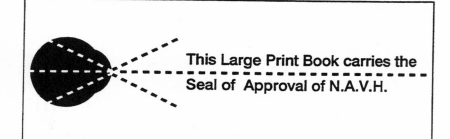

This Large Print Book carries the
Seal of Approval of N.A.V.H.

THE
HELLION
BRIDE

CATHERINE COULTER

G.K. Hall & Co.
Thorndike, Maine

Published in 1996 by arrangement with
The Berkley Publishing Group.

G.K. Hall Large Print Romance Collection.

The text of this Large Print edition is unabridged.
Other aspects of the book may vary from the original edition.

Set in 16 pt. News Plantin by Juanita Macdonald.

Printed in the United States on permanent paper.

Library of Congress Cataloging in Publication Data

Coulter, Catherine.
    The hellion bride / Catherine Coulter.
       p.   cm.
    ISBN 0-7838-1294-9 (lg. print : hc)
    1. Large type books. I. Title.
  [PS3553.O843H44 1995]
  813'.54—dc20
                                         95-9760

To

Penelope Williamson

*An excellent friend and a superb
writer. A woman of infinite good taste,
witness every Tuesday at the Cantina.
Nora's wrong. It won't be s-l-o-w-l-y.*

CHAPTER 1

Montego Bay, Jamaica
June 1803

It was said she had three lovers.

Rumor numbered those three as: the pallid thin-chested Oliver Susson, an attorney and one of the richest men in Montego Bay, unmarried, nearing middle age; Charles Grammond, a planter who owned a large sugar plantation next to Camille Hall, the plantation where she lived, a man with a long-faced, strong-willed wife and four disappointing children; and a Lord David Lochridge, the youngest son of the Duke of Gilford, sent to Jamaica because he'd fought three duels within three years, killed two men, and tried unsuccessfully, because of his phenomenal luck at cards, to spend his grandmother's entire fortune that had been left to him at the tender age of eighteen. Lochridge was now Ryder's age — twenty-five — tall and slender, with a vicious tongue and an angel's face.

Ryder heard about these men in surprising detail — but nearly nothing about the notorious woman whose favors they all seemed to share

7

equally — on his very first afternoon in Montego Bay in a popular local coffeehouse, the Gold Doubloon, a low sprawling building whose neighbor was, surprisingly enough to Ryder, St. James's Church. The crafty innkeeper had gained the patronage of the rich men of the island through the simple expedient of using his beautiful daughters, nieces, and cousins to serve the customers with remarkable amiability. Whether or not any of these lovely young girls carried any of the innkeeper's blood was not questioned.

Ryder had been made welcome and given a cup of local grog that was dark and thick and curled warmly in his belly. He relaxed, glad to be once again on solid ground, and looked about at the assembled men. He silently questioned again the necessity of his leaving his home in England and traveling to this godforsaken backwater all because the manager of their sugar plantation, Samuel Grayson, had written in near hysteria to Douglas, his elder brother and Earl of Northcliffe, describing in quite fabulous detail all the supernatural and surely quite evil happenings going on at Kimberly Hall. It was all nonsense, of course, but Ryder had quickly volunteered to come because the man was obviously scared out of his wits and Douglas was newly married and to a young lady not of his choice. Obviously he needed time to accustom himself to his new and unexpected lot. So it was Ryder who'd spent seven weeks on the high seas before arriving here in Montego Bay, in the middle of the summer in

8

heat so brutal it was a chore to breathe. At the very least, what was happening was a mystery, and Ryder loved mysteries. He heard one of the men say something about this girl with three lovers. Had the men no other topic of conversation? Then one of her lovers had come in, the attorney, Oliver Susson, and there had been a hushed silence for several moments before one of the older gentlemen said in a carrying voice, "Ah, there's dear Oliver, who doesn't mind sharing his meal with his other brothers."

"Ah, no, Alfred, 'tis only his dessert he shares with his brothers."

"Aye, a toothsome tart," said a fat gentleman with a leering smile. "I wonder about the taste of her. What do you think, Morgan?"

Ryder found himself sitting forward in the cane-backed chair. He had believed he would be bored on Jamaica with backwater colonial contentiousness.

He found himself instead, grinning. Who the devil was this woman who juggled three men in and out of her bedchamber with such skill?

"I doubt it's cherries he tastes," said the man named Morgan, tilting back his chair, "but I tell you, young Lord David licks his lips."

"Ask Oliver. He can give us his legal opinion of the tart in question."

Oliver Susson was a very good attorney. He blessed the day he arrived in Montego Bay some twelve years before, for he now controlled three sugar plantations since all three owners were in

England. Not one of the owners seemed to mind that he was a competitor's attorney. He sighed now. He had heard every provocative comment and he never showed any emotion save a tolerant smile.

He said with an easygoing bonhomie, "My dear sirs, the lady in question is the queen of desserts. Your jealousy leads your tongues to serious impertinence." With that, he ordered a brandy from a quite striking young woman with wild red hair and a gown that offered up breasts as creamy as the thick goat milk served with the coffee. He then opened an English newspaper, shook the pages, and held it in front of his face.

What the hell was the woman's name? Who was she?

Ryder found that he really didn't want to leave the coffeehouse. Outside, the grueling sun was beating down, piles of filth and offal on all the walkways, thick dust that kicked up even when a man took a single step. But he was tired, he needed to get to Kimberly Hall, and he needed to soothe Grayson's doubtless frazzled nerves. Grayson was probably even now at the dock wondering where the hell he was. Well, he would discover all about this so-called tart soon enough.

He paid his shot, bid his new acquaintances goodbye, and strode out into the nearly overpowering heat of the late afternoon. It nearly staggered him and he found himself wondering how the devil one could even want to make love in this inferno. He was immediately surrounded by

10

ragged black children, each wanting to do something for him, from wiping his boots with a dirty cloth to sweeping the path in front of him with naught more than twigs tied together. They were all shouting "Massa! Massa!" He tossed several shillings into the air and strolled back to the dock. There were free blacks in the West Indies, he knew, but if they were free, they couldn't be more ragged than their slave brothers.

On the small dock, the smell of rotting fish nearly made him gag. The wooden planks creaked beneath his boots, and there was a frenzy of activity as slaves unloaded a ship that had just docked. Both a black man and a white man stood nearby, each with a whip in his hand, issuing continuous orders. He saw Samuel Grayson, the Sherbrooke manager and attorney, pacing back and forth, mopping his forehead with a handkerchief. The man looked older than Ryder knew him to be. When he looked up and saw Ryder, Ryder thought he would faint with relief.

Ryder smiled pleasantly and stretched out his hand. "Samuel Grayson?"

"Yes, my lord. I had thought you hadn't come until I chanced to see the captain. He told me you were the most enjoyable passenger he's ever had."

Ryder smiled at that. The fact of the matter was, he hadn't slept with the captain's wife, a young lady making her first voyage with her much older husband. She'd tried to seduce him in the companionway during a storm. Captain Oxenburg

11

had evidently found out about it. "Oh yes, I'm here, right enough. I'm not a lord, that's my older brother, the Earl of Northcliffe. I'm merely an honorable, which sounds quite ridiculous really, particularly in this blistering sun, particularly in the West Indies. I believe a simple mister in these parts is quite sufficient. Good God, this sun is brutal and the air is so heavy I feel as though I'm carrying an invisible horse on my shoulders."

"Thank God you are here. I've waited and wondered, I don't mind telling you, my lor— Master Ryder, that we've trouble here, big trouble, and I haven't known what to do, but now you're here and, oh dear, as for the heat, you'll accustom yourself hopefully and then —"

Mr. Grayson's voice broke off abruptly and he sucked in his breath. Ryder followed his line of vision and in turn saw a vision of his own. It was a woman . . . really, just a woman, but even from this distance, he knew who she was, oh yes, he was certain this was the woman who dangled three men so skillfully. When she bade them dance, they doubtless danced. He wondered what else she bade them do. Then he shook his head, too weary from the seven weeks on board the comfortingly huge barkentine, *The Silver Tide*, that he simply didn't care if she were a snake charmer from India or the whore of the island, which, he supposed, she was. The intense heat was sapping his strength. He'd never experienced anything like it before in his life. He

12

hoped Grayson was right and he'd adjust; that, or he'd just lie about in the shade doing nothing.

He turned back to Grayson. The man was still staring at her, slavering like a dog over a bone that wouldn't ever be his because other bigger dogs had staked claim.

"Mr. Grayson," Ryder said, and finally the man turned back to him. "I would like to go to Kimberly Hall now. You can tell me of the troubles on our way."

"Yes, my lor— Master Ryder. Right away. It's just that she's, well, that's Sophia Stanton-Greville, you know." He mopped his forehead.

"Ah," said Ryder, his voice a nice blend of irony and contempt. "Onward, Grayson. Pull your tongue back into your mouth, if you please. I see flies hovering."

Samuel Grayson managed it, not without some difficulty, for the woman in question was being helped down from her mare by a white man, and she'd just shown a glimpse of silk-covered ankle. To render men slavering idiots with an ankle made Ryder shake his head. He'd seen so many female ankles in his day, so many female legs and female thighs, and everything else female, that he by far preferred an umbrella to protect him from the relentless sun than seeing anything the woman had to offer.

"And don't call me master. Ryder will do just fine."

Grayson nodded, his eyes still on the Vision. "I don't understand," he said more to himself

13

than to Ryder as he walked to two horses, docilely standing, heads lowered, held by two small black boys. "You see her, you see how exquisitely beautiful she is, and yet you are not interested."

"She is a woman, Grayson, nothing more, nothing less. Let's go now."

When Grayson produced a hat for Ryder, he thought he'd weep for joy. He couldn't imagine riding far in this heat. "Is it always this unmercifully hot?"

"It's summer. It's always intolerable in the summer here," said Grayson. "We only ride, Ryder. As you'll see, the roads here are well nigh impassable for a carriage. Yes, all gentlemen ride. Many ladies as well."

Grayson sat his gray cob quite comfortably, Ryder saw, as he mounted his own black gelding, a huge brute with a mean eye.

"It's nearly an hour's ride to the plantation. But the road west curves very close to the water and there will be a breeze. Also the great house is set upon a rise, and thus catches any breezes and winds that might be up, and in the shade it is always bearable, even in the summer."

"Good," Ryder said and clamped the wide-brimmed leather hat down on his head. "You can tell me what's been happening that disturbs you so much."

And Grayson talked and talked. He spoke of strange blue and yellow smoke that threaded skyward like a snake and fires that glowed white and an odd green, and moans and groans and smells that came from hell itself, sulfurous odors that announced the arrival of the devil himself, waiting to attack, it was just a matter of time. And just the week before there'd been a fire set to a shed near to the great house. His son, Emile, and all the house slaves had managed to douse the flames before there'd been much damage. Then just three days before a tree had fallen and very nearly landed on the veranda roof. The tree had been very sturdy.

"I don't suppose there were saw marks on the tree?"

"No," said Mr. Grayson firmly. "My son looked closely. It was the work of the supernatural. Even he was forced to cease going against what I said." Grayson drew a very deep breath. "One of the slaves swore he saw the great green serpent."

"Excuse me?"

"The great green serpent. It symbolizes their primary deity."

"Whose primary deity?"

Grayson actually looked shocked. "One forgets that Englishmen don't know about these things. Why, I'm speaking of voodoo, of course."

"Ah, so you believe all this the work of the supernatural then?"

"I am a white man. However, I have lived in Jamaica for many years. I have seen things that would make no sense in a white world, perhaps things that could not exist in a white world. But the strangeness of the things happening, sir, it gives way to doubts."

Ryder had no more belief in the supernatural than he had in the honesty of a gaming hell owner. When Grayson paused, Ryder was frowning. "Forgive me, but I have no doubts. Simply mixing certain chemicals would produce the smoke and the strange-colored flames. It is a flesh and blood man, no great green serpent behind this. The question we must answer is why and who. Yes, who would do this?"

But Grayson clearly was not convinced. "There is another thing, Ryder. After the French Revolution, there was a revolt on Haiti led by a man named Dessalines. He butchered all the whites and forced many priests and priestesses of voodoo to leave Haiti. These people are powerful; they spread throughout the West Indies, even into America itself, and with them they took their demons."

Ryder wanted to laugh, but he didn't. It was obvious that Grayson felt strongly about this voodoo nonsense. And Grayson was right about one thing: a white man couldn't accept such things as being real, particularly not if he'd lived his entire life in England. He said, "We will see soon enough, I imagine. Ah, I didn't know you had a son."

Grayson puffed up like a proud rooster then he fidgeted with his light gray gloves. "He is a good boy, sir, and he does a lot for me — for the Sherbrookes — now that I am getting on in years. He is waiting for us at Kimberly Hall. He didn't wish to leave the plantation house unprotected."

16

They passed dozens more children, all of them ragged, all of them black, children of the slaves working in the fields, but these children were silent at the sight of the two white men riding in their midst.

Grayson said, pointing to the right and to the left of the narrow rutted road, "We are in the mangrove swamps now. Take care whenever you ride this way for crocodiles come out of the swamps and many times appear like fat logs lying across the road. They will normally eschew the presence of humans, but there have been stories where they didn't, very unpleasant stories."

Crocodiles! Ryder shook his head, but he kept one eye on the sides of the road. The smell of the fetid swamp water was nearly overpowering. He urged his horse forward. There came a flat stretch, the Caribbean on their left and field after field of sugarcane on their right, even climbing the hills that lay in the distance. And there were goats everywhere, sitting on low stone fences, chewing at flowers left on graves in the church cemeteries. There were egrets sitting on the backs of cattle, cleaning them of ticks, Ryder knew. And there were black men, tall, their bare upper bodies oily with sweat, working in the sugar fields, wearing only coarse trousers made of stout osnaburg. They didn't seem to notice the heat, their rhythm steady, as they plowed or pulled weeds or dug deeper trenches between the sugar plant rows. And there were women as well, their heads covered with bright bandannas, bending and straightening like the men in a steady rhythm. Not far away sat a white man on a horse, an overseer, sitting under a lone poinciana tree, its feathery, fernlike leaves shimmering in the sunlight, to see they didn't slack off. The whip in his left hand ensured their continued work.

It was utterly foreign to Ryder. It was exotic, too, with the thick, sweet smell of the frangipani trees that were thick alongside the dirt road, and the startling blue of the water coming into sight at unexpected moments. He was pleased he'd done reading on the voyage here. He wasn't completely ignorant of the local flora and fauna. But he hadn't read about any damned crocodiles.

"We are nearing Camille Hall," Grayson said suddenly, his voice falling nearly to a whisper.

Ryder raised an eyebrow.

"It's her home, sir. Sophia Stanton-Greville's home. She lives there with her uncle and her younger brother. There is one plantation between Camille Hall and Kimberly Hall, but as I understand it, her uncle is soon to buy it and thus add substantially to his holdings."

"Who is the owner?"

"Charles Grammond. Some say he wishes to move to Virginia — 'tis one of the colonial states to the north — but it is a lame reason, one with little credence, for he knows nothing of the colonies or their customs and manners. He has four children who haven't become a father's pride, all of them sons, none of them ambitious or willing to work. His wife is difficult, I've heard it said.

18

It's a pity, yes, a pity."

Ryder was certain he'd heard the man's name in the tavern. He said slowly, "I understand that this woman, this Sophia Stanton-Greville, has three men currently in her bed. I seem to recall that one of them is this Charles Grammond."

Grayson flushed to the roots of his gray hair. "You have but just arrived, sir!"

"It is the first topic of conversation I heard at the coffeehouse, the Gold Doubloon, I believe the name is. And I heard it spoken of in great detail."

"No, no, sir, she is a goddess. She is good and pure. It is all a lie. There are many men here who are not gentlemen."

"But it is the gossip, is it not?"

"Yes, it is, but you mustn't believe it, Ryder. No, it's a vicious lie. Don't mistake me. Customs, the local mores, if you will, are different here. All white men have black mistresses. They're called housekeepers here and it is considered a respectable position. I have seen men come from England, some to work on the plantations as book-keepers, some to earn their fortune, and most change. They take wives and they take mistresses. Their thinking changes. But a lady remains a lady."

"Has your life changed, Grayson?"

"Yes, for a while it certainly did. I was my father's son, after all, but my wife was French and I loved her dearly. Only after her death did I succumb to local custom and take a mistress or a housekeeper. Life here is different, Ryder, very different."

Ryder subsided, letting his body relax and roll gently in the comfortable Spanish saddle. He closed his eyes a moment, breathing in the salty fresh smell of the sea, the coastline no longer obscured by thick clumps of mangrove. "Why is Grammond selling out then, in your opinion?"

"I'm not completely certain, but there are, of course, rumors. It was a sudden decision, that I do know. He and his family are leaving next week, I have heard it said. The plantation is quite profitable. It is said he lost a lot of money to Lord David Lochridge, a young wastrel with whom you must avoid gambling, sir, at all costs. It is said he has sold his soul to the devil, and thus his incredible luck."

Ryder turned to face Samuel Grayson, saying in a meditative voice, "There is every bit as much talk here as there is in England. I had believed to be bored. Perhaps we will have some mysterious manifestations this very night, to welcome me here. Yes, I should enjoy even a ghostly spectacle, if it is possible. Isn't this young Lord David reputed also to be one of her lovers?"

Ryder wondered if Grayson would have an apoplectic attack. He opened his mouth, realized that his employer was seated next to him and closed it. He managed to say in a fairly calm way, "I repeat, Ryder, all of it is nonsense. Her uncle, Theodore Burgess, is a solid man, as we say here in Jamaica. His reputation is good. He is amiable, his business dealings honorable. He loves his niece and nephew very much. I imagine that the vicious rumors of Miss Stanton-Greville's reputation hurt him very much. He never speaks of it, of course, for he is a gentleman. His overseer, however, is another matter. His name is Eli Thomas and he is a rotten fellow, overly cruel to the slaves."

"If Uncle Burgess is such a fine man, why does he have this crooked stick as his overseer?"

"I don't know. Some say he must have Thomas else the plantation wouldn't make any money. Burgess is too easy on the slaves, you see."

"And this Charles Grammond is selling out to the woman's uncle? This Theodore Burgess?"

"Yes. Perhaps Burgess feels pity for Grammond and is simply buying the plantation to assist him and his family. Burgess is the younger brother of Miss Sophia and Master Jeremy's mother."

"How do the girl and boy happen to be here on Jamaica?"

"Their parents were drowned some five years ago. The children were made wards of their uncle."

"I haven't heard the name Stanton-Greville. Are they English?"

"Yes. They lived in Fowey, in Cornwall. The house and grounds are in a caretaker's hands until the boy is old enough to manage for himself."

Ryder was silent, chewing over all the facts. So the girl had been raised in Cornwall. And now she was here and she was a tart. His thinking turned back to the problem that had brought him

21

here. Ryder strongly doubted the supernatural had anything to do with the problems occurring at Kimberly Hall. Oh no, greed was the same all over the world. Gaining one's greedy ends evidently conformed to local custom. He said, "Did Mr. Grammond have any problems before he agreed to sell to this Burgess?"

"Not that I know of. Oh, I see the direction of your thoughts, Ryder, but I cannot credit them. Burgess, as I said, has a fine reputation; he is honest; he gives to local charities. No, if Grammond were having financial problems or if he were being besieged as we are at Kimberly, Burgess certainly wouldn't be behind it."

Ryder wondered if Grayson spoke so positively about the Sherbrookes. He'd never met a man before in his life who deserved such accolades. Well, he would soon see. The island was small; society intermingled continuously and he would meet this Mr. Burgess and his niece soon enough.

Grayson directed them inland, away from the blessed breeze from the water. The air was heavy with dirt and the sickly sweet smell of the sugarcane. They came shortly to the top of a rise and he looked back at the Caribbean, stretched as far as the eye could see, brilliant blue, topaz in shallower water, silver-capped waves rolling onto the white beaches. He wanted nothing more than to strip off his clothes and swim in the Caribbean until he sank like a stone.

"All this is Sherbrooke land, sir. Ah, look upward at the top of the rise, in amongst the pink cassias." He heard Ryder suck in his breath and smiled. "They're also called pink shower trees. They're at their most beautiful right now. And there are golden shower trees, and mango trees and the ever-present palm trees. There, sir, just beyond is the great house. You cannot see it from here, but the coastline curves quite sharply just yon and is quite close to the back of the house."

Ryder drew in his breath yet again.

"Most of the great plantation houses here on Jamaica are built in the traditional manner of three stories and huge Doric columns, only here we have verandas and balconies off nearly every room, for fresh air, you understand. You will see that all the bedchambers are at the back of the house and all have balconies that face the water. The back lawn slopes down to the beach and is always well tended. You will be able to sleep, even in the deepest part of the summer, though I think you're doubting that right now."

"You're right about that," Ryder said, wiping the sweat off his face with the back of his hand.

It was nearly midnight. Ryder had thoroughly enjoyed himself in the warm water of the Caribbean for the past hour. There was a half-moon that lit his way. It glittered starkly off the waves. He felt for the first time as if he really were in paradise. He chose to forget the awful heat of the afternoon. It was so beautiful, the black vault of the sky overhead with the studding of stars, so calm, so silent, that he felt peace flow through him.

He wasn't a peaceful man. Thus, it was an odd feeling, but he didn't dislike it. He stretched out naked on his back, knowing full well the sand would likely find its way into parts of his body that he wouldn't like, but for now, it didn't matter. He stretched, feeling himself relax completely. He closed his eyes and listened to the sounds he hadn't heard before. He'd read about the coqui or the tree frog, and thought he heard some chirping into the soft darkness.

He also knew a turtledove when he heard it and sighed as the sounds became more distinct, each adding to his relaxation, his sense of well-being.

It was just so damned exotic here, he thought, stretching yet again, only to have the sand make him itch madly. He jumped to his feet, ran splashing through the surf then flattened into a dive into the next good-sized wave. He swam until he was exhausted, then walked slowly back to the beach. He realized he was ravenous. He'd been too hot to eat much at dinner and the strangeness of the food hadn't added to his appetite.

There were coconut trees lining the perimeter of the beach and he grinned. He'd seen a black man shinny up a coconut tree earlier. His mouth was already watering. But it wasn't as easy as it looked and Ryder ended up standing on the beach, rubbing a scraped thigh, staring with malignant hatred at the coconuts just beyond his reach.

There were other ways for the son of an English

earl to get at a damned coconut. He found a rock and aimed it carefully at the coconut he'd selected. He was on the point of throwing it when he heard something.

It wasn't a coqui nor was it a turtledove. It wasn't like anything he'd ever heard in his life. He held himself perfectly still, lowering the rock slowly, silently. He listened hard. There it was again, that strange sort of low moaning sound that didn't sound remotely human.

His feet were tender, for he was an Englishman after all, but he managed to move silently enough through the trees that lined the beach. The sound became louder the closer he got to the great house. He ran lightly up the grassy slope toward the back of the house. He eased around the side so he could see onto the front lawn. He stopped behind a breadfruit tree and looked out onto the beautifully tended grounds. The sound came again and then he saw a strange light welling up from the ground itself. It was a narrow, thready light, blue, and it smelled of sulfur, as if it were coming up directly from hell and the moans were of the souls entrapped there. He felt gooseflesh rise on his body; he felt the hair rise on the back of his neck. Then he shook his head. This was beyond absurd. He'd said with absolute certainty to Grayson that it was naught but a mixture of chemicals. It was true, it had to be.

He saw candlelight flicker in one of the rooms on the second floor of the house. Probably Grayson and he was most likely scared silly. Then he heard a hiss from behind him and turned very slowly, the rock ready now, his body poised.

It was Emile Grayson.

Ryder smiled. He liked Emile. He was about Ryder's own age, intelligent and ambitious. He, like Ryder, wasn't the least bit superstitious, though he hadn't once disagreed with his father during dinner or their talk afterward.

"What is it?" Ryder said behind his hand in a deep whisper.

"I don't know but I do want to find out. Now you're here to help me. I've tried to make some of the male slaves keep watch with me but they roll their eyes back in their heads and moan." Emile paused just a moment, then added, "One slave did help me. Josh was his name. We kept watch several nights together. Then one morning he was found dead, his throat cut. I've had no more volunteers."

"Very well," said Ryder. "Go around to the other side of that damned light and I'll ease closer from this way."

Emile slithered like a thin shadow from tree to tree to work his way to the other side of the thready light. A neat trap, Ryder thought, pleased. Blood pumped wildly through him. He hadn't realized really how very bored he'd been during the voyage because he'd bedded two ladies, both of them charming, and from long experience, time passed more smoothly if one made love during the day and if one slept with a woman cuddled against one's chest during the night.

When Emile was in position, Ryder simply straightened, the rock still held in his right hand, and walked directly toward the light. He heard an unearthly shriek.

The light became a thin smoke trail, bluer now, the odor foul as the air of hell itself. A few chemicals, he thought, that's all, nothing more. But who was doing the moaning?

He heard a shout. It was Emile. He began to run. He saw the figure then; white flowing robes covered it, but there was a very human hand showing and that hand held a gun. Ah, was that a pillow slip over the man's head? The hand came up and the gun exploded toward Emile. Ryder yelled at him. "You bastard! Who the hell are you!"

Then the figure turned and fired at him. Ryder felt the bullet pass not three inches from his head. Good God, he thought, and ran straight for the figure. The man was tall and fit, but Ryder was the stronger and the more athletic. He was gaining on him. Any moment now he would have him. He sliced his foot on a rock and cursed, but it didn't slow him.

Then suddenly, without warning, he felt a shaft of pain sear through his upper arm. He stopped cold in his tracks, staring down at the feathered arrow tip that was sticking obscenely out of his flesh.

Damnation, the man was escaping. Emile, shouting hoarsely, was at his side in another moment.

He said blankly, "Where the hell did that bloody arrow come from? The man had an accomplice, damn him!"

"It's nothing! Get him, Emile!"

"No," Emile said very calmly. "He will come back."

With no more words, Emile ripped off the white sleeve of his shirt, then turned to Ryder, and without pause, without speech, he grasped the arrow firmly and pulled it out.

"There," he said, and began to wrap the shirtsleeve around the small hole that was oozing blood.

Ryder felt momentarily dizzy but he was pleased that Emile had acted swiftly.

"Yes," he said. "There." He looked up. "The bastard got away, curse him. Both of them." He looked back down at his arm. "When you've got me wrapped up, let's go examine the light and smoke, or whatever it is."

But there was no more smoke, no more thin thready blue light. There was, however, a faint sulfurous odor and the grass was scorched.

"Now," Ryder said grimly, "there are two of us. We'll catch the bastards who are doing this." He paused, feeling a burning sensation in his upper arm. "Why? Ah, that's the question, isn't it?"

"I don't know," Emile said. "I've thought and thought and I just don't know. No one has approached my father about selling the plantation, not a soul, nor is there any gossip, just that some voodoo priests or priestesses are displeased with us for some unknown reason. Please, Mr. Sherbrooke, come into the house because I want to clean the wound. We've got a good store of medicines and basilicum powder is just what we need."

"My name is Ryder."

Emile grinned. "Given the circumstances, all right, Ryder."

Ryder suddenly laughed. "Some guard I am," he said and laughed more. "I probably astonished our villain more than I frightened him. Jesus, I'm stark naked."

"Yes, you are, but I hesitated to point it out, particularly when the bastard was so close."

"I know. It's also difficult to call a man Mr. Sherbrooke when he's wearing naught but his hide."

CHAPTER 2

Camille Hall

He struck her ribs with his fist just below her right breast, hard enough to slam her against the wall. Her head snapped back and hit the top edge of the thick oak wainscoting.

Slowly, stunned, she slid down to the floor.

"Why the hell didn't you tell me, you stupid little fool?"

Sophie shook her head to clear it. She raised her hand and lightly touched her fingertips against the back of her head. A dizzying shaft of pain brought bile to her throat.

"Don't you dare tell me I hurt you. If it is so, it is your own fault."

It would naturally be her own fault. He was always careful never to strike her where it would show. Never. She moved her hand to her ribs. The pain made her suck in her breath, but that made it hurt even more. She took short, very shallow breaths and waited, praying that her ribs weren't broken, praying the nausea would subside. If he had broken some ribs she wondered how he would explain it. But he could come up with some plausible explanation. He always had in the past.

He was standing over her now, his hands on his hips. He was pale, his eyes narrowed with fury. "I asked you a question. Why didn't you tell me that Ryder Sherbrooke had arrived in Montego Bay?"

She opened her mouth to lie, but he forestalled her. "And don't tell me you didn't know. You were in town today, I saw you go myself. I gave you permission to go, damn you."

"I tell you I didn't —" She stopped, hating her cowardice, hating her voice that sounded thin as the batiste of her nightgown. She was silent a moment, feeding the rage that was bubbling up inside her. She looked at him squarely in his hated face. "I wanted him to be here, to catch you. I prayed he would come. He wouldn't believe any of that voodoo nonsense. I knew he could stop you."

He raised his fist. Then slowly, he lowered it.

He actually grinned at her and for a moment she saw what other people saw — a man with humor and wit, a gentle man, a somewhat diffident man of breeding and unquestioned gentility. In the next instant it was gone and he was back as she knew him to be. "If Thomas hadn't shot him with the arrow he might have. I was totally taken off guard. Certainly Grayson's son, Emile, has been something of a thorn in my flesh, but this young man, naked as a satyr, running at me yelling at the top of his lungs, came as quite a shock. Then Thomas got him."

Sophie paled. "You killed him? You killed the owner?"

"Oh no, Thomas shot him through his upper arm. Thomas is always careful. Strange thing, really, the fact that Sherbrooke was naked and carrying a rock, howling at me just like a damned Carib. Thomas says he was probably plowing one of the slaves when he came out to investigate the sulfur and the smoke and all those hideous moans we've perfected. I was relieved that Emile Grayson stopped and saw to Sherbrooke."

She said nothing. By keeping the information to herself, she had endangered a man's life. It hadn't occurred to her that he could be in any real danger. She'd been a fool and he'd been the one to pay for it. She'd paid too, but that was nothing new. At least he would be all right and she would be as well, eventually. She slowly deepened her breathing as the pain in her ribs eased a bit.

Uncle Theo moved away from her now. He pulled the chair away from his small writing desk and sat down in it, crossing his legs at the ankles and looking at her, his arms settled on his lean belly. "Stupidity doesn't suit you, Sophia," he said finally, shaking his head. "How many times do I have to tell you that obedience is the only choice you have? Loyalty to me is your only choice. You just might ask yourself what would happen to you and your precious Jeremy if I had been caught. You're underage; you're the whore of the island; you would have no money, no place to live; you would end up selling your body on the streets and Jeremy would end up in some workhouse. Perhaps he could be someone's apprentice bookkeeper and spend all his time in the trashhouse. No, miss, you will not try to do me in again or I swear to you —" He paused, rose quickly, and strode back over to her. She shrank back against the wall, she couldn't help it, as he came down on his haunches beside her. He grabbed her chin in his palm and jerked her head toward him. "I swear to you, Sophia, I will kill you if you try such a thing again. Do you understand me?"

She said nothing. He saw the hatred in her eyes and said more softly now, "No, I won't kill you, I'll kill that pathetic brother of yours. Oh yes, that's what I'll do. Now do you understand me?"

"Yes," she said finally. "Yes, I understand you well enough."

"Good." He rose then offered her a hand. She stared at his slender long fingers, the well-buffed nails, then looked him in the face. Very slowly, she pushed herself upright. He lowered his hand.

"You're stubborn but I don't dislike it in a woman. You hate me as well, and that is amusing. Now, if you were my mistress I would enjoy whipping that insolent look out of your eyes. Take yourself back to bed. I have plans to make. Ryder Sherbrooke is here finally. God, I waited a long time for Grayson to act, for the Earl of Northcliffe to react and send someone out here. And he sent his brother, just as I'd hoped. Now it is time to put my plan into motion.

"Ah, yes, my dear, since you have seen a frankly impressive number of naked men, let me tell you that this young man is built very well. He's an athlete and his body is lean and strong. Aye, you'll find that Sherbrooke is a fine specimen." He paused again, looking off into nothing in particular. "I think this will work quite nicely, but I must think about it in more detail. The man is not a fool. I was, I suppose, expecting another Lord David, but Sherbrooke isn't at all like that young wastrel. I will tell you in the morning what you will do."

At eight o'clock the following morning, Sophie was trying to fasten the front buttons of her gown. Every movement hurt. The flesh over her ribs had turned a fierce yellow and purple during the night. As she worked another button into its hole, she felt the pain so deeply she doubted it would ever ease. She stopped, bending over like an old woman. She'd sent her maid away; she couldn't allow Millie to see her, for it would start gossip and she couldn't allow that.

She couldn't allow that because of Jeremy.

When there came a light knock on her door, followed by her young brother's head coming around, she smiled despite the pulling pain. Jeremy came into the bedchamber. "Don't you want breakfast? It's growing cold and you know how

Uncle Theo is. You won't get a bite to eat until luncheon."

"Yes, I know. Let me finish with these buttons."

Jeremy prowled around her room, forever curious, filled with a nine-year-old's energy. Always on the move, always restless, always ready to work as hard as any slave, only he couldn't.

She finally finished with the buttons. She happened to glance in the mirror and saw that she hadn't brushed out her hair. She looked pale and frowzy and about as seductive as a broken conch shell. Some whore she was. There were dark circles under her eyes. Ah, but it hurt to pull the brush through the tangles. Every stroke sent waves of pain through her chest.

"Jeremy, would you brush my hair for me?"

He looked startled and cocked his head to one side in silent question. When she merely shook her head, he came to her, frowning. "Are you tired or something, Sophie?"

"Yes, I'm something." She handed him the brush and sat down. He did a poor job of it but it was sufficient. She managed to pull back the mass of chestnut hair and tie it at the nape of her neck with a black velvet ribbon.

"Now, Master Jeremy, onward to breakfast."

"You're ill, aren't you, Sophie."

It wasn't a question. She touched her fingers to his cheek for she saw the worry in his eyes, and the fear that something was seriously wrong. "I'm all right. Just a touch of a stomachache, I

35

swear to you. Some of Tilda's wonderful muffins and I'll be right as rain."

Jeremy, reassured, skipped ahead of her. It was, at least, skipping to her. Perhaps to others it looked like clumsy ill-coordinated movements, but not to her. No, he was a happy little boy and he was doing marvelously well. She loved him more than anyone in the world. He was hers, her responsibility. He was the only person in the world who loved her, without question, without reservation.

Uncle Theo was in the breakfast room. The veranda doors, green-slatted, as were all the floor-to-ceiling doors in the house, were open and a slight breeze stirred the still air. In the distance the sea glittered beneath a blazing early morning sun. Just outside the open doors, the air was thick with the overripe summer scent of roses, jasmine, hibiscus, bougainvillea, cassia, frangipani, and rhododendron. During the hottest part of the day, the scent was nearly overpowering. But now, early in the morning, it was a paradise of smells and it stirred the senses. However, Sophie felt no stirring inside her this morning at the beauty of it. There was very little of anything that held beauty for her now. There had been very little of beauty for the past year. No, now it was closer to thirteen months.

Thirteen months since she'd become a whore. Thirteen months since other plantation owners' wives cut her directly whenever she chanced to see them shopping in Montego Bay. They didn't cut her here at Camille Hall; they admired her dear uncle much too much to hurt him like that. No, they were coldly polite to her here.

"There aren't any muffins, Sophie," Jeremy said. "Do you want me to ask Tilda?"

"No, no, love. I'll have some fresh bread. It's fine. Sit down now and eat your breakfast."

Jeremy did, with his usual enthusiasm.

Theodore Burgess looked up from his newspaper, the imported London *Gazette*, only seven weeks old, for English ships were regular in their arrivals.

He studied her face for a long moment, was content at the lingering pain he saw in her eyes, and said, "You and I will meet after you've eaten, my dear. There are things to discuss, and I know you always wish to accommodate yourself to my wishes. Ah, do eat a bit more. I know the heat is enervating, but you are growing too thin."

Jeremy continued oblivious, content to smear more butter on his roasted yam.

"Yes, Uncle," Sophie said. "In your study then. After breakfast."

"Yes, my dear, that is exactly what I wish. As for you, my fine lad, you will accompany me to the stillhouse today. There are some processes I wish you to learn. It will be hot as the fires of hell itself but we shan't stay long. Just long enough for you to learn something of the rum-making process and the steps Mr. Thomas takes to prevent the slaves from stealing and drinking all our profits."

The pleasure in Jeremy's eyes made her ribs hurt all the more.

Samuel Grayson had seen Ryder come back into the house, his thick pale brown hair dark with sweat, his white shirt stuck to his back, his face flushed red from the sun. He'd ridden over the plantation the entire morning with Emile, and now, at midday, he imagined Ryder was holed up someplace cool. He found him sitting on the veranda that gave off the billiard room. He was in the deepest shade, the one place where the breezes flowed continuously. He said quietly, seeing that Ryder's eyes were closed, "It's an invitation, Ryder, from Theodore Burgess of Camille Hall. There is to be a ball this Friday and you are to be the honored guest."

"A ball," Ryder said, opening his eyes. "Jesus, Samuel, I can't imagine trying to dance in this infernal heat. Surely this Burgess fellow isn't serious."

"There will be slaves waving woven palm fronds about to keep the air stirred up. Also the Camille Hall ballroom, like this one, is lined with slatted doors, all opening up from ceiling to floor. It will be quite pleasant, I promise you."

Ryder was silent for a moment. He was thinking about the woman who was sleeping with three men. He wanted to meet her.

"There's a boy waiting for your response, sir."

Ryder gave him a languorous smile. "We'll go, naturally."

Grayson left to write an acceptance and Ryder closed his eyes again. He didn't move much; it was too hot. He knew he couldn't go swimming just yet else he'd be baked within ten minutes by that inferno of a sun and his face and arms were already a bit burned. Thus, he sat there quietly and soon he slept.

When he awoke, afternoon shadows were lengthening and Emile was sitting beside him, his long legs stretched out in front of him.

"Your father says I will become accustomed," Ryder said. "I think he's lying to me."

Emile grunted. "A bit, but the summers are particularly brutal."

"Is it ever too hot to make love, I wonder?"

Emile laughed. "Yes, it is. I hear we are to go to a ball at Camille Hall this Friday night."

"Yes, I am to be honored. I think, however, that I would prefer swimming, perhaps even trying to shinny up a coconut tree again or even chase a villain who is wearing a sheet."

Emile grinned. "It should be amusing, Ryder. You will meet all the planters and merchants from Montego Bay and their wives. You will hear so much gossip your ears will ache. There is little else to do here, you see, except drink rum, which most do to excess, unfortunately. Also, Father is much taken with Sophia Stanton-Greville, and she is Burgess's niece and hostess. I don't doubt he would challenge any man to a duel if he dared say something insulting about Father's goddess."

"I also understand that she is a whore."

"Yes," Emile said, not looking at Ryder, "that's what is understood."

"This displeases you. You've known her a long time?"

"Her parents were drowned in a storm four years ago on a return voyage from England. Sophie and her brother, Jeremy, were given into the guardianship of Theodore Burgess, her mother's younger brother. She has lived here since she was fifteen. She is now nineteen, nearly twenty, and her exploits with men and thus her reputation began over a year ago. You are right, it displeases me and disappoints me even more. I had quite liked her. She was a spirited girl, fun and without guile or vanity. Indeed, I once thought that we might — but that's not important now."

"You know it as a fact then?"

"She meets her lovers at this small cottage that fronts the beach. I chanced to visit the cottage following a night she spent with Lord David Lochridge. David was still there, naked, and drinking a rum punch. The place reeked of sex. He seemed quite pleased with himself. He was rather drunk, which surprised me because it was only about nine o'clock in the morning. He spoke of her freely, her attributes, her skills at pleasing a man, her daring at flaunting convention."

"This woman wasn't there?"

"No. Evidently she leaves her men to wake up by themselves, that's what David said. However, there are slaves there to tend to them. None of the men seem to mind her habits."

"You believed this Lochridge?"

Emile's voice was emotionless, but still he didn't look at Ryder. "As I said, the place reeked of sex. Also, he was too drunk to make up something that hadn't happened. I don't like him particularly, but there was no reason for him to lie. The cottage is on Burgess land."

Ryder swatted a mosquito. He said, his voice meditative, "So she turns eighteen and decides to flout convention. It doesn't make a lot of sense, Emile. Surely no man would wed her now. Why do you think she started making herself available in the first place?"

"I don't know. She was always a strong-willed girl, spirited, as I told you, and very protective of her little brother. One of the planters called her a hellion because once she was angry at his overseer for calling her brother names and she smashed him on the head with a coconut. The man was in bed for a week. That was about two years ago. She could have wed any gentleman on the island for it is known that she is handsomely dowered. I have always been given to understand that females don't wish to have sex as much as men do. Thus, why would she want it so badly to give up everything that women are raised, even expected, to want?"

"There is always a reason for everything," Ryder said. He rose and stretched. "Thank God, I do believe it's cooling off just a bit."

Emile grinned up at him. "I heard Father order

41

Cook to make you something cool for dinner, a bowl of fresh fruit, perhaps, and some iced-down shrimp. No baked yams or hot clam chowder. He doesn't want you to shrink away for lack of sustenance."

Ryder swatted another mosquito. He looked off over the sugarcane fields shimmering beneath the sun, to the endless stretch of blue sea beyond. So beautiful it was, yet so alien. "As I said, there is always something that drives men and women to behave as they do. There are three different men involved, I understand, and there were probably others before these three. There is of course a motive, and you know something, Emile? I rather fancy that I will amuse myself and just find out what it is that makes this hellion part her legs for so many men."

"It is depressing," Emile said, and he sighed.

By Friday night, Ryder was actually beginning to believe that he could endure the heavy still heat, even though he was sometimes so hot it hurt to breathe. He had even swum that afternoon, but not long, for he didn't want to burn too badly. To his disappointment, after the incident his first night, there had been no other strange occurrences. No burning sulfur; no sheeted man; no moans or groans; no guns or bows and arrows.

Nothing at all out of the ordinary had occurred. He had met Samuel Grayson's "housekeeper," a young brown woman with merry eyes, a compact body, and a ready smile. She lived in Grayson's room and worked in the house during the day. Her name was Mary. As for Emile, he also had a "housekeeper," a thin slip of a girl who answered to Coco. Her eyes were always downcast in Ryder's presence, and she never uttered a word that Ryder heard. She couldn't have been more than fifteen. Emile paid her no attention whatsoever, except, Ryder assumed, at night, when he took her to his bed. She cared for his clothing, kept his room straight and clean, and was utterly docile. Ryder was amused and put off by this custom, one considered quite respectable on Jamaica by all parties concerned.

Grayson, of course, had offered him a woman, and Ryder, for the first time in his adult sexual life, had refused. It simply seemed too cold-blooded to him, too contrived, too expected. That was it, he didn't want to do the expected thing. He laughed at his own conceit, at the affectation of his own behavior.

The three men rode to Camille Hall at nine o'clock on Friday night. It was just growing dark and the moon was full, the stars lush overhead. Ryder had never seen such a sight as this; it still made him stare.

They could see the lights of Camille Hall from a mile distant. There were carriages despite the condition of the main road, and at least three dozen horses, all tethered close to the great house and watched by a dozen small boys. The house glistened and shimmered. All the veranda

43

doors were wide open.

Ryder saw her immediately. She was standing next to an older man at the very entrance. She was gowned in white, pure virginal white, her shoulders bare, her chestnut hair piled on top of her head with two thick tresses falling over her shoulder to lie on that bare white flesh. Ryder looked at her and smiled just as she looked up and saw him. He saw her go very still. He realized, of course, that there was something akin to contempt in that smile of his. He removed it. He relaxed. It didn't matter if she slept with every man on the island. It simply didn't matter.

But motives interested him. She interested him.

He walked beside a worshipful Samuel Grayson toward her. He saw upon closer inspection that she wasn't the heavenly beauty that Grayson saw her to be. She looked much older than nineteen. Her eyes were a fine clear gray, her skin as white as her bare shoulders, too white. But she was wearing more makeup than a girl her age should wear. She looked more like a London actress or an opera girl than a young lady at a ball in her own home. Her lips were thick dark red, kohl lined her eyes and darkened her brows. There was rouge on her cheeks and a heavy layer of white powder. Why did her uncle allow her to look a harlot in his own house? And that damned white virginal gown she was wearing, it was the outside of too much. It was as if she were mocking her uncle, mocking all the people present, perhaps even mocking herself.

Ryder heard the introduction and took her hand, turning it over and lightly kissing her wrist. She jerked and he released her hand slowly, very slowly.

Theodore Burgess was of a different ilk. A tall man, thin as a stick, with a gentle face yet stubborn chin, he seemed inordinately diffident. He also seemed oblivious of the nineteen-year-old girl who flaunted herself beside him. He shook Ryder's hand with little strength and said, "A pleasure, sir, a pleasure. Mr. Grayson has spoken often of the Sherbrookes and his esteem for the Sherbrooke family. You are most welcome here, sir, most welcome. You will dance, of course, with my sweet niece?"

Was the damned fellow an idiot? Was he blind?

The sweet niece looked like a painted hussy. Ryder turned politely and said, "Would you care to dance this minuet, Miss Stanton-Greville?"

She nodded, saying nothing, not smiling, and placed her hand lightly on his forearm.

He realized that she'd said nothing at all to Emile. She'd ignored him. More tangled and unexpected behavior. He became increasingly fascinated. His curiosity rose accordingly.

"I understand you and Emile have known each other since you were practically children," he said, then released her to perform the steps in the minuet.

When they came together again, she said, "Yes." Nothing more, just that flat, emotionless "yes."

"One wonders," he said when she was near him again, "why one would ignore one's childhood friend when one reached adulthood. Yes, one wonders."

It was several minutes before her hand was in his once more. She said, "I suppose one can wonder about many things." Nothing more. Curse the chit.

The minuet ended. To Ryder's relief, he wasn't sweating by the end of it. Grayson hadn't lied. The ballroom, brilliantly lit by myriad candelabras, was nonetheless fairly cool, what with the breeze coming from the sea from all the open doors, and the ever-swinging palm fronds waved by small boys all dressed in white trousers and white shirts, their feet bare.

Ryder returned her to her uncle. He said nothing more. He turned away, Grayson at his side, to be introduced to other planters. He looked back once to see her standing very straight, her shoulders squared. Her uncle was speaking to her. He frowned. Was the uncle berating her for wearing so many cosmetics on her face? He hoped so, but doubted it. Personally, if it were up to him, he'd hold her face in a bucket of water then scrub it with lye soap but good.

He danced with every daughter of every Montego Bay merchant and every planter within a fifty-mile radius. He was fawned over, complimented on everything from the shine on his boots to the lovely blue of his eyes — this by a seventeen-year-old girl who could manage naught else but giggles — simpered at until he wanted to yawn with the boredom of it. His feet hurt. He wanted to go sit down and not move for a good hour. Finally, near to midnight, he managed to elude Grayson, three purposeful-looking planters, two more purposeful-looking wives with daughters in tow, and slip out onto the balcony. There were stone steps leading down into a quite lovely garden, redolent with the scent of roses, hibiscus, rhododendron, so many more brilliantly colored blossoms that he couldn't identify. He breathed in deeply and walked into the garden. There were stone benches and he sat down on one and leaned back against a pink cassia tree. He closed his eyes.

"I watched you come out here."

He nearly jumped off the bench, she startled him so badly. It was Sophia Stanton-Greville and she was standing very close to him.

He looked up at her, not changing expression, making no movement whatsoever now. "I wanted to rest. I am not yet accustomed to the heat and every girl in that bloody ballroom wanted to dance."

"Yes. I understand that's what one does at balls." She sounded cold, very aloof. She sounded as if she disliked him. Then why had she followed him out here? It made no sense.

He relaxed further, stretching his legs in front of him, crossing them at the ankles, crossing his arms over his chest. His posture was insolent. Never in his adult life had he been so rude in the presence of a woman. He said in a voice that matched her coldness, "What do you wish of me, Miss Stanton-Greville? Another dance perhaps, since it is a ball, as you so graciously pointed out?"

She stiffened, and again he wondered why the hell she was even here. She looked out into the darkness. "You don't behave as most men do, Mr. Sherbrooke," she said at last.

"Ah, by that do you mean that I don't drool on your slippers? I don't stare at your very red mouth or your doubtless delightful breasts?"

"No!"

"Then what is it that I don't do?"

She turned away. He saw her fingers pleating the soft muslin folds of her gown. She was very slender, and although her gown was cut high in the new fashion made popular by Josephine, he could tell that her waist was narrow. He wondered about her legs and hips.

She said, turning to face him, this time a ghost of a smile on her painted mouth, "You are brazen, sir. Gentlemen don't speak so baldly, surely not even in England."

"Not even to painted tarts?"

She sucked in her breath and he could have sworn that she actually reeled back in shock. She raised an unconscious hand to her cheek, and began to rub at the powder.

She stopped suddenly. She dropped her hand to her side. She smiled now, and the utter control of it made his eyes gleam. "No," she said calmly, "not even to painted tarts. I had been told you had some wit. I had thought to hear it, but evidently gossip was mistaken. You are rude and a boor."

He rose to stand over her, very close, but she didn't move away from him. "Now you draw blood," he said, "and you don't do it too badly. But not all that well either." He withdrew a handkerchief from his pocket and swiftly wiped it over her red mouth. She tried to jerk away, but he grabbed her about her throat and wiped her mouth yet again. He threw the handkerchief to the ground. "Now," he said, leaned down and kissed her hard on her mouth. He kissed her for a very long time. After but a moment, he gentled, and she knew his expertise was great, greater than any she'd known before. His mouth was caressing hers, his tongue seeking entrance, but not demanding. She allowed him to continue, not moving, not reacting.

Suddenly his hands were cupping her breasts and she jumped, she couldn't help it. "Shush," he said, his breath warm and tart with the rum punch he'd drunk. "Let me feel you. Is your skin as soft and warm as I believe it to be?" Just as suddenly, as he spoke, his hands were down the front of her bodice and cupping her bare breasts. He paused a moment, lifting his head, and staring down at her. "Your heart was pounding, but not fast enough, I don't think. Your breasts are nice, Miss Stanton-Greville. Is this why you came out here in search of me?

You wanted me to fondle you? Perhaps you even wanted me to take you here in the garden? Perhaps right here beneath this beautiful cassia tree? The scent is strong; perhaps strong enough to cover the smell of sex."

She said nothing, merely stood very quietly, allowing him to caress her breasts. He kissed her again, deepening the kiss this time, his open palm against her heart. The heartbeat quickened just a bit and he smiled into her mouth.

"Is that it? Do you think to compare me to your other men? You won't, you know."

His breath was very warm, his tongue gentle and easy against hers. But she wasn't kissing him back. She was passive. He didn't understand her. He wanted a response from her and by God he was going to have it. He pulled his hands out of the bodice of her gown, grabbed the shoulders of the gown, and jerked it to her waist. In the pale moonlight her breasts showed soft and white. Not large breasts, but very nicely shaped, full and high, the nipples a pale pink. He leaned down and began kissing the warm flesh.

It was then that she laughed, a teasing, wicked laugh. He straightened from the sheer surprise of it and looked down at her. Graceful as a dancer, she spun away from him. However, she did nothing to cover herself.

"You are not bad, in the way of men," she said, her voice light and caressing, her breasts pale in the moonlight, her shoulders back, thrusting them outward. "No, not bad at all. You are bold, arrogant, a man who doesn't wait for a lady to issue an invitation. You should show more restraint, sir. Or perhaps it is an invitation you want, and you haven't the patience to wait for it?"

"Perhaps," he said, "perhaps. But I don't share, Miss Stanton-Greville. When I take a woman I am the only man whose rod comes inside her. There will be no comparisons, at least no immediate ones."

"I see," she said, that damned voice of hers now lilting and more seductive than any woman's voice he'd ever heard in his life. "For the moment then, you may admire me, sir," she said, and he stared at her breasts as she slowly and with infinite fascination pulled the gown back to her shoulders, gently easing it into place. When her gown was straight and she looked as if she'd done nothing whatsoever out of the ordinary, she said, "No, Mr. Sherbrooke, you have moved too quickly. You have displeased me with your excesses. You demand, not ask. On the other hand, I do not dislike your arrogance. It is refreshing. You do not mince matters. You speak what you think. I will think about you, Mr. Sherbrooke. I have decided that I will ride with you in the morning. You will meet me here at eight o'clock. Do not be late. I dislike waiting for men."

He wanted to tell her to take her riding habit and her horse and her damned orders and go to hell, but he didn't. He was looking at her mouth, clean now of the damned red paint. A

51

beautiful mouth, truly. And she was still a mystery. Ryder couldn't resist a mystery.

He smiled at her as he reached out and lightly stroked his fingertips over her jaw. "An order for you. Do not paint your face. I don't like it. You will excuse me now, Miss Stanton-Greville."

He left her without a backward glance. He was whistling.

Sophie stared after him, unmoving, until he disappeared into the darkness. Her heart was pounding and she felt light-headed. She was terrified of him. She hadn't lied, he was like no man she'd ever known. She sank down on the bench and put her face in her hands. What was she going to do?

CHAPTER 3

Ryder smiled as he looked at the ormolu clock in the main salon of Kimberly Hall. It was now fully eight o'clock in the morning. She would be looking for him to arrive momentarily, yes, any minute now, and she would expect to see him riding up to the front of Camille Hall, just as Her Highness had bade him do.

Only he wouldn't be there.

When it was eight-thirty, he rose and stretched and went into the small breakfast room that opened onto a side garden. Both Emile and his father were there. Two house slaves were serving them, one of them Samuel's housekeeper, Mary, and she smiled at Ryder merrily, waving him to his seat as if he were her guest.

Ryder asked for fresh fruit and bread from the tall black man, James, who, like every black man, woman, and child on Jamaica, wore no shoes. It still disconcerted Ryder a bit. He downed the hot black coffee that tasted so rich here on Jamaica, saying nothing, for he was thinking about Sophia Stanton-Greville and trying to picture the look on her face now that she must realize he wasn't coming. He smiled as he chewed on the bread.

"I heard it said last night that you were riding this morning with Miss Stanton-Greville."

Ryder didn't look up at Samuel Grayson. He was afraid that if he did, he'd grin like a sinner, for Samuel sounded jealous. How many men were besotted with the damned girl? And, how the devil did anyone know about the plans he and Miss Stanton-Greville had made? Rather, the supremely confident order she'd given him.

"I would say that the persons reporting the phenomenon were wrong, wouldn't you? I'm here, eating my breakfast. James, please tell Cora the fresh bread is quite good."

"It was her uncle who told me," Samuel said. "He asked me if you could be trusted. He loves his niece very much and he is very anxious that no man take advantage of her."

Emile choked on his coffee.

Ryder leaned over and smacked him on his back. "Are you all right?"

"I won't stand for this, Emile," his father said harshly. "You will not speak badly of her, do you understand me? You will not act the leering young man."

"I said nothing, I merely choked."

"Damn you, boy, I won't tolerate your damnable impudence!"

"Samuel," Ryder said smoothly, interrupting him. "There is not a consensus of opinion on

54

the virtue of Miss Stanton-Greville. Surely you know that."

"It matters not," Grayson said. "I know the truth."

"Let us speak of other matters then. There have been no further demonic spectacles. I'm disappointed, and yet at the same time, I do wonder why they ceased so abruptly with my arrival."

Emile said slowly, "It's true. Since you spent some hours in the bay before my father brought you to Kimberly, everyone or practically everyone would have known within twenty-four hours that you had arrived."

"Which means," Ryder continued thoughtfully, "that if they were meant to cease upon my arrival then the person responsible hadn't heard of my arrival before that first night."

"Exactly," said Emile.

"I am still not certain that there is a person behind this," Grayson said. "It isn't natural, all that you saw. You said yourself, Ryder, that there was no sign of the fire where you'd seen one. Perhaps it wasn't a person in a white costume, perhaps it was simply another manifestation of voodoo evil."

"It was a flesh and blood man," Ryder said firmly. "Also, the arrow that went into my arm was shot by a very real person. Thus, there were two villains at Kimberly that first night. A question, Samuel — do you know of any man nearby who is good at archery?"

"Good God," Emile said, startled. "I hadn't

thought to ask. Yes, Father, let's think on that."

Both men were silent for several moments. Ryder ate the chilled fresh fruit and the crusty fresh bread. He thought of Sophia Stanton-Greville, waiting. Both the thought and the bread were delicious.

Samuel said, "Yes, I know a man who excels in the sport of archery."

"Who?" Emile and Ryder asked at the same time.

Samuel waved his hands in dismissal. "No, no, it makes no sense. I was thinking of Eli Thomas, Burgess's overseer. He is noted for his skill, but again, no, it makes no sense. Why would he come here and shoot Ryder? Also, David Lochridge is a devotee of the sport as is a Mr. Jenkins, a merchant in Montego Bay. There are doubtless others in the vicinity. Certainly too many to draw any sort of meaningful conclusion."

Ryder smiled. Another part of the puzzle brought out onto the table. Another link to that wretched little tart at Camille Hall who'd teased him and practically let him make love to her in the Camille Hall gardens with a hundred guests but yards away. He toyed with an orange slice. "Since the men who visited us that first night of my arrival didn't know I was here, why then, we can begin to narrow the list, because I met many gentlemen that first afternoon in the Gold Doubloon."

Emile got a piece of foolscap and a pen. They listed all the names Ryder could remember.

"Many aren't accounted for," Emile said. "More than many more. The count boggles the mind."

"Such as two of her lovers," Ryder said easily. "We can mark off Oliver Susson."

"Yes," Emile said, and his father threw his napkin down on the table and strode from the room.

Ryder frowned after him. "Why does he wish to be blind to this girl and what she is?"

Emile looked across the breakfast room to the oil painting of a sugarcane field. "He had selected her to marry me. He won't give up the idea. I think also that he is taken with her. Her wickedness teases him. You've noticed Mary, his housekeeper, is a little tease, and he is very fond of her. I tell you, Ryder, even if Sophia took him as one of her lovers, he would still defend her. You mustn't take his anger to heart. He is my father and he means well."

Ryder nodded and continued to eat.

Emile said after a moment, "You were to have ridden with her, weren't you?"

Ryder grinned at him. "Yes, but I will never allow a woman to dictate to me. I will tell her what I wish of her and when I wish it. I will do the asking, not she the telling."

"This should prove interesting."

"I trust so," Ryder said and drank the rest of his rich black coffee. "Do you have the time, Emile?"

"Yes, it's nearly nine-thirty."

"I believe I will go riding."

Emile gave him a crooked grin. "Good hunting."

"Indeed," Ryder said.

"Where is he?"

Sophie turned to face her uncle. "I don't know. I assumed he would be here at eight. He did not say he wouldn't come."

"You angered him, damn you!" He raised his fisted hand, but one of the house servants was coming onto the veranda. He lowered his arm.

He lowered his voice, but the anger was strong and vicious. "You put him off! You didn't succeed, Sophia. I am displeased with you. Must I do all the planning? No, don't say anything. I will decide what is to be done now. You've botched it and I wonder if you did it apurpose."

He began to pace the veranda. Sophie watched him with a disinterested eye and kept silent. She prayed that Ryder Sherbrooke would have the good sense to keep miles away from Camille Hall and away from her.

Burgess paused and approached her, sitting in a cane-backed chair close to hers. "You took Lord David to the cottage last night, did you not?"

She nodded.

"All went well?"

"Yes. But he was jealous of my attention to Ryder Sherbrooke. His is not a steady character. He is childish and self-absorbed. Once he has drunk sufficiently, he is not difficult for me to handle, but last night his jealousy . . . well, it doesn't matter now. It turned out all right."

"You dealt with him?"

"Yes."

"Grammond will be leaving next week."

"Yes."

"You may detach yourself from Lord David now. There is no more use for him."

"He will not go easily," Sophie said. "He's young and arrogant and considers himself to be my stud. He will not take it kindly that I no longer want him."

"You will think of something." Theo Burgess rose and walked into the house, leaving her alone with her endless round of useless thoughts.

When Ryder Sherbrooke rode up some ten minutes later she wished she could yell at him to leave, curse his male stubbornness. She knew men and she knew what he was doing. He was teaching her a lesson; he was teaching her that he would not take commands from a woman. He was punishing her, humiliating her. Well, let him try. If only he knew it was her wish never to see him again, that she would give just about anything for him to book passage on the next ship back to England. She didn't move, merely watched as he cantered up the long drive, dismounted, and tied his stallion to the post some ten feet away from her.

He strolled over to her, leaned negligently on the veranda railing, and said easily, "Good morning."

He frowned for she was wearing that awful paint on her face. It looked garish and tawdry in the morning sunlight.

"I told you to wash your face. You look absurd. You may be the tart, but there is no reason to advertise it."

Sophie stood up slowly. She looked at him for a very long time, saying nothing. Then, in that light, teasing voice, she said, "Are you here to take me riding or to dictate terms for a surrender?"

"Surrender," he repeated. "That sounds quite charming to me, particularly with regard to you, madam. First, go wash your face. Then I will take you riding."

"You are nearly two hours late, sir!"

"Am I? Dear me, how remiss of me. On the other hand, I didn't wish to ride two hours ago. Now I do. Go wash your face. I will give you ten minutes, no more."

"I wouldn't go to the trashhouse with you, damn you! Get out of here! Go back to England and be a boor there."

"Mr. Sherbrooke! How delightful to see you, sir. My niece mentioned that perhaps you would be coming to take her riding. Sophia, where are you going, my dear? Mr. Sherbrooke surely would appreciate your charming company."

Ryder was amused to see her so neatly trapped. "To freshen myself, Uncle."

"Excellent. Mr. Sherbrooke and I will have a cozy chat until you return. Such a sweet girl,

60

my niece. Sit down, Mr. Sherbrooke, do sit down. Should you like a rum punch?"

"At this hour? No, thank you, Mr. Burgess."

"Ah, do call me Theo. I'm not quite that old."

"Then you must call me Ryder."

"I understand your brother is the Earl of Northcliffe?"

"Yes. He would have come here himself but he had recently wed."

"Ah. Do you plan to remain on Jamaica?"

"Only until we have dealt with the ghostly manifestations that seem to have plagued Kimberly Hall for the past four or so months."

"Mr. Grayson has spoken to me of these things. It's common knowledge that there are evil ceremonies and equally evil priests and priestesses on Jamaica who are capable of anything."

"They have stopped."

"Really? I'm vastly relieved, Ryder, but I wonder why."

"So do I." Ryder wanted to ask him about his overseer and his archery skills but it was too soon. He wanted to keep the upper hand. He sat back in his chair and gave Mr. Burgess a guileless smile.

A house slave brought lemonade at Mr. Burgess's request. It was delicious. Ryder noted that Miss Stanton-Greville had far exceeded her ten minutes. He finished his glass of lemonade and gently set the glass down on the polished mahogany-topped table next to him. He rose and extended his hand to Theo Burgess.

"I fear it grows late, Theo. Evidently your niece has become occupied with more important matters than riding with me. Good-bye."

He walked away, whistling, nonchalant as a clam.

Theo Burgess stared at him, then yelled, "Sophia!"

Ryder didn't pause. He strolled out onto the drive toward his horse. He heard a noise from above, and curious, looked up. She was standing on the balcony some twelve feet up and in her hand was a basin. He moved, but not quickly enough. A good amount of water whooshed down in a thick arc and landed squarely on the top of his head.

He knew he heard a laugh, but then she was crying out. "Oh dear, what have I done? Oh, Mr. Sherbrooke, how could I be so very careless! Dear me, I really should have looked. Do forgive me, sir. Do come in and I will give you a towel. Oh dear, oh dear."

He would give it to her. She'd gotten him quite nicely.

He called back, "Thank you, Miss Stanton-Greville. Actually the water feels very good in this heat."

"I will be right down with a towel, sir." She added with a voice of gentle sweetness so false he was forced to grin, "And do call me Sophia."

He turned back to the veranda and saw something very unexpected. It was Theo Burgess's face and it was ugly and mean and something very frightening moved in his pale brown eyes. Then, suddenly, whatever Ryder thought he'd seen was gone, and Burgess was distraught and concerned and waving his hands as he moved quickly toward him, even wringing his hands, exclaiming, "Come here, Mr. Sherbrooke, do come here and sit down. Ah, my niece was careless, but surely she will make it up to you."

"I have no doubt she will try," Ryder said.

The brazen jade.

Sophie had washed only the most vulgar of the makeup off her face. But Ryder Sherbrooke's face was shiny and dripping with nice clean water. She smiled at him, her eyes glittering her triumph even though the words that came out of her mouth would do justice to a contrite nun. She prattled nonsense like a brainless twit. She hung about him, offering to pour him more lemonade, offering him four more towels, perhaps even five for he was so *very* wet, even offering him a comb for his hair, even offering to comb his hair.

Finally, Ryder said, "No, thank you, Sophia. I feel quite dry. No more of your ministrations. I do hope that the bucket you accidently spilled on me contained fresh water and only fresh water?"

She blinked rapidly, her face paling creditably, then flushing, and settled finally into a patently false mask of chagrin. "Oh dear, I think so, but you know . . . oh certainly Dorsey must have changed it and cleaned out the bucket, but then again, sometimes she is lazy so perhaps not.

63

Wait, sir, and I will ask." Then she struck a pose. "But you know, if Dorsey didn't clean it out, she would never admit it. So we will never know. Oh dear." She jumped to her feet and as she passed him, she sniffed rather loudly and wrinkled her nose.

She was quite good.

He rose to stand beside her. "Sniff again, Sophia. Yes, is there anything untoward? No? Excellent, I see that your face must weigh a bit less than it did. There are still cosmetics, but not enough to make me send you back to your room. Further, you have no more water to wash your face with, do you? Perhaps I now have some of your powder on my head? Come, let's go riding before it becomes too hot."

A boy appeared leading a beautiful bay mare with two white stockings. She nipped Sophie's shoulder. Sophie laughed, and patted her nose. "You naughty girl! Ah, you are ready for a gallop, aren't you?"

Ryder frowned. A completely different voice and a low, quite charming laugh.

He didn't help her to mount. She expected it, he saw that, but he merely mounted his own stallion and waited, not even looking at her.

The boy gave her a foot up. She looked over at Ryder, her expression as bland as his sister Sinjun's when she'd managed to beat him at a game of chess.

"Where would you like to go, Mr. Sherbrooke?"

"Since I am to call you Sophia, why don't you call me Ryder?"

"Very well. Where would you like to go, Ryder?"

"To the beach, to that very cozy little cottage I've heard so much about."

She didn't miss a beat, but he would swear that he saw her eyes widen, just a bit, in shock. But she said very coolly, "I think not." She gave him a seductive smile and a toss of her head. Her riding habit was of pale blue, her hat was a darker blue with a charming feather that curved around her face. It was very effective, that feminine head toss. "Besides, I do believe the cottage is perhaps still occupied. My uncle lends it out, you know. Yes, one never knows just who might be there."

"Oh? Your uncle, you say?"

Sophie kicked her mare, Opal, into a canter and off they went down the long, wide drive of Camille Hall.

She was brazen. There wasn't an ounce of shame in her.

He followed her, content to let her take the lead. They rode onto the road, following it only for a half mile or so, then she turned off it toward the sea. When they broke through the thin stand of mango trees, Ryder sucked in his breath. He'd never seen anything so beautiful in his life.

There was a stretch of beach that went on and on, disappearing around a bend a goodly distance to the east. The sand was stark white, pure and clean. The water was a light turquoise. The mango trees gave way to coconut trees that lined the perimeter of the white sand. The tide was going out and the different hues of the sand and water were startling in their beauty.

"It's incredible," he said before he thought to censor and give her only what he wanted her to hear. "I have never seen anything quite like it."

"I know. It is my favorite stretch. I swim here a lot."

He got control of himself and raised a brow at her. "Would you like to swim now?"

"I normally swim in a sarong. I don't have one with me."

"No matter. I really would like to see you. I already know that your breasts are quite adequate. Not all that large, but fine, really. No man I know of would complain about their size or their weight or their softness. But there is the rest of you — your hips, your belly, your legs, and your woman's endowments. I think a man should be able to see what he'll be getting himself into before he takes the plunge, so to speak."

She turned her head away, but for only a moment. "Oh? And do you believe a woman should have the same consideration, sir?"

"You may call me Ryder since it's likely we're going to become quite close. Why, certainly women should be given every consideration. Would you like to see me naked, Sophia? Now?"

66

He thought he'd gotten her, but not a moment later he knew he was wrong. She gave him the hottest smile he'd seen in his adult life. She ran her tongue over her lower lip and leaned her upper body toward him. "Why, I think that would be nice, Ryder. Perhaps you could pose for me. I could sit over there beneath a coconut tree and tell you which way to turn so I could gain every perspective I wished of you. A man's buttocks, flexed, you know, are sometimes quite delightful."

Good God, he thought, picturing exactly what her words had conjured up in his mind.

He flushed. He actually turned red to the roots of his hair.

Sophie saw that flush and her satisfaction wasn't at all subtle. She shook her finger at him. "Really, Mr. Sherbrooke, it's never wise to bait your hook when you don't know what you'll catch." It was difficult, but she'd managed it. She'd won for the moment. She'd been so outrageous she'd made him blush. She knew she must be the first woman to have accomplished such a feat, for he was polished, this Englishman with his clear blue eyes, polished and cynical and very sure of himself. But she'd known exactly what she was saying, for the first time she'd taken Lord David Lochridge to the cottage, he'd already been three-quarters drunk. He'd stripped off his clothes, eager to show her that his body was firm and muscled, much nicer than that old man, Oliver Susson's, and how once she saw him, she'd dismiss all the other men. He'd posed for her, even turning his back to her and flexing his buttocks, and thus it was he she was seeing when she'd said those words to Ryder Sherbrooke.

Ryder was furious with himself. He was so furious with himself that he wanted to howl. He wanted to dismount and kick himself. But he didn't. He wouldn't allow her the upper hand. Ha, she had it. He had to get it back. It was intolerable that a woman, a damned tart, could do him in.

"I enjoy taking chances, Sophia," he said finally, creditably in charge of himself and his voice again. "I haven't yet caught a shark or a piranha. Perhaps I've hooked an angelfish and the good Lord knows they're quite enjoyable to eat." He gave her an intimate smile, but Miss Stanton-Greville merely looked at him, one eyebrow arched, and Ryder would swear she had no clue as to what he was talking about. No, impossible, she was just toying with him again, pretending to innocence this time.

She said on a laugh, "Perhaps I should show you a rooster-tail conch. They're quite lovely but somewhat dangerous. They can cut you when you least expect it. Then there is the trumpet fish who is quite loud to other fishes and they avoid him. All in all a rather boorish fellow, one would say."

"I'm at a distinct disadvantage in this," Ryder said. "You could continue indefinitely whereas I have used up the sum of my marine life knowledge."

68

"Again, it isn't wise to bait your hook —"

"Yes, I know. I wouldn't want to hurt a tender mouth. However, some fish have tough little mouths and even tougher minds. As for their bodies, who can say? I wonder about their taste. Sour, do you think? Perhaps even deadly? Surely not sweet and juicy."

"Your similes are drifting rather far afield. Let's canter up the beach. There are some rather interesting caves in the low cliffs just beyond that bend ahead."

He followed her, appreciating the sea breeze that cooled him. He was angry with himself, not with her. She was what she was. The only problem was he wasn't certain exactly what that could be.

She dismounted, shaking her skirts, and led him up a narrow path that skirted jutting rocks and narrow crevices. There were gnarled bushes along the way. Finally, both of them panting from the heat, she stopped and pointed. There was a narrow opening into the side of the hill in front of them. Ryder stepped into the black stillness then out again. "So there really are caves. Have you explored it?"

"Yes. It's deep and has no other opening that I could ever find."

"Have you supplies in there?"

"What do you mean?"

"Oh, things like blankets, perhaps a sheet, a bottle of rum or two? Champagne to toast a successful completion?"

"I see. Do I come here occasionally with other people, that is what you're wondering." She looked momentarily thoughtful, nothing more. "No, not to date, but it isn't a bad idea. As I told you, it's quite possible there is a guest in the cottage even as we speak. It would be nice to have another place available to one, don't you think?"

"I think a man would have to be pretty desperate to be naked as a snake in a cold, damp cave, despite the skills of his companion."

"On the contrary. I have found gentlemen to be much alike. They tend to forget themselves entirely. They could be on the moon and dismiss it as unimportant when they are otherwise occupied."

Ryder suddenly remembered telling his brother that he would forget his very name once he was inside a woman, forget everything for the pleasure was so intense. Once again, he flushed. This time he managed to control it enough so he prayed she wouldn't notice. If she did, she didn't say anything. Damn her.

"To keep many men content when each knows about the other tends to support your theory."

"Crying uncle, Mr. Sherbrooke?"

"No, those are facts. A man has to be stupid not to face up to facts. My name is Ryder. I shouldn't like it if you screamed Mr. Sherbrooke when you have your first orgasm with me. It would make me feel very strange."

She didn't look a bit embarrassed. What she

looked was appalled and utterly scornful. He merely smiled at her. "Would you like to go back to the horses? Incidentally, do horses get sunburned?"

She gave a lilting laugh.

It was late in the afternoon. Sophie sat in her bedchamber, wearing only a light shift for the air was heavy and still. She sat very quietly in a cane chair that faced the sea, in front of the open balcony. She was utterly silent. She felt utterly defeated.

She wouldn't be able to handle Ryder Sherbrooke. He wasn't like any other man she'd ever met, any other man she'd manipulated and seduced. It was true that she did him in, but that was because he'd simply never met a woman who spoke so baldly before. But he was already accustoming himself to her.

What to do?

She knew her uncle was in her bedchamber even though she hadn't heard the door open.

"Tell me what happened."

She still didn't turn to face him. She said in a flat voice, "We rode. I showed him Penelope's Beach and one of the caves. He is a man, Uncle, but a man unlike the others. He made no move to kiss me, no move of any kind, but he spoke frankly of sexual things."

"You will seduce him. Perhaps tomorrow night."

She turned then to face him. He was sitting on her bed, his back against the headboard. His face was framed by the mosquito netting, and for an instant, just the veriest instant, he looked good and kind and gentle, the man and mask he presented to the world now one and the same.

"You don't understand. He does what it is *he* wishes to do. He will tell me when he wants to bed me, not the other way around. I could probably walk around him naked and if he felt he didn't have complete control over me, over the situation, why, he would smile, say something outrageous, and stroll away. He would not even bother to look back to see my reaction."

Theo Burgess frowned. She was right. He'd spoken to Ryder Sherbrooke long enough that morning to see her point. It was valid and it irked him.

"Fine," he said, rising now. "We will simply get him to the cottage another way."

She said nothing. She felt very cold suddenly, very cold and very weary.

"Did he say anything about his wounded arm?"

She shook her head.

"He isn't a stupid man. I imagine he inquired as to who hereabouts could shoot a bow and arrow. He plays a game, but you and I, Sophia, we are the ones, the only ones who know the rules."

She hated the rules. They were his rules, not hers.

That evening she had to tell Lord David

Lochridge that she wanted nothing more to do with him. She had no idea how to accomplish it, for he was young and filled with himself, and she knew that he wouldn't be able to imagine anyone not wishing for his wonderful self anymore.

Theo Burgess came up with the way to do it. For the first time in a very long time, Sophie laughed.

It was very late. Sophie arrived at the cottage. David's horse was tethered outside. When she entered he saluted her with a rum punch. He didn't appear too drunk yet. That should make it easier.

He rose immediately to embrace her. She danced away from him, laughing, her hands in front of her. "No, David, first we must talk."

"Talk," he said blankly. "How very strange you've become. Why talk?"

"I have something to tell you. It's only fair that you know the truth since I am very fond of you. I don't want you to be hurt, to perhaps go mad as many do, I am told."

Lord David drank the rest of his rum punch. "This is talk," he said, "talk that is very curious. What do you mean, Sophie?"

"I have the pox."

He turned utterly white. "No!"

"Yes," she said in a low, very sad voice. "The pox. There is no doubt."

"You didn't get it from me, damn you!"

"Oh no, certainly not. If I had, I wouldn't have to warn you, would I now?"

"Oh God," he said and actually moaned. "What if you've given it to me?"

"I don't think that would have been possible, not yet. You are still safe. But I fear it wouldn't be wise for us to continue as lovers."

He looked wildly about the small cottage where he'd spent a good dozen nights over the past two months. He looked at her, wondering, wondering at the strange fancies, the odd fragments of dreams, as he sometimes did when he was sober enough to assemble his thoughts coherently. But now, those fancies were nothing, less than nothing. Jesus, the pox!

"I'll go now, Sophie. I'm sorry. Good-bye."

"Good-bye, David. Don't worry. You'll be all right."

She watched him grab his hat, smash it on his head. He was actually running from the cottage, then galloping as if the great green serpent itself was after him. In this instance, Uncle Theo had been quite right.

She wondered if he was also right about David's reaction once he calmed down.

"He won't say a word to anyone. We needn't worry about that. No, he'll fear ridicule if he does. When he finds out that he hasn't caught anything, why then, he'll look at the other men and just smile and wish them the worst. That is his character, you know."

"He's that kind of man," Sophie said.

Before she fell asleep that night, Sophie wondered how Ryder Sherbrooke would have reacted had she told him she had the pox. She had an idea he would search her face for the truth then demand to examine her himself.

He was that kind of man.

CHAPTER 4

Emile told Ryder upon his return from Montego Bay late the following morning that Lord David Lochridge was no longer one of Sophia Stanton-Greville's lovers.

Ryder blinked. "Good heavens, she's worked very quickly. Astonishing, I would say, but difficult to accept. Didn't you tell me he was at her cottage just two nights ago?"

Emile grinned, pushed back a chair and sat down. "You don't suppose she's clearing out all the flotsam for you, do you?"

Ryder was thoughtful for a long moment. He said finally, very firmly, "One could be tempted to think so at first blush. However, I still can't see her doing something so blatant. She's a subtle female when she sees it is called for and, more importantly, she isn't stupid. She's many things, but not stupid."

"Really, Ryder, perhaps you're entirely wrong. Perhaps she wants to bed you. Perhaps she admires you and wants you, pure and simple. No ulterior motives. You aren't a troll, you know."

"There is nothing either pure or simple about Miss Stanton-Greville. As much as I would like to preen myself on my manliness, on my utter magnetism with women, I would be a fool to do so. No, Emile, if she does indeed want to add me to her string, there's an excellent reason for it."

"Fine. But why kick out Lord David, I wonder?"

"Perhaps," Ryder said, stroking his long fingers over his jaw, "just perhaps he's outlived his usefulness." But he was remembering his order to her that he wouldn't be one of many men in her bed. He would be the only one. He shook his head. No, he wouldn't be drawn into that conceit. This was really quite interesting.

"What does that mean?"

"I mean that everyone behaves a certain way for very solid reasons. If she dismissed Lord David, then there were very good grounds for her to do so. Remember, we spoke of motives. Lord David is young, handsome, a likely candidate if a woman wished to take a lover. But Oliver Susson? Charles Grammond? They're middle-aged, overweight, or stoop-shouldered . . . no, Emile, the selection isn't random."

"Lord David is saying, of course, that he was tired of her but no one believes him."

"No, indeed."

"I stopped by the Grammond plantation to bid my good-byes to the family. They're leaving at the end of the week. I drank some rum with

Charles and learned one thing of interest, but not until that boss-wife of his left the salon. What we had heard is true — he lost a bundle of money to Lord David. Didn't my father tell you of Lord David's phenomenal luck at cards?"

"Yes, he did and several others as well warned me to avoid him. This is interesting, Emile. So, as a result, he must leave Jamaica after selling his plantation, which, just as a matter of happenstance, is situated next to Camille Hall. Mr. Theodore Burgess — because he's such a fine, compassionate fellow — is buying the plantation. I do wonder what he's paying Grammond for it?"

"I can find out," Emile said. "I should have thought of asking but I didn't. Besides, his wife came back into the room. She quite terrifies me."

"No matter. There are more pieces of the puzzle falling in place with each passing day. Lord, it's hot."

Emile gave him an unholy grin. "It's not even noon, Ryder. I had thought to ask you to visit the stillhouse with me."

"Kill me first, for it's as close to hades as men have managed to get whilst still flesh of this world. I have wondered how the slaves tolerate it."

"They are quite used to it. Also, they all come from Africa, a country even more inhospitable than Jamaica."

"Still," Ryder said, then shrugged at the sight

of Emile's housekeeper, Coco, shyly peeping around the door.

Emile turned and frowned at the girl. "What is it, Coco?"

The girl showed another inch of herself, but her eyes were on her bare feet now. "I — I must speak with you, massa. I'm sorry, it's important." Emile turned back to Ryder. "Usually she doesn't say boo to anyone, thus it must truly be important, so I'll speak to her. Excuse me for a moment."

Ryder wondered what Emile's housekeeper wanted. Then he felt the heavy, still air close in around him and he thought only of being naked in a snowbank on the very top of Ben Nevis, and wallowing and wallowing until he was freezing. He even thought fondly of a thick white fog swirling around him, making him cold to his very bones as he walked St. James's street to White's. Even a London drizzle, frigid and miserable, dripping down the back of his neck, sounded remarkably inviting at the moment.

He wondered why Sophia Stanton-Greville had dismissed Lord David Lochridge. He believed he knew why she'd taken him as a lover in the first place. He wondered how the devil he would verify what he believed to be true. But primarily, he wondered exactly why he'd been selected as her next lover. For the life of him he couldn't think of a thing to be gained by having himself in her bed.

Theo Burgess was pale with anger when he came into her bedchamber. "Damn your laziness. He hasn't shown himself in two days."

"I know," she said, turning slowly to face her uncle. "It's a game he's playing with me."

"Game or no, I want you to ride over to Kimberly Hall and do whatever you have to. I want him at the cottage and soon, Sophia."

He walked over to her, looked quickly around, saw there was no one in sight, and slapped her. She reeled back, bumping into a chair and careening to the side. She fell. She didn't move.

"Stand up. I'm not certain you understand just how very serious I am about this."

"I understand."

"Damn you, stand up or I'll have your brother fetched and just see how much he enjoys pain."

Sophie stood up. This time she was prepared for the blow, but still the fist in her ribs dropped her to her knees. More bruises, and the ones from his last beating had just begun to fade. She shook with rage and pain.

"Now I trust you understand. Get yourself dressed and put on your cosmetics. You're pale and sickly looking. That little tap I gave your face just might discolor a bit. Cover it up. Go now and hurry."

"Ryder Sherbrooke doesn't like my face painted."

"Then do as he would like. Don't just lie there like a lame dog."

An hour and a half later, just as the three men were preparing to sit down to luncheon, James announced the arrival of Miss Sophia Stanton-Greville.

Emile shot Ryder a quizzical look. Ryder was frowning slightly. He hadn't thought she would come here, to him. It wasn't her style, at least he hadn't thought it would be. Something must have happened to get her here, that, or someone must have put the spurs to her to come.

Samuel Grayson gave James a fat smile and actually rubbed his hands together. "Do show her in, James. Oh yes."

When she came into the dining room, a vision in a pale yellow riding outfit, with only a minimum of cosmetics on her face, Ryder's eyes glittered. He knew her face wasn't completely clean because to do a good scrubbing would require utter compliance to his wishes. She would give up a single battle, but not the war.

She was all laughter and charm. She was gay and witty and she played with incredible boldness to Samuel Grayson's besottedness. She cast Ryder sloe-eyed looks, remarkably seductive, really. As for Emile, she ignored him for the most part. She readily accepted Samuel's luncheon invitation.

Ryder was content to sit back and watch her perform. He had no intention of entering the fray until he had her alone. And he did indeed want to be alone with her. As for Emile, he was clearly distracted.

Near the end of the meal, Sophie raised laughing eyes to Ryder and said, "I'm here actually to ask Mr. Sherbrooke to visit a fascinating cave one of our field slaves just discovered. It is much larger than the one I showed him on Penelope Beach and it isn't quite so cold and damp because the entrance is larger and thus more sun can come in."

"You would make a charming guide, my dear," Samuel Grayson said in a voice so infatuated that it made Ryder nauseous. "Ryder normally stays out of the sun during this part of the day, the suffocating heat, you know, and he isn't yet used to it."

"Perhaps Mr. Sherbrooke would consider himself to have sufficient fortitude, to be a man of strong enough will, to bear up under the heat when the end result would be this charming cave."

Ryder recognized a bucket of bait when it hit him in the face. Ah yes, question a man's virility and he would leap onto the hook with no hesitation.

"I don't know," he said slowly. "Perhaps another time, Miss Stanton-Greville. I'm really quite fatigued."

"Sophia," she said, her voice testy.

"Yes, Sophia. You know I'm not all that strong and my fortitude appears to be at low ebb. Yes, I am a weak man, one who must take care of his precarious health."

"Surely you can survive a simple ride to the beach!"

"Do you have an umbrella I can hold over my head on the way there?"

"A hat should be sufficient."

"I'm also worried about my horse," he said. "He pretends to be a mean devil, but underneath he's just as weak and low-ebbed as I."

She sucked in her breath. He was slippery as a spotted moray eel. Then she smiled. "Very well, then. I'm off to visit the cave. Good-bye, Mr. Grayson. Thank you for the delicious luncheon."

"But you didn't eat anything," Grayson called after her.

Emile began to laugh. His father spun on his heel and hurried after Miss Stanton-Greville.

"You have her going every which way, Ryder. I fancy this has never happened to her before."

"Yes. But enough is enough. I think I will have to follow her now. She just learned an important lesson in control. Now it's time for a frontal attack."

"No flank? No coming around the back?"

"You're becoming impertinent, Emile," Ryder said, grinned from ear to ear, and left.

Sophie didn't know what to do. She let a small slave lift her onto Opal's back. She sat there, staring blankly ahead of her. What to do?

She couldn't simply return to Camille Hall because Uncle Theo would know she'd failed. She shuddered at the consequences of that, unconsciously touching her fingertips to her cheek. It was a bit swelled from his blow. The powder covered it, but it didn't bury the memory of the pain, the humiliation. She would have liked to shout to that smug bastard, Ryder Sherbrooke, that she didn't wear makeup to look like a tart. She wore it to hide bruises, at least she had at first until Uncle Theo decided she looked more worldly, more seductive, painted like a whore. Of course he also realized that he could hit her more often without chance of discovery if her face was covered with cosmetics.

She had no choice. She would ride to the beach and loiter about before she returned home. Then she would lie to him. She would tell him that Ryder Sherbrooke had kissed her, had told her he wanted her. But then why wouldn't he want to take her to the cottage immediately? In her uncle's mind, a kiss made a man think instantly of bed. In her experience her uncle was quite right. Her brain closed down. She would deal with that when she had to.

Her decision made, Sophie urged Opal forward and made for the beach. It was called Monmouth Beach and it lay a mile farther east from Penelope's Beach. It was littered with jagged rock formations, the sand was a dirty brown from the swirling tides that crashed over and around the rocks. The cave was real. A slave had found it but yesterday. Opal picked her way carefully through the rocks, avoiding tide pools and battered tree limbs.

She didn't want to go to the damned cave. She pulled Opal to a halt, dismounted, and looked around. Within minutes, she was spreading the saddle blanket beneath a coconut tree and sitting in the shade, staring out over the brilliant blue sea. Her thoughts were, oddly, of her parents, of the last time she'd seen them four years before.

Her mother had been as strong-willed as a bull, beautiful of face and bountiful of figure, Corinna by name, a woman who loved her children very much, too much to take them on the journey to America, a journey she considered too fraught with danger. Her father had said "nonsense," but he didn't have her mother's strength of character and thus Sophie and Jeremy were fetched from Fowey, Cornwall, by their uncle Theo after the drowning of their parents, and brought to Jamaica. She remembered clearly her grief as well as her gratitude to her uncle. She had loved him, then.

She prayed her parents' deaths had been quick. Even now after four years she still repeated that prayer. Somehow she just knew that her mother had eased her father at the very end. It was the way her mother had been. She closed her eyes and felt the cool breeze from the sea on her face. She slipped out of her riding jacket and unfastened the top buttons of her linen blouse. She removed her riding hat, laying it gently atop her jacket, smoothing its curling feather as she did so.

Within minutes she was asleep.

When Ryder saw her mare, he smiled. So, she had come here after all. Perhaps that cave was really something. Then he saw her, leaning against that coconut tree, sound asleep.

Despite the heavy humid air, here on the beach, out of the sun, it was cool enough. He dismounted a good distance away from her, tethering his stallion close enough to some sea grass so he could graze.

He stood over her, staring down at her face, still now, and he realized that she looked very young despite the cosmetics that still coated her face. Very young indeed. Why, he wondered, why had she taken all those men to her bed?

Now she wanted him.

He dropped silently to his knees beside her. Very gently, very slowly, he began to unfasten the remaining buttons on her blouse. She wore a very plain batiste chemise beneath. No fancy frills or lace. He frowned and finished with the buttons.

But he couldn't peel the blouse off her because it was tucked into her riding skirt. He wanted her to remain asleep a bit longer.

He pulled the blouse back as far as he could then took a knife from his pocket and slit the chemise down the front to just below her breasts. Ah, he thought, as he eased the light material back, her breasts.

They were beautiful breasts. She stirred, but didn't awaken.

He waited a few minutes, then slowly eased her down until she was lying flat on her back. He waited longer, hoping she would remain asleep. She turned on her side, moaned just a bit, then fell back again. Smiling, Ryder then began to work up her riding habit, slowly, ever so slowly, until it was bunched at mid-thigh, and he could see the plain garters that held her stockings in place. Very nice legs, he thought, long and sleekly muscled.

He was still looking at her legs when he eased down beside her and waited for her to awaken.

He wasn't quite certain how he expected her to react when she did wake up. He supposed she'd look up at him, be a bit aroused already, and hold out her arms to him. He waited, picturing his hand easing up her inner thigh to touch her intimately, and she'd be eager, and she'd beg him to take her here, now. He looked at her mouth.

She awoke in the next instant, and out of that lovely mouth came an actual scream, loud and embarrassed and utterly horrified. The scream dwindled into a squeak then a gasp.

He sat up next to her. She was staring stupidly from him to her naked breasts down to her legs.

"Damn you, what did you do to me!"

"I kissed your breasts and you moaned and arched your back. You thrust your breasts into my face so I was forced to slit your chemise open to help you get what you wanted. But you're a greedy woman. You wanted more, so you came down upon your back and lifted your hips and I helped you by pulling up your skirt."

"No, no, damn you, that's a lie!"

Her face was red and she was actually sputtering. Ryder frowned. This was unexpected. Where were her teasing smiles, her outrageous, coy, very sexual remarks? He watched as she regained control, watched the blankness disappear from her eyes, watched the control and that damned cool smile set itself into place.

What Sophie was thinking was, *Did he see the bruises on my ribs? Dear God, please no.*

She got herself in control. Slowly, giving him a very tempting sideways smile, she pulled the sides of her chemise over her breasts and began to work the buttons closed again, all the while keeping her legs exposed to him.

When she'd finished, she slowly rose and stared down at him. She smoothed her skirt, then put her hands on her hips.

"You damned bastard," she said, surprised at the mildness of her voice. "Damn you, you came."

"Yes, I decided my manhood couldn't tolerate your obvious scorn."

"Most manhoods couldn't. You are no different."

"No, probably not."

"You had no right to do what you did to me."

"I wanted to take you off guard. I find you excessively unpredictable whenever I manage to do it. You shrieked, just like a maiden aunt. Most delightful. It sweetens the pot, one could say, all these varied and unexpected sides of you. I wonder how many other sides you will show me if I'm quick enough to catch you showing them."

"You have had your fun, Ryder."

"Oh, I haven't as yet begun, as you will see. But I do have a question for you, Sophia. Why did you dismiss Lord David Lochridge from your harem?"

"Harem? I think you're confusing your genders."

"It's the same concept. Why, Sophia?"

She shrugged and turned away from him for a moment, looking out over the sea. She was silent for a very long time.

Finally, she turned back to him and that damned flirtatious mask was well in place. "He bored me. He was a boy in a man's body. He cared only for his own pleasures, his own amusements. I grew tired of him, that's all."

"You're lying."

"Oh? Why would you say that?"

"You wish me to believe that you dismissed him because you wanted me and you remembered my demand that I be the only man in your bed and thus in your body?"

"Yes, I remember you saying that."

"What about Oliver Susson? Will you dismiss him as well?"

She shrugged, saying nothing.

"I won't become your lover until you do."

"Surely you are a bit overenthusiastic in your demands, Ryder. Surely it isn't up to the lady to make herself more appealing to the gentleman.

I am already appealing; you should be slavering over me even as we speak. You should be begging me to allow you in my bed."

He laughed, a rich, deep laugh. "Sophia, let me tell you something. You are pretty, yes, even with the absurd paint on your face, but understand me. I have bedded many women whose beauty reduces yours to mere commonplace, to nothing out of the ordinary. From what I have seen of your body, it is pleasing enough. But understand me, I won't play your games. I won't wait in the wings while you spread your legs for seemingly every gentleman in the vicinity. I am not an uncontrolled boy, anxious to plow every female belly he can manage. I am a man, Sophia, and I have developed standards over the years."

"Years! What are you, twenty-five, twenty-six?"

"I had my first sexual encounter when I was thirteen. What about you?"

In that moment, he saw anger in her, at him, and it was barely leashed. He saw uncertainty then, as if she were arguing with herself whether or not to cosh him on the head if she could manage it. Then she smiled at him, that coy, teasing smile that made him hard as a rock.

"In short, Miss Stanton-Greville, get rid of the others — all the others — or I will never bed you. I find I am already losing interest quickly."

"Very well," she said. "I will dismiss Oliver. Will you come to the cottage tonight? At nine o'clock?"

"Are there any others?"

"No."

"Ah, you already dismissed Charles Grammond, the poor fellow who lost all his money to Lord David?"

"That's right."

Ryder found that he was brooding, picking, but knowing at the same time that she would elude him. She would show him glimpses of herself, but she wouldn't drop her guard unless he pulled something totally unexpected, caught her completely off guard, like baring her breasts or pulling up her skirt.

He rose to stand beside her. He said nothing, merely stared down at her. He grasped her upper arms in his hands and pulled her up against him.

"Perhaps I don't wish to fall into the same bed that has held so many other of your men. Perhaps I would like to sample what you have to offer me right here, right now."

He kissed her, but she jerked her face away and his lips landed on her jaw.

He merely smiled down at her, clasped his arms beneath her hips and raised her, pressing her belly hard against his groin. He was hard and he knew she could feel him.

"Put me down, Ryder."

Her voice was calm and controlled. He didn't stop smiling. "On the other hand," he said close to her mouth, "perhaps I don't really wish to come into you right now. Perhaps what I really wish to do is pay you back. Give you a taste of retribution. Yes, that's exactly what I want to do."

He carried her to the water's edge. She knew his intent and began to struggle. He laughed as he waded out into the water, ruining his soft leather boots and not caring. He waded until the water lapped around his thighs.

She was screaming at him, pounding her fists against his chest, his arms, his shoulders.

He lifted her high in his arms and hefted her a good four feet into deeper water. She landed on her back, arms flailing wildly, and sank like a stone.

"There, you hellion," he shouted when her head cleared the water. Her chestnut hair was matted and tangled over her face and shoulders. She looked quite pathetic. "Don't attack me again unless you want to pay more reparations."

He laughed again and strode back to his horse. "I mean it, Sophia. I am a gentleman most of the time unless circumstances dictate another behavior. Understand me. I will never allow you to do your worst to me again without complete and utter retaliation."

As she stumbled through the water, her skirts dragged her first to one side and then to another. Her boot went into a hole and she went down on her face. She managed to regain her balance and rose, shaking her fist at him. He was on his horse's back, riding away down the beach. He was still laughing.

He stopped and she heard him shout over his

shoulder, "Tonight. Nine o'clock. Don't be late! Ah, and make certain the place is aired out."

Sophie paced the cottage, aware that her uncle was watching her from the corner of his eye. She said finally, "I'm afraid of him."

"Don't be a fool," Theo Burgess said. "He's just a man, a young man, not all that experienced, surely."

"You're wrong. I get the impression he's slept with more women than there are on Jamaica. Him and his damnable standards."

Theo shrugged. "Get him drunk. You know how to do it. It's nearly time for him to arrive. I'll be close by. You know what to do."

"Yes," she said and wished, quite simply, that she could drop to the ground and die.

But that would leave Jeremy alone.

She stiffened her back, but the fear wouldn't go away. She had to get control, she had to manipulate him. She was good at it, for she was bright, and the good Lord knew she'd had a lot of practice.

At exactly nine o'clock, there came a light tap on the front door of the cottage.

Sophie opened the door. He stood there, giving her a lazy smile.

As he stepped past her into the cottage, he said, "Your attempt at a seductive gown is more of a success than not, I should say. However, harlot-red really isn't your color. I think a soft green would be more the thing. To avoid laughter, you should avoid any shade of white. Also, the whalebone pushing up your breasts is an artifice I deplore. A woman has breasts or she doesn't. A man who knows women isn't fooled. But you will learn. Come into the light so I can see your face."

Sophie followed him dumbly. She was right to be afraid of him.

He clasped her chin in his long fingers and raised her face into the full candlelight. "Ah, no makeup, or hardly any. I am pleased that you wish to satisfy my demands. Now, should you like to strip for me now or should we talk for a while? Who are your favorite philosophers, for example? Ah, I can see by your expression that you have read the great minds throughout all the centuries. Yes, there are so many you are very likely completely conversant about. Let's select only the second half of the last century. French."

She drew back, moving away from him to stand behind a wicker chair. "I like Rousseau."

"Do you now? Do you read him in French or do you read him in English?"

"Both." She turned away from him and quickly poured him a glass of rum punch. She handed it to him. "It's warm tonight. While we speak of Rousseau, why don't you drink a bit."

"I don't like Rousseau. I find him nauseatingly imprecise in his thoughts and rather foolish, truth be told, in his aspirations of the earth's possible perfection in his hands, using, naturally,

94

his absurd methods."

Ryder raised his glass and toasted her. He drank it. It was tart and cold and quite delicious. He hadn't realized he was so thirsty. He didn't particularly care for rum, but this didn't taste all that much like rum. He took another drink. It was really very good.

"I think Rousseau is a gentle man, one who wishes what is best for both men and women. He believes that we should quit the infamy and decadence of the world and return to a simpler life, return to nature."

"As I recall, this matter of nature was never defined."

Ryder drank more punch. It slid down his throat, tasting better than anything he'd ever drunk in his life. He finished the glass and handed it back to her. She poured him another.

"As I said, the fellow is a fool. What he should have preached is that men must control women or they will lose all sense of what and who they are, for women can control men through sex. The more skilled the woman, the more dangerous she is to a man. You, for instance, Sophia. I wonder what you want from me. I wonder what I have that you could possibly lust after, other than my body, of course. It is true that I am a Sherbrooke and thus the plantation belongs to my family, however —" Ryder broke off. He felt suddenly quite warm; he felt, really, quite wonderful, relaxed, but yet the need for her was growing hot in his blood. She looked soft and sweet to him, so willing, so anxious to please him. Now she was holding out her arms to him and she was speaking to him, but he didn't understand her words, which was odd, but he really didn't care. He downed the rest of the rum punch, rose from his chair, and walked to her. He took her into his arms and began kissing her. Her breath was warm and sweet and she opened her mouth to him and he reveled in her. His hands swept down her back to cup her buttocks. As he had that afternoon, he lifted her against him and moaned at the delightful sensation.

He released her for a moment, then stepped back and began to pull her gown from her shoulders.

She laughed softly, so very sweetly, and slapped his hands away. "No, Ryder, you'll rip the material and it was expensive. I had it made just for you. I am sorry that you dislike the color. I will have another made in the shade of green you deem proper for me. Now, let me remove it. Let me become naked just for you. Yes, sit down here and watch me. Tell me what you want me to do. Here's another rum punch to cool you whilst you watch me."

Ryder took one sip of the rum punch. He leaned his head back against the chair cushion. His eyes were slitted as he watched her, standing in front of him, her hands on the buttons at the front of the harlot-red gown.

It was the last thing he remembered.

"He's unconscious."

"Excellent," Uncle Theo said, stepping into the

cottage. He walked to Ryder and examined him closely. "Yes, this is excellent. No, Sophia, don't leave. I would like you to see him. It is quite possible that being the sort of man he is, he will question you, and you must be prepared. If there is a mole or a birthmark on his thigh, why then, you must be able to remark upon it."

She stood back as her uncle dragged Ryder Sherbrooke to the wide satin-sheeted bed. He undressed Ryder swiftly, for he'd had a lot of practice. When Ryder was sprawled on his back, quite naked, Theo laughed. "My God, he's still aroused. Look at him, Sophia. Didn't I tell you he was an excellent specimen?"

She didn't want to, but she did look. She supposed he was beautiful, for he was lean and nicely muscled, light brown hair covering his chest and thinning out to his belly, but she found him terrifying, particularly his sex, which was thick and hard. Uncle Theo turned him over on his stomach. His flesh was smooth, his back long, the muscles deep and firm. There were no moles or birthmarks.

Uncle Theo turned him again onto his back. "Ah, he is ready because in his mind it's you he will bed." Theo turned and called out, "Dahlia! Come in now, girl."

A very beautiful young girl, no more than sixteen, with light brown skin and brown eyes, stepped into the cottage. She sauntered over to the bed and stared down at the naked young man. She stared a good long time.

"He be a treat," she said and gave Theo Burgess a big smile even as she lightly touched Ryder's belly.

"Excellent. I won't have to pay you then."

"He not that much a treat," she said. She slipped out of her dress. She was naked beneath, her breasts pendulous and very large, her hips round and supple. Sophie turned away only to have Uncle Theo grab her arm. "I think you should watch, Sophia. Again, he might ask questions, make comments and —"

"I won't!" she yelled in his face, jerked free of him, and ran from the cottage.

She heard Dahlia laughing softly, heard her say in an utterly happy voice, "Ah, look at how much bigger he get and all I do is touch him with my fingers! Ah, yes, massa, this nice boy be a treat."

Sophie fell to her knees. She felt nausea roil in her belly but she wasn't sick. She was beyond being ill. At first she would have been, but not now. No, too much time had passed. She'd seen too much. She hugged her arms around herself and rocked back and forth.

She heard Dahlia crying out in the cottage, heard her laughing and groaning and encouraging Ryder to come deeper into her, to caress her breasts. She wondered if Uncle Theo were standing there, watching. She knew he'd done it before. She wondered if he'd taken Dahlia to bed himself. She heard Ryder then. Heard him moan, heard him yell. Oh God, it was too much.

She crept away.

CHAPTER 5

Ryder woke slowly. His first reaction was one of incredulity, for he felt both slightly drunk and sated. He also felt utterly relaxed, but strangely vague. But it was morning, he knew that, and he was drunk? He'd never been drunk in his life upon waking. It made no sense. Nothing made any sense at the moment.

He sat up in the strange bed, and held his head in his hands, trying to understand. He realized then that he was naked, and remembered where he was and what he had done here in this bed for most of the previous night. Actually, he should be completely exhausted but he wasn't.

He'd been in this bed with Sophia Stanton-Greville.

God, she'd been incredible, her skills beyond the ability of any woman he'd ever bedded before. He rose slowly, shaking his head to clear it. The front door opened and an old female slave came in, giving him a wide toothless grin, saying in just short of a cackle, "Good morning, massa. Aye, 'tis fine you be this mornin'." He started to cover himself, but the old woman merely shook her head. She couldn't have cared less if he was wearing a gentleman's morning wear or was as naked as the Sherbrooke Greek statues he and his brothers had gawked at when they'd been boys.

She offered him a bath and breakfast. True to form, Sophia had left him alone. He was just one of many. She hadn't cared enough to stay with him. Oddly it hurt and made him angry, in equal parts. He was just another man and she'd not cared.

He eased himself down into the bath. He tried to remember the previous night in detail, but most of the specifics eluded him, which was surely very strange. He remembered kissing her at first, then he could almost feel again her mouth caressing him expertly and he shuddered with the memory. He remembered her riding him hard and fast, his hands kneading her large breasts, caressing them, lifting them, and he'd screamed like a wild man when his climax had hit him.

She'd screamed as well. And she'd spoken to him, urged him on, telling him what she liked, telling him what a man he was. He remembered it quite clearly, her voice soft and deep. He remembered her breasts in his hands and how they'd thrust forward when she'd arched her back over him.

Ryder didn't remember pleasuring her though, and that was odd for he hadn't lied to her. He was an excellent lover. He never left a woman unsatisfied. But he hadn't taken her in his mouth as she had him. He couldn't remember kissing her either, except at the very beginning of the evening, and surely that was even more odd, for Ryder loved kissing, sliding his tongue into a woman's mouth, stroking her, bringing her closer and closer as he used his hands on her body to heighten her pleasure.

Why hadn't he kissed her? Was she so abandoned that she could climax with him simply inside her? He hadn't even fondled her with his fingers, at least he couldn't remember doing so. He shook his head again, shaking away a slight dizziness. He still felt mildly drunk and he hated it, and the damnable vagueness.

He rose from the bath and the old slave handed him a towel. She didn't show any interest in his body at all. No, he thought, the anger building stronger than the drunkenness, she was so used to seeing naked men here — Sophia Stanton-Greville's men — that she didn't even pay attention anymore.

He dressed in freshly pressed clothes — good God, did the cursed woman think of everything? — and ate fresh fruit and warm bread. He shook his head at the offered rum punch. Jesus, he thought, watching the old slave drink it when she thought he wasn't looking. The drinking here was beyond good sense and control. He should know, he'd done enough of it the previous night.

When he left a few minutes later, he turned in the doorway of the cottage and looked back

101

toward the bed, now freshly made up by the old slave. The interior still smelled of sex.

He hated himself for what he'd allowed her to do to him. She'd obviously kept control the entire time. He again remembered her shriek of pleasure and wondered if it had been feigned. Odd, for he wasn't certain and surely that couldn't be right. Ryder knew women. No woman could feign pleasure with him. But she could have and he simply didn't know. He remembered then the glasses of rum punch he'd drunk when he'd arrived the previous evening at the cottage. How delicious it had been, how cool and refreshing, and then all he remembered was the warmth he felt, the hard arousal, the urgency, the incredible sex that had gone on and on until he'd finally fallen like a good soldier in battle.

He walked to his horse. Sitting beneath a mango tree was Emile, chewing on a piece of turtle grass, his hat pushed to the back of his head.

"So," Emile said only, rising, and dusting off his breeches. "Are you ready to go home?"

"Yes," Ryder said. "I'm more than ready."

Emile asked him no questions. As for Ryder, he was cold sober now, his head so clear it ached. The more he tried to remember each detail of the previous night, he found he simply couldn't call it forth. Except that he'd spewed his seed in her mouth, his back arcing off the bed the release had been so powerful, that and her sitting astride him, riding him hard, her hands busy on his body, pushing him until he couldn't bear it, and again, he'd screamed his release.

Something wasn't right. In fact, something was very wrong. He was still frowning when he and Emile rode down the long Kimberly Hall drive. Ryder listened with half an ear to the rhythmic humming and singing of the slaves as they worked in the fields.

"Emile," he said finally, "have you ever seen a crocodile in the middle of the road in the mangrove swamps?"

"Yes, I have. It's terrifying, really."

"Something is very wrong," Ryder said.

"What do you mean?"

Emile was dancing around the issue. He didn't want to call Sophia Stanton-Greville a whore if Ryder was now enthusiastic about her. He was uncertain; he was trying to be diplomatic.

From one instant to the next, Ryder realized the truth, clear and shattering. It was her breasts! He'd fondled Sophia's breasts two times. He knew the texture of her flesh, the size of her, her weight, his hands could even now mold themselves in the shape to hold her breasts.

The woman who'd taken him twice the night before wasn't Sophia Stanton-Greville. The breasts were all wrong. It was that simple. If it hadn't been Sophia, then it had been another woman, and that meant something that made him want to howl in fury. He turned to Emile and said, "There was something in the rum punch she gave me last night." There, he'd said it aloud. And it was true, of that he was certain. But he couldn't tell Emile he was basing everything on the size and feel of breasts.

Emile was clearly incredulous. "You mean to say she drugged you? Good God, why?"

"I woke up alone, just as you told me would happen. What was strange was that I was still feeling drunk. Something else even stranger is that I can remember certain things, but all the details of the night are gone from my memory." He shook his head for there was something of a flaw in his theory. "If there was something wrong, if she has indeed been drugging men's rum punch, why wouldn't her other lovers have come to realize it and said something or confronted her with it?"

"I would say that you are the man with the most experience of all the men she's taken to that cottage. Perhaps the others simply remembered the pleasure and didn't question a thing."

"Perhaps," Ryder said. "Perhaps." He was thinking that more than likely, none of the other men had ever seen and caressed Sophia Stanton-Greville's breasts as he had. Just that other woman's, and thus the fools didn't realize the truth. Perhaps he wouldn't have either, at least at first.

He laughed aloud then. She'd be brought down all because of her breasts.

At five o'clock that evening, Ryder realized there'd also been a man there. He could actually hear his voice, but he couldn't remember the words he'd said. Did that make any sense? It had to. Who the hell had stripped him naked? He certainly couldn't remember taking off his own clothes, much less Sophia Stanton-Greville's.

She'd drugged him, seduced him, then brought in another woman to make love to him. It was clear enough. Ah, yes, and there was Uncle Theo who'd come in to see to his clothing. It must have been Burgess, there was no one else.

Ryder rose from the chair, a very grim smile on his mouth. He bathed and dressed carefully. He was coldly and calmly furious. He was going to drop in at Camille Hall. He had no doubt that he wouldn't be invited to stay for dinner.

Sophie wanted to eat in her room but Jeremy came bursting in upon her. "What's the matter, Sophie?"

Always he was afraid that she would become ill and die as their parents had died. She hastened to reassure him. "I'm just fine, love. I've quite changed my mind about eating here in my room. Give me a moment and I'll comb my hair."

Jeremy sat in a chair watching her brush her hair, chatting all the while.

". . . Uncle Theo had Thomas take me with him to the north field today, just for two hours, not more, because of the heat. It was fascinating, Sophie, but several times Thomas used his whip on a slave. I didn't think it was necessary but Thomas said he had to because they were lazy and had to taste the whip to remind them what would happen if they didn't work. He kept calling them lazy buggers."

Thomas was a cruel monster. Sophie hated him. She fastened her hair at the back of her head with a black velvet ribbon. She rose and looked in the mirror. In the old pale yellow muslin gown she looked about sixteen. The only discordant note was the faintly greenish bruise on her left cheek. She had no intention of putting on the powder. It didn't matter. Besides, in the dim evening light, no one would notice. And if Uncle Theo did, why it would probably give him pleasure.

She said over her shoulder, "If you were master here, Jeremy, would you keep Thomas as your overseer? Or another man like him who would whip the slaves?"

Jeremy chewed on his lower lip, swinging his legs, his energy overflowing despite his mental contemplation.

"I don't know," he said at last. "Uncle Theo seems to think Thomas is very good. He trusts him and allows him to do just as he likes. It's just that —"

"What?"

Jeremy shrugged and rose. "Well, I've known most of the slaves since we came here over four years ago. Most of them are my friends. I like them and they like me. I don't understand why you would want to hit someone you liked. And it's so hot in the fields, Sophie. I know I wanted to rest after a while. They never get to rest."

She ruffled his hair and kissed his brow, risking

a little boy's horror at such a motherly act. Jeremy squirmed away from her and out of her bed-chamber. "Come on, Sophie!"

She drew to a stop at the bottom step of the stairs. She stared, her heart pounding. There, standing in the large open foyer, was Ryder Sherbrooke, looking like an English gentleman from his brushed pale brown hair to his glossy Hessian boots.

Uncle Theo had just welcomed him in.

Ryder looked up and saw her. He blinked, he couldn't help it. The tart in the red gown from the night before bore no resemblance to this young girl standing there, mouth agape, staring at him as if he were the devil himself come to claim her for the fourth circle of hell.

Theo Burgess turned at that moment and a spasm crossed his face. Damn the girl, she looked like a virgin of fifteen, certainly not like she should look. He wanted to hit her for her defiance; he disregarded the fact that Ryder Sherbrooke was entirely unexpected.

"Hello, Sophia," Ryder said very calmly. "Your uncle has seen fit to take me in. I am to dine with you. Ah, and who is this?"

"I'm Jeremy, sir. I'm Sophie's brother." Jeremy walked with his clumsy gait, his hand out-stretched.

Ryder smiled down at the boy and shook his hand. "How do you do, Jeremy? I hadn't realized Sophia had such a large younger brother."

"Sophie says I grow faster than the swamp

grass. I'm nine years old, sir."

"He's a good lad," Theo said, his voice testy.

Sophie was standing there, frozen, waiting. Would Ryder look at Jeremy with contempt or pity? She didn't know which was worse. People had looked at him with both and it was all horrible. Ryder had been a perfect gentleman thus far but she didn't trust him, not an inch. Perhaps he hadn't yet realized that Jeremy wouldn't grow up to be perfect like him.

Jeremy beamed up at the man he recognized immediately as a real gentleman. He was young and handsome and well dressed, and there was a very nice smile on his face, a smile that reached his eyes. Jeremy also realized that he must be here because of Sophie. He turned to his sister and called out, "He's having dinner with us, Sophie. Isn't that grand?"

"Yes," she said, forcing a smile that was ghastly. "That's just grand."

Ryder saw the marked resemblance between brother and sister. He also saw that Jeremy had a lame left leg, probably a clubfoot. It was a pity, but it didn't seem to slow the boy down a bit. He was a handsome lad and seemingly well adjusted. He chattered all the way into the dining room to Ryder, who found him both amusing and intelligent. He reminded him very much of Oliver. Ah, how he missed Oliver and the other children.

Theo Burgess tried to sidetrack Jeremy, but it didn't work. It seemed that the man was truly fond of the boy. He didn't order him to be quiet. He merely shook his head at him and smiled at Ryder as if to say, What can I do?

Sophie said nothing at all.

"My sister is the best rider in the entire area," Jeremy said. "Maybe on all of Jamaica, but I've never been to Kingston so I can't be certain."

"Thank you, Jeremy," Sophie said, smiling at her knight, a quite beautiful unconscious smile that made Ryder draw in his breath. She looked about fifteen and that smile lit up her face. It made her look very different, very appealing, really, and he didn't like it. At that instant he realized it was the very first time he had ever seen her smile.

What the hell was going on here?

He looked down at the delicious curried shrimp with pineapple. He speared a shrimp and chewed it thoughtfully. The boy was speaking again, telling his uncle and Ryder about his hours spent with Thomas in the fields.

Sophie noticed that he didn't mention Thomas whipping the slaves.

The dinner was pleasant, finished off by mango pie topped with warm cream. The rich Jamaican coffee was thick and black and wonderful, as usual.

Ryder bided his time. He enjoyed the boy. He shook his hand when he was dismissed to his bed. When Theo Burgess asked him if he would like to adjourn to the veranda where it was much cooler, he readily agreed. Every man he'd met on Jamaica imbibed rum in the evenings. It was time for the ritual to begin. It was time to put his plan into action.

He wasn't surprised when Sophie excused herself to follow Jeremy upstairs. Nor was he surprised when Theo called after her, "You will join us, my dear, when you have seen to your brother. Don't forget, Sophie."

"I won't forget, Uncle," she said, and Ryder heard something odd in her voice, something he didn't understand at all. "I'll be down shortly."

Ryder set out to make himself a congenial companion. He was amusing, his anecdotes of the first order. He encouraged Theo Burgess to talk and once he started, Ryder sat back, thinking about what he hoped would happen.

When Sophia came out on the veranda, she was carrying a tray and on that tray were glasses of rum punch. Ryder wasn't at all surprised.

"How delightful," Theo said. "I'm glad you remembered, Sophie. I trust the punch is up to the Burgess standards? I assume you enjoy a rum punch in the evenings, Ryder?"

"Why, most assuredly, sir," Ryder said.

So this was it.

He accepted the glass Sophia handed to him. He thought her hand shook a bit. But no, he must have imagined it.

Theo proposed a toast. Ryder clicked his glass to theirs and then pretended to drink.

He then rose, glass in hand, and walked to the wooden railing, leaning his elbows on it, and

110

looking out toward the glistening sea in the distance. There was a half-moon and the scene in front of him was spectacular. But he really didn't see it. He turned to face Sophia and Theo, made a toast to this beauty he really didn't see, and again pretended to drink. As he turned away again, he dumped the contents of the glass into the vivid pink blooms of the hibiscus bush just below the veranda. He hoped he hadn't killed the plant.

Now it was time to act. He turned, smiling widely, showing his empty glass, and said, "Why don't we take a bit of a stroll, Sophia?"

She didn't want to. She wanted him to just leave. She didn't want him to be sprawled naked in the cottage with Dahlia leaning over him, fondling him. She didn't want to hear him yell again in his man's release.

"Yes, Sophia, go along, my dear."

"Do bring us each another glass of that delicious punch."

"Yes, an excellent idea," Theo said and he felt the blood speed up, felt the triumph. Sophia had been quite wrong about Sherbrooke. He was only a young man, not all that intelligent or sly, quite easy really, quite predictable. In a sense it was disappointing. There was no challenge in him, not really. Sophia had been wrong.

Sophie brought each of them a fresh glass. Again, Ryder accepted the glass she thrust toward him. He offered her his arm. "Let's walk a bit. It's a beautiful night, isn't it? You can tell me

111

some more of the island's history."

"Oh yes."

He drew her into the garden on the eastern side of the house. It was darker here, but the scent of all the flowers was stronger, nearly overpowering. There was no one about, just the two of them, each with a glass of rum punch in his hand.

He said easily as he walked slowly beside her, "You don't look the whore tonight."

"No."

"However, last night was something of a sensation, wasn't it? Quite memorable, but not really, but surely I am quite wrong. It must have been memorable."

"Yes, of course it was. You seemed to enjoy yourself."

"And you, Sophia? Did you enjoy yourself as well?"

Still, she kept walking, and showed him only her profile. "Naturally. I wouldn't have wanted to make love with you had I not expected pleasure from it. You are quite competent as a lover."

"You screamed quite loudly when you climaxed."

She was silent as the night.

"I found your skills quite adequate, more than just quite, actually. Did you enjoy taking me in your mouth? You took me so deeply I feared I would gag you. But you didn't gag, at least I don't think you did."

"I think such things should be left to the cottage, don't you, Ryder?"

"Let's stop a moment. What is that bush over there? Yes, that one with the wispy yellow leaves?"

He took her glass from her, saw her stiffen slightly, then ease, as relaxed as could be, when he set both glasses on a stone bench. And he knew, simply knew, that she was memorizing that her glass was the one on the left. Well, it wouldn't matter. When she turned away from him, he slipped the packet of powder from his pocket and quickly poured the contents into her glass, stirring it with his finger.

"It's a yellow poui tree, actually, it's just very small as yet."

She turned and waved him forward. "You see, the flowers are in clusters. They're quite delicate and won't last long, perhaps only another week."

He admired the yellow poui tree.

When he turned back, she was already at the stone bench and she'd picked up her glass. She was obviously taking no chances. As he'd assured Emile she wasn't stupid.

He picked up his own and raised it in a toast. "To our evening. You gave me great pleasure. I trust we will spend another together very soon."

"Yes," she said and clicked her glass to his. She sipped it, found it remarkably delicious, and drank deep.

"Finish it off, Sophia, and if you like, we'll stroll about a bit more."

His rum punch went onto the ground and hers

113

went straight down her throat.

Ryder said, "You have beautiful breasts, but I've already told you that. However, I remember last night that your breasts seemed even larger. Isn't that curious? I suppose it must have been my lust, my fevered urgency for you that made me imagine such a strange thing."

"Perhaps."

"Why do you say perhaps?"

"You'd drunk a bit more than you should have, but you seemed to enjoy it very much. I didn't wish to take away from your enjoyment."

"It was very kind of you."

She kept walking. Why wouldn't he simply collapse? He'd drunk two glasses, surely it was enough. Uncle Theo had made it stronger tonight. But he sounded chirpy as a blue jay and his step was light and bouncy. She hated him and herself. If it weren't for Jeremy, why she'd . . . she didn't know really what she would do.

Ryder stopped and turned to face her. "I'd like to kiss you, Sophia. Odd, but I can't remember kissing you at all last night, except of course just a few forays before you pushed me away so you could strip off that scarlet whore's gown for me. It's odd, for kissing is something I much enjoy. Why didn't we kiss, Sophia?"

"You wanted me quickly. As you said, there was fevered urgency. There was no time."

"Now there is." He kissed her and she let him. She tried to force herself to kiss him back but she couldn't. She was a fraud and a cheat and she was very, very afraid of this man. Ryder was well aware that she was letting him touch her, not reacting, suffering him. It was enraging, but he wasn't overly surprised and oddly enough his anger soon stilled.

He gently pushed her away, holding her in the circle of his arms. "How do you feel, Miss Stanton-Greville?"

She looked up at him. "Why so formal, Ryder? After all, you are now my lover. None other, just you, and you will remain my lover, won't you?"

"Oh yes. You're marvelous. If I close my eyes, why I can see you taking me into your mouth, I can feel your tongue on me, the warmth of you. Yes, you gave me great pleasure. Tell me though, Sophia, isn't there something I can give you? Something you would like to have? I had thought to bring you a piece of jewelry but I didn't have time to go to Montego Bay. What would you like, sweetheart?"

Yes, she thought, bitterness filling her, he had to pay the whore. She wished she could tell him Dahlia's name and send him to her; let her get the gift. But no.

"Well," she said slowly, giving him a dazzling smile, "perhaps there is something I would enjoy."

"Yes? Just tell me and it's yours. A bauble, perhaps? A diamond or a ruby? Of course I want you again, tonight."

She didn't tell him. She sighed softly and fell

against him, quite unconscious.

Well, hell, Ryder thought, as he lifted her. She'd succumbed more quickly than he'd expected. He gently laid her out of sight in the midst of colorful jasmine bushes, smoothed down her skirt, and rose. He gave her a small salute.

And he thought, as he walked quickly back to the veranda, now it's your turn, Uncle Theo. I suspect you'll be fairly easy, you old bastard.

And Theo Burgess was remarkably easy. There was only one old slave to see him when he carried Theo over his shoulder, quite unconscious, to his bed.

Sophie woke slowly. She felt strangely suspended, somehow separate from herself. Her head felt light, her thoughts scattered and vague. She felt slightly dizzy. It was morning, the sun was shining through the window.

But that couldn't be possible. The morning sun didn't shine in her window.

She forced herself to sit up in bed. She shook her head, wondering at the strangeness of how she felt. She felt somehow drunk but surely that was odd.

She swung her legs over the side of the bed. It wasn't her bed. She realized then that she was perfectly naked.

She cried out. She stared blankly around her. She was in the cottage, quite alone. She simply sat there, tugging the sheet over herself, staring at the far wall. What had happened?

Ryder Sherbrooke had happened. Somehow he'd discovered what she and Uncle Theo had done to him. And he'd gotten revenge.

She wondered if he'd taken her as Dahlia had taken him two nights before. How did one tell? She rose slowly, dropping the sheet. The room was warm and she felt perspiration on her brow from the heat of the room, and from the heat of her fear.

What had he done to her?

She looked down at herself. She looked just the same. She remembered long ago that Uncle Theo had assured her that she'd remain a virgin. But how could one tell if a female was a virgin or not? She hadn't asked him. God, she didn't know.

What to do?

Sophie saw her clothing lying neatly over the back of a wicker chair. They were the same clothes she'd worn the night before. He'd brought her here to the cottage and stripped her to her skin. It was beyond embarrassing. She had to know what he'd done to her. She had to find out what he knew.

She thought of Uncle Theo and blanched. Then, of course, she realized what must have happened. Ryder had drugged her, then Uncle Theo. He'd done a fine job of it. He'd paid them back in kind.

She dressed quickly and combed her hair, tying it at her nape with the same ribbon she'd used the night before. She looked at herself in the mirror. Did she look different? Was that how one knew that one wasn't a virgin anymore?

She looked pale, nothing more that she could see. She had to know. She left the cottage and walked quickly back to Camille Hall.

Uncle Theo wasn't there. A slave told her that the massa hadn't come down yet.

She realized then that it was only seven o'clock in the morning. But she couldn't wait. She called for Opal to be saddled.

CHAPTER 6

Ryder was alone on the front veranda drinking a cup of coffee. It was still very early, but he knew, deep down, that she would come and very soon. She wouldn't be able not to. She would have to know what he'd done to her and he couldn't wait to tell her.

When he saw Opal cantering up the drive, he smiled in anticipation, both his body and his mind becoming instantly more alert. He didn't rise, merely sat back and watched her ride closer and closer.

Sophie dismounted and tethered Opal to one of the black-painted iron posts. She was shaking. That would never do. She wiped her hands on her skirt and forced her shoulders back.

She walked up onto the veranda and simply looked down at him. She hadn't expected him to rise as a gentleman should in the presence of a lady and, indeed, he didn't. After all, she was about the furthest thing from a lady that breathed.

Ryder smiled up at her, a predator's smile, a quite evil smile really. "Good morning, Sophia.

You haven't changed your clothes, I see. You couldn't wait to see me again, then? Would you like some breakfast? Coffee, perhaps? You must keep your strength up, particularly after your exertions last night."

He was going to toy with her. Very well then, she wasn't an inexperienced twit when it came to men. She'd well learned most of their vagaries during the past year, their little conceits, their need to dominate and rule. She smiled back at him and tossed her head. "I should like some coffee, thank you."

"Do sit down."

She waited for him to return, her mind working feverishly, but blank of ideas. When he handed her the cup, she took it and sipped it slowly, all the while watching him take the wicker chair opposite her. He leaned back, as indolent as a lizard warming himself in the sun, and crossed his arms over his chest. He leaned the chair back on its hind legs. She wished it would tip over and he would cosh himself on his damned head.

"It's very early for a visit," he remarked to the wisteria that was spilling wildly over the railing of the veranda.

"Yes," she said, "very early indeed, yet you are up and dressed, almost as if you were waiting for someone to arrive. It will be hot today."

"It's hot every day. Did you wish to speak to me about something in particular? Or perhaps you wanted to see Samuel, who's so besotted with you he nauseates me with his endless effusions?

Or perhaps Emile, your childhood friend whom you now ignore?"

"You."

He gave her a lazy nod, then fell silent. The silence stretched long between them.

"Well?" he asked at last. "It's not that I have something urgent to do, it's just that I do bore rather easily. You are pushing the limits, Sophia."

"What did you do to me?"

"I beg your pardon?" An eyebrow shot up a good inch. He was pleased with the utterly sincere puzzlement in his voice.

"Damn you, don't play with me further. Please, did you take me to the cottage?"

"Yes."

"Did you take off my clothes?"

"Yes. I also folded them neatly for you. I am a man of orderly habits."

"Did you . . . that is to say, did you become intimate with me?"

"Do you mean did I become intimate with you before I folded your clothes neatly? Or after?"

She said nothing, merely stared at him. He shrugged, looked at her breasts, and smiled. "Become intimate, Miss Stanton-Greville? Why in heaven's name wouldn't I have taken you, or, as you so quaintly put it — become intimate with you? Isn't that the whole purpose of having a lover? Your body is mine, you told me that quite clearly. I don't particularly like females in my bed who are more unconscious than not, but parting your legs and coming into you did indeed serve my purpose . . . my purpose as your lover, naturally. You did arch your back just a little bit. No, unfortunately, I don't think you enjoyed it, even though you did moan once or twice." He struck a thoughtful pose. "But wait, I recall you moaned when I kissed your breasts, or perhaps it was when I was caressing your buttocks and I turned you on your stomach. You certainly didn't scream as you did the other night, though. Of course, you were in no shape to ride me, so it was I who did the mounting and the riding. You're quite soft, Sophia, and very giving. You gave me some measure of enjoyment. Last night, of course, I was full-witted and felt every shred of feeling to be felt from plowing your belly." He was just getting into the full swing of his splendid monologue when she jumped to her feet and yelled at him, "Damn you, stop it! Just stop it! You forced me, you raped me! You're an animal!"

"Forced you," Ryder said blankly. "An animal? Surely not, Sophia. I'm your lover."

"You drugged me! You took me when I was unconscious. You're no lover, you're a perfidious bastard! I hate you!"

He laughed then, a full, deep, rich laugh that made her skin crawl. God, she wanted to hit him, to hurl something heavy at his head, to kick him. She couldn't stop herself. She rushed from her chair and at him, her hands fisted. It took a lot of strength, but she managed to push his chair

122

backward, sending him sprawling. Unfortunately she didn't move back quickly enough. Ryder caught her ankle and jerked her down over him. He held her wrists so she couldn't strike him.

He looked up at her face, flushed with fury, at her breasts, heaving up and down, and said, happy as a vicar at a wedding, "How passionate you are, Sophia. Perhaps next time you can be as full-witted as I was this time and we can speak together while we make love. It will enhance your enjoyment, and mine as well, I hope, not that I'm complaining all that much."

She struggled and he was well aware of her body pressing onto his. She was truly enraged, quite unaware that her belly was grinding against him. He was hard; surely she felt him. But he had her firmly held. He merely waited until she realized she couldn't hurt him. But she struggled a good three minutes more. Finally, her voice low and mean, she said, "Let me go, damn you to hell."

"You know, Sophia, no woman has ever attacked me before with evil intent. Attacked me with laughter and sexual intent, certainly, for I much enjoy playful women and many of them seem to know it. But this violence? I'm uncertain of the rules here. Should I hold you another five minutes to be certain you're well tamed?"

She felt rage and fear. Tears were burning her eyes. She had no more words. She simply shook her head.

Ryder saw the tears but he knew she wouldn't

let them fall. "If I release you, will you try to do me in again?"

She shook her head again, and he guessed she was now really beyond words. He had won. Quite simply he'd demolished her. She deserved it. He released her wrists. She rolled to her side and was on her feet in an instant, staring down at him.

Ryder rose slowly. He set his chair back in its place, then motioned for her to be seated again.

It was as if it had never happened, she thought numbly, for the first words out of his mouth after he'd sat down again were, "Drugged you? That is what you said, isn't it? What a novel idea. What a grotesque thought. Who ever would think of something so perfidious as drugging? Why, that lacks all honor, all honesty. The deceit of such an act boggles the mind. Goodness, it's very early in the morning for such jests, but since I have nothing urgent to do, as I told you, and you certainly aren't boring me now, why, do continue spinning your fairy tales."

"I was a vir—" Her voice fell like a stone off a cliff. Good God, telling him she was a virgin would make him howl with laughter. She shook her head, trying to get hold of herself. He knew about the drugging; she'd been almost certain. "You drugged me. You must have put something in my rum punch. And then you took advantage of me." The words weren't what she would have liked to have said but there was nothing else in her mind. They were the ineffectual words of

124

an outraged maiden. She also realized that if more words were to come out of her mouth, they wouldn't be the right words either and he would only laugh all the more at her.

"Did I tell you that my very first afternoon in Montego Bay I heard you had three lovers? I heard descriptions of the three men in question. Why, Oliver Susson even came in and was needled mercilessly about you, all envy of course. Now, unless you took all these gentlemen in strange and exotic ways, then it's impossible that you've been a virgin for a very long time. Ah, yes, don't look so surprised, Sophia, and please don't protest. There are few words I know well that begin with 'vir.' I am relieved that you stopped yourself before you finished out that truly ludicrous lie. Virgin . . . another deceit that boggles the mind."

"No," she said, defeated. "I won't lie." But she was thinking, *I didn't feel any different this morning. I even looked in the mirror. I looked just the same, yet he says he took me and knew I wasn't a virgin.* She didn't understand this, but she remained silent. Evidently a man couldn't tell whether or not a woman had been touched. Evidently a man had to take a woman's word for her innocence. Given her reputation, her word was worthless and she knew it, so that was that. She was about as innocent as any harlot in Montego Bay. She saw he was grinning at her, and that grin was filled with triumph and satisfaction and more than a dollop of malice.

"Please, Ryder, please tell me the truth. What

do you know? How did you find out? What do you want? I admit it's over now, I know that even if Uncle Theo doesn't yet, but, please, oh God, please —" She stopped. What was she prepared to ask him anyway? There was nothing she could do now to prevent him from doing precisely what he wanted to do. She could hear his laughter if she attempted to tell him about Jeremy. Slowly, feeling as numb as a slept-upon arm, she rose from the chair. She stared at him blindly, turned, grabbing up her skirts, and ran down the front steps of the veranda.

He called after her, his voice loud and carrying, "It was your breasts that did you in, Miss Stanton-Greville. From that I deduced you must have drugged me. You see, it wasn't all that remarkable of me to have figured it out. Yes, indeed, a woman's breasts are hers alone, not to be pawned off on another. The other breasts were nice really, but much too large. No, I prefer yours."

She didn't turn but he would have sworn that her entire body jerked at his words.

Ryder watched her run away. He let her go. He didn't say another word. So she'd wanted to protest that she was a virgin. He shook his head at that nonsense. Even though another woman had bedded him, he still doubted very strongly that Sophia was as innocent as she looked now, as she'd looked the previous night, in that mussed girlish muslin gown, her face washed clean of cosmetics. No, it was highly unlikely. She'd led him on, teased him expertly, enticed him, let him fondle her breasts as would an experienced courtesan, setting the pace unless he managed to knock her off guard.

He watched her gallop her mare full tilt down Kimberly Hall's drive. He watched her until she disappeared from his sight.

He rose and stretched. He really had to decide what he was going to do now. It was a pity he hadn't discovered the purpose of the game with him, but he would, he didn't doubt it for a single moment.

Uncle Theo was waiting for her in his study. His face was pale and his hands were shaking slightly. He wore no kindly gentle mask for her. She knew fear, and kept as much distance as she could between them. She shut the door behind her and watched him slowly rise.

"Where the devil have you been?"

She expected this, and recited in a low voice, "I awoke in the cottage, naked in the bed, quite alone. I had to know what happened so I rode to Kimberly Hall. Ryder said he'd taken me since he was my lover, and what was all the fuss about.

"I accused him of drugging me. I started to tell him I was a virgin but I didn't because I knew he wouldn't believe me."

"He drugged both of us, the damnable bastard!"

At that, Sophie felt a fierce joy, despite what

Ryder had done to her. It was over now, finally over.

"Damnation! How did he know? None of the others ever wondered about a thing."

"I don't know." But he saw she was lying, and knowing there was no hope for it, she said quietly, "Very well. He said he knew that the breasts of the woman of that night weren't mine. He had fondled me before, twice, seen me, felt me. That was how he knew. He said all women were different from each other."

"That's absurd! He knew Dahlia's breasts weren't yours!" he cried, his words slightly slurred because his tongue was thick with rage. "Ridiculous. You're lying, damn you, Sophia!"

Theo Burgess stopped cold, whirled about and stared at his niece. "By God," he said very quietly, "you told him, didn't you? You went to him and you told him. You fell for his charm and his man's body and you told him!"

"No! I despise all men! He is no different."

"You hate me so you used him to get back at me. Well, it won't work. I'll figure something out and you'll do as you're told. Oh no, it's not over, Sophia. It won't be over until I say it will."

"It is over. He knows. Not all of it, but he knows enough. He will do something and you can't stop him."

"He knows because you told him. Don't lie to me further, you damned little bitch!"

She saw the darkening of his eyes and knew what was coming. He was on her in an instant.

128

He struck her hard and she slammed against the doorframe. She grabbed the knob to keep herself upright, then wished she hadn't, for he struck her again. Rage flowed through her, rage and strength she didn't know she possessed. The pain disappeared, leaving only the rage. She whirled away from him, regaining her balance. She picked up a lamp from a table and hurled it at him. It struck his arm.

He was screaming at her, cursing her, and she knew that if he got to her again, he wouldn't stop until she was dead.

A slave's face appeared at the veranda window, then quickly disappeared. She ran behind his large desk, grabbing books and throwing them at him, but he kept coming, closer and closer, and his fists were large, his knuckles white with the strain, his face brutal.

She saw the letter opener. She didn't think, she was beyond thought. She grabbed it and ran straight at him.

"I won't let you hit me again! Never again! I hate you!" She struck as hard as she could. She felt the end of the blade slide into his shoulder with sickening ease.

She was crying, her vision blurred. She looked at the letter opener, the mother-of-pearl handle sticking obscenely out of his flesh. She watched him look from her to the letter opener. His expression was bewildered.

"You stabbed me," he said slowly. He looked up at her again and he screamed, "I'll take care of you now, you damned little bitch! I've given you everything, you and that miserable little cripple. Stab me, will you."

He caught her arm, bent it until she knew it would snap, then released her, shoving her hard against the wall. She was trapped now in the corner of the room, and he was on her, hitting her again and again . . . her ribs, her face, again and again.

Until she slumped unconscious onto her side.

When she came to, she was still lying on the floor where she'd fallen, sprawled on her side. The pain drove all efforts at coherent thought from her head. Her body clenched and twisted in on itself; she moaned softly, unable to keep the sounds to herself. At least he hadn't killed her. Nor was her arm broken. That was something.

She lay there for several more minutes, not moving, scarcely breathing. She had learned to deal with pain but it was more difficult this time. He'd showed no restraint at all. He'd beaten her here in his study, a room that the slaves could enter at any time. Usually he was so careful, waiting until she was in her bed and coming into her room and beating her there with little to no chance of discovery.

Had he beaten her so badly because he had no intention of continuing his gentle, kindly fiction to anyone, the slaves included? Did he finally accept that it was over and he simply no longer cared? Even had she not stabbed him, she knew he still would have beaten her badly.

Perhaps he was dead. If so, she was a murderess.

Sophie tried to sit up. The pain was bad but she managed it. She couldn't remain here. If a slave came in and saw her, the truth would be out all that much sooner, and then Jeremy would find out as well and her mind balked at that. He wouldn't keep still. He would try to protect her. He would attack Uncle Theo. She saw both of them in a heap with their few possessions in a pile of refuse in the middle of Montego Bay. Oh, Jeremy, oh no, not her little brother. She'd been responsible for him for four years. She would be until she died.

No, she had to be wrong. Uncle Theo wouldn't do anything immediately. No, at the very least, she'd wounded him. He would be too weak to do anything yet. But he'd sworn to her that it wasn't over yet. He'd beaten her because he'd been so furious at Ryder Sherbrooke. No, he'd try to continue the fiction, he simply had to. Yes, she was wrong.

She drew a deep breath, gripped the edge of the desk, and pulled herself to her feet. She felt dizzy and nauseous but finally she managed to control it. She had to get out of here until she could keep from crying out in pain. She would need all her cosmetics this time to hide what he'd done to her.

She passed a mirror but didn't look at herself.

She crept out the side door of the study, holding her sides. She walked the near mile to the cottage, bent over like a frail old woman, breathing in short, jerking gasps.

It was too much. This time she had to do something. It had to end. Either she did it or Ryder Sherbrooke would. But she didn't think she'd have time to take action. She hurt too badly. Time seemed to stop. She wondered if she would die. She thought of Ryder. He was furious and primed for revenge. What he'd done to her was just the beginning, and that gave her hope.

When she finally reached the cottage, she began to cry. She couldn't stop crying nor did she try. The tears burned down her bruised checks.

She staggered into the cottage and, very slowly, walked to the bed. She eased herself down on it and let the pain flood over her in relentless waves.

Ryder wanted more answers. He was through with games. He rode to Camille Hall. Sophia wasn't there. The house slave didn't know where she was. The slaves he saw were acting strangely but they wouldn't tell him anything. Uncle Theo wasn't there either, not that Ryder was ready to face him down just yet.

Ryder paused a moment at the end of the long drive, wondering where she could have gone after she'd ridden away from Kimberly Hall. Then he knew. Without hesitation, he directed his horse to the cottage. If she wasn't there, she'd probably ridden to Penelope Beach, her private place, she'd told him.

At first he thought he'd been wrong. There didn't seem to be anyone about. He walked through the door and became very still.

She was lying on her side on the bed, fully dressed, her legs drawn up. She appeared to be deeply asleep.

Ryder walked very quietly to the bed and stared down at her. He took her arm and pulled her onto her back. He sucked in his breath in disbelief. All burgeoning ideas of further punishment fled his mind; incredulity took its place, then a rush of sheer rage. He stared down at her face; he couldn't believe it. Jesus, what had happened to her? But of course he knew. Uncle Theo had beaten her.

Even her heaviest cosmetics wouldn't cover these bruises. He realized his hands were fisted. She moaned and he saw her hands flutter about her chest.

As gently as he could Ryder undressed her. He guessed that she was as much unconscious as she was asleep. When he got her gown and slippers and stockings off her, he was still left with her chemise.

Again he drew his knife and cut it off her. The sight that met his eyes made him go very still. From just beneath her breasts to her belly she was covered with ugly bruises. Uncle Theo had hit her hard many times. He'd shown no mercy. It came to Ryder then that the night before when he'd stripped her, it was possible that there had been remnants of bruises over her ribs. But he couldn't be certain. The light had been dim. But now the evidence was there for all to see.

Jesus, the man was an animal. Lightly, he touched his fingertips to the worst of the bruises, just below her left breast. She moaned softly, flinging her arm out, then letting it fall. She'd come here to the cottage to hide away as would a wounded animal.

He straightened. The first thing he needed was laudanum, explanations could wait. When she awoke he could only imagine how bad her pain would be. He would have to leave her to fetch medicine. That, or he could simply wrap her up and take her back with him to Kimberly Hall.

She began to cry, low deep sobs that tore at him. Tears seeped from beneath her lashes. She was unconscious and still she was aware of the pain to such an extent that she was crying. Was she crying about all the rest of it as well? The months upon months of deception?

Ryder didn't hesitate. He wrapped her as gently as he could in a blanket and carried her out of the cottage. It was not easy to get her and himself onto his horse's back but he finally managed it. He prayed she would remain unconscious until he could get her back to Kimberly Hall.

When he arrived at Kimberly Hall, Emile was standing on the front steps, pulling on gloves. He started forward, eyes widening in surprise.

"What the hell is this, Ryder?"

"Come with me and I'll explain what I can. First, Emile, get some laudanum, water, strips of cotton, cream, whatever. If I'm not mistaken, her dear uncle Theo beat the hell out of her."

"Jesus," Emile said and hurried away.

Ryder carried her to his bedchamber. It simply didn't occur to him to take her anywhere else.

He pulled back the mosquito netting and laid her as gently as he could upon her back. He covered her with the blanket. He didn't want Emile to see her naked.

When Emile came back into the room, he said, "My father wants to know what's going on. I put him off. You should tell him what you think appropriate."

"Thank you, Emile. Just leave the things. I'll take care of her."

Emile hesitated. "Would you like Mary or Coco to help you?"

Ryder just shook his head. "No, I'll see to her. I don't suppose there's such a magical item as real ice here?"

"Of course. Ah, you want it for her face, to reduce the swelling. I'll fetch some immediately." Emile quietly shut the door on his way out.

Ryder peeled the blanket off her and set to work. When he knotted the last of the strips of cotton over her ribs, having made certain they weren't broken, he rose slowly, studying his handiwork. She was still unconscious.

He had a glass of water with laudanum ready

the moment she woke up. He studied her face as he waited. Slowly he reached out and gently glided his fingertips over her brow, her nose, her jaw. He slipped his finger into her mouth and pressed against her teeth. Her teeth were still strong and nothing was broken, thank God. Ah, but the pain she would suffer.

Sophie didn't want to wake up. She knew if she did, she wouldn't be pleased about it. And she wasn't. The pain hit her in vicious waves and she gasped with the force of it.

His voice came from above her. He was saying over and over that she would be all right, that he would make certain Uncle Theo never hurt her again. She was to trust him. "Trust me," he said yet again.

She opened her eyes then and stared up at Ryder Sherbrooke.

"Trust you?" she said, shuddering with the pain those two simple words brought her.

"Yes, please, Sophia. Trust me. I'll see that everything will be all right. Here, drink this."

Ryder saw equal amounts of pain and wariness in her eyes. He understood, he couldn't blame her, but he was determined. He gently lifted her head and forced all the drugged water down her throat.

He eased her back down. "Now, don't say anything. There will be time later to find out exactly what happened. No, don't try to talk. Just listen. Nothing seems to be broken. I've bound up your ribs. Your face is another matter. I'm going to wrap ice in a cloth and cover your eyes with it. Hopefully the cold will keep the swelling down, all right? If you feel something very cold, don't be alarmed. Now, just hold still."

Her eyes were closed when a light knock came on the door. It was Emile and he was carrying cloths and a bucket of ice chips.

"Thank you," Ryder said. "If Theo Burgess shows up here, come and get me."

Once alone with her again, Ryder wrapped the ice in the cloths and laid them over her eyes and across her face. She flinched and he said quietly, "Just hold still, Sophia. It will numb your face and the pain will lessen. Also, I gave you laudanum. Don't worry, please."

She tried to force the words from her mouth. "Jeremy," she said, but knew it was but a whisper of sound in her mind. She felt the laudanum pulling at her and tried one more time. "Jeremy."

Ryder's face was very close to hers. He made out her brother's name. He felt a frisson of alarm. If Uncle Theo had beaten her so badly, what would he do to the boy?

"Uncle Theo, I stabbed him. He won't come here, at least not today."

"You what?"

"I . . ." Her head lolled to the side.

Ryder didn't hesitate. He found Emile, who was pacing in the front entrance hall downstairs. "Have Coco stay close to her. The laudanum I gave her put her to sleep. Tell James not to allow anyone from Camille Hall in here. No one. As for your father, Jesus, tell him whatever you think best."

Emile nodded and was gone in an instant. Ryder took his place pacing. When Emile returned, he said, "Now what?"

"You, my friend, you and I are going to beard the lion in his den. Hopefully the damned lion isn't dead. I'll tell you all about it on the way."

Sophie gritted her teeth. The pain kept coming, kept pounding through her, surging and swelling until she thought she couldn't bear it. Then it would lessen, retreating and flattening as a wave receding from the shore, but she knew it would return again and again and there was nothing she could do about it. It wouldn't ever stop, not ever. She was trapped in it, helpless, and completely alone. She'd failed and now she was paying with this ghastly pain. There was nothing she could do to help anyone.

"Please don't cry, Sophie, please. Here, drink some water. Ryder said you'd probably be really thirsty."

She sipped the water, nearly choking. Then she realized that it was Jeremy who was here with her. Jeremy, her little brother. She raised a hand and pulled away the cloth from over her eyes. She could open her eyes without too much effort. The swelling had gone down. She saw Jeremy was standing there beside her, worry and fear etched deeply into that beloved face.

"I'm all right, Jeremy," she whispered. "Don't

worry. I probably look much worse than I really am."

"Shush," Jeremy said. "Ryder said you'd try to talk to me, and he said I was to tell you to be quiet. He said I could tell you what was happening. All right?"

"Yes."

"You are to lie very still. Ryder said that you'll be just fine. He said nothing was broken, but your ribs and your face are badly bruised. He said to be very still, Sophie."

"Yes."

"Uncle Theo changed," Jeremy said slowly, and he was frowning as he said it. He didn't understand, that was clear to her, but she didn't say anything, merely waited for him to continue. "He saw me come into the house with Thomas and he started yelling. He was holding his shoulder and I saw blood seeping through his fingers. He screamed at me that he was through with the two of us."

"He didn't hit you, did he?"

"Oh no. He just told Thomas to lock me in my bedchamber. He said he'd take care of me later. He didn't hurt me like he did you. But he was very angry and he was calling you a liar and a slut and a whore and other words I didn't understand. He said I was nothing but a crippled little bastard and he'd see to it that I never, ever inherited Camille Hall or got control of our home in Fowey. He said he'd see you in hell where you belonged."

Oh God, Sophie thought, wishing she could reach out and fold Jeremy in her arms. Yet he sounded very calm, detached, as he spoke, and that frightened her even more.

"I was going to climb down the trellis off my balcony when the door burst open and Ryder came in. He said we were leaving. He said you were here and he was bringing me to you. He said everything would be all right."

"Uncle Theo?"

"He wasn't there. I guess he went off with Thomas to see to his shoulder. Did you hit him, Sophie?"

"Yes, I stabbed him with a letter opener."

He seemed to take her bald words quite in stride. "I was afraid, Sophie," Jeremy said after a moment. "I was afraid that he would send in Thomas with his whip and he would whip me like he does the slaves. And I didn't know where you were or what he'd done to you."

She felt such relief that for an instant, the pain faded into near insignificance. She didn't hear the door open, but suddenly Jeremy turned and his face lit up.

"Is she all right?" It was Ryder's voice, low and deep.

"Yes, sir. I told her to be quiet, just as you told me to, and just let me talk. She's been pretty good. She tried, sir. She did stab him."

"Yes, I know. Now, my boy, would you like some pineapple betty? Cook said every young man she knows loves her pineapple betty."

Jeremy shot a look back at his sister.

"No, it's all right. I'll be here. Go ahead, Jeremy."

Ryder didn't say anything until Jeremy had left the room.

"Are you ready for some more laudanum?"

"No, please, it makes my mind fuzzy."

"It's better than the pain. Jeremy is safe and I swear to you he will remain under my protection. There is no reason for you to be a martyr. No, keep quiet, Sophia. Here, drink this."

She did and within minutes her eyes were closed and her breathing had deepened.

Then she said in a soft, slurred voice, "My name is Sophie. I've always hated Sophia."

"I prefer Sophie as well," Ryder said, but she was asleep.

He placed fresh ice packs over her face then settled back in a chair. He stretched out his legs, crossing them at the ankles. He steepled his fingers and lightly tapped his fingertips to his chin. His eyes never left her. What the hell was he to do now?

He thought fondly of home, of his brothers and Sinjun, his sister. He thought of his brother's new wife, Alex, and wondered how she was faring with the earl, a very stubborn man.

If Samuel Grayson hadn't written all in a dither about strange happenings here, why then he would still be in England, enjoying his children, enjoying his mistresses, riding the southern cliffs, the wind whipping his hair in his eyes, without a worry in the world.

Now he had two big human worries. He realized that his life to this point had been exactly as he'd ordered it up. He'd done precisely what he'd pleased because providence had made him the second son, and thus his brother was the Earl of Northcliffe. An equal share of good fortune was the immense wealth left to him by his uncle Brandon. He realized with a start of self-contempt that he'd played with his life, taking what he wanted, never really thinking about consequences because he'd even managed to control those quite well. Most who knew him liked him, he knew that. He was charming, he brought laughter into a room with him, he was honorable in his dealings. He shook his head, seeing himself clearly. He was honorable for the simple reason that there was never any reason for him not to be honorable, no challenges to his honor, to his integrity; he'd never really had to prove himself. One could praise him about the children, perhaps, but that was different, that was something deep within him that he had to do. It was a pleasure to do; it was easy to do; they made him feel blessed, not put upon.

But now things had spun quite beyond his control. He didn't want to be involved in this mess, but he was. He stared over at the beaten girl on his bed. She'd managed to stab the bastard. She had guts. He couldn't walk away from this. He couldn't walk away from her. He cursed quietly, with great fluency.

There was nothing for it.

CHAPTER 7

Sunlight poured in the bedchamber, warming Sophie's face. She opened her eyes and queried her body. The pain was less than it had been yesterday. Two days now, two days of lying here and wondering what had happened and what would happen now. She hated the helplessness. She had to get up; she had to do something, what she didn't know, but she knew the first step was to get her feet on the floor. She managed to pull herself upright, groaned with the rush of pain in her ribs and fell back again, panting. She closed her eyes and waited, counting slowly to ten. At least she could close her eyes, even blink, without pain. The ice Ryder had kept on her eyes for the past two days had markedly reduced the swelling. Ah, but her ribs. She tasted blood and knew she'd bitten her lower lip. But it didn't matter. Who cared? She got control of the pain, finally. Still, she didn't move. She was afraid to move, it was that simple. When she finally opened her eyes again, Ryder was standing beside the bed, looking down at her.

"Good, you're awake. I've brought you break-fast. I'll bring Jeremy along to see you once I make certain you're in good enough condition not to scare the devil out of him. I had to let him see you the first time because he wouldn't believe that you were alive. But it did scare him; he was brave about it and continues to hold up well. I am proud of him and so should you be as well." He smiled at her as he spoke, and he was very matter-of-fact. The last thing she needed was an outpouring of sympathy and pity, and he knew it.

"I did what I thought best for him and for you. No, hold still. I'm going to lift you. Don't try to do anything yourself."

When she was propped up against the pillows, he set the tray on her legs. "Before you eat, per-haps you need to relieve yourself?"

"No," Sophie said, staring at the fork beside her plate.

"Don't be unnerved. It really doesn't suit you. Surely you can handle any impertinence out of a male mouth. Come now, after the long night you must have to —"

"All right, yes! Would you please take this tray and leave me alone."

He grinned down at her, pleased with her out-burst that brought color to her face, and called out, "Coco, come here and assist Miss Stanton-Greville."

He turned back to her. "I suppose you would like me to remove myself?"

"At the very least."

"Ah, it pleases me to allow you to resharpen your knifely wit on my poor male head."

She paled. It infuriated him. He leaned down, his hands on either side of her face. "Dammit, Sophie, don't think about your uncle! Lord, had I been with him, I wouldn't have stabbed him, I would have wrung his mangy throat. Now, stop it."

"You don't understand."

"I understand a lot more than you think I do."

She looked up at him, wondering, but afraid to ask him what he meant. "Thank you for keeping Jeremy away." He merely nodded and left the bedchamber.

When he returned, Sophie was eating her breakfast. No, he was wrong, she was actually pushing the soft baked yams around her plate. She didn't look quite as frightful as she had the day before or the day before that. He needed to examine her ribs, but he would wait a bit for that.

"Eat. I won't leave you alone until you finish everything. Does it hurt to swallow and chew? I imagined that it still did and that's why you have the soft yams again. I had Cook put some brown sugar on them."

"Thank you. They're quite good, really. I'm just not very hungry."

"You're worried and I told you not to. Eat."

"Why are you being like this?"

He turned toward the open wooden doors that gave onto the balcony. "Like what?" She waved her fork at him, winced because the slight movement brought her pain, and continued silent.

"Well, I really can't see myself making love to you in your current condition. No, don't throw the yams at me, you might hurt your ribs. I will tell you something. Even the bruises in all their splendid color are preferable to those cosmetics you smeared on your face."

"My uncle demanded the cosmetics. He said they made me look more like a woman should, more sophisticated."

"Yes, and I imagine you also had to use them to cover bruises. Am I right?"

"I will be well enough to travel very soon now."

"Oh? Where do you intend to travel to? A young girl with a little boy and no money?"

He regretted his sarcasm, though she'd deserved it, and said quickly, "I will decide what will be done after you're completely well again. You're not to concern yourself about anything. As I told you, Jeremy is just fine and I'm keeping a close watch on him. When I'm not with him, Emile or Samuel is. All right?"

"Why are you being so nice?"

"Does that come as a shock to you? I suppose you're really not used to nice men."

"No."

"Finish your breakfast and then we'll talk. It's time, don't you think? I cannot continue to battle shadows. I must know the truth."

"You're so smart I would have thought you would have already figured out everything. Didn't you just tell me that you understood more than I gave you credit for?"

No, he thought, he wouldn't strip her just yet to see her ribs.

"I don't like the way you're giving orders, Ryder. I'm sorry, you are being nice to Jeremy and me, but after I'm well again, I will see to us. We are not your responsibility and —"

"Shut up, Sophie. You're really quite wearying."

"Go to the devil!"

He grinned at that. "Who was it who told me you were a regular hellion?"

"Some miserable man, I doubt not. Hellion — what nonsense! None of you can bear the thought of a woman making decisions for herself, being responsible for herself. You must always rule and order things to your own satisfaction, and you dare to call it protecting her. Well, let me tell you, I won't have it, do —"

"Shut up, Sophie. If you want to expend ire, why, then, let's redirect it. Let's talk about Uncle Theo."

"Is Uncle Theo alive? Are you certain?"

"Yes, I am certain. Your aim wasn't all that good."

"It is not a good thing to stab one's uncle."

"Nor is it a good thing to beat one's niece."

She sighed, leaned her head back, and closed her eyes. He studied her in silence for several minutes. Her hair was loosely braided and hung lank and dull over her right shoulder.

"Would you like to bathe? To have your hair washed?"

Her eyes flew open and there was such hope and excitement that he laughed. "Very well, if you finish your breakfast, I will see to it."

She ate everything on her plate and promptly fell asleep. Ryder removed the tray and sat down on the chair beside her bed. What a damnable mess. He realized fully that he was in it up to his neck, perhaps beyond. What he was going to do about it was still unknown. He looked at Sophie — yes, she did look like a Sophie, young and vulnerable and soft. She didn't look like an elegant, cold Sophia. He looked beyond the ugly bruises and saw the fine high cheekbones. Her nose was thin and straight, her eyebrows nicely arched and slanted, her lashes thick. Perhaps in another time, in another place, in different circumstances, he would have taken her as his mistress and shown her that men could really be quite useful when it came to making a woman happy. But the time was now, and the circumstances were godawful. He continued to study her. She was really quite nice-looking and that realization surprised him. Her chin wasn't rounded and soft, it was stubborn and solid, that chin, as was her jaw. He imagined she was a hellion even when she was a little girl. Ah, but she was loyal. She would do anything for Jeremy. Anything at all.

And now what was there for her to do?

He had bath water brought to the bedchamber

and poured into the large copper tub. Now was as good a time as any to have a look at her ribs. Very slowly he drew the sheet down. He was unfastening the buttons on one of Samuel's borrowed nightshirts when her eyes flew open. She stared up at him, not moving, not saying a word.

"What are you doing?"

"I'm going to look at your ribs. The bandages must come off in any case if you're to have a bath."

"No."

"Sophie, I know your body very well, as well, I imagine, as you know mine. I admit the circumstances are a bit peculiar here but I am the only one who has taken care of you. You will hold still and let me look at your ribs. If you continue being stubborn about it, I will tie you down."

"No, damn you!"

"You won't get your bath."

"No."

"How many men have seen your body besides me? Surely more than the three you entertained when I arrived. Surely you can't have an ounce of modesty left."

She turned her face away. He eased her out of the nightshirt then methodically began to untie the bandages from her ribs. He paid no attention to her breasts, to her white belly. He was staring at her bruised ribs and feeling bile rise in his throat. He wanted, quite simply, to kill Uncle Theo with his bare hands.

He gently ran his fingertips over each rib. "Tell me how bad the pain is," he said. Her breathing was shallow. His hand brushed against her left breast.

She shuddered.

"All right. You're better. Now, I'm going to help you into the bathtub."

Why not, she thought. It didn't matter. He was quite right. He had seen her and taken her and probably looked his fill of her the night he'd drugged her. It made no difference. She allowed him to ease her to the side of the bed. She was naked and he was holding her, lifting her now to her feet. Her knees gave, and when she fell against him, he held her upright, pressing her against him. His breath was warm on her temple. She would have been terrified of him but she felt too weak, and the pain was rippling through her. He knew, of course, damn him.

"Is the pain bad?"

"No, I'm just weak, that's all. Ryder, I can manage, truly. Would you leave me alone now?"

"Be quiet, Sophie."

He eased her into the copper tub. She sighed with pleasure and he grinned down at her. He unbraided her hair and smoothed out the ripples.

She managed to wash most of herself and he washed her hair. It took a long time, and she was white with fatigue and trembling with weariness when they were finished. And pain, he guessed. He toweled her dry as matter-of-factly

150

as he'd rub down a lathered horse. That thought made her smile and he saw that small smile and wondered at it as he wrapped her hair in another towel.

He carried her to a rocking chair by the open louvered doors and sat down, holding her in his lap. "Time for a rest for both of us. You've worn me out. You've a lot of hair. Lean your head against my shoulder. That's right."

"I'm nothing to you."

"What does that mean?"

"I mean that I'm naked and you have seen me and taken me and yet you don't care. I'm nothing to you."

His arms tightened about her and he felt her wince and immediately loosened his hold.

"Would you prefer me to slaver all over you and make you uncomfortable by staring at your breasts?"

"No, you already did that. It was just a game to you, it meant nothing. It's just that —"

"That what?"

"I don't understand you."

"Sometimes I don't understand myself," he said. He began to rock her back and forth. She was asleep within two minutes.

No, he thought, he didn't understand and it was driving him mad.

He carried her back to bed and laid her on her back. He decided to leave her ribs unbandaged. Very gently he removed the towel from her hair and smoothed out the tangles with his fingers, fanning her hair about her head on the pillow to dry.

He looked at her flat belly and at the soft nest of hair below. She really was quite lovely, he thought, as he pulled a sheet over her, and she'd known men in only one context. They wanted her body, nothing more. Well, she had a very nice body, but he wasn't moved at all.

He had no intention of ever being moved by this woman, at least any more than he already was.

He was eating luncheon with Samuel, Emile, and Jeremy, when James came into the room and said, "Mr. Thomas is here, Mr. Sherbrooke. He wants to see you."

Jeremy's fork fell to his plate, his face suddenly white. Ryder nodded to James, saying, "Show him into the salon, James. I shall be there presently. Now, Jeremy, pick up your fork and eat those delectable shrimps. I asked your sister to trust me. I'm asking the same of you. If you don't get color back into your cheeks, I'll stake you out in the sun. If you think I will allow Thomas or anyone else to get near you, you are sorely mistaken. Do you understand me, young man?"

"Yes, sir," Jeremy said, his eyes searching Ryder's face. Ryder saw the fear, the uncertainty, and he felt something move deep inside him. He buffeted the boy's shoulder as he passed his chair. "Emile plans to teach you all about rum this afternoon."

"I already know a lot about rum."

"Emile will show you things you've never seen before, won't you, Emile?"

"Indeed."

"Eat your lunch. You'll need your strength."

Ryder heard Jeremy say to Emile as he left the dining room, "Do you whip the slaves, sir?"

"No," Emile said matter-of-factly. "They're our workers. Without them we wouldn't produce much sugar. We depend on them. If I hurt them, why then, they couldn't work and then where would we be?"

"Thomas beats the Camille slaves."

"Thomas is a stupid man. Ryder will doubtless see to his education."

Ryder smiled in anticipation. He wished he'd spoken to Sophie but he hadn't wanted to awaken her. Well, doubtless Thomas was here because Uncle Theo still wasn't well yet. Good. It seemed that she'd plunged that letter opener nice and deep.

Sophie woke up just as the sun was lowering, splashing the sky with all shades of pinks and reds. She was alone. She rose and relieved herself, then found the man's nightshirt she'd been wearing and slipped it over her head. Her ribs ached and pulled but the awful tearing pain was now bearable.

She walked slowly to the balcony and raised her face to the still evening air. Soon she would be well enough to leave Kimberly. Soon she would have to leave Kimberly, she and Jeremy. But where would she go?

Ryder was right about that. She had nothing, no money, nothing except a harlot's reputation.

She stared blankly into the pink and golden twilight, listening to turtledoves, frogs, crickets, and the myriad other night creatures that she normally didn't hear because she was so used to them.

Ryder paused in the doorway. He saw her standing there in the ridiculous loose nightshirt, her hair thick and flowing down her back. She looked sixteen. But he knew when he saw her eyes there would be weary cynicism there.

"Come back to bed," he said quietly, not wanting to startle her.

She turned slowly. She was no longer weak and hurting. She was standing now, a grown woman, and she had to deal with him. She said calmly, "I'm tired of that damned bed. I wish to remain standing for a while. You said you wanted to speak to me. Let's do it."

She was back to normal. It pleased him enormously. "As you will," he said easily. "Thomas was here."

Had he expected her to gasp? To shudder with fright? To totter toward him and beg for his protection? She didn't do any of these things. Her expression was remote and remained remote. She looked calm and serene. She was really very good. He walked to her and stopped directly in front of her. He raised his fingertips and lightly touched her chin, the tip of her nose, ran his fingertips over her eyebrows. "The bruises are fading. By tomorrow you won't be such a fright."

She didn't move. "Then I won't request a mirror until the day after tomorrow."

"As I said, Thomas came here."

"I assume you handled him?"

He grinned. "No, I pleaded with him to allow you to remain here for a little while longer. He beat me into the floor but decided to let you stay. However, he said he'd come back and —"

She jerked. It was just a small sort of shiver really, but he'd discovered that during the past few days he'd become attuned to her, noticing small movements, small reactions, that gave her away.

"Don't be a fool," he said. "Now, let me tell you about a very unmemorable meeting. Lord, the man's a villain and utterly without a conscience. I met him in the salon. Did you know that James, our footman, isn't fond of Thomas? Why, I do believe James's eyes got meaner than a snake's when he said the man's name."

"Thomas is an animal. James has a brother who is owned by my uncle. Mr. Grayson tried to buy him but my uncle refused. Yes, Thomas is a swine."

"Well, yes he is. Hush now and let me tell you of our rather boring conversation."

Ryder had walked into the salon in high good humor, nearly rubbing his hands together in anticipation. He stopped, smiled, and said, "I believe your name is Thomas? Fancy seeing you here at Kimberly Hall without your bow and arrows and that very charming white sheet both you and your master enjoy wearing. I particularly applauded the white hoods. Ah, but my manners. Would you care for some coffee?"

"I have come for Mr. Burgess's niece and nephew."

"Oh?" Ryder smiled benignly at the overseer. He was tall, exceedingly thin, save for a belly that protruded between his vest and his breeches. His hair was grizzled and very short and there was beard stubble on his jaw. He looked as if he hadn't slept much or bathed or changed his clothes in several days. His eyes were cold, very cold, and Ryder doubted if he'd ever been filled with the milk of human kindness.

"I do owe you for that arrow you put in my shoulder."

"I'm sure I don't know what you're talking about," Thomas said. "If you please, Mr. Sherbrooke, Mr. Burgess is anxious to see his niece and nephew. He is naturally concerned for their welfare."

"Ah, doubtless that is so. How could anyone ever question his feelings? However, whatever makes him think they could be here?"

"There is talk. Everyone knows. The gossip is that Miss Stanton-Greville is living here openly as your mistress, and in return for her favors, you also took in the boy. It distresses Mr. Burgess. Bring them down now and they won't bother you again."

156

"Why don't you sit down, Thomas."

"Damn you, Sherbrooke, you have no right —"

"No right to what? To rescue a girl who's been beaten senseless? To take a small boy out of a locked room?"

"Hellfire, one of her lovers beat her! I locked the boy in his room to protect him!"

"One of her lovers beat her," Ryder repeated slowly. "Which one, I wonder? Perhaps Oliver Susson? Now, he's certainly a vicious brute, isn't he? No, I think you must be mistaken. He'd already been dismissed, and according to my sources, he didn't seem at all upset by his dismissal. Who else? Charles Grammond, perhaps? I hear his wife's a regular tartar, perhaps she did it?"

"Damn you, Sherbrooke! Get them!"

Ryder smiled. "You will now listen to me, Thomas. I think you're a conscienceless bastard. I will have no more dealings with you. Your master, however, is another matter. Tell him he will hear from me shortly. Now, if you attempt to bring back some of your cronies to Kimberly Hall and cause a ruckus, I will come after you. I will kill you and I will do it very slowly. Do you understand me?"

Thomas didn't know what to do. He'd told Mr. Burgess that this man wasn't like the other men here on Montego Bay. This man was hard and smart. "As I told you, Sherbrooke, one of Sophia's lovers beat her. Her uncle tried to stop it. If she's told you differently, it's because she's ashamed of her notoriety. Now, be sensible. Why would you want to be saddled with a little cripple and a whore?"

Thomas didn't get out another word. Ryder smashed his fist into his jaw, a hard, clean blow. Then he drew back his right arm and sent his fist into the man's belly. Thomas yelled as he fell like a stone to the floor.

"James! Ah, I'm glad you're here. Didn't go very far, did you? Well, I very much do need your assistance now. Please ask another strong man to take this vermin back to Camille Hall and dump him there. In the dirt. On his face."

"Yes, massa," James said and he was smiling. "Dat man a bastid, a real bastid. He look good flat on de floor. No, not a bastid, he be a serpent."

"His fangs should be dangling loose, at the very least," Ryder said as he rubbed his knuckles. He frowned down at Thomas. "He's got a big belly. That's not good for a man. No, not at all healthy."

He rubbed his knuckles again as he finished speaking, thinking again how good it had made him feel to vent his rage on that mangy bastard. He looked at Sophie and grinned just as he had before to James. "That's all that happened. Nothing more. James and another fellow took him away."

She said, "I'm glad you hit him. I hope you struck him very hard. I've wanted to many times. He's a horrible man. Good heavens, you enjoyed that!"

"Perhaps," Ryder said with obvious relish.

"The man's a rotter." He fell silent then and he gave her a brooding look. "However did you manage to get yourself into this ridiculous mess?"

"What do you mean, sir? Ah, you wonder why I chose of my own free will to become a whore? Perhaps why Jeremy decided to become a cripple? I would that you be more specific."

"You were much easier to handle on your back. You're all vinegar again."

"A pity, for you will never see me like that again."

"Not even when I make love to you again?"

Another very small jerk of her shoulders. Yes, he was getting to know her quite well.

"Sit down, Sophie. I'll keep my distance. I don't wish to frighten you."

That got to her. Ryder was pleased; he was even grinning shamelessly when she said, "You don't frighten me. No man frightens me."

"As a matter of course I would believe you. You appear quite skilled with men. However, I am not other men and I do frighten you. You will admit it eventually and then, I daresay, you'll be more careful around me. Sit down before I pick you up and set you down."

She sat down, smoothing the nightshirt over her legs. It occurred to her then that it must surely be odd to be here in a bedchamber with a man wearing only a man's nightshirt, and that made her smile.

She said then without preamble, "Kimberly Hall belongs to you, not to your brother, the

159

Earl of Northcliffe."

Ryder stared at her, his mouth open. "What did you say? No, that's absurd, that's utter nonsense. Wherever did you get such an idea?"

"Be quiet and attend me. Kimberly Hall belonged to your uncle Brandon. When he died, you inherited his fortune. However, Oliver Susson neglected to attach the specifics of this property to the will he sent back to your family. At the time it was truly an oversight. Also, at the time, I believe your father had just died and thus there was some confusion because the new earl hadn't sold out yet of the army. Thus, everyone believes that Kimberly belongs to the family — your older brother — not you, to be exact."

"By God," Ryder said, staring at her.

"Are you not rather rich for a second son?"

"Yes."

"Well, now you are even richer for this plantation is yours."

"I begin to see why Oliver Susson was one of your lovers."

"Naturally."

"I did tell Emile that there were always motives. Particularly where you are concerned, Sophie. You would never have become a slut without very strong motives."

"Understand me, Ryder. I don't care if you own all of Jamaica. My uncle wanted this plantation and he thought my talents would give him an excellent chance at it. Don't get me wrong, I was to be used just to soften you up. In his

160

final estimation, he didn't think you would care about living here, or care about the uncertainty of sugar profits, and thus, you would sell out to him, stuff the guineas in your aristocratic pockets, and sail happily back to England."

"And at the appropriate time I would have been told by Mr. Susson that Kimberly Hall belonged to me."

"Yes."

"And with you as my delightful mistress — you and that other woman with the big breasts of course — I would be delighted to sell to your uncle. Did he intend to send you back with me to England? As my mistress?"

"I don't know what he planned."

"Why did you agree to this?"

Her look was hard and cold. "Don't be absurd. You're so excellent at assigning motives, why have you let down here? Jeremy was to be his heir if I cooperated. If I didn't cooperate, he said he would throw both of us out. Jeremy is lame; he would never be able to make his way here."

"And naturally, you could."

She didn't react in any way, merely said in that same cold voice, "Quite probably."

"Lord David became your lover so that he would fleece Charles Grammond."

"Yes and he performed admirably."

"And Charles Grammond was your lover so he would be quite amenable to selling his plantation to your uncle."

"Yes."

"How did you ever manage to rid yourself of Lord David?"

She smiled. It was an impish smile, a young smile, and he found himself reacting to it. He realized it was the first genuine smile he'd ever seen from her. "I told him I had the pox."

"Good God, that's wonderful."

"I would have probably told you the same thing once you had sold Kimberly to my uncle."

"Ah, but the difference is that I wouldn't have simply believed you."

"That's what I told my uncle. I told him you weren't like the other men. I told him you weren't stupid. I told him that he should be very cautious with you, perhaps even fear you. He refused to heed me."

"You aren't making much sense about this fear business, but no matter. He didn't listen to you. He wasn't afraid enough of me, more's the pity."

"No. He measures all men with himself as the standard. He'd heard you were a womanizer, a young rakehell with no more morals than a tom-cat. He thought it would be marvelously easy."

"I'm not a —" He stopped and frowned down at his bruised knuckles. Jesus, what an appalling thought. His mind shied away from it. He swallowed, then shrugged negligently. "Well, he was wrong, wasn't he?"

"About you being a womanizer? A tomcat? No, surely not. If you'd been like the other men, you wouldn't have realized that it wasn't me."

"Are you telling me that you didn't sleep with

any of them? That it was always this other woman?"

She looked at him steadily. "Would you believe me if I told you that I had not?"

"Probably not." He raised his hand to cut her off. "No, attend me, Sophie. I have never before met a woman with such a repertoire of feminine tricks as you have, and believe me, I've been treated to the best. I wish I knew the female equivalent of a rakehell or a tomcat. You surely fit the mold. You're remarkable in your scope of seductive devices for one so young. Now, enough of that. It's not important. Back to your dear uncle. It still takes me aback that I own Kimberly Hall."

"It's true."

"But what if I hadn't come here? What if my brother had come instead?"

"Uncle Theo considered that unlikely. You see, he knows all about your family. He even hired a man back in England to find out everything he could about the Sherbrookes, about you. The man wrote back with a goodly number of details."

"He did all this before he and Thomas began their little scare campaign?"

"Oh yes. It was all well planned. Uncle Theo knew that Samuel Grayson was superstitious and could be manipulated. He knew if he played on his fears, why, he was bound to write to your brother, begging for help. And he did. He even told my uncle that he was going to write. Of course, my uncle encouraged him to write, encouraged him in his superstitions, stoked the fires, so to speak."

"I begin to believe that Uncle Theo deserves to have me wring his miserable neck."

"The man my uncle hired wrote that your brother had many responsibilities and that it was highly unlikely that he would come; your younger brother is at Oxford studying to become a man of the cloth. That left you and your fifteen-year-old sister. Naturally it was you who came. Everything went just as he'd planned. He simply misjudged you, that's all. He assumed you'd be like Lord David — frivolous, narcissistic, rather stupid, and wanting only to sleep with me. He was wrong; he simply wouldn't recognize that he'd failed. You never for a moment believed there was anything supernatural about the incidents, did you?"

"Of course not," Ryder said, his voice clearly abstracted.

"Nor did you ever want to become my lover."

"No. Yes. I don't know. I don't share."

"What are you going to do?"

"Oliver Susson agreed not to say anything to my brother or to me until your uncle decided it was the right time?"

She nodded.

"Did Jeremy know any of this?"

"No, I tried to protect him as best I could. Also, Uncle Theo was always very careful to treat him well, both in private and in public. Even now, everyone believes both Jeremy and I are very lucky. Indeed I imagine the gossip is that Uncle Theo is too loving, too sentimental, to even realize that his niece is a whore."

"Yes, that's what I've heard. You're tired. It's time for you to rest and for me to do some thinking. I want this mess resolved and soon."

She didn't sleep for the simple reason that she was too frightened about the future. But she did lie on that damned bed for three hours, her mind squirreling about frantically.

CHAPTER 8

Sophie walked quietly down the upstairs corridor of Kimberly Hall to the bedchamber where Jeremy was sleeping. She wanted to speak to her brother, to reassure him, to make him promises that she prayed she'd be able to keep.

She quietly opened the door and peered in. The room was small, but as in all the other chambers, there were floor-to-ceiling louvered doors that gave onto a balcony and those doors were wide open. She smiled. Jeremy many times slept on his balcony at Camille Hall. He was probably doing the same here. The mosquitoes never bothered him.

He wasn't in his bed. She still smiled even as she walked slowly to the balcony. He wasn't there either. Her smile froze.

Oh God.

She'd seen him today, briefly, and he'd been very quiet, too quiet. He'd looked at her for a very long time and she'd known he was troubled, but she hadn't said anything to him because Ryder had come in. And that was why she'd wanted to see him now.

But he was gone.

Of course she knew where he was. He'd gone back to Camille Hall to face down Uncle Theo for beating her.

Uncle Theo would hurt him badly, perhaps even kill him, for now there was no reason for him to pretend to kindness, to affection, for either of them. She realized she was breathing in huge gulps that made her ribs throb and ache. She leaned forward, hugging her arms around her.

When the pain drew back, she still didn't move, just stood there, very still, staring out onto the beautiful scene before her, but not really seeing the glistening waves beneath the near full moon. The stars were points of cold white in the sky, a sky empty of shifting clouds. Slowly, she turned and went back to her own bedchamber. She found her gown in the bottom of the armoire. It was ripped and soiled but she didn't care. She dressed quickly, ignoring the pulling and aching in her ribs, her mind set on what she had to do. She merely shook her head when she realized she had no petticoats, no chemise, no stockings, nothing but the gown.

Nor could she find her shoes. No matter, she'd go barefoot. She crept down the front stairs as quietly and stealthily as a thief, and into the small estate room that was also the Kimberly Hall library. There was a gun case there, thank God, a tall oak affair with glass doors. It wasn't locked. She knew guns and thus picked out a small derringer. If she had to protect Jeremy, she would shoot whoever it was at very close range. She had no intention of missing.

She slipped out of Kimberly Hall five minutes later, walking quickly down the graveled drive, ignoring the small rocks digging into the soles of her feet, welcoming the evening breeze that stirred tendrils of hair on her forehead.

It was a beautiful night, a still night. Her heart pounded in slow, steady strokes. If only she knew how long Jeremy had been gone. She was afraid, but she was calm. It was about time she took over responsibility for herself and for Jeremy. Dear God, please give her enough time to prove herself.

It took her twenty minutes to walk to Camille Hall, cutting through canefields, keeping in the shadows as much as possible. She cut her feet but ignored the jabs of pain, even ignored the blood when she felt it sticky and cold on the soles of her feet.

There was light coming from several windows, but she couldn't see anything, no shadows, no sign of her uncle or of Thomas or any of the servants. Where the devil was Jeremy?

She ran bent over from bush to bush, getting closer and closer to the great house. She slithered up onto the side veranda to where her uncle's study was located. It was then she heard the voices.

It was Uncle Theo, and he sounded amused. He also sounded quite drunk. "So, you little bas-

168

tard, you decided to come back here and whip me, eh?"

"Yes. I'm not a bastard. My mother was your sister and she was my father's wife. I'm here because of what you did to Sophie. I can't allow you to hurt my sister and get away with it. You *beat* her!"

"She deserved it, and as soon as I get my hands on her again, I'll whip her until she's begging for mercy."

"I won't let you. Ryder won't let you."

Ryder Sherbrooke, the young man Theo wanted very much to kill. Ah, but he had the boy here, the useless little cripple. He grinned down at Jeremy. "And just how do you think you'd ever stop me, whelp? You couldn't even keep your whip. I have it now, don't I?"

"I will think of something."

There came the hissing sound of a whip cutting through the air. Then she heard a sharp cry. It was Jeremy. Uncle Theo had struck him with the whip.

She thought she'd felt all the rage of which she was capable. She'd been wrong. The wooden door was partially open. She slipped through it very quietly to see Uncle Theo, his shoulder heavily bandaged, wearing a dressing gown, standing over Jeremy, the whip raised again in his right hand.

"I'll give you another taste, Master Jeremy, just to show you how important you are!"

"If you do, you filthy wretch, I'll put a bullet

through your belly. I don't want you to die quickly. I want you to lie on the ground, holding your belly, feeling your guts rotting from the inside out while you scream and scream."

Theo Burgess froze, but just for an instant. Slowly, very slowly, he lowered the whip and turned to face his niece.

"So, you discovered the little cripple was gone and came galloping to his rescue."

She ignored him. "Come here, Jeremy. Keep your distance from him. That's right, come to me now."

Jeremy's face was white with pain, his eyes hollow with failure. She understood both feelings very well, and said, "It's all right. This time, we've won. You're very brave to come here. That's good, come to me now and we will leave soon."

"You think so, do you, slut? Don't count on it. All I have to do is call out and at least ten slaves will be here to do my bidding in an instant."

"It won't matter because you'll be belly-shot. Go ahead, Uncle, yell as loud as you want because it's the last sound you'll make without agony. I want to kill you very badly. You're a coward, whipping Jeremy, who's half your size. I suppose your utter lack of any feeling surprised even me, but just for a moment."

Theo Burgess didn't know what to do. He shook his head, trying to clear his thoughts from all the rum he'd had to drink for the damnable pain

170

in his shoulder. He believed the girl. She'd stabbed him, hadn't she? Lord, he should have continued hitting her until she was dead, but he'd had to stop because the blow she'd dealt him was making him dizzy and light-headed. He looked at her now, feeling renewed pain in his shoulder, despite the huge amounts of rum he'd drunk, remembering the bitter torture of that damned letter opener, remembering how Thomas had pulled it out and how he'd tried to keep silent but had failed and screamed. Even then it hadn't been fair. He hadn't fallen into blessed unconsciousness. Oh no, he'd stayed with the torment and it hadn't let up for a very long time. He'd sworn to make her pay. He had to make her pay and he would.

He said at last, very pleased with the indifference of his voice, "You know, my dear, if you kill me, you won't have a thing."

"The rum has curdled your wits. Jeremy is your heir. He will have everything."

"Oh no. He isn't my heir for the simple reason that I don't have a will."

"Will or no will, we are your closest relatives, and thus when all is said and done, Jeremy will inherit Camille Hall. Of course my father's house in Fowey is also his."

"Did dear Oliver Susson tell you that when he was plowing your belly?"

"That you believe your own fiction rather points to a failing mind, doesn't it, Uncle? I have two bullets in this derringer. Jeremy, let me see

171

how badly he hurt you."

Her brother turned his back. The single stroke of the whip had cut through his shirt. Thank God the skin wasn't broken, but the long diagonal welt was ugly and red, the flesh rising around it. She sucked in her breath. "You're a monster, truly. Now, as I said, I have two bullets. If that whip had drawn even a fingertip of blood, I would have shot you in your belly. However, you are lucky, Uncle. I won't shoot you at all, this time. I'm simply taking Jeremy back with me to Kimberly Hall. You will leave us alone, do you understand? You won't come there nor will you send Thomas again. Now, we will leave. Don't move an inch."

"And just what will you do when Ryder Sherbrooke tosses you and the boy out of Kimberly?"

"That isn't your concern."

"Thomas told me you were installed in Ryder Sherbrooke's bedchamber. Everyone knows now that you're his mistress. Your reputation is —"

She actually laughed. "Look at my face. Can even you imagine a healthy man being interested in bedding me now? My ribs are even more violent shades of purple and green than my face. Believe me, even if I wanted to be in his bed, even if he'd wanted me there, I would have been unable. You saw to that. Now, Uncle, I want to leave here with Jeremy."

"To go back to that damned Englishman?"

"You're a damned Englishman, remember?"

"As I said, he'll remove you quickly enough.

I hear he bores easily and no one woman could ever hold him. My agent in England wrote that he had women climbing over themselves to become his mistress. No, you ugly little slut, you couldn't hold him for more than a night."

"I don't want to hold him. I don't even want to be in the same room with him. He can have a dozen more mistresses for all I care. However, he does seem honorable, something new in my experience in a man. He has protected Jeremy. I grow tired of this. Jeremy, go outside. I'll follow."

"But, Sophie —"

"Go!"

The boy backed away from her, his face white and set.

She lowered the derringer to the level of Theo Burgess's left knee. "Perhaps," she said in a very low, very mean voice, "just perhaps I've changed my mind. I would like to know that you're hobbling about for the rest of your damned life, a cripple, a no-account cripple."

Theo Burgess shrieked, "No, damn you, no!" He rushed toward her, flailing his arms madly.

Suddenly the candelabra crashed to the floor and the room was plunged into darkness.

Sophie's finger inadvertently jerked the trigger. The derringer fired, a monstrous loud noise in the small room. She heard an anguished yell. Someone struck her arm but she managed to hold onto the derringer, and this time she pulled the trigger on purpose. Then something struck her on her temple and she slumped to the floor. She heard Jeremy yelling and she smelled something acrid, something she vaguely recognized. She managed to open her eyes, trying desperately to hang on. She saw only darkness and a strange glowing orange light. And the sounds — snapping and hissing and a windy sort of whoosh.

The light muslin draperies were aflame, billowing upward as if caught in a great wind, flaming outward, the heat intense. The room was on fire.

"Jeremy," she whispered, "run, please, you must run. Go to Ryder. He'll take care of you. You can trust him." She choked on the smoke even as she closed her eyes and her head lolled back on the wooden floor.

She awoke coughing, her throat raw and burning. She felt someone's arms around her, felt a man's hands rubbing her back as she coughed and wheezed. She heard his voice: "It's over, Sophie. Jeremy is safe. It's over. Shush, don't worry now and don't try to talk."

Ryder. His voice, his hands on her back. She leaned against him, shuddering from the rawness in her throat, trying not to swallow because it hurt so much.

"Where is Jeremy? Is he all right, truly?"

"Be quiet and I'll tell you everything. We're here at Camille Hall. Jeremy had very nearly managed to pull you out of the room all by himself by the time Emile and I got here. The fire is out and the damage isn't too bad. Only the study was pretty well destroyed and the veranda outside charred a bit. Naturally there's smoke damage and the smell in the house is godawful. Uncle Theo is quite dead."

It hurt so much to talk, to say the words, but she did, wheezing them out. "I must have killed him. My derringer went off and I heard him yell."

"Did you now? Well, that was well done of you. However, when you're well enough again, I will have to thrash you at the very least for what you did. If Coco hadn't seen you running barefoot down the Kimberly Hall drive, why then you very probably would have died in that fire, Jeremy along with you, for the boy wouldn't have left you in there to die."

"The magistrate, Mr. Sherman Cole, will see that I'm hanged."

"I see no reason why he would want to hang you."

She tried to pull away from him but he held her firmly.

"Yes he will. He wanted me to take him as my lover but there was no reason to and so Uncle Theo had me refuse him. He was nasty about it, and threatened me. Uncle Theo thought it was amusing. He said he could handle Cole if the need ever arose. And he also said I was to keep up a light flirtation with him so that if Uncle Theo ever needed something from him, he'd come running when I smiled at him."

175

"But you didn't keep flirting with him?"

"No, I slapped him and stomped on his instep when he tried to kiss me. He's repellent. It was about three months ago."

"I see. Well, then, my dear girl, I guess it must be I who shot Theo Burgess, trying to save you and Jeremy. But why? After all, Burgess is known only as the loving, ineffectual uncle, isn't he? I must think on this. Perhaps there is another resolution to all this. Yes, let me think on it."

"Where is Thomas?"

"I don't know. I haven't seen him. I'll ask."

"I wanted to shoot Uncle Theo in his knee so he'd be a cripple like Jeremy, to make him live with a limp just as Jeremy has had to do — dear God, he'd actually taken a whip to Jeremy — but I swear to you, I didn't pull the trigger intentionally. The candelabra suddenly crashed to the floor and everything was dark and I jerked accidentally on the trigger. Then someone hit my arm and I pulled the trigger on purpose to protect myself."

"Tell me all of it and don't leave out a thing. Quickly, I don't know how much time we have."

By the time she was finished speaking, her throat was so raw she could barely speak in anything but a hoarse whisper.

"I'm giving you over to Samuel now, both you and Jeremy. He'll take you back to Kimberly Hall. Now, no more words from you, no arguments, no nothing. I'm in charge now and you will do exactly what I tell you to do. The first

176

order is that there is to be no talking from you for at least twenty-four hours."

"My head hurts."

Ryder frowned down at her and lightly touched his fingertips to the bump over her temple. "Good God, you didn't tell me that someone struck you on the head."

"I forgot."

"All right, talk, but make it quick." When she'd finished, he was frowning. She opened her mouth, only to feel his palm over her lips. "No, now be quiet. Here's Jeremy. Emile was seeing to him while I talked to you."

The boy was on his knees beside her, stroking her filthy face, her hands. "Oh, Sophie, your feet! What happened? What did you do?"

She'd forgotten her damned feet.

Ryder yelled for a lantern. When a slave brought it, he lowered it and looked for a long time at her feet, saying nothing. Then, "From the top of your head to your very toes, you've managed to do yourself in. Jesus, Sophie, your feet are a mess. See that Coco bathes them when you get back to Kimberly."

Ryder watched Samuel drive away with Sophie and Jeremy. He himself had carried her to the carriage. He was hot and sweaty and covered with smoke and grime from the fire. He was also in a devil of a mess and in an equally foul mood.

Where the hell was that bastard, Thomas? Actually, truth be told, Thomas worried him more than Theo Burgess. At least Theo tried to keep up appearances; Thomas couldn't give a good damn about anything. Ryder had no doubt that it was Thomas who had struck Sophie and hurled the candelabra to the floor.

Ryder left Emile in charge of Camille Hall and took himself back to Kimberly for a few hours' sleep. When he awoke he was told that Miss Stanton-Greville was still sleeping. He frowned but said nothing. He was thinking about her damned bloody feet, curse her. Just after he'd finished eating breakfast, Mr. Sherman Cole arrived from Montego Bay.

Sherman Cole looked like the father of one of Ryder's mistresses, a draper in Rye who was greedy and sly. He was very fat, double chins wobbling over his collar, had a monk's tonsure of gray hair, very sharp eyes, and thick lips. The thought of him trying to kiss Sophie made Ryder want to gag.

Still, he shook the man's hand and offered him coffee. Mr. Cole wanted not only coffee, but sweet buns, which, when a tray was set before him, he eyed with more intensity than Ryder would have had gazing upon a beautiful naked woman.

Ryder merely sat opposite him and looked over his right shoulder, unable, for the most part, to look at the man's face. It was not an elevating sight. He listened to the man speak even though his mouth was many times full and thus his words a bit slurred.

"Yes, Mr. Sherbrooke, as you know, I am the magistrate, the man in charge of all civil and criminal disturbances. I am the law here on the island, the power of the law resides with me. I was shocked to learn that you were involved, that you had brought Miss Sophia Stanton-Greville back to Kimberly with you. I don't know how you came to be involved with her, but I am certain you will tell me soon enough. Please have the girl fetched here. I will question her now."

My God, Ryder thought, steepling his long fingers. He looked over them at the man who had just consumed four sweet buns. The man was not only a pig, he was also pompous, condescending, and thoroughly irritating. As to his manners, he had none. There were crumbs on his coat and on his chin. The man needed to be stripped and tossed to the crocodiles in the mangrove swamps. It would doubtless keep them busy for at least several days.

"I think not, Mr. Cole," Ryder said mildly. "You see, she is suffering from breathing in too much smoke and thus cannot speak without a lot of pain. Perhaps in several days you can return and she might be better."

Mr. Cole frowned. He wasn't used to having anyone go against his expressed wishes. He was the man in charge; he was a leader of men, truly the law here, and it was his word, his orders, that counted. "I want to see her," he said again, obstinate as a pig.

"No."

"See here, Sherbrooke —"

"*Mr.* Sherbrooke, Cole."

Sherman Cole was quite obviously taken aback and becoming angrier by the minute. But he wasn't stupid. Was Sophia Stanton-Greville already this man's mistress? Was he set on protecting her? He pursed his lips. He held himself silent, having learned that a man or woman felt compelled to fill in silences and thus provide him with information, but this young man didn't say a word. He sat back in his chair, his fingers still steepled, and, damn his eyes, he looked bored.

It was infuriating. Mr. Cole drew a deep breath, looked quickly down at the tray but saw there were no more sweet buns there, and frowned again. Food helped him sort through his thoughts, it always had, even when he'd been a child. "I want her," he said.

"A pity. You must accustom yourself, sir. You will never have her."

"That isn't what I meant! My dear young man, I am married, my wife is a charming lady, really quite charming. I mean that I must speak to her, and I must tell you, Mr. Sherbrooke, that I suspect foul play here. I suspect that she murdered her uncle in cold blood and then set fire to the great house."

"This is a rather remarkable theory. May I inquire as to what brought you to this incredible conclusion?"

"The girl isn't what she seems to be, rather she is exactly what she seems, only her uncle wouldn't recognize it or accept it. You must have heard — perhaps you even have firsthand information — she's a slut, a high-priced harlot with no morals at all. I think her uncle finally realized the truth and she killed him when he threatened to toss her out. Aye, that's what happened." He stopped, gave Ryder a patented hanging judge's look, and announced, "I am here to see justice done."

Ryder laughed, a deep, rich laugh. "Your theory is beyond amusing, Mr. Cole. However, you must realize that it is also rather libelous."

"I have a witness, Mr. Sherbrooke."

"Do you now?"

"Yes, Thomas, the overseer."

Ryder laughed again, more deeply, more richly, more genuine amusement than before.

"Sir!"

"Mr. Cole, Thomas is a villain, as I must assume you already know. I don't believe it wise to take testimony from a villain. I propose another theory, one that differs from yours quite substantially. However, there is just as much motive, just as much rationale for mine, as for yours. Thomas is a bounder. I suspect that Mr. Burgess discovered Thomas was cheating him, that or he was abusing the slaves too much, and he fired him. Put very simply, Thomas killed him. As luck would have it, Miss Stanton-Greville and her brother were there at Camille Hall and thus she proved to be a perfect scapegoat for Thomas."

"Thomas is a man and she is a —"

"No, he's a bastard, no-account, cruel, mean as a snake."

"That doesn't excuse Miss Stanton-Greville. Why, she's nothing more than a —"

"I wouldn't say anything were I you, Cole. She and her brother are under my personal protection. Indeed, I will be applying shortly to become the guardian to both of them. Oliver Susson will be handling the matter."

"Ah, I see the truth of the matter now."

"Do you, now? Pray, just exactly what do you see?"

"She is, as I intimated before, your mistress."

Ryder said in a voice reminiscent of his father's whenever he was tired of an individual's impertinence and wanted him gone, "Perhaps she will be someday. I'm not as yet certain I wish to bed her and keep her. However, I do feel an obligation to Jeremy and she comes along with him. He is, after all, Theo Burgess's heir. His interests must be protected and I can see no other man to do the job. Now, Cole, do you wish to say anything else? No? Why then, why don't you have Thomas fetched in your august presence? Perhaps with your obvious interrogation skills you can induce him to tell the truth." Ryder rose and merely waited for Cole to heave himself to his feet, which he did, reluctantly.

"I just might find more evidence to convict her!"

"More, Cole? As of this moment, you haven't even a pinch, nary a dollop. Get Thomas and you've got your killer. Now, I have many matters to attend to. I trust you will excuse me. Oh, should you care for more sweet buns to take with you?"

Sophie quickly ran back up the stairs. She'd seen Mr. Sherman Cole ride up the drive. She'd had to know what he would say. Nothing he said was unexpected. Ryder had handled him brilliantly. But then Ryder had spoken. . . . She felt deep, very deep pain and it wasn't in her ribs or in her burned throat.

"I am not as yet certain I wish to bed her and keep her."

He was no different from any of the other men. She guessed that he would demand her in his bed as payment for seeing to Jeremy's protection. Then he would tire of her and that would be that. At least she'd be free, at last. She and Jeremy would live in peace at Camille Hall. Everything would be all right. In a year and a half she would be twenty-one and deemed old enough to become his guardian.

She managed to climb into her bed and pull the sheet to her chin before he was standing there in the doorway, looking at her, saying nothing for a long time.

"Mr. Cole was very amusing."

"Was he? Am I to be arrested?"

"You still sound like a foghorn. No, you won't be arrested. I venture to say that Thomas just might be the one to hang. Wouldn't that solve all our problems?"

She turned her face away from him and said in a very low voice, "Why was Coco awake so very late last night? You said she was the one who saw me leaving."

"Coco is pregnant. She was feeling ill and thus had her face in the cool night air on the balcony."

"Oh."

"Would you like to hear everything that is going to happen now?"

She wanted to scream at him that she'd already heard everything and for him to shut up and just go away, but she couldn't. She merely nodded.

He censored judiciously, so well in fact that if she hadn't overheard the entire exchange between the two men, she wouldn't have suspected a thing.

Ah, but he left out the damning things.

"I don't think so," she said when he finished.

"You don't think so what?"

"I don't need you to volunteer your services as guardian. I am nearly twenty. Mr. Susson can be Jeremy's guardian until I reach twenty-one, then I will be his guardian. Camille Hall now belongs to him. Yes, I will be his guardian."

"No."

"You are very nearly as young as I am. How could you possibly set yourself up to be my guardian? It's absurd."

"I am nearly twenty-six, not so very young an age."

"Not so great an age either."

He grinned suddenly. "My brother would like to hear you say that. The poor fellow is only twenty-eight and all the Sherbrookes were pounding and pounding at him to get himself wedded and produce an heir."

"What happened?"

"He did marry, just before we received the letter from Samuel Grayson."

"Well, I feel sorry for his poor wife if that is why he married her. To breed heirs."

"I wouldn't feel sorry for Alexandra," Ryder said slowly. "I must admit, however, to being interested in learning what has happened between the two of them. But that's all beside the point. I will go to Montego Bay and speak to Oliver Susson. I will tell him the race is lost, so to speak. I will engage him to handle this situation and if he does it well, why then, I won't beat him to a bloody pulp."

She was quiet. Too quiet. He frowned down at her. "Attend me, Sophie. This is what is going to happen so accustom yourself. If you try to leave Kimberly Hall again, Emile has instructions to sit on you."

"Why are you doing this? Do you even realize what you're doing? You are volunteering to take a nine-year-old boy into your guardianship along with his nineteen-year-old slut of a sister. Why would you want this kind of responsibility?"

"I don't know," Ryder said. He tried to shrug it off, but couldn't quite manage it. He said slowly, "I am twenty-five. I am the second son, an honorable, not a lord. All my life I've done precisely what I wanted. All my life I've laughed and played and loved and enjoyed myself. When my father died, well then, there was Douglas to take care of things because, after all, he was the new earl. He was the responsible one. And I continued as I had. There was no reason for me to change. No one expected anything else from me. As for the other, well, none know of it and it is none of their business and besides it is no great or grave responsibility."

"What other?"

He simply shook his head and looked irritated with himself.

Sophie held herself silent.

He shrugged. "So," he said, "now I am responsible for both you and Jeremy. You will depend upon me and upon no one else. Just me. No, just shut your mouth, Sophie, and shake hands with your new guardian."

He hadn't really expected her to do anything but continue to squawk. She thrust out her hand and he took it in his. She stared up at him, saying in her tortured raw voice, "I do trust you with Jeremy. I do."

"You must learn to trust me with yourself as well."

"Oh no."

"How are your feet?"

"My feet? Oh, I forgot about them. They're fine, nearly well, in fact."

"Yes, I'll just bet they are." Ryder pulled the sheet off her. Her feet were lightly bandaged. Blood had soaked through the white cloth. "Why is there blood on the bandages?"

From walking on them downstairs and then running back upstairs.

"I don't know." Actually, she hadn't felt a thing. Odd, that.

"Sophie, it's obvious you got out of that bed. What did you do?"

"I had to relieve myself."

"Yes, certainly, that sounds like the exact truth. And reaching the chamber pot — all of six feet away — did this. Where did you go, Sophie?"

She looked at her hands. There was still grime under her fingernails. She said absolutely nothing.

"You need a guardian more than Jeremy does."

She looked then at her feet and wondered how she could have possibly forgotten them. Even dashing up and down the stairs to eavesdrop on Ryder and Mr. Cole hadn't hurt her. But now, looking at them, seeing the bloody bandages, she began to feel throbbing pain.

"I will see to them. There's no reason for you to remain, Ryder."

He cursed, fluently and loudly.

Within ten minutes he'd removed the bandages and was washing her feet with soap and hot water. She was trying to keep from crying out. He saw her white face and gentled. He called her a fool and kept cleaning the cuts. He called her a stupid twit when he lightly rubbed at a gash that was ugly and still bleeding.

When he poured alcohol over both feet, she

nearly leapt off the bed it hurt so bad. But he grabbed her shoulders and forced her onto her back. "I know it must sting like the very devil but you deserve it. Damn you, don't move. I don't know where you went walking but I'll find out and don't think I won't. Now, I'm going to do it again, just to make sure. If you dare to move, I will tie you down. Scream instead."

She yelled at the top of her lungs when he forced both feet into an alcohol bath. He held them there and she choked on the pain and on her tears.

Jeremy came flying through the door. His fists were up, his face was red with anger and determination.

Ryder stopped him with a look and a simple, "I'm helping her. Come here and hold her hand."

Jeremy clutched Sophie's hand until finally Ryder was satisfied that he'd done all he could. He lifted her feet out of the alcohol and swung them back onto the bed. "Now, we're not going to do anything for the moment, just keep them on top of this clean towel. No walking or I'll thrash you and I daresay Jeremy will help me."

"Yes, Sophie, don't you move. How could you? Coco took care of your feet last night. What did you do?"

"I'm your sister," she said, her voice so raw and hoarse that she was barely understandable. Jeremy didn't understand but Ryder did, and he did sympathize. He was no relation whatsoever

188

to Jeremy, yet Jeremy was perfectly willing and ready to obey him, not her. He leaned down and patted her white cheek. "Jeremy will visit with you for a while. Keep an eye on her, my boy, and don't let her move except to relieve herself. You're in charge, Jeremy. Don't let me down."

"Oh no, sir."

Ryder gave her a small salute. He gave Jeremy a wink, and left.

CHAPTER 9

He shook his head and shook it again. He simply couldn't get over her feet. She'd obviously walked somewhere — certainly a farther distance than to the chamber pot — and it had been only a short time before, for the blood on the bandages was quite fresh.

Then he knew, of course. She'd seen or heard Sherman Cole arrive and she'd been terrified. She'd come down and doubtless listened at the door.

His jaw tightened when he remembered his words about her to Sherman Cole and the man's words about her. Ryder's had been the more damning because she'd come to trust him, at least with Jeremy. He'd given her a clout that was both unexpected and beyond cruel. Ryder realized he was standing in the middle of the entrance hall, simply standing there, doing nothing, looking at nothing in particular when James said, "Suh, you need something?"

"No, James. Was Miss Stanton-Greville downstairs a few moments ago?"

190

"Yes, suh, she was. In old Mr. Grayson's night-shirt, her hair all wild, that ancient nightshirt flapping around her poor bandaged feet."

"Thank you, James."

"Yes, suh. Ah? suh, will dat Thomas get his neck stretched out?"

"I hope so, I surely do."

Ryder walked out onto the veranda. He saw Emile riding up and waved him down.

"Camille Hall is running as smoothly as I can make it at the moment," Emile said as he dismounted his horse. "The inside smells revolting still but the slaves are working hard scrubbing away the soot and grime. I left Clayton, one of our bookkeepers, over there to meet with the Camille Hall bookkeepers and the head drivers. He's a sharp fellow and a good organizer. He will keep everyone working. I will return this afternoon to see what they've accomplished."

"No sign of Thomas?"

"Nary a shadow. I directed the grizzly job of getting Burgess buried. His body had simply been overlooked, if you can believe that. Jesus, Ryder, it was a mess. At least it's done and over with. How are Jeremy and Sophie?"

"They're fine. Keep an eye out, Emile."

"Certainly. Where are you going?"

"To Camille Hall. Sophie and Jeremy need clothes."

Emile frowned after him.

Clayton was a vigorous, harshly tanned, wiry

little man who seemed to be moving even when he was standing still. He met Ryder at the door and began talking nonstop.

Ryder listened carefully to the man as he studied the great house, mentally noting what would have to be done, then dismissed Clayton and made his way upstairs. A giggling young girl with her hair wrapped in a colorful scarf showed him to Sophie's bedchamber. Her name, she pertly informed him with a sloe-eyed smile, was Dorsey. Sophie's bedchamber adjoined her uncle's. He looked over at that adjoining door and imagined it opening and Theo walking in, a whip in his hand.

He opened the armoire doors and saw at least half a dozen of the most garish gowns he'd ever beheld. All silks and satins, the colors too brilliant, all gowns much too old for her, gowns shrieking that she was a woman who knew men and would make a man scream with pleasure. There was nothing else hanging in the armoire save those utterly repulsive gowns.

In the drawers beneath, however, he found gowns that he could well imagine her wearing — soft pastels, light muslins. There were also her underthings — all well sewn and beautifully embroidered, but not what a whore would wear, all lawn, cotton, and linen, no silk, no satin. He shook out a nightgown and held it up. It was batiste, white, and looked as if it would be worn by a little girl.

He made a pile of clothing he would take back

to Kimberly. He did the same thing in Jeremy's room.

All the clothes would be delivered in the early afternoon.

When he arrived back at Kimberly, hot, sweat making his shirt stick to his back, he couldn't believe his eyes.

There was Sherman Cole and with him were four men, all armed. Cole was yelling at Samuel to bring down the harlot. She was a murderess and he was here to take her back with him to Montego Bay.

Ryder rode his stallion through the men, stopping only at the first step to the veranda.

Cole whirled around. "You! It doesn't matter, sir, I will take her, and I have the men with me to do it."

Ryder waved a negligent hand to the four men, all of whom looked vastly uncomfortable, their faces flushed scarlet in the heat.

"Why don't you come in, Mr. Cole? I am sure there are some rather tasty buns for you to enjoy while we straighten out this confusion."

Cole shouted, "No! I want her, now!"

"I'm fatigued from this infernal heat," Ryder said, dismounting, and walking past Sherman Cole, "and from your infernal yelling. Either you accompany me inside or you can stand out here baying in the sun until you melt."

Samuel hurried after Ryder. Cole, taken aback yet again by this damned young man, followed more slowly. He could hear low conversation among the four men and wondered if the bastards were going to leave him here alone. None of them had wanted to come with him. Well, let them leave. He'd bring her back himself. Then he'd lock her in that room and he'd keep the key. She would be dependent on him for the very water she drank.

Ryder faced him in the salon and said without preamble, "You say Miss Stanton-Greville killed her uncle?"

"Yes, and this time I have enough proof. She shot him twice, one of my men found the derringer." He pulled it out of his pocket and dangled it in front of Ryder. "You'll see that it has two chambers. Both are empty."

"Interesting."

"Get her. It's obviously a woman's gun. Get her. I will take her back with me."

"Take her back where, Cole?"

The man's color was high and it went higher. "Why, there is a house we use to keep prisoners in. More a large room, really, but it will suffice for the likes of her."

Ryder could only shake his head. He should allow Cole to see her now — with her bruised face, bent over like an old woman because of her battered ribs, not to mention her bloody feet. Surely his ardor would cool at that sight. If he took her to this house, he would force her. Rape her endlessly. Ryder felt a knot in his gut and he rubbed his hand over his belly as he said easily, "I think not, Cole. Why don't you and your men ride back to Camille Hall. There's a nice fresh grave for you to dig up."

"What the devil are you talking about, sir?"

"Simply this, Cole. It seems that Theo Burgess wasn't buried immediately and thus Emile Grayson was able to examine the body before he saw him buried. It turns out Burgess wasn't shot. He was stabbed three times in the chest. Now, would you like to examine his body yourself? Emile did say that it was quite a messy job. You understand, of course. The heat and all. No? Well, then, why not take yourself and your men off and find Thomas."

"But this derringer —"

"It's mine," Samuel Grayson said. "I appreciate your returning it. And you're quite right, sir, it is a lady's gun. It belonged to my wife."

Cole ignored him, his eyes hard on Ryder. "But what was she doing there?"

"I thought it was her home," Ryder said, an eyebrow climbing upward.

"I will examine the body myself."

"Fine. A man called Clayton is there. He is a Kimberly bookkeeper but he is overseeing things at Camille Hall. He will doubtless provide your men with shovels. It won't be pleasant work, but I'm sure you know that. Good Lord, isn't this heat something? I might add that Emile was rather green when he returned after getting it done. Several more hours have passed. Ah well, how much more unpleasant can it get? Go now, Cole, I'm tired, and speaking with you tires me even more. Good luck with your digging. The result, I daresay, will be even less pleasant than the process."

Ryder turned away then and walked through the open doors onto the front veranda. He said nothing more, merely waited for Cole and his men to leave, which they did, Cole muttering threats under his breath.

"He was really stabbed?" Samuel asked.

"I have no idea. Emile didn't say."

"Are you saying that you just made that up?"

Ryder cocked an eyebrow at Samuel. "Why, yes. It makes for an interesting theory, doesn't it?"

"I'm still worried, Ryder. Cole is determined. He's a dangerous man, despite your contempt of him. We've just bought a little time, that's all. He wants her badly."

"She scorned him, you know. Struck him when he tried to kiss her."

"He isn't the kind of man to ever forget something like that." Samuel shook his head. "Something must be done and soon. Ah, that poor child."

"You mean Jeremy? I agree but he is young and adaptable. He will be just fine."

"No! I meant Sophia."

"Oh, her. I trust she's kept to her bed?"

"Yes."

Ryder said nothing more, merely walked back into the house and headed up the stairs.

When next he visited her, it was late afternoon.

Sophie was wearing one of her nightgowns. She looked fresh and clean and very young. Her face was only faintly bruised now and she looked very bored. She frowned at him and said, "It is difficult to bathe and not get your feet wet."

"It's a sight I should have enjoyed witnessing. Perhaps you could bathe again this evening for my entertainment? I suppose that vicious snarl means I am to be denied. Well, it doesn't matter. I have come to talk to you."

"Talk, then."

"Feeling restive, are we?"

"I want to go home. I heard that one of your bookkeepers is overseeing things at home. That isn't right, Ryder. I should be there. Our people are perfectly capable of dealing with the problems themselves. I really must go home."

"Well, you can't just yet, so be quiet. As for Clayton, Emile says he's a diplomat so you needn't worry about lacerated sensibilities. Cole was here again after your lovely hide, but I told him that your uncle was just buried and it turns out he was stabbed, not shot."

She stared at him. "You're jesting."

"Who knows? It got Cole out of here. But I will tell you true. I think Thomas really did kill him and that he was the one you shot. Of course, that means it wasn't a mortal wound for he later spoke to Cole, giving his spurious evidence. But he's gone to ground now. I want to find him and toss him into the mangrove swamp. Yes, that's what I'll do."

"He won't return to Camille Hall. I really do want to go home, Ryder. There is so much to be done. There is no reason for Jeremy and me to remain here any longer. My ribs are much better now and my feet — well, I won't walk much, all right?"

"And just what would you do if Mr. Sherman Cole arrived with his men to remove you to Montego Bay?"

She paled. He remained unmoved.

"Actually," he said, looking beyond her right shoulder, "I've decided that we're all going back to England."

"You're mad!"

"Quite possibly. Jeremy needs schooling. He will go to Eton."

It was a dream come true, only Sophie didn't want it to come true this way, no, not through him. "No," she said. "I won't allow it."

"You have no choice at all," he said and smiled at her.

"I do have a choice. I won't be your mistress, Ryder, I won't."

"I don't recall having asked you. At least not in the past three days."

"I heard you! I heard what you said to Mr. Cole!"

"In that case, you must know that my ardor for your lovely self is quite in doubt now. After having examined you quite thoroughly I'm not sure at all that I am interested anymore. You are adequate for your environs, perhaps, but back in England? I don't know about that."

She picked up a heavy book of Shakespeare plays and flung it at him with all her might. He caught it square in his chest and grunted. Actually, she felt more pain in throwing the heavy tome at him than he felt at the blow. She paid it no mind. She threw a pitcher of water at him, a much easier shot, soaking the front of him.

There was nothing else to throw. She lay back against the pillows, panting and heaving, her forehead damp with perspiration. He hadn't moved, even to wipe the water from his face. "That's the second time you've attacked me," he said mildly. "What do you think I should do about it?"

"You should stop trying to take over my life."

"I want you to be well again."

"So do I!"

"Ah, but my reasons for wishing it are quite different from yours. I want you well and thus able to fight me. I want to hear you yowl when I've bested you, which I will do. I want to hear you curse me. I want you to hurl yourself at me again and again, because I know you, Sophie, I know you don't give up easily. When I have bested you, then you will get what you deserve."

"I wish you had never come here."

"Oh? And who should have come in my place? My little sister, Sinjun? I must admit that she would have found all this vastly amusing, but I'm not certain she would have dealt with you as well as I. She is very straightforward and honest, you see, utterly without guile. Or perhaps my pious younger brother, Tysen, who is right now at Oxford preparing himself for vicardom. He, I doubt not, will marry an equally pious girl who will be nauseatingly proper and good. Still and all, however, it's possible that Tysen would have been the recipient of one of your drowsy-eyed smiles and stuttered himself off the island and quite probably drowned. Now, as to the earl, why, my dear girl, he would have eaten you for breakfast. He has no patience, not like I have. He doesn't like games, either, not like I do. He doesn't indulge wholeheartedly in the sport women usually provide, not like I do. No, he would have put a stop to you immediately and walked away, dusting his hands. So, all in all, I think you were very lucky I came here, and I do promise you, Sophie, I swear it, that you will be bested by me, but in my own good time."

"A man's threats — always violence, always bragging and braying about the pain you will inflict."

"Oh no, I intend no pain."

"Very well, dominance. It's every bit as bad as physical violence. All men must know that they rule, even if it's just over a single woman."

"I believe we've been through similar charges before."

"Go to the devil, Ryder. You and all men are despicable. As for your repulsive family, I hope they all rot."

"Even Sinjun?"

"If she is like you, then yes, damn you."

Ryder wasn't used to explosions like this. He frowned at the newness of it, the abruptness of it, although since he'd met her, she'd knocked him off balance more times than he'd experienced in his life. But this — well, what could he expect? Her uncle had beaten her, probably countless times, out of the demented fun of doing it and to make her perform as he demanded. "You don't bore me," he said abruptly. "Actually, I find you quite amusing and I haven't even made —" He stopped cold in his tracks. No, he wasn't about to tell her that he hadn't taken her that night at the cottage when he'd drugged her. He had a clear flash in that instant of himself staring down at her and how he'd wanted very much to touch her, to caress her, but he hadn't. He wasn't that cold-blooded.

"Well, Sophie, do you want to be my mistress for a time?"

"No."

"Ah, you find Oliver Susson more to your taste? Really, my dear, he's not at all a sterling specimen of manhood, although he is cooperative, which is a good thing for him. And that is the reason I haven't been up to see you earlier. I rode to Montego Bay to visit with Mr. Susson. Let us say that he now understands very clearly what he is to do. He will work to see that my guardianship is handled immediately. He apologized profusely for his ethical lapse and assured me that he would perform these duties without financial remuneration." Ryder paused for a reaction, but she held herself silent. She was well hidden from him, an act she was quite good at. He wanted to draw her, to bait her into fury, and thus continued in a mocking voice. "Naturally, the thought of losing you upset him dreadfully. He even went so far as to say that he would marry you, though he knew it would greatly affect his reputation in Jamaica. I thought there were actually tears in his eyes once he learned that he would never again enjoy you at the cottage."

"He never did enjoy me. He did, but not in the way you think."

"Oh? You say you were never at the cottage with him?"

"Yes, but I didn't —" She stopped. It was no good. She said abruptly, "All you have to do is look at my face and my ribs, Ryder, and know that I did nothing with any of these men willingly."

"Reluctant all the way, huh? Perhaps I believe you with a pathetic bastard like Sherman Cole. But with all the rest of them? I'm sorry, Sophie, but I do remember that first night with you and how you played the coquette to perfection. You didn't turn a hair when I pulled your gown to your waist and fondled your breasts. Oh no, you handled me with great skill — ah, the promises, the anticipation you built up in me. I positively festered with lust."

"Will you get me some bandages so I can wrap up my feet? I must get up, Ryder. I am so bored

202

I want to scream and your conversation is rendering me nearly insensible."

So much for goading her into an excess of bile, he thought, and simply nodded. He himself wrapped up her feet, pleased that they looked better than they had that morning. Nice feet, he thought, narrow, highly arched. He said as he studied her toes, "When I finished my conversation with Mr. Susson, I checked on shipping schedules to England. There are several ships due in from England very soon now. We will have time to tie up all loose ends. I firmly intend for the three of us to be on the next ship back home."

"Sir, are you helping my sister again?"

Ryder slowly lowered her foot back onto the bed. He turned to see Jeremy standing in the doorway. He said under his breath, but Sophie heard him, "I really must remember to close that bloody door." He grinned at the boy. "Come in, Jeremy. Your sister is flushed from the heat and I was just trying to amuse her. She is bored, you know, and wants for diversions."

"You were holding her foot."

"Yes. She had a cramp in her toes but it is better now. As you can see I'm also bandaging her feet again. She is bored."

"I will read to her. Goodness, Sophie, whatever is the Shakespeare doing on the floor? You must be more careful. Some of the pages are twisted. Goodness, page four hundred and thirty is torn."

"You're right, Jeremy. She tore the second scene in *The Taming of the Shrew*."

"Go away, Ryder," she said. "Just go away."
He did, whistling.

Sophie didn't know what had awakened her. At one moment she was dreaming deeply, and her mother was there with her, laughing and brushing her hair and talking about the future and all the fine young men who would want to marry her when they went to London upon her eighteenth birthday. The next moment, she was wide awake, jerking upright in bed, frozen still and listening.

The sound came again. Movement coming from outside.

Her heart began to pound, fast, shallow strokes. Slowly, she pulled off the single sheet covering her and eased out from beneath the mosquito netting. It was very late and very silent except for that other sound. It was a person and he was moving along the balcony outside, quietly but not quietly enough for her sharp ears.

She stepped onto the floor. Her feet were still bandaged but it had been two days since the fire at Camille Hall and the pain was nearly gone now. She walked slowly, tiptoeing to the open door and peering out. She heard nothing but the soft grating sound of a lone coqui. Then in the next instant, she saw a shadow, a long shadow, the shadow of a man, and he was moving stealthily around the side of the house.

She picked up the water pitcher beside her bed, the one she'd hurled two days before at Ryder, unceremoniously dumped the remaining water into the chamber pot, and walked out onto the balcony. There were no barriers. The balcony curved around the entire second floor of the house, a good eight feet deep with a twelve-foot overhang to protect from the sun. She crept after the man. Suddenly she was right behind him and she froze. He was silent, staring into a bedchamber.

It was Ryder's room.

She saw him raise a knife in his hand. God, it was Thomas and he was going to kill Ryder.

She waited until he stepped into the bedchamber then ran quickly after him, the thick bandages on her feet silencing them. She peered around the open doorway to see Thomas now standing by Ryder's bed. He had the knife raised. She saw a bulky bandage around his chest. She'd shot him, not her uncle. Ryder had been right.

But her aim hadn't been good enough, worse luck.

Slowly, he pulled back the mosquito netting.

Sophie screamed and screamed again, yelling like a banshee, shrieking like a mad voodoo priestess. She ran toward Thomas, the pitcher raised high.

Ryder awoke to see the silver flash of a blade over his body, a harsh scream echoing in his head. Jesus! He jerked away, rolling off the other side of the bed, but he tangled himself in the mosquito netting.

Sophie saw him roll quickly to the opposite

side of the bed, but he didn't jerk the mosquito netting out of the way. He fell hard to the floor, tangled in the yards and yards of netting.

Thomas was running around the side of the bed, breathing hard, not even looking at her, intent upon getting to Ryder.

"Thomas!"

He jerked toward her then and she saw the hatred twisting his face.

"Thomas, I shot you, not Ryder! What's the matter, are you afraid of me? You miserable bastard, you *are* afraid of me, a girl, half your size. Coward, murdering, sniveling coward! Why did you kill my uncle? Did he deceive you, cheat you?"

Thomas went berserk. He was trembling, making slashing downward and upward motions with the knife. "I know you shot me, you damned bitch! After I kill him I will deal with you. First I'm going to have me some fun with you and then I'll let you beg me not to kill you. On your knees, you little slut, on your knees in front of me begging and begging." He was stalking her, Ryder now forgotten.

Sophie didn't have time to question the wisdom of her attack. If Ryder didn't free himself quickly, she would very shortly be in grave difficulties. She moved behind a wicker chair, shoving it forward toward him.

Every nerve was tingling in her body. She felt dread, fear, and, oddly enough, excitement at the danger. Her eyes glittered as she looked at his hated face.

"You gutless coward!" she screamed at him, taunting him. Then just as quickly, she stepped to one side of the chair, looked beyond him, and yelled, "Yes, Ryder, kill him now!"

Thomas whirled about to face his new attacker, a man, and thus more of a threat.

It was a mistake.

Sophie rushed up behind him and struck the heavy pottery pitcher over his head. It cracked hard against his skull. Thomas groaned softly and slumped to the floor. The knife fell from his fingers and lay beside him, the long silver blade obscene in the pale light of the bedchamber.

Ryder pulled the mosquito netting off himself and slowly got to his feet. He walked over to Thomas, kneeled down, and felt the man's pulse. He was alive, just barely.

"You gave him a fine cosh," he said, still studying Thomas. "You did shoot him. Here, in the ribs. He must have still been in some pain." Ryder looked up at her then. She was standing there, silent as a stone, swathed in one of her voluminous white nightgowns, her hair loose down her back, her face as white as the Valenciennes lace at the collar of her gown. She was still holding the broken-off pitcher handle, clutching it like an amulet.

"Thank you, Sophie," he said, and slowly rose.

She drew in a sharp breath. He was naked and he didn't appear to be aware of it. He walked to a lamp and lit it. He turned to face her and at that moment, Samuel, Mary, Emile, Coco,

James, and several other house slaves burst into the room. Coco promptly fainted. Emile caught her, luckily, and set her on Ryder's bed. "She's pregnant," he said and shrugged.

Ryder smiled and raised his hand. "It's all right. Thomas is the one on the floor. He came to kill me. At least I was first on his list. Sophie saved me."

"Ryder," Emile said on a strained laugh. "I'm delighted it's over and both of you are all right. Sophie saved you? She always was a daring girl, and anyone to attack someone dear to her got the brunt of her fury. But, my dear fellow, you are quite naked. This is the second time you've been thusly unattired."

"So I am," Ryder said, bemused. He walked over to a chair and shrugged into a dressing gown. "It's so bloody hot, you know. Sophie, are you all right?"

She still hadn't said a word. In fact, she hadn't moved an inch. He walked to her and gently touched his fingertips to her cheek. "Are you all right?"

"Sophie!"

It was Jeremy and he shoved and pushed his way into the room and ran clumsily to his sister.

She came alive then and held him against her. She stroked his tousled hair, saying very softly and calmly, "I'm fine, love, just fine, and so is Ryder. Thomas, however, isn't. That's grand, isn't it, Jeremy? No more villains to hurt us or anyone else. No more villains at all."

"Unfortunately the world abounds with villains," Ryder said. "But there is now one less. Emile, why don't the two of us tie this one up and take him to the mangrove swamp and leave him there for the crocodiles. I surely do like that notion."

"I do too," Emile said.

"We must notify Sherman Cole," Samuel said. "Surely now he will believe that Thomas murdered Burgess."

"I suppose you're right," Ryder said on a mournful sigh. "Perhaps Emile and I can take him into Montego Bay. Perhaps we can have a slight accident on the way, by the —"

"Mangrove swamp," Emile said, grinning.

"It's the middle of the night," Ryder said. "Let's tie him up and stuff him in some dark closet. Is there anyplace secure here, Samuel?"

"Yes, the icehouse."

Within five minutes Thomas was securely bound and carried out to the icehouse, a guard set over him. Finally Ryder's bedchamber was empty again but for Sophie and Jeremy. He was still holding her, clutching at her really, for she was all that was left of his world.

Ryder didn't think, he merely dropped to his haunches and said quietly, "It's all right, Jeremy. Truly. Sophie's safe. Now, my lad, why don't your sister and I take you back to bed?"

"A glass of milk first, Jeremy?"

The boy shook his head. "No, I'd throw it

up. This was scary, Sophie, too scary. I'm tired of being scared."

"Me too, love, me too."

"I as well," Ryder said and ruffled the boy's hair when he stared at him, disbelieving.

It took a good thirty minutes to settle Jeremy. They both remained with him until he fell asleep. Ryder followed Sophie back to her bedchamber.

"Come outside and let's sit a while. Like Jeremy, I'm too excited to sleep just yet."

They sat in two wicker chairs, enveloped in silence, the terror fading slowly, very slowly.

"Thank you, Sophie."

"You're welcome."

"How did you know?"

"I just heard an odd sound, one that didn't belong to the night, and it woke me up. I saw this shadow and followed it. Then I knew it was Thomas and he was here to kill you."

"You reacted very quickly," Ryder said, and he sounded a bit annoyed. "I have never known a female to act so quickly and so competently. You didn't hesitate. You didn't swoon and give a pathetic little yell. You screamed your head off. You even had your weapon with you."

"As you recall, I had used that same pitcher before. I knew it was sound. You were tangled in the netting. What was I supposed to do? Let him gut you like a trapped fish? Also, a delicate feminine little whimper wouldn't have accomplished much. Besides, I was next and then possibly Jeremy."

"Yes, you were next," Ryder repeated slowly. "He would have succeeded if you hadn't been there. You know that, don't you? I am not a particularly light sleeper."

She shrugged as if she didn't give a good damn and it infuriated him, this strength in her, this bravado, that was or wasn't real — he didn't know and wondered if he'd ever know. He rose quickly to his feet and stared down at her. He was shocked at his own behavior. Never before in his life had he come face to face with a dog-in-the-manger attitude in himself. It was too much. She'd turned the world and all his experiences and beliefs inside out. "I am pleased that I am someone dear to you."

"What are you talking about?"

"Emile said you were ferocious when it came to protecting those dear to you."

"I told you, Ryder, he would have killed me after he'd taken care of you. I'm not stupid."

"How are your feet?"

"Fine. I'm nearly well."

"Good," he said, and jerked her to her feet. He pulled her against him before she had a chance to react. He grabbed her chin in his hand and held her still. He kissed her closed mouth, hard.

"I don't like this," he said against her mouth, his breath hot as the urgency that burned deep within him. "You are not as you should be. I cannot understand you. I won't put up with it anymore. Damn you, be a woman!"

He kissed her again. He felt her belly against

him and his hands were wild down her back, caressing her, stroking down over her buttocks, pulling her upward hard against him.

She wrenched away from him. She didn't say a word. She just kept backing away from him, one step at a time, a single, small step, farther and farther away from him. She wiped the back of her hand across her mouth.

He knew such fury he was shaking with it. "After all the damned men you've had, you dare to wipe the taste of me off your mouth?"

She dropped her hand to her side and took another step backward.

"You go much farther and you'll end up in Samuel's bedchamber. You'll have to kick his housekeeper out of his bed, but I'm certain he'd be more than pleased to have you instead of Mary."

She shook her head, still silent.

"Damn you, say something!"

She turned on her heel and ran.

CHAPTER 10

Thomas escaped. No one was precisely certain how he'd managed to free himself from the icehouse, but there were two Kimberly slaves unconscious and bound in the bushes nearby. They'd been clobbered, but not killed, and that surprised Ryder. They hadn't seen a thing. Ryder suspected that some of Thomas's cohorts from Camille Hall had rescued him, and perhaps it was these cohorts who had kept him from killing the guards like one would swat flies. He was long gone, dammit. No crocodiles for him, dammit even more. Ryder sent out search parties. He sent word to Sherman Cole. Then he brooded about Sophie.

Ryder hated to brood. He'd done very little of it in his life for the very simple reason that he'd never felt the need to take himself apart from his fellow man and commit himself to brooding. It had always seemed to him to be a singularly boring way to pass the time. But now he felt the need and it was sharp and deep inside him. It was also unexpected and unwelcome and made him uncomfortable; nor did he particularly know how to do it properly.

Damn her for making him ponder and muse and agonize and absorb thoughts and feelings he didn't want or need.

He jumped to his feet, furious with himself and with her, and determined to end it once and for all.

She wasn't in her bedchamber — his former bedchamber, rather. She was dressed and sitting quietly in a chair on the balcony. Her eyes were closed, her hands folded in her lap. She looked to be asleep. She was wearing one of the pale blue muslin gowns he'd brought back from Camille Hall for her, a high-necked affair with lace that nearly touched her chin. He paused, just looking down at her for a very long time. Her hair was clean and pulled back with a pale blue ribbon at the nape of her neck. There were only the faintest bruises on her face now. She looked scrubbed, fresh, and immensely innocent, and too young.

Innocent, ha. But that was the crux of the matter, indeed it was, and he wouldn't stand for it anymore. He lightly touched his hand to her shoulder.

She opened her eyes slowly and stared up at him, her expression not changing. She didn't jump or exclaim.

She said only, "Ryder."

"Hello," he said, and he felt something odd and sweet touch him as she spoke his name. It made him angry and she felt it. She tensed beneath

214

his hand. He pulled back, his hand dropping to his side, and took the chair opposite her.

"This is the second time we've sat here on this balcony like an old married couple reviewing the events of the day."

"Hardly," she said. She gave him a smile that didn't reach her eyes, a hard smile, and had he but realized it, a smile that cloaked an immense vulnerability. "If I didn't know better I would think you were agitated about something. Difficult to believe, I know. You, Ryder Sherbrooke, a man to whom the worries of the world are practically unknown. No, certainly that can't be it. You are not like normal people with normal concerns."

"I believe you have said quite enough. It always surprises me how you can go immediately on the attack with little or no buildup. Instantly, you are at the jugular, biting and nipping away. But you won't draw me this time or sidetrack me. That is always your purpose with me, isn't it? No, don't bother to deny it or bait me more. Now, I want to know something from you and I want the truth."

"Very well."

He sat forward, his hands clasped between his knees. "The truth, Sophie. I mean it."

"If you have to remind me, if you have to look as serious as an idol, I doubt you'll believe a truth when you hear it."

"Did you sleep with any of those men willingly? Did your uncle force you into being a harlot or

215

were you a harlot before and your uncle merely molded you into doing what he wanted you to do and with whom?"

"No."

"Damn you, Sophie, don't you dare —"

She rose suddenly, her skirts swirling about her ankles, and he saw that she was barefoot. Still bandages, but no shoes. He didn't like that. It made him angrier.

"Answer my question, damn you!"

"Ask me a single question, then, and I will answer it." Her back was to him, her shoulders straight, and he knew that chin of hers was probably thrust up a good two inches.

"Very well. Did you sleep with any of those men willingly?"

"No."

"Not even Lord David Lochridge?"

"No."

"Had you slept with any men before your uncle coerced you into bedding those of his choosing?"

"No."

"I see," he said, but he didn't, not really. His brain wasn't functioning with its usual clarity — doubtless because of the brooding — and it was making him equal parts frustrated and furious. "Damn you, how old were you when you had your first man?"

She turned to face him then and she was still smiling that hard, cutting smile. "If you're to be believed, why then, the first man had me when I was nineteen. And that first man was you."

She laughed at the infuriated expression on his face. "You see, Ryder, you refuse to believe me because you're a man and men must place women into very neat slots. A woman is innocent or she's not. There is no middle ground for a woman. A widow is all right, perhaps, but even then men assume that she will bed any number of them willingly, indeed, enthusiastically, because she's used to having sex and knows what it's all about.

"I have come to believe that once a woman has known a man intimately, she really isn't to be trusted after that. Goodness, if the man is her husband she just might cuckold him. Of course, a husband can't cuckold his wife. A husband can continue doing whatever he pleases. If he can't get a woman to willingly bed with him, why he simply buys a woman for the night. Or, like you — a rich man — he keeps mistresses. And the man remains utterly respectable. Indeed, his credit rises with both men and women. It is nonsense and not fair. I will tell you the truth again, Ryder. I have never been with a man intimately —"

"More of your unenlightened philosophy of life — how trippingly it flows from your mouth. You, Sophie, are more ignorant than a slug. You know nothing of men and women and what is important between them and how —"

She actually stamped one of her bandaged feet. "I never want to know! I sincerely doubt that there could be anything equal or fine or just between a man and a woman. I don't think you

217

believe it either, Ryder. Don't you dare sneer at me. I will tell you again and it's the truth. I have never been intimate with a man, except you and you had to drug me and —"

"Damn you, I fondled and caressed your breasts and you allowed me to do it! You let me kiss you and you kissed me back expertly. You let me put my tongue in your mouth. By God, when you woke up on the beach and saw that I'd nearly stripped you and taken you then, what did you do? You smiled at me and teased me and invited me to be your lover. You promised you would dismiss the others. I would call that pretty damned intimate."

"— then you took me to the cottage, and I have no memory of that at all, as you well know. So, no, I'm no longer innocent, I suppose. I had assumed a man could tell if a woman was without experience and vice versa, but apparently it isn't so because you didn't apologize and admit that I had been a virgin when you took me."

Ryder rose very slowly. His face was red, the pulse in his throat was swelled and throbbing. He picked up his chair and hurled it with all his strength over the railing. A shout came from below. He gave her a look of utter loathing and strode off the balcony and out of the bedchamber.

Samuel Grayson found Ryder in the north cane-field. He was speaking to one of the head drivers, a black man named Jonah who could snap a man's

218

neck with one huge hand. Ryder wore a hat. His shirt was open nearly to his waist and his chest was shiny with sweat and darkened from the sun. Samuel set his jaw and rode to the two men.

Ryder finished his questions to Jonah, thanked him, then turned to give a salute to Samuel.

"A good man," Samuel said, looking after Jonah.

"Yes. I would certainly like to have him on my side during a fight. Thinking of him as an enemy makes my blood curdle."

"I must speak with you, Ryder."

Ryder took off his hat, fanned his face, then rubbed his sleeve over his forehead. "Let's go find some shade. Perhaps to the beach, if that's all right with you, Samuel."

They rode to Monmouth Beach. Ryder was aware of a slight deepening of recognition inside him, a warming that somehow pulled and tugged at him, which was quite foolish, of course. It was just a beach, for God's sake, a place that was pleasant, nothing more. Certainly it had nothing to do with her. They dismounted and settled themselves beneath a coconut tree. The breeze was steady and cool. Ryder felt the sweat drying and it brought a very nice chill to his skin. He sighed with pleasure and leaned back bonelessly against the trunk.

Samuel said without preamble, "I want to marry Sophia Stanton-Greville. Then I will be the boy's guardian. Camille Hall is the very next property to Kimberly. Emile and I will be able to oversee all operations and ensure that the boy's inheritance is secure."

Good God, this was a shocker, but it shouldn't have been, not really. Ryder knew Samuel was infatuated with her, had known it from the beginning, and had found it, at first, somewhat amusing. It was no longer amusing. He heard himself say in a faraway voice, "I will shortly be Jeremy's guardian. As for Sophie, who knows? But, Samuel, there is no need for you to do anything."

"But you don't really want to be the boy's guardian. I know you want to return to England as soon as possible. Your life is there. You're taking the boy and Sophie with you because you don't see any other choice. But there is now a choice. They both belong here, not in England. I know there is a house and some property in Cornwall, but surely it isn't as important as the plantation is here. I will hire a tutor for Jeremy. He will be educated and someday he will assume his inheritance. Sophia will have security, a family, people around her who care about her."

Ryder felt suddenly very cold. He turned away from Samuel, suddenly afraid of what his expression might give away. He stared out over the sea. Where the devil had all his carefree laughter gone? "I see," he said at last. "You have thought a lot about this. I suppose you are one of these people who care for Miss Stanton-Greville."

"Yes."

"You also realize you're old enough to be her father."

"I naturally realize that as well and it concerns me. I had wanted Emile to marry her for their ages are closer, but he believes her a whore. He respects her at least now, for she did save your life, and that is something. Still, he looks at her with a sneer and in that assessing way a man looks at a woman he thinks just might want to bed him — the way you look at her. I want to protect her. I want to care for her. Once I marry her, Emile will keep his opinions to himself. Indeed, he might come to change them for they are quite wrong. She is a good girl, a wholesome girl. She has been maligned and her uncle is the only one at fault. I'm glad the man is dead."

"She plays the whore to perfection."

"If that is true, it is her uncle's doing. Everything she has done he's made her do. But he could not have made her agree to sleep with all those men."

"You believe, then, that all the men have simply lied about bedding her at the cottage?"

"They must have."

"Emile said she was a hellion."

"I don't think she could have survived had she not been strong-willed, had she not been able to endure. She has protected her brother to the best of her ability. I have wondered about the gossip, indeed, have listened to all the men who have claimed to have been her lover. She couldn't do such a thing; it's that simple. It isn't in her nature."

"But wouldn't she do anything to protect Jeremy?"

"Almost anything, yes, but not degrade herself, not that. She didn't hesitate to save your life either. If that makes her a hellion, why then, it is a good thing, at least I would imagine you believe it to be."

"Yes, she did save me, didn't she? Listen to me, Samuel, you must also realize that if you marry her neither of you will be received by the families here, or, even if you are received, she will be snubbed. She is already ostracized."

"I intend to change all that," Samuel said. "I will claim to all that she came to my marriage bed a virgin. I will tell the truth about her uncle."

"The only result to that assertion would be laughter. Be sensible, Samuel. No one will ever change their opinion."

"I will try, I must."

"When I spoke to Oliver Susson today he also said he would marry her."

"I wouldn't allow Oliver to get near her."

"If you want to shelter her from all the men she's entertained — forced to by her uncle or not — you would end up spending your lives as hermits. The list of men visiting that damned cottage of hers is long, Samuel."

"You are wrong, Ryder. I will change opinions. My word is respected here."

"No," Ryder said.

"Excuse me?"

"I said no. You won't marry her."

Samuel felt stirrings of anger at the young man. Even though he was Kimberly Hall's owner, Ryder Sherbrooke had no right to dictate personal matters to him. His reasons for his actions were sound. He rose slowly to his feet. "You have no say in the matter, Ryder. It is my decision, not yours."

Ryder smiled. "Actually, Samuel, it is Sophie's decision and she will say no."

"Why? Because you ruined her and thus she wouldn't want to shame me by accepting me as her husband? Don't look so bloody surprised. I knew very well you wanted her, that you wanted to dominate her, to bring her to her knees, if you will. You made it a test of manhood. Ah, yes, you behaved just like a new hound in the pack. You had to prove your virility and power with this woman, to yourself and to others. It was a competition. You had to show the world that you could have her, and in having her make her say that the others weren't important to her, just you. I'm not blind. Also, I was standing beneath the balcony a short time ago, and I heard what she said and your accusations as well. I heard her telling you that she'd been innocent until you'd taken her to the cottage.

"You have ruined Miss Stanton-Greville and you have made no move to remedy the situation. The only remedy that would occur to you would be to make her your mistress, and she a young lady of excellent birth and breeding. She is also a young lady of principles. Have you even given a thought to the possibility that you could have gotten her with child? Of course you haven't. Well, I care about her and I will marry her and if she is pregnant, then she won't birth a bastard. Damn you, keep that supercilious eyebrow of yours down! Can you swear to me that when you took her at the cottage she wasn't a virgin?"

Ryder said very quietly, "No, I can't swear."

"What you refuse to admit is that you breached her maidenhead, that you took a virgin. She is no harlot, and well you know it. I have told you what I intend. I have given you that much courtesy. At least I'm offering the poor girl a choice, which is more than you've thought to do."

Ryder picked up a small pebble and flung it toward the water. It bounced in the surf. "Just how do you plan to protect her when Sherman Cole comes to arrest her so that he can hang her for murdering her uncle?"

Samuel Grayson looked away from Ryder, out over the sea. "So you believe it better for you to take her away from here along with Jeremy? She would be your mistress, that, or she would be completely alone with no money, no friends, no way to support herself? That is some solution, I warrant!

"God save us all from men who think the world is theirs to command and women there for their selfish pleasures. I have also observed your notion of honor, sir; it burrows deep into your pride, into the years upon years of privilege and wealth you and your family have enjoyed. But the other? The worth of a single girl? Her honor? Her reputation? There is none, there is only your domination of her and her surrender to you, this competition you and all young men revel in. And then you walk away, thinking no more about the girl and what you've done to her. No, it will be done my way. If Sherman Cole arrests Sophie, why then, I don't know. But by God I will think of something. Good day." Samuel strode away from him, striking his riding crop against his thigh in his agitation.

Ryder stared after the man. He felt as if he'd just been verbally thrashed by his father. His father had been better at it as he recalled, but Samuel wasn't bad. He snorted as he watched Samuel mount his horse.

He leaned back against the tree trunk again and closed his eyes. Of course he didn't see the entire world as his to command, just a small bit of it perhaps. So what was wrong with that? He wasn't selfish; he wasn't greedy. He took but he didn't take too much. He didn't hurt people. And he did give, certainly he did. Jane could tell anyone that as well as his sister, Sinjun.

Was he such an unfeeling, selfish bastard? Had his aims been all that ignoble? Was he really the leader of the hounds? No, all that nonsense about proving his virility was just that, nonsense. He was himself and he wasn't all that bad, not at all. He was honorable because it was bred into him, Samuel was right about that, so what was the matter with it? But he felt guilty nonetheless and he felt a fraud, dammit, which wasn't fair.

"Well, hell," he said to an incredibly huge green turtle who was making a sluggish trail toward the water's edge. "Well, hell," he said again.

Samuel Grayson looked at Sophie with bleak eyes. Ryder had been right. She'd refused him without hesitation, but very nicely. She looked tired and somehow defeated. He hated it but didn't know what to do about it.

She tried to smile at him, but there were tears in her eyes. "You know I cannot," she said again, for he had remained silent. It seemed he'd used up all his words on Ryder Sherbrooke.

He said finally, his voice tired as his soul, "No, I don't understand. This shame of yours, it is nonsense. I am not a randy young man with expectations of purity, Sophia. I would that you reconsider."

Again, without hesitation, she said, "No, I'm sorry, Samuel." His name felt odd on her lips, for he'd been Mr. Grayson to her the entire four years she'd lived on Jamaica, but when a man proposed, she supposed it wouldn't be polite to treat him like your father.

"I apologize if this embarrasses you, Sophie, but I know about what Ryder did to you. I know this is your shame. I am sorry for it."

"He told you?"

"No, certainly not. But he knows that I know. Is it possible you are with child?"

226

She paled and clutched a chair back. She was shaking her head violently even as she whispered, "Oh no, I couldn't be, it wouldn't be fair. Oh Lord, what am I to do?"

"You can marry me and be safe. I don't care if you are pregnant with his child."

She marveled at the goodness in him, the genuine caring for her, and knew regardless that she couldn't marry him, not ever. "No, I would never do that, never."

Samuel sighed. "Ryder was right."

She stiffened. "What do you mean?"

"He said you would refuse me because he'd bedded you."

She laughed, actually laughed, and Samuel stared at her dumbfounded. "Well," she managed at last, "at least he believes me to have some honor. Me, the whore of Jamaica! Ah, but it is too much."

Ryder heard that laughter and found himself walking swiftly toward it. It was strained and he felt the wildness of it to the very depths of him, a barely contained fierceness. It scared him to his toes. He quickly opened the door of the drawing room only to draw up in some embarrassment. He didn't know who he'd expected to be with her, but not Samuel Grayson. Good God, Samuel had said something to bring that on?

"Oh," he said. "Samuel, Sophie. Excuse me."

"No, Ryder, it isn't necessary," Samuel said. "You were right. She won't have me. Now, I must needs see to some work. No, stay here, I will be off. I believe I will ride into Montego Bay and see what Sherman Cole is up to. Perhaps Thomas has been caught." Ryder didn't say a word until Samuel had closed the door after him.

Ryder felt a spurt of relief so profound that he trembled with it. He didn't want to accept the relief because accepting made him so furious with himself that he wanted to howl. He looked at her standing there in one of her modest muslin gowns, her feet bare as an urchin's, no bandages now, and he said, "I assume all those sweet girlish gowns I brought over from Camille Hall for you were from your precottage days?"

Her eyes narrowed. Her hands fisted at her sides. Then she smiled at him, one of those drowsy-eyed smiles, and when she spoke, her voice was soft and mocking, and his body reacted before he could stop it. "Ah, Ryder, certainly they're from before. Boring little confections, aren't they? Could you ever doubt it? But what was I to do? You left all my other gowns at Camille Hall. Why don't you pretend that I'm wearing a bright scarlet satin cut nearly to my waist and come here and fondle me again? Be bold, Ryder, be a man and rip the gown right off me. Wouldn't you enjoy that? A real man asserting his strength and power. Goodness, it makes me shudder just to think about it. You could bend me back over your right arm. Really, don't I deserve a reward for saving your poor Mr. Grayson from a fate worse than death?"

He didn't move. Then he cursed. Then he

shouted at her, "Stop that damned act!"

"Act? You mean you don't think I'm a harlot anymore?"

"Yes, no. I don't know, curse you."

"Did dear Samuel begin to change your mind?"

"No."

Just as suddenly as she'd assumed the polished harlot role, she became more vulnerable than he could bear. Because she couldn't control it, and she didn't want him to see that vulnerability, she whirled about and walked quickly to the veranda. But he had seen it and followed on her heels. She was wringing her hands as she said in a terrified whisper he barely heard, "What if I am pregnant?"

He did not pretend to misunderstand her. "Did you never think of that with all the other men? Did you always take precautions with them?"

"No."

More of her verbal confusion. He should have told her that if she were pregnant, it certainly wasn't with his seed. And if she were, just by chance, as innocent as she claimed to be, why then, they should be speaking of a possible religious birth.

He should tell her that he hadn't taken her. He should, really, but he didn't. Because if he did tell her she just might marry Samuel Grayson, and he knew he couldn't allow that to happen.

"When was your last monthly flow?"

She jerked with shock. He watched, fascinated, as she forced herself back into control. She looked him straight in the face, didn't say a word, then turned and walked quickly away.

He frowned after her. Her look had been one of utter scorn; she'd needed no words, for her expression had been quite enough. He should teach her how to sneer. She would do it well.

When Samuel Grayson returned to Kimberly four hours later, he was sweating profusely and he looked frantic. He said to both Emile and Ryder without preamble, "Sherman Cole is digging up Burgess's body tomorrow morning. It's the talk of Montego Bay. Thomas is still at large. Cole says that after he arrests Sophia, he will offer money to Thomas to come out of hiding and testify against her. He says he doesn't believe the story of Thomas coming here to murder you, Ryder. He also claims you were lying about Burgess being shot. I heard he is paying a lot of money to three men to dig Burgess up and examine him. He says he will arrest her immediately, try her, and hang her, all within the week. He says that none of us can stop it."

"So," Emile said, "the end is near. No matter what I think of her personally, I don't wish to see her hung."

His father snorted in disgust. "You blind young puppy! Well, Ryder, soon you won't have to worry about her. Soon it will be just Jeremy." He turned to his son. "I need you to be at Camille Hall when Cole goes there tomorrow morning. We must have warning. Go tell Sophie to stay close to the house."

After Emile had left the salon, Samuel said, "Now there is no choice. I will tell you, Ryder. There is the *Harbinger*, a big stout barkentine, in port right now. It is returning to England with the morning tide. Sophia and Jeremy must be on that ship."

"Yes," Ryder said. "They must." He grinned, splaying his hands in front of him. "I know, I know. I cannot send her to England with no protection. No money. No one to look after her."

"You cannot as yet leave Jamaica."

"I know, not until all this guardianship business is completed. There's Sherman Cole to be dealt with, of course, as well as that mangy bastard, Thomas, to be found."

"Then what will you do?"

"It appears my choices have just dwindled alarmingly. Get the vicar over here and I will wed her. She and Jeremy will be aboard that ship even as Sherman Cole is over digging at Camille Hall. Once they reach England, she and Jeremy will go to Northcliffe Hall, to my family. They will take care of them."

"And when you return to England, Ryder?"

"Don't push, old man. You've got your way. You've saved the girl, using me to do it."

"She will make you a fine wife."

Ryder cursed him and left to go find his soon-to-be bride.

Marriage! It was a truly appalling thought, but there was no hope for it. He thought of his brother, the earl, and prayed that his own recent marriage was shaping up, but in truth he'd had grave doubts when he'd left England, despite the pluckiness of Douglas's new bride. All because he'd come to Jamaica he would find himself leg-shackled. His life had been progressing just as he'd ordered it up.

He sighed. He might as well get it over with. He found her in the late afternoon at Monmouth Beach. Her mare, Opal, was grazing nearby on swamp grass. She was seated in the shade of an Indian almond tree, staring out over the water, her legs crossed, tomboy style.

He loosed his own horse, then strode to her, stood over her, his hands on his hips, and said, "I rode to Camille Hall. They said you had been there, overseeing the indoor work. You shouldn't have gone back there yet. You're not well enough."

She didn't look up. "Nonsense," she said.

He leaned down and jerked up the skirt of her riding habit. "Then why aren't you wearing shoes?"

She slapped her petticoats and skirt back down. "Go to the devil, Ryder. Camille Hall belongs to Jeremy now. He is still there. In truth I became overtired and came here to rest a bit. Now, what do you want? More truths from the resident harlot's mouth?"

"No."

"Then what do you want?"

He looked at her with acute dislike. He shook his head and said, "As of thirty minutes ago, you and I have no choice in the way we must now proceed. You will come back to Kimberly with me. You have much to do before tomorrow morning."

"What the devil are you talking about?" she asked with a cold indifference that nearly made his eyes cross with rage.

"Look at me, damn you!"

She sighed and looked up. "Your language is foul. You're also standing with your back against the sun and I can't really see your face. Forget your display of manliness and sit down, Ryder."

He did and crossed his legs, like hers. "You will listen to me now, Sophie. I dislike you speaking to me like that. That was no manliness display; I was just standing there, like anyone would just stand there."

She nearly smiled. She began to sift sand through her fingers. He truly didn't perceive the natural arrogance that was deep within him. All wish to smile vanished as he continued, saying, "Now, there is no other solution. I have thought and thought, but it does no good. I have argued with myself. I have brooded, a pastime I abhor. I have presented myself with all the reasons why it is the height of foolishness, the very depths of idiocy, but nothing has worked. Very well, then, I will have to marry you."

She stared at him. "You're mad."

"Yes. However, I will do it. I can't seem to find another choice for myself. I will marry you. You and Jeremy will be aboard a ship leaving for England early tomorrow morning. You will wed me this evening. When you reach England, you and Jeremy will journey to my family at Northcliffe Hall, and they will take care of you until I come home."

"You're doing this because you're afraid I'm with child? Your child?"

"No. Sherman Cole is digging up your uncle tomorrow. Then he will arrest you. He's even offered money to Thomas to come out of hiding to testify against you. Therefore you will marry me, and you and Jeremy will be long gone by the time Cole is rubbing his fat hands together contemplating having you completely in his power. No, don't say anything. You have to leave Jamaica. Ah, do you want to know what you're getting in a husband? You won't have a title because I'm the second son, as you know. However, I am rich enough even for you, I imagine. Hell, now that I own Kimberly Hall, I daresay I can give you whatever your heart desires."

"Excellent. All right, my heart desires that I will be Jeremy's guardian and that it will be I who will see he receives a gentleman's education."

"Don't do this, there is no time for further games on your part. We will wed. It will be done. Be quiet. I'm not jesting about Cole and his intentions."

She jumped to her feet. "I can't believe this. Are you certain? But —" She stared down at him, silent now. She turned and picked up her skirts and ran down the beach.

"Sophie! Come back here! Your damned feet!"

She ran faster. He, fool that he was, was worried because her damned feet weren't yet completely healed. He ran after her, and because he was stronger, his legs longer and unhampered by petticoats and skirts, he caught her quickly. He grabbed her arm and jerked her around to face him. He pulled her up against him and kissed her hard.

She struggled and jerked and tugged, but even when he released her mouth, he didn't let her go. "Do you prefer the hangman to marriage with me?"

She shook her head.

"Ah, but before the hangman you would doubtless have Sherman Cole slavering all over you when he rapes you."

"You don't have to say anything more."

"Good, because I was growing a bit impatient."

"This is absurd. I am very ordinary, Ryder. I am common. I have no secrets, nothing to interest you. I'm not ignorant because I have read a lot, a pastime I know gentlemen consider frivolous in women, mayhap even harmful for their brains. Believe me, I am nothing at all, merely a backwater colonial with no pretensions to anything. Why do you feel responsible for me? It is not your fault that my uncle is dead."

"Shut up." He kissed her again but she was struggling frantically against him, and he didn't

235

want to risk hurting her ribs. He contented himself with merely holding her. He felt the heat of her, felt her breasts heaving against his chest, and he closed his eyes a moment.

"Do you forget how much you dislike me, Ryder? You think me a horrible woman. You scorn me and what you believe I am. Why are you doing this?"

He looked over her shoulder at the jagged black rocks that jutted out into the sea. "I have to. Call it my honor. Call it an attack of scruples. Samuel said I'd ruined you. Perhaps you are even now carrying my child. Now, in addition to your ruination and a possible babe, there is the matter of saving your neck. Now, come back with me. We both have a lot to do."

She fell into step beside him. She stared blindly ahead of her. She didn't believe that life could change so drastically and so very quickly.

She looked at his profile, pure and clean and strong. He would be her husband.

She shivered.

CHAPTER 11

The vicar, Mr. Jacob Mathers, was a wizened little man with a shock of white hair sticking up like a rooster's comb. He knew all the gossip, naturally, but to his credit he took no part in it. Truth be told, he was more a listening man, particularly if he had a glass of rum punch in his hand. He listened and listened even more, and then disregarded the most of it. He had been a close friend of Samuel Grayson's for over twenty years, and thus, when an invitation to dinner arrived, he accepted gladly. After dinner was over and he learned what his other duty was to be, he blinked once, looked at Samuel for guidance and received a smile and a nod. If this was what Samuel believed was right, then Jacob would do it.

He would marry these two disparate people. When Ryder Sherbrooke had told him with a smile that he also wanted him to accept Kimberly Hall hospitality until the following afternoon, he readily agreed. He knew all about Sophia Stanton-Greville's reputation and that Sherman Cole wanted to arrest her very badly, for what reason he imagined he already knew. Human failings were, after all, his primary business. However, he wasn't a stupid man nor an unkind one, and curiosity wasn't necessarily a good thing. In this instance, he didn't really want to know all the ins and outs.

Everyone arranged themselves. Mr. Mathers had a remarkably deep voice, mellifluous and soothing, perhaps more so than usual because of the three glasses of rum punch he'd drunk at dinner. Soon, he was near the end of the brief ceremony. He was relieved that the young lady hadn't fainted. She was very pale, her eyes dark and blank, and her responses were barely above a whisper. As for Ryder Sherbrooke, the young man looked every inch the English aristocrat. He stood tall and straight; his voice was strong and steady. If he felt the same terror his bride felt, he was hiding it very well.

Ryder was wondering what Sophie was thinking. He knew well enough that she hadn't wanted to marry him. It was only the thought of being hung that had turned the tide. Not a very enlivening judgment for the groom. He doubted now that even if she'd believed she was pregnant with his child, she would have accepted him. Well, it would soon be done. He realized with something of a shock that he wanted it to be done. He wanted her as his wife. He wanted her safe, her and Jeremy.

He squeezed her hand when she whispered a

very faint, "I do." Her refusal, his thinking continued as he looked down at her, must denote some sort of honor, some sort of honesty. Nor did she seem to want him, but that made sense to him given her experiences. He would soon change her mind about that. He wasn't a clod and she would be his wife. He thought of all the women he'd enjoyed since he'd come to manhood, how he'd pleasured them and teased them and laughed with them. And now, he must tie himself to the one woman who didn't want him. She was marrying him because she had no choice. At least they were even on that, he thought. He would never have considered marriage with her, despite the fact that she did, on occasion, give as good as she got. No, his honor demanded it, nothing more.

Sophie was pleased that she'd gotten her response out of her mouth. However, she was disgusted that she had sounded like a bleating goat, but the truth of the matter was, even though he was saving her, and she was well aware of what he was saving her from, he scared her to death.

Once he had her as his wife, he would be free to do anything he pleased with her. She knew that; her uncle had told her that often enough. She didn't believe he would beat her, no, Ryder wasn't that kind of man. What scared her was having him take her body, have it as his right, however and whenever he pleased. On the other hand, he'd already had her, and thus he'd seen her body, just as she'd seen his. Surely he hadn't hurt her. She'd felt nothing the next morning, not a bit of pain or discomfort. No, he hadn't hurt her.

And it would just be for one night.

She was scared. She fingered the soft muslin gown Coco had sewn for her throughout the afternoon. It was lovely and it was snowy white. That made her smile. "You'll look like a virgin sacrifice," he'd said when she'd shown him the nearly completed gown.

She wished the vicar would just be done with it. She felt sick to her stomach. She was terrified, not only of Ryder, but of Sherman Cole. She wondered if she and Jeremy truly would be aboard the ship tomorrow and be safe, once and for all.

She remembered when Ryder had come to fetch her for dinner. He'd come into the room, all elegant and handsome as the devil's right hand, and he'd just smiled at her.

"You're beautiful, you know that?"

She merely shrugged. "Passable, I would say."

"No, beautiful. Are you ready? The vicar is here. We'll have dinner first, then the ceremony. I'm sorry about you not having anyone from Camille Hall, but we can't risk it."

"You don't have to do this, Ryder."

"Be quiet," he said quite pleasantly, offered her his arm, and walked beside her down the wide staircase.

Ryder felt her quiver when he said his vows. "Don't," Ryder said quietly. "Don't stiffen up

240

on me. Trust me, Sophie. It will be over soon and then nothing bad will ever touch you again."

She didn't believe him but it didn't seem to be the thing to say to him now that he would be her husband. She saw Jeremy smiling just like he'd been offered the world. Ryder had won him over with an ease that astounded her.

It was over. There were congratulations. Samuel looked delighted and immensely relieved. Then he turned to Sophie, hugged her against him, and said quietly, "It will be fine for you now, my dear. I have always believed that things happen for a reason. You and Jeremy were meant to leave Jamaica and return to England. You will trust your new husband. Once he realizes the right way, he embraces it without hesitation. Yes, Sophia, trust him, for he's a very good man."

She looked over at her new husband. He was hugging Jeremy against him and the boy was chattering faster than a magpie and Ryder was laughing and nodding.

Suddenly, without warning, all the happy chatter began to die away. Ryder looked up to see Sherman Cole standing in the doorway of the salon.

Sophie wanted to sink into the mangrove swamp. She didn't move. She watched Ryder stride over to Cole.

"What a pleasure, Mr. Cole. However, you weren't invited. What do you want now?"

Sherman Cole looked around the room. He stared at Sophie, standing there like a pale statue, in her wedding gown, her white wedding gown. He saw Samuel standing there beside her, her arm in his, and he said, "Good God, you think to protect the little slut by marrying her off? Has that fool Grayson really married her? He actually married the little tart?"

Ryder sighed. "Did I not warn you before? You are slow of wit, sir, and an unspeakable embarrassment."

"But he can't be married to her! Look here, Samuel, it will make no difference! She murdered her poor uncle. I will come for her tomorrow, once we've examined Burgess's body. You will have only one night with her, no more, so be certain you enjoy it! And then it will be my turn, that is to say, I will see that justice is well done and —"

Ryder hit him cleanly in the jaw. Sherman Cole went down in a graceless heap. Ryder grabbed the man beneath his arms and heaved and tugged until he'd managed to drag him behind a chair. His legs still stuck out. He pulled the chair out a bit more and shoved Cole completely behind it. Then he moved the chair back in place. He looked over at Sophie, grinned, and rubbed his hands together.

"That was fun," he said when he rejoined her. "Emile, when he rouses himself, why don't you see him back to Montego Bay. I like the notion that he believes Sophie is married to your father. He will remain unworried and quite pleased with himself."

"Now," Samuel said, "let us go into the dining room. I want to toast both of you with that champagne James unearthed for you."

She remained still and pale. Ryder frowned down at her. "Stop it," he said, and when she didn't, he pulled her against him and kissed her. Not hard, but very lightly, his mouth barely touching hers, gently pressing, but not demanding. Then he said into her mouth, "I am your husband. I will protect you. Cole won't touch you."

She was afraid. She didn't move. When he finally released her, he wasn't frowning, but he still looked thoughtful. She hadn't kissed him back, but then again, she'd just had another unpleasant shock.

"You know something, Sophie, I did indeed protect you this time. On the other hand, to be completely honest, I wanted very much to hit him, so I can't be certain that my motives were all that pure. But let's be kind and assume they were. Now, can I believe that you would likewise protect me?"

"I already did."

He grinned at her. "Yes, you were a marvel. Will you continue to be my Amazon? Will you continue to protect me?"

"You aren't Jeremy."

"No, I'm not. I'm your husband and, in the future scheme of things, I'm more important."

"Yes," she said on a sigh. "I will protect you, Ryder."

"Good."

Ryder looked back over his shoulder once. He saw Cole's feet sticking out from beneath the chair. What the devil had the man wanted? It was a long ride to and from Montego Bay. Had he merely come to gloat? To terrify Sophie? To try to intimidate the rest of them?

Ryder forgot Cole. Tonight he would have her. Very soon now. No more than three more hours and he would have her naked and in his arms and in his bed. He would have to sate himself on her to make up for the weeks they would be separated.

He was humming as he walked beside her into the dining room. He seated Sophie on his right hand then took the master's chair. He lifted her hand and kissed her fingers. She didn't move.

"Emile will take Cole away," he said. "Perhaps he'll find out how and what Cole found out and why he came here tonight."

"I wish I could have hit him," she said.

He was pleased. "Would you really? Well, perhaps I can find him again and bring him back to you. Show me your fist."

She did and he neatly tucked her thumb under. "Whenever you hit someone, don't let your thumb stick out. You could get it broken. That's it."

"You bruised your knuckles."

"Ah, but don't you see? One must weigh the bruises against the fun of it. Now, my dear, you're a new bride. Raise your glass and lightly touch it to mine. Yes, that's right. Now smile. Good."

244

She sipped the champagne. It was wonderful, cool and tart.

She took another longer drink.

Conversation at the table was brisk. As each new bottle of champagne was uncorked, the laughter and noise increased. The vicar recounted a jest about a saint who was accidentally sent to hell. He told it with all the enthusiasm of a devout sinner.

Ryder laughed until he looked at his wife. "You're too damned quiet. You ate almost no dinner."

"I didn't want this to happen," she said, eyes down on the plate with its slice of pineapple cake.

"It's happened. Get used to it. Accept it."

"I suppose there's nothing else to do," she said, and took another drink of her champagne.

"Are you planning to drink yourself insensible?"

"No, I don't think that's possible."

"Oh, it is, believe me. Young men do the most ridiculous things, you know, like drinking themselves into unconsciousness, singing at the top of their lungs even while they're falling flat on their faces under a table."

He was smiling at her charmingly, laughing, seducing her with the best weapons in his arsenal. It wasn't working.

"You're tired, Sophie?"

"Yes," she said, then realized the import of her words and actually jerked back in her chair.

"How are your ribs?"

"They hurt dreadfully as do my feet and —"

"You're a very bad liar. You didn't use to be, but you are now, now that I know you."

"You don't know me, Ryder. You truly don't."

"I will come to know you. It is something I want very badly. It's unfortunate we will be separated. I will give you a letter to present to my brother the earl once you arrive at Northcliffe Hall. Also I will give you sufficient funds so that you and Jeremy can rent a carriage at Southampton and several guards. Promise me you will hire guards."

She promised.

He was looking at the swell of her breasts above the soft lace over her bosom. "You're thin at the moment, but I don't mind. I'll fatten you up."

"Since I am with child, that will most certainly happen."

Lies, Ryder thought. It was damned difficult to keep up with them. Still, he said easily, "The child, as I've told you, isn't necessarily a foregone conclusion. It's possible that you're pregnant. I hope that if you aren't pregnant you won't be too disappointed."

"I don't feel well. I must be pregnant."

That was interesting, he thought. He sat back in his chair, twirling the stem of his champagne glass between his long fingers. "You know, Sophie, there's no reason for you to be embarrassed around me. No, please don't waste my time or yours denying it. I told you I know women. Please strive to remember that you're not a virgin since I took you. And I did look my fill at you. I even kissed that very cute birthmark of yours behind your left knee. So, you see, there is no need at all for embarrassment."

"That's true, I guess, but still —"

"Still what?"

"I wasn't really there when you did all those things to me."

"You will simply have to trust me."

"Trust you the way you trusted me?"

"All the past lurid machinations are over, all the druggings are over, though I still admit to a burgeoning of rage when I think of you and your uncle stripping me and offering me up to that other girl. What was her name, by the way?"

"Dahlia. She looked at you and said you were a treat."

When Ryder grinned she quickly added, "But not enough of a treat for my uncle not to pay her."

"Did you watch me with her, Sophie?"

"Just for a moment because my uncle said I had to, that you were the kind of man to share intimacies with his mistress and thus I had to be prepared to be intimate in my speech back to you, but I couldn't bear it, and left the cottage."

"It was a very nasty game. Now, my dear wife, you and I are going upstairs."

Not ten minutes later, she was staring at him across the bedchamber. He'd shut and locked the door. Then he was striding confidently toward her, smiling, looking at her with the victor's gleam in his blue eyes.

She did look like a virgin sacrifice, he thought, staring at her. He supposed it was at that moment he accepted the fact that she was indeed a virgin, that all her supposed lovers had enjoyed Dahlia, that Samuel had been right when he'd said that she simply wouldn't play the whore, no matter the cost.

He wondered briefly if he should tell her that she was still a virgin, and that he'd told her a magnificent lie to prevent her from marrying Samuel Grayson. Even as a silent thought, it didn't sound all that promising as a way to bring her around. It made him sound like a bastard, truth be told. No, no, he'd keep it to himself. He had all the time in the world to tell her whatever he wanted to tell her. The truth could wait a bit longer.

He took her in his arms. He didn't kiss her, just said as he looked down at her, "I know you have seen some of what men and women do together in bed. I know from firsthand experience that you know how to seduce a man, how to tease him until he's hard as a stone and willing to say anything, promise anything, to you. However, I know you've never experienced any of it, even with me, because of the odd circumstances. We are going very slowly, Sophie. I don't want you to hark back to the repugnant experiences you've had. They're not important now.

Only you and I are important. Do you understand me?"

"I don't want this, Ryder. I need time."

"You will have all the time you wish after tonight, at least seven weeks of it. I'm not like those other pawing cretins. I will please you, I will make you forget all their annoying habits."

His hands were on her back, lightly stroking up and down, slowly, soothing, as if she were a child, as if she were a wary animal to be tamed. She saw Lord David, felt his hands on her, his mouth on hers. And Oliver Susson and Charles Grammond, and Dickey Mason, another man her uncle had ruined with her help. There were two others, one of them now dead, the other a drunkard who'd left Jamaica in disgrace. Dear God, it was too much. She hated it. She hated herself and she hated him for forcing her into this marriage. She pulled away from him suddenly, taking him by surprise, and he let her go.

She walked quickly to the balcony, not turning to face him until she was to the railing.

When she turned back, he was where she'd left him, standing in the middle of the room, only now he was taking off his coat. She froze, watching him. Next came his cravat. Then he was unfastening his shirt and vest. Then he sat down on a wicker chair and pulled off his boots. When he rose again, his hands on the buttons of his britches, she yelled, "No! What are you doing? Stop it!"

"Why?" he said. "I can't offend your maiden's

sensibilities. Good God, woman, you've seen me naked. Not only have you seen me naked, you've seen my sex swelled. You've seen my eyes glazed with lust. There's nothing new for you. Didn't you see all the other men as well?"

She stared at him, unmoving. He was soon naked, and as he had been before, his sex was swelled, but he made no move toward her. Instead, he held out his hand. "Come here, Sophie. It's time we began our married life together."

"I don't feel well," she said.

"Very well," he said more to himself than to her, and walked toward her.

Her wedding gown defeated her. She tried to duck around him but the skirts tangled between her legs and she couldn't move quickly enough. She tripped on the lace hem and felt the material rip beneath her left arm. She hadn't meant to hurt the gown. It was so beautiful, she hadn't meant it. Ryder's impatient voice brought her back to another misery.

"No more fighting me, Sophie. It's done. You're my wife. No more, do you hear me? We've only tonight and I want to consummate this damned marriage."

"Let me go."

"Not on your life. I'm going to undress you, Sophie. You will not fight me. You took a vow to obey me and it's time you took that vow seriously."

She raised her head and looked at him straightly. "From my uncle's domination to yours. I want to be free, don't you understand? A man is born with the taste of freedom in his mouth, but the chances that a woman can ever gain freedom are remote. It's just as I knew it would be. You're no different from the others. All of you are animals, selfish and brutal."

"I'm quite different from the others. I'm your husband until the day I stick my spoon in the wall."

She was standing stiff as a pole, watching him.

He had, suddenly, the most awful presentiment that she would never come to want him. No, that was absurd. He wouldn't allow it.

He sighed. "All right. Sit down. Let's talk for a little while."

She sat and he saw the relief flood her face, damn her. "Now, do you have more proclamations of men's dishonesty and general brutishness?"

She didn't look at him. She said at last, "I suppose it is stupid of me. You already took me and looked your fill at me and I suppose you didn't hurt me because the next morning I felt nothing. But you see, I didn't know you were looking at me, I didn't know anything." She raised her head and looked at him straightly. "It is difficult, Ryder."

"I'll make it easier. All you have to do is trust me. Now, about your freedom. I shan't lock you up, Sophie, if you believe that's what men do to their wives. For the most part I imagine you will do precisely as you please. If by freedom you mean you can't sail to the ends of the earth by yourself, that's quite true and the reasons are obvious. You are a woman and thus weaker than a man. You could be hurt. But in the future who knows? Perhaps we will visit faraway places together."

It wasn't at all what she'd meant by freedom but it didn't matter now. It was moot.

"I won't ever hurt you, Sophie, or beat you or threaten you. I think men who do are utter bastards. Your uncle was a conscienceless villain. He wasn't normal; he was twisted. I'm not like that. None of my friends are like that. I will never hurt you."

"I have no reason to believe you."

"You have no reason to disbelieve me." Ryder rose and offered her his hand. "Come inside. It's time to go to bed. I'll help you with the gown."

No choice, she thought. No more choices at all. She went with him. Soon her gown was open on her back and he was gently easing it down. He dropped a light kiss on her shoulder and felt her flinch.

"Take the gown off now. I assume you will want to keep it since it's your wedding gown. Doubtless you can repair that rip. It doesn't look too bad to me. Do you have space in your valise for it?"

"Yes."

She wanted to mend the gown now, truth be told. The night stretched out before her in a terrifying long number of minutes. But even Sophie knew from the look on Ryder's face that she'd pushed him far enough. She saw her uncle's face in its stead, the fury darkening his eyes when she'd pushed him. She remembered the pain of his fists, the rippling of her flesh when they struck. She was soon standing only in her chemise and stockings.

"You didn't wear slippers at your own wedding," he said, bemused. "I had thought you were taller. Let's get those stockings off, I want to look at your feet."

She sat on the edge of the bed wearing only her white muslin chemise, Ryder on his haunches in front of her, completely oblivious of the fact he didn't have any clothes on.

"Your feet are healing nicely," he said. "There are only a couple of cuts that still look tender. On board ship, don't wear slippers unless you have to and be careful of the decks, you could get splinters. Now let me look at your ribs."

He took her hand and drew her upright. He bent down to take the hem of her chemise in his hands. He stopped cold. He wanted to howl and laugh at the same time at the damnable irony. It was his wedding night and he'd been done in.

There was blood on her chemise.

"You don't feel well, Sophie?"

"Not very well. I'm not lying to you, Ryder. My stomach is cramping a bit."

"No wonder," he said and sighed very deeply. "I'm sorry if this disappoints you, but you're not pregnant."

She gasped as she looked down at herself. She turned white.

"No need to be embarrassed. Have you cloths?"

She shook her head.

"All right. I'll send Coco to you. Would you like some laudanum? Is the cramping bad?"

"No. Yes."

Fifteen minutes later Ryder stood beside the bed, wearing a dressing gown, looking down at his wife's pale face. Despite the heat she'd pulled the sheet up to her nose. He'd forced the laudanum down her throat, saying in a very irritated voice, "I swear not to ravish you whilst you're unconscious." To which she'd replied in an equally irritated voice, "Why not? You did before."

That had stopped him cold. He looked down at her now. "So much for the vaunted Sherbrooke luck," he said more to himself than to her, and lifted the sheet. He eased in beside her. "No, Sophie, don't have a fit and don't squirm around so much, you might fall on the floor. I won't force you to have me tonight. Hush now. The laudanum should be taking effect soon. That's right, just close your eyes and breathe deeply. Would you like me to rub your belly?"

He didn't expect an answer and he didn't get one. A short time later he heard her breathing evenly into sleep.

He took her hand in his.

The sky was beginning to lighten into morning.

Ryder stood on deck of the *Harbinger* beside Sophie. "Don't forget to give my brother the letter," he said for the third time. "And don't worry. He will take good care of you and Jeremy. My mother could be a bit of a problem, but she's unaccountable. If she chooses not to be charming to you, simply ignore her, all right? You'll have quite an ally in Alex, I doubt not. Have you put the money I gave you in a safe place?"

"Yes, Ryder."

"Does your belly feel all right this morning?"

"Yes."

"You promise to hire two guards at Southampton?"

"Yes."

He frowned at her. "You think I'm treating you like a child, don't you?"

"Yes."

"Look, Sophie, I've never had a wife before, never really had any responsibilities of this sort before except of course for the chil—" He broke that off and shook his head at himself. He couldn't seem to keep his tongue quiet in his mouth around her. He would tell her about the children, but in his own time, in his own way. She was looking at him, an eyebrow lifted in silent question, but he merely shook his head, and continued. "In any case, you and Jeremy are mine now and I want to make certain you will be all right."

"We will be fine. Don't worry. Are you sure your family won't toss us out on our ears?"

"I won't lie to you. They will be very surprised.

I hadn't planned to marry, at least for a very long time. I would appreciate it, Sophie, if you would try to make my family believe you are at least a bit fond of me, that you don't look upon me as a ravening beast."

Captain Mallory appeared at Ryder's elbow. There was a wide grin on his broad, ugly face. " 'Tis time for you to remove yourself, Mr. Sherbrooke. Your bride will be fine. Give her another hug and a kiss and get off my ship."

He smiled down at Sophie. "Can I have a kiss?"

She raised her face, her lips pursed. He lightly touched his fingertip to her lips, pressing slightly, then he kissed her very gently, with very little pressure. He felt a shudder in her but didn't know if it was from fear, nervousness, or wonderful lust. Somehow he doubted the latter.

"You will be careful," he said yet again, patted her cheek, walked over to Jeremy, hugged the boy tightly, ruffled his hair, and said, "Keep her spirits up, Jeremy. I'll return to England as soon as all this nonsense is taken care of. Be a good boy. Another thing. I'm quite fond of you so you will be careful of yourself as well."

He strode down the gangplank. He watched it hauled onto the ship's deck. He watched the sun rise full in the sky now and stood very still listening to Captain Mallory shouting his orders. He waved a final time to his bride and his new brother-in-law.

He continued to wait on the dock until the

ship was gone from view. He turned then, smiling. She was safe now, completely safe. He whistled as he mounted his horse to return to Kimberly Hall.

At one o'clock that afternoon Sherman Cole arrived. Ryder smiled as he watched the man dismount and walk toward the veranda where he sat, a glass of lemonade in his hand. Samuel and Emile came out of the house and Ryder felt the relief radiating from them.

"What an unexpected surprise," Ryder said, and yawned deeply. He didn't rise. "Have you come to bring more discord, make more threats?"

"Damn you to hell, Sherbrooke!"

Ryder's eyebrow went up. "I beg your pardon? I truly didn't strike you that hard, though you deserved it."

"I was certain you'd lied, I would have wagered all I possessed that you had lied, damn you. And you did, of course, to protect that little slut."

"Where are all your bully boys?" Emile asked quickly before Ryder could rise from his chair and flatten Sherman Cole again.

"They're looking for Thomas."

"I wager you'll have to pay him quite a bit of money once you catch up to him. He probably won't trust you. You'll have to convince him that you want him to help you hang Miss Stanton-Greville."

"Pay him! Ha, I will hang the bastard! He lied to me, he made a fool of me."

Now this was the wrong play, Ryder thought, blank-brained. This is a comedy, not a tragedy.

"What do you mean?" Samuel asked.

"Burgess wasn't shot, nor was he stabbed, as Sherbrooke here said. He was garroted. Dammit, she couldn't have killed him, she doesn't have the strength."

He turned away, stomped to his horse, mounted, and rode away, never once looking back.

Ryder didn't move. "Dear God," he said at last, "I didn't have to marry her. I didn't have to ship her and Jeremy back to England. To be only twenty-five years old and be done in by irony."

"It's better done," Samuel said. "One never knows what Cole will do next."

But Ryder was immersed in contemplation of his fate. Well, perhaps it wouldn't be such a bad fate. One would have to see about that. He sighed and rose. He shook his head and said, "Garroted, the bastard was garroted."

He shook his head again. "I'll be damned," he said, and walked to the stables.

CHAPTER 12

The English Channel, seven weeks later

Sophie and Jeremy stood side by side on deck, the fog-laden wind blowing into their faces, tightly holding the wooden railing because the water was choppy, the waves splashing high and rocking even the solid barkentine with their force. Jeremy was nearly squealing with excitement because he'd been the first to see the English shoreline through the thick fog bank. Gravesend, he'd shouted. As for Sophie, she wanted to shout hallelujahs as the English coast neared. She felt equal parts of anticipation and belly-deep fear as she watched the billowing fog bank just off port. Nearly home, but not really hers and Jeremy's home in Fowey, but Ryder's home — Northcliffe Hall.

The trip had been long and uneventful. Captain Mallory and his first mate, Mr. Mattison, both puff-chested Scotsmen who had nearly identical bald heads, had kept Jeremy and her entertained with the best tall tales they'd ever heard.

Sophie had tried to structure the days as best she could. She gave Jeremy French lessons an hour each morning. Captain Mallory tutored Jeremy in astronomy and navigation, the first mate taught him geography and gave him access to his collection of novels and plays that filled his small cabin to overflowing. Jeremy was nearly through the Restoration. As for Sophie, she too had nearly read her way through all the first mate's books as well. She occasionally wondered what she'd do when she turned the last page and closed the last book.

One afternoon several days before, Sophie and Jeremy were playing chess in their small cabin. A light rain splattered against the single porthole. The room was warm. Sophie played with verve and enthusiasm, but not much strategy. Jeremy, on the other hand, excelled in patience and tactics. He invariably beat her soundly, but it was slow torture, and Jeremy was heard to groan frequently.

She said after she'd moved her queen's bishop, "We will be home soon. Rather, we will arrive in Southampton."

"Yes, Ryder told me that a carriage would get us to Northcliffe Hall all in one day. He didn't want us to have to stop at an inn for the night because we're alone. He said I had to grow another foot at least before I could protect you properly." Jeremy smiled then and added, "Ryder's going to teach me how to fight."

"I'm delighted it pleases you so, but heed me, love, one doesn't necessarily need a man. I'm not a fool or helpless."

"Of course you're not like most girls," Jeremy

said, not looking up at her, his entire attention now on the position of his pieces and his burgeoning strategy. "Ryder said you'd say something like that. He also said that he was responsible for both of us now and that was the end to it."

"Perhaps you would like to discuss some of the plays both of us have read."

Jeremy easily accepted her change of subject. "I was reading one of the Restoration plays and Mr. Mattison saw it. I thought he'd throw it overboard he was so upset. He turned red in the face and actually sputtered at me. Even the top of his head turned red. It was a remarkable sight."

Sophie chuckled. "Some of those plays are fairly racy. Perhaps you'd best show me what you plan to read before you read it."

Jeremy frowned as he looked up at his sister. "I've got to learn all about men and women sometime, Sophie. In the plays they act pretty silly and do the most outlandish things. As for the other part of it, it just seems strange to me."

"I think you're right about the strange part," Sophie said. She thought of Ryder and felt a pang of something — guilt? Anger? She wasn't certain. She did know, however, that she missed him — his wit, his outrageousness, the way he teased her until her eyes nearly crossed with rage. She looked up when Jeremy moved his queen's bishop pawn.

"Oh ho, it appears you want to trample my center." She moved her king's knight, a mindless move really, then sat back in her chair, her arms folded over her chest. "That should take care of your foolish hopes."

Jeremy said as he fiddled with a rook, "You're not very happy, Sophie. You miss Ryder, don't you? I know I do. He's a great brother-in-law. I'm glad you married him. I'm glad we left Jamaica, because we are English, you know. But still it's kind of scary." He finally released the rook and moved his queen's bishop instead. "Do you think his family will like us?"

"I pray so, Jeremy." Nor did she miss Jamaica. All the happiness she'd experienced on Jamaica could be weighed in her left hand.

"Well, I don't see why they wouldn't like us. We're nice and we know how to use our forks at the dinner table. You shouldn't have moved that knight. It was a bad move. I'm not just going to trample your center. I don't have to. Checkmate, Sophie."

"Why," she said aloud, "don't I ever learn?"

Sophie shook away the memory. She prayed every night that she and Jeremy wouldn't be shunted aside by Ryder's powerful brother, Douglas Sherbrooke. After that she simply stared off into space. She didn't know what to pray for. She couldn't begin to imagine her future. The wind whipped her hair into her eyes and she slapped it away.

Seven interminable weeks. It was nearly over. She wondered how much longer it would be before Ryder returned home. She would have to be a wife to him, whatever that would mean.

She immediately shied away from that.

Jeremy waved to Clancey, the third mate, a young man full of high spirits and liking for children. "Aye," he'd told Sophie at the beginning of the long voyage, "I was one of nine nippers, and there was only me ma to see to us. Don't ye worry about Jeremy here. He be a good lad. I'll see he don't go headfirst into the briny deep." Sophie liked him. He appeared utterly disinterested in her; some of the other sailors looked to be interested but they kept their distance, thanks to a frank discussion the captain had given them. "As the only woman on board, ma'am," he'd told her, "you will still be careful." And she had.

She was bored. She was also worried.

She made herself dizzy trying to structure the future for her and Jeremy.

Southampton at eight o'clock on a drizzly, foggy morning was an alien landscape with men yelling on the docks, drays and wagons of all sizes being loaded and unloaded. As it turned out, the first mate, Mr. Mattison, escorted them to the Outrigger Inn and hired a carriage and two outriders, just as Ryder had demanded.

Ryder had his way even here. She'd had no choice in the matter. She smiled up at Mr. Mattison and offered him her hand. "Thank you. You were kind to us. Good-bye."

Jeremy begged to ride on top of the carriage

with the coachman, but Sophie said he couldn't until after the fog burned off and the sun came out.

The weather remained horrible.

Jeremy fidgeted until Sophie released him to ride with the coachman. It was after a lunch of codfish and strawberries that Sophie's stomach rebelled. Four hours later when the carriage pulled into the long winding drive of Northcliffe Hall, there was no one inside the carriage. Sophie and Jeremy sat huddled together against the drizzling rain, the driver pressed against Jeremy's other side.

An hour before Sophie had ceased to care. She felt trickles of rain snake down the back of her neck. She was shuddering from cold. There was gooseflesh on her arms.

"Goodness, Sophie, it's so big!"

She looked and swallowed. Northcliffe Hall was overwhelming, a huge Palladian mansion of three stories. She couldn't imagine real people living in that awesome structure. The two outriders, bored and wondering why the devil their escort had been needed in the first place — good hell, the girl had ridden on top like a serving wench — accepted payment from Sophie and took themselves off. As for the coachman, he scratched his head, stared from Sophie to Jeremy and back again and said, "Well, miss, this is the fancy cove's abode what ye wanted to come to. Northcliffe 'All. All right an' tight. Be ye sure this is where ye should be?"

Sophie wanted very much to say no, but she merely nodded, paid the man, and watched him bowl down the drive. She and Jeremy were left in front of the wide, deep stairs of the mansion, their two paltry valises sitting forlornly beside them on the gravel drive. Rain dripped off the end of her nose.

Had Sophie but had more than the hundred pounds Ryder had given her, she would have turned on her heel and left immediately. She would have walked to Fowey. She would have carried Jeremy to Fowey when he got tired of walking. But again she had no choice. She stood there for another minute, feeling more alone than she ever had before in her life, just staring up at the three-story mansion with ivy rich and green up the west side of it until Jeremy tugged on her sleeve.

"Sophie, I'm wetter than a wharf rat. Let's go in."

She shivered, picked up both their valises, and began climbing the deeply grooved marble steps. "That sounds like a verbal gift from Clancey. Contrive to forget it, Jeremy."

"Do you think they'll let us stay?" Jeremy whispered, his eyes large now with fright as they neared the incredibly huge double doors. There were large brass lion heads for doorknobs. The lions' mouths even had brass teeth. The doors looked more solid than a live oak tree.

"Of course," she said, and began another series of devout prayers.

There was an overhang just in front of the massive doors and Sophie pulled Jeremy out of the cold drizzle. She looked at the bellpull. There was no hope for it. The poor relations had arrived.

She pulled the bellcord with all her might. She jumped at the full-bodied ringing that seemed to reverberate throughout the mansion. They hadn't long to wait.

The door opened without a creak or a groan. A footman in dark blue and green livery stood before them. He was small and slender and he didn't say anything, just stared at them and blinked.

He was an older man, as bald as Captain Mallory and Mr. Mattison had been. He opened his mouth then and said, "Would you care to go to the servants' entrance?"

"No," Sophie said, and forced a smile. She could well imagine how the two of them looked.

"I saw you arrive, both of you sitting on top of the coach. Perhaps you're looking for employment? Then you must speak to Mrs. Peacham. As for the boy, I don't —"

"We are here to see the Earl of Northcliffe. You will show us to him immediately, if you please."

Her speech was upper class, no doubt about that, but there was a faint lilt to it, a sort of strange drawl that Jamieson couldn't identify. So she wanted the earl, did she? She and the boy looked like beggars. Wet beggars. He could tell the girl's gown was too short. Doubtless they wanted charity. The gall of these two. He drew himself up, ready to tell the minx what she could do with her demands when there came another man's voice. "What have we here, Jamieson?"

"Ah, Mr. Hollis, sir. These two just climbed off a carriage box. This one here's demanding to see the earl. I was just endeavoring to —"

Mr. Hollis looked at Sophie. She looked back at him. He smiled and stepped aside, ushering them in.

"Do come in, ma'am, and the lad too. Ah, the weather isn't what one would wish, is it? You are both wet and cold. Come with me. Jamieson, take the bags, please, and place them at the foot of the stairs."

"Who is he?" Jeremy asked behind his hand. "Is he the earl?"

"I don't know."

"This is all very strange, Sophie."

Their footsteps resounded in the immense entry hall. A huge chandelier hung overhead, its crystals glittering in the dim afternoon light. Italian black and white marble squares stretched in all directions. There were paintings on every wall, and even several suits of armor set on either side of a huge fireplace. Sophie remembered their snug Georgian house in Fowey. They'd had a chandelier there as well, only it wasn't as large as a room. When Ryder had spoken of his home, she'd never imagined anything like this. There were maids and more footmen, all looking at them, and, Sophie knew, whispering about them behind their hands.

She wanted to be sick. Her chin went up.

Mr. Hollis led them down a vast corridor into a small room that, luckily, had a blazing fire burning in the grate.

"I will inform the earl of your arrival. Now, may I give him your name, ma'am?"

"Yes," Sophie said. Suddenly, she grinned, for it really was too much. "Please tell the earl that his sister-in-law and brother-in-law have arrived from Jamaica."

The man's dark eyes never registered anything but calm acceptance. If she wasn't mistaken, there was even a sudden gleaming in his eyes. "I see. Do remove your cloaks and dry yourselves. I am quite certain the earl will wish to see you immediately."

They were left alone in the small room. The draperies were drawn against the chill afternoon. It looked to be a lady's salon, with its feminine desk and pale green and yellow furnishings. There was a pile of books on the floor beside a comfortable wing chair. It was a lovely room and so unlike any room in Jamaica.

It was so bloody cold. She'd forgotten how very different England was from Jamaica. She helped Jeremy off with his cloak, then removed her own. They stood in front of the fireplace, hands extended to the flames.

"You did that well, Sophie. I was so scared I couldn't think of a word to say."

"They can't shoot us, at least I don't think they can. But what they will do —" She shrugged, saying no more. Her tongue felt as if it had a cramp in it.

The door flew open and in strode a young girl with thick, curly brownish-blond hair and the most beautiful blue eyes Sophie had ever seen. Actually, they were exactly the same color as Ryder's eyes; the girl's hair matched Ryder's as well. She looked exuberant, full of life — just as Ryder did — and she was grinning at them. "Ho! What's this? I saw you climb off that carriage. My, you're wet and doubtless miserable. I myself am so very tired of this blasted rain. Do forgive me, but I'm Sinjun, you know, the earl's sister. Who are you?"

Sophie had to grin back. There wasn't really a choice. This girl was exactly as Ryder had described her. She was tall, lanky, lovely really, and friendly as a puppy.

Sophie stepped toward her. "I am Sophia Stanton-Greville. Well no, that's no longer correct. I am Sophia Sherbrooke. I am Ryder's wife and this is Jeremy, my brother."

Sinjun could only stare at the wet, frowzy girl standing there in front of her in a girlish muslin gown that was too short for her, a gown that Ryder would have found utterly distasteful.

This was excessively odd.

"Oh dear, is it true? It's difficult to believe, you know. Ryder married! Imagine such a thing. It leaves the brain numb. I never thought he would take a wife because he absolutely adores so many ladies and —"

"I believe that is quite enough, Sinjun."

The earl, Sophie thought, and went very still. He didn't look at all like either Ryder or Sinjun. He was massively built, all lean and muscular, very tall, his shoulders broad as the front door, and dark as a Moor, his hair black as midnight, his eyes just as dark. He looked ruthless and mean and severe and she couldn't imagine him doing anything but tossing her and Jeremy out on their wet ears. He was looking at her, taking in every detail. Sophie knew what she and Jeremy looked like. It wasn't promising. Her chin went higher. She remembered Ryder telling her that his brother, the earl, would have demolished her in no time had he been the one to come to Jamaica. He wouldn't have enjoyed playing her games as Ryder had.

Then, quite suddenly, the earl smiled. It changed him utterly. Sophie heard Jeremy release a pent-up breath. "Forgive my sister here for bombarding you the moment you arrived. It wasn't well done of you, brat. Now, I am Douglas Sherbrooke, Ryder's brother. Welcome to North-cliffe Hall."

Sophie gave him a curtsy, saying quietly, "I am Sophia and this is my brother, Jeremy. We left Ryder on Jamaica to conclude business, but he will return here very soon. It is all very complicated." She paused, not another word swirling to the forefront of her brain, thrust her hand into her reticule and retrieved Ryder's letter. She thrust it at the earl.

He smiled at her quizzically as he took the letter, saying, "Please be seated. Sinjun, make yourself useful and have Mrs. Peacham send some tea and some cakes. Our guests look a bit tired."

"Yes, Douglas," Sinjun said, rubbing her hands together. "Wait until Alex hears about this, she's my other sister, you know. I just —"

"Go, brat!"

Sinjun went, but not before she winked at Sophie.

"Forgive my sister's impertinence," Douglas said as he opened the letter, "but no one has ever managed to curb her tongue."

"Her tongue is friendly. I didn't mind."

"Nor did I," said Jeremy.

"Actually, I don't either. Excuse me a moment," the earl said, and lowered his eyes to the letter.

Sophie didn't know what Ryder had written. She had wondered many times during the voyage, one time even going so far as to hold the envelope over a candle hoping to loosen the wax. She'd drawn it back. With her luck, if she did open it, it would show and the earl would believe her a sham. She pictured him pointing a long finger at her as she was dragged out the door. She stood there, stiff and miserable, waiting like a condemned prisoner in the dock. The earl read the letter through very slowly. When he looked at her there was a softening about his mouth. There was also a glittering in his dark eyes. He looked very human now. Sophie noted these changes with relief. She had learned to read men quite well in the past nearly two years.

"Ryder tells about some nasty business that has nearly been concluded satisfactorily."

Sophie hoped she wasn't the major part of the nasty business. "I see," she said, waiting, wary and very still.

"He also writes that I am to call you Sophie. He writes that Sophia sounds like a Russian princess who has ice water in her veins. He says you're warm and sweet."

"He wrote that?"

"My brother always gets to the kernel of the matter, Sophie. He doesn't waste time on trivialities. As for you, Jeremy, Ryder says you are the best of brother-in-laws and I am to immediately put you on a horse."

"Ryder really said that? But it is too bad of him, sir, for I am his *only* brother-in-law!"

"Yes, that is true as well. He requests that I look after the two of you until he comes home."

Both brother and sister merely stared at the Earl of Northcliffe. Douglas Sherbrooke realized fully that they'd been perfectly terrified of him. When Hollis had told him that his sister-in-law was waiting to see him, he'd laughed and wondered aloud at the gall of some of Ryder's women. "A child is with her, you say? Goodness, a boy about ten years old? It doesn't make sense, Hollis. Ryder isn't old enough to have fathered a boy that age!" But Hollis hadn't laughed with him. He'd looked utterly austere and said as he looked past Douglas's right shoulder, "Do not treat her badly, my lord. You are quite wrong. She is who she claims to be."

It was true they both looked like drowned urchins. It was even truer that Sophie wasn't a remarkable beauty, not like the women Ryder would normally rave about. But there was something lovely in the cast of her features, and he wasn't blind to the pride and stubbornness in her, or the character. His brother had married her. It was difficult to accept even with the evidence standing in front of him. It was difficult to accept even though Hollis had been convinced immediately. The earl shook himself and tried to find something to say. He was rescued by the entrance of Mrs. Peacham herself, the Sherbrooke housekeeper for twenty years.

"Master Ryder's wife, just imagine that! But you're not at all comfortable, are you, in those wet clothes? Oh, but aren't you a sweetling and just look at all that pretty hair! Goodness me, I'm Mrs. Peacham, and I'll take care of you and you'll not have to worry about a thing."

Sophie was overcome. She nodded. "I'm not all that wet now."

"Ah, and here is Hollis. You wish to meet the wife as well, Hollis?"

"Most assuredly, my lord. I am Hollis, ma'am.

If you require anything at all, you have but to ask me."

Tea was dispensed. Mrs. Peacham and Hollis took themselves off. Sinjun was joyfully consuming scones and nudging Jeremy in his ribs as she pointed out the tastiest ones to him. He'd already moved closer to her.

Sophie took a bite of lemon cake. It was delicious. She looked nervously at the earl, who was thoughtfully studying her. The room was warm and pleasant. They'd been welcomed. They'd even been fed. Ryder had told his brother to call her Sophie. He'd told his brother to give Jeremy a horse. It was suddenly too much. Then, the earl smiled at her and offered her more tea.

Sophie burst into tears.

"Oh dear!"

"Sinjun," the earl said calmly, "I want you to take Jeremy to the stables and select a suitable mount for him. Go now. If it's still raining, why then, describe the horses to him."

Sinjun grabbed Jeremy's hand and nearly dragged him from the room. She said fiercely, leaning down to his ear, "Don't worry. Douglas will take care of your sister. I imagine she has had a very difficult time. She will be all right, Douglas will see to it. He's wonderful, you know."

Douglas waited a moment, then said to Ryder's weeping wife, "You have done very well. I believe I myself would have cracked under the pressure of coming here to a strange house filled with people you don't know, people who could make your life quite unpleasant. But you're here now and the people here accept you and welcome you and everything will be fine."

Sophie hiccuped and wiped the back of her hand across her eyes. The earl handed her a handkerchief and she blew her nose.

He moved back to lean against the very feminine desk, his legs crossed at the ankles, his arms crossed over his chest.

"Ryder stands the same way," Sophie said. "Only he does it to intimidate me. You look fine doing it."

Douglas smiled. "My brother tries to intimidate you? How peculiar of him. Usually Ryder has but to use his charm to receive any gift he wishes."

Sophie blew her nose again, then tucked the handkerchief into her sleeve. "That's what he kept telling me."

"Ryder had to remind you of his considerable charm? How very odd of him. Would you like to meet my wife now? By that time Mrs. Peacham will have prepared a room for Jeremy and aired your bedchamber. Later, if you wish, you can tell me more of what occurred on Jamaica. As I told you, Ryder wrote of important things, not the other superfluous things."

Sophie nodded and tried to swipe some of the wrinkles from her gown. She still looked wilted but she was nearly dry now. She caught a look of herself in a mirror in the hallway. She looked a fright. She made a distressed sound, her hand flying to a strand of hair that hung damply down the side of her face.

The earl said easily, "Don't mind that mirror. It lies always. My wife has remarked upon it. Even my wife's sister, Melissande, who is so beautiful it makes your teeth ache just to look at her, avoids that mirror. I regret that my wife can't come here to meet you. We must go to her. Also, you don't have a red nose. She does."

The Countess of Northcliffe was in bed, propped up with pillows. Her nose was indeed red, her eyes watery, and she was sniffling. Her hair was a marvelous shade of red and was braided loosely around a very pretty, pale face.

The introductions were made.

The countess stared at the girl who stood still as a Sherbrooke garden statue.

"As least you're wearing clothes," the countess said.

"I beg your pardon, my dear?"

"Oh, I was just thinking that Sophie is standing as still as our garden statues."

"And the statues, Sophie, are, unfortunately, quite bare of fig leaves and of shirts or trousers. My wife's mind has slipped a notch with this cold. It brought her low two days ago. She dislikes being kept in bed; she desires to be up and about, ordering all of us around mercilessly."

"He adores to tease me. Goodness, you've been crying. What happened? Douglas, weren't you kind to her?"

"No, Alex, I was vicious. I berated her for daring to come here. I told her she could sleep for two nights in the stables but then she would have to leave. However, I did give her my handkerchief."

"Well, it is true that Ryder actually marrying a wife is enough to overset one's thinking."

"He couldn't very well marry a monkey, Alex. I will bring up Jeremy later to see you. Keep your distance, Sophie, I don't wish Ryder to return home only to find his bride in bed with a red nose and a foul disposition."

The earl patted Sophie's arm, gave his wife a mock bow. "If my wife makes you uncomfortable, simply tell her to mind her own business. On the other hand, I have always found her utterly discreet and an excellent confidante. She also has an adequate sense of humor." He touched Sophie's arm once again, then took himself off.

"He is wonderful, is he not?" the countess remarked.

"That's what Sinjun said."

"It's true. Even when he behaves in a manner that provokes one to the point of madness and wanting to cosh him, he is still wonderful. I sound besotted, don't I? Well, I daresay it will go away in twenty or so years."

"I have wanted to cosh Ryder since the first moment I met him."

"Just excellent," said the countess and blew her nose. She then sneezed, lay back against her pillows and moaned. "I am so sorry not to be able to see to your comfort. But Douglas, you know, I'll wager at this very moment, he's ensuring that a maid will be assigned to you and that she will see to your clothes and that one of the footmen will see to your brother — Jeremy? Yes, a very nice name, yours as well. Please, sit down and tell me all about Ryder. That's right. Now you're more comfortable."

"He isn't wonderful!"

Alex merely looked at her new sister-in-law. "I see," she said slowly. "Do tell me more."

Sophie felt an ungrateful fool. She bowed her head and her hands fidgeted with her skirt. "I'm sorry. He is your brother-in-law and you must be fond of him. It's just that he married me only to save me from being hung. He didn't want to. He doesn't even like me. It all came about because he felt sorry for me. I do think he came to believe that I was indeed a virgin, at least before he drugged me and took me to the cottage and . . . and took off my clothes and did other things, except I don't remember because, as I said, he had drugged me."

Alex said not a word. Suddenly she felt miraculously better. She even sat up higher against her pillows. She didn't have to blow her nose. Her brain felt clear as a summer sky. Her silence was not uncomfortable. She smiled at Sophie, and Sophie, without a whimper, gave it up. "It's not that he's unkind or cruel or anything like that. Indeed, he saved me as many times as I saved him, no, more times, to be truthful. It's just that I am afraid of him and I didn't want to marry any man even though he said there was no reason to be embarrassed because he'd already done everything he'd wanted to me. He kept telling me to trust him but how could I given all that had happened?"

"I see," Alex said again. She waited, but Sophie said no more. Well, it didn't matter. This was fascinating and Alex didn't doubt that there would be more confidences very soon. She said quite easily, "This is now your home. I hope you will be happy here. There is only one person who could perhaps be a bit troublesome to your peace of mind and that is your mother-in-law, mine as well, more's the pity. But too much pleasantness would likely prove boring. She keeps me on my toes. She detests me, but I don't pay her much mind. She wanted Douglas to marry my sister, Melissande, but — Ah, but it's as complicated a tale as yours is, I fear. You and I will be able to entertain each other in both the tellings. In any case, I won't be able to protect you for a couple of days. Lady Lydia just might take a liking to you, but I doubt it. Hers is not a particularly amiable disposition. Ah, here's Douglas. Oh, yes, Sophie, you are taller than I, but perhaps my maid can alter several of my gowns to fit you until we can bring a seamstress here."

"Oh no, I couldn't!"

But the countess said in the most imperious voice, "Don't be a ninny. The last thing we need is to have Lady Lydia see you in a gown like the one you're wearing, and she will forever relegate you to the underbelly of females."

Douglas laughed. "She's right, you know. After I have shown you to your bedchamber, you will return here and get yourself properly begowned. I will endeavor to keep my mother occupied until dinner." Even as he said the words, he sounded uncertain. Sophie could only stare at him, this man who looked as if he were master of the world. He walked to the bed, leaned down and kissed his wife's mouth, then said into her ear, "Many seams will need to be taken in, sweetheart. Your miraculous bosom is one of a kind, you know."

Sophie heard him. She stared some more, she couldn't help it. This stern man Ryder said would destroy her before breakfast was teasing his wife about her bosom? Perhaps, just perhaps, she didn't know men as well as she believed she did.

The earl straightened, gently ran his knuckles down his wife's cheek, then said to Sophie, "We will leave her to her misery for a while. You can return to take care of clothing in an hour, all right?"

Sophie nodded. There was nothing else to do.

CHAPTER 13

"What is going on here, Alexandra? I was told by Jerkins, who was told by Dora, who had over-heard Mrs. Peacham talking to Hollis, that Ryder had married. Married! It is absurd. It can't, simply can't be true. It's one of his floozy women trying to pass herself off as a decent person and fool us. She wants money, her sort always does. I even heard there is a child involved. This is out-side of too much. I'm here to assist you in re-moving her, Alexandra. You're sick and thus I am not surprised that the girl has taken you in. Good grief, is this she? She's in your bedcham-ber? She looks just as I thought she would — a slut, a fright, a sham. Get out, young woman, get out!"

The woman was actually shooing at her with her hands. Sophia stood still as the wing chair in front of the fireplace, staring at the woman, the distinctly unfriendly voice sounding in her ears, loud and imperious. She didn't have time to gather a response; she felt paralyzed.

"Oh dear," Alex said, and she suddenly looked

very ill indeed. She even closed her eyes a moment.

Sophie stood in the middle of the room, wearing one of Alex's gowns. The gown came only to her ankles and it was frankly loose on the bosom, for Sophie didn't have Alex's magnificent endowment, as the earl had pointed out. What had the woman meant — one of Ryder's women?

Alex girded her mental loins and scooted higher on her pillows. "Dear Lydia, this is Sophie Sherbrooke, your new daughter-in-law. Sophie, this is Ryder's mother, Lady Lydia Sherbrooke."

"I don't believe it," said the dowager countess, hands on hips, voice flat and hard. "Just look at you! And that rag you have on, girl, it passes all bounds. It's ugly and cheap and you look quite the sham in it. No, you shan't take me in as has this other daughter-in-law of mine who shouldn't be either."

"Actually, ma'am, it's one of my gowns. We're having it altered for Sophie."

Lady Lydia wasn't at all daunted by this proof of her error, and not at all remorseful about the insult she'd just dished out to her daughter-in-law, for she usually dished out too many in the course of a day to remember more than a fraction of them. Her hands remained on her hips and her nostrils still quivered with indignation. She wasn't about to budge. She gave Sophie another long look, and said, "Well, the color is all wrong for her. Sallow, that's what it makes her, utterly sallow. Now, young woman, you dare to say you're married to my son. Well, you can't be. Ryder has always laughed when anyone mentioned marriage. He is content as he is with all his women. Therefore, you are a liar, an adventuress, doubtless a —"

"Sorry, Alex, I lost track of her, but I'm here now. Hello, Mother."

It was the earl, and he was actually out of breath. Sophie was tempted, but only for an instant, to laugh as she pictured this fiercesome man racing up the stairs and to this bedchamber to muzzle his mother.

"Ah, I see you've met Sophie. Her little brother is also here. Jeremy is with Sinjun, I believe."

As if recalling that he was the master, the earl strode like the lord he was into the room, giving Sophie a wink as he passed by her. He paused a moment and looked her up and down. He said to his wife, "You see, it is just as I said. You are quite unique. Now, Mother, would you like to welcome Sophie to Northcliffe Hall?"

The earl sat down on a very feminine chair that all but groaned under his weight, but his dark eyes were calm and deep on his mother's face, and if Sophie had been in the older woman's slippers, she would have stammered something quite inoffensive and slithered out of the room. She prayed she would never have to cross swords with this man. He was honed as the sharpest of knives.

"Well, what am I to think?" Lady Lydia said, her voice peevish. "Come, Douglas, don't tell me you believe her. Just look at her. Why, dear Ryder wouldn't look at her a second time."

"I imagine he had to, Mother, for they are married. You see, Ryder wrote me a letter introducing her and Jeremy. I would appreciate it if you would accord her one of your lovely smiles and welcome her here."

Sophie would have smiled like a fool if those quietly spoken, utterly calm words had been directed at her. Lady Lydia fidgeted a moment, then said stiff as a poker, "You are here. My son, who is also the earl and thus must be accorded respect and patience, has accepted you. We will see if you remain once my other son returns."

Back straight as a broom handle, Lady Lydia marched from the bedchamber.

The earl said to his pale-faced wife, "Have you been giving my mother lessons, my dear? That straight back of hers rivals yours at your most arrogant. Surely you must have instructed her."

"I wish you'd been faster," Alex said.

"Sorry, but as I said, she moves very rapidly when she wants to. The gown does make you look a bit sallow, Sophie. You must avoid shades of yellow. They look lovely on Alex, but you need pale pastels, I believe. Have you a soft pink, Alex?"

Alex owned three such soft pink gowns. Within fifteen minutes, the countess was tucked down for a nap, the maid had taken the pale pink gown away to alter, and Sophie was in her bedchamber, staring at the huge cherrywood armoire that held a goodly number of men's clothes. Ryder's clothes. She was in his bedchamber.

It simply hadn't occurred to her that she would be put in his bedchamber. To await him. What to do?

Ryder's bedchamber.

She walked over to the window that gave out onto the front drive. She saw Jeremy walking with his slow hitched gait beside Sinjun from the stables. She'd slowed her own step to match his. He was speaking with great animation, using his hands, just like his father, and Sinjun was looking down at him, smiling and nodding. Sophie felt a surge of gratitude. The sun had come out in the late afternoon and the beautiful grounds were lush and green, the flowers in bloom, not the suffocating sort of lush bloom on Jamaica, but nonetheless, it was beautiful. She wondered where the naked Greek statues were kept.

With Ryder living here, she would have imagined his windows looking over the statues. She found herself walking around the bedchamber, opening drawers in the dressers, seeing her underclothing next to his. It was disconcerting. It was frightening. She very quietly closed the dresser drawers. She lay on the bed and stared up at the ceiling.

It was a blustery day, cold with dampness heavy in the air. Sophie dismounted Lilah, the bay mare the earl had given her to ride, tethered her to the skinny branch of a yew bush, and walked to the edge of the cliff. Waves crashed on the rocks some fifty feet below. The beach was littered with driftwood, tangled seaweed, huge boulders, and very dark sand that looked wet and cold. She was shivering, and it surprised her still. She'd been cold ever since she and Jeremy set foot in England. She wrapped her arms over her chest and didn't move for a very long time. The savagery of the scene below held her silent. She stood there very quietly, rubbing her arms, her hair blowing about her face, soon free of its knot at the back of her neck.

This was the earl's thinking place, Sinjun had told her. However, her sister-in-law had added, a twinkle in her incredible Sherbrooke blue eyes, Douglas hadn't visited here very much at all since he'd married Alex and not at all since he'd decided to keep her as his wife. It was just as well; Sophie liked having the barren cliff and the churning water below all to herself. She'd spent hours here during the past week, escaping Lady Lydia's tongue and all the curious Northcliffe Hall eyes.

She sat down on a rock, arranging her riding skirt over her legs. Her mare suddenly whinnied and she looked up. It wasn't the earl riding toward her or even Sinjun, who came here quite often and simply sat at her feet, quiet and undemanding, but a man she'd met in the village several days before. His name, if she remembered aright, was Sir Robert Pickering. He was well into his thirties, married and a father of five daughters.

He reminded Sophie of Lord David Lochridge, even to the assessing, very possessive way he'd looked at her when Alex had introduced them. She'd disliked him then, and his arrival here, on Sherbrooke land, made her dislike show on her face. She knew his sort, indeed she did, and she braced herself.

Sir Robert dismounted and strode to her. He stood over her, hands on hips, just smiling down at her.

"I was told I'd find you here. I trust you recall who I am? Certainly you do. All ladies remember gentlemen who look at them as I did you. You know, my dear girl, once Ryder returns you will be in dire straits, and he must return very soon now. Indeed, I expected him to come sooner. You must know he keeps many women and not one of them has he ever allowed to stay at Northcliffe Hall."

Oh yes, she knew his sort quite well. Sophie gave him a lazy look and yawned. "This is Sherbrooke land. I would that you leave now. And no, I don't remember your name at all. For the life of me I cannot imagine why I should."

She'd angered him a bit and it pleased her. She yawned again. He said, "My name is Sir Robert Pickering, and oh no, I shan't leave just yet. I wish to speak to you. I came here to find you. To come to an agreement, if you will. It is all the talk of the district, you know, how you, this simple maid from Jamaica, arrived with the little lame boy as your shill and pulled the wool over the Earl of Northcliffe's eyes. Of course, he is still so besotted with his new wife that it is no wonder he accepted you. It is even said that Lady Lydia avoids a room when you are in it. But your fun will soon be over. Who knows when Ryder will come back? As I said, it must be very soon. He won't allow you to remain, you know. You will be unmasked. He will not bed you in his home. He is discreet. He is very likely to be angry with you for your gall and impertinence. I think you are a quite pretty girl. Thus, I am willing to provide for you, and the little lame boy, but you must leave Northcliffe now. I will install you in a cottage I own some miles from here."

"I see," Sophie said, hating him so much her hands shook to shove him off the cliff. Sinjun had said on a giggle that he had a shocking reputation and all the ladies felt sorry for his wife, who, the poor woman, was continually with child. He was tolerated because his father had been a very popular man.

"Will you accept my offer, then?"

Sophie controlled her anger. She clearly saw his pretensions, his conceits, his fateful pride that would make him do and say very stupid things. She even smiled at him now.

"Tell me something, Sir Robert. Why are you so certain that I'm not married to Ryder Sherbrooke? Do you think I look like one of Ryder's women? Do I look like a girl who would be a man's mistress?"

"No, you do not and that pleases me. Actually, the half dozen or so women I know Ryder has kept are quite varied. Some are so beautiful they make a man's rod swell, others are simply pretty, but their bodies — all their bodies are magnificent. Now, as I already told you, Ryder has a reputation. He enjoys dozens of women. He would never tie himself to just one. Thus, you are one of his mistresses. There is no other way for it. Did I tell you I was one of her ladyship's confidants, just as my father was before me? No? Well, Lady Lydia would like to see you at Jericho. I enjoy obliging her. I will take action. Will you accept my offer?"

Sophie rose slowly. She dusted off her riding skirt. She smoothed out her gloves. As for her hair, she stuffed it as best she could under her riding hat. How very odd that it wasn't she who was regarded as the slut here, it was Ryder. She was only a slut by extension, for her husband couldn't be a husband and thus she had to be a liar. She gave him a remote look and said, "I would wager, Sir Robert, that you are the type of man to pin a maid against the stairs and fondle her."

He looked taken aback, then he nodded slowly at her, as if she'd just confirmed something he'd been thinking. He said, "I knew you would be brazen behind that demure façade of yours. There's just something about you, something that teases a man, that makes him want to throw up your skirts. A man looks at you and knows that you are well aware of what he wants of you. Your eyes, perhaps. You'd like that, wouldn't you? Like for me to take you right here."

"Your conceit is remarkable. If you come near me I will throw you over the cliff."

He laughed, moved quick as a snake, and grabbed her arm, jerking her against him. She felt no fear, just vast annoyance. Men, she thought, they were all the same, no matter what the country. She remarked the clump of hair on his jaw that his valet had missed while shaving his master. She smelled the pea soup on his breath. She waited, looking bored.

It enraged him. He crushed her against him and tried to find her mouth. But she eluded him. She knew he didn't understand, didn't accept that she wouldn't have him willingly. He grabbed her hair to hold her head still.

"You really shouldn't do this," Sophie said, still calm. "I won't allow much more."

"Ha," he said and managed to find her mouth. He touched her flesh, but that was all. Her hands were raised and fisted, her knee ready to come up and kick him in the groin. There was a furious yell behind him. Sophie felt him jerked like a mangy dog off her.

It was Ryder and he looked beyond angry. He looked vicious.

For a brief moment, she was so glad to see him she wanted to yell with it. He looked fit and tan and strong and she saw that his Sherbrooke blue eyes were alight with rage. She calmly watched him strike Sir Robert in the jaw with his fist. The man went down on his knees. Ryder reached for him again. Sophie laid her hand on his arm. "Don't, Ryder. He isn't worth bruising your knuckles and that is what would happen. He will already have to find an acceptable explanation for the wonderful bruise you've given him. Let him go. He is a worm, after all."

Ryder felt her words flow over him. He felt his rage lessen. His toes, however, still itched to kick the man in the ribs.

"Did the cretin hurt you?"

"Oh no. In fact —"

Sir Robert stumbled to his feet. His rage was directed at Sophie, not at Ryder, who'd struck him. It was, Sophie knew, the way men reacted. They always blamed the woman. She drew herself up and waited for his venom.

"She tried to seduce me, Ryder! Welcome home. I was here and she came and tried to seduce me!"

Ryder struck him again, and this time he grinned while he did it.

Sir Robert remained on the ground. "No one believes her tales, no one, particularly your mother. She claims to be your wife, Ryder, and everyone knows that's a patent falsehood. She wanted me, she's flirted shamelessly with all the men who've met her, she —"

Ryder knelt down, jerked him up by his collar, and said not two inches from his face, "She is my wife. Her name is Sophia Sherbrooke. You will tell all these randy men that if any of them come near her again, I will kick them into next week. As for you, Bobbie, you irritate her again and I'll kill you. You say anything about her and I'll kill you. Do you understand, Bobbie?"

Sir Robert nodded finally, and it was toward Sophie he shot a malignant look. He shook his head even as he backed away from Ryder toward his horse. "You are really married to her? To one single woman?"

"Did I not tell you she was my wife?"

Ryder said nothing more. He watched Sir Robert climb back onto his horse and kick the poor beast sharply in the sides. It wasn't until he was out of sight that Ryder turned to Sophie. She was standing there silently, the wind whipping her hair across her face, just looking at him, saying nothing. He smiled at her, reached out his hand and lightly touched his fingertips to her cheek. He wound a tress of hair between two fingers.

"It's been a very long time," he said, not moving himself. "They told me at the stable that you liked to come here. Hello, Sophie."

"Hello."

"Is this the first time Bobbie has bothered you?"

"Yes. I would have handled him, Ryder. There was no need for you to play knight to my damsel in distress."

His eyes narrowed. "I saw your knee ready to do him in. But I wanted to thrash him, Sophie. I am pleased you allowed me my fun. You understand that, don't you? You know men so well, after all."

"Yes."

"Why were you letting him kiss you?"

"He very nearly pulled my hair from my scalp."

Ryder shook himself. "This is bloody ridiculous. The last thing I want to talk about or think about is that damned lackwit Bobbie Bounder, as we called him when we were boys." He smiled down at her. "Come here."

She didn't move. She felt her heart begin to pound, slow, heavy beats. He came to her, pulled her into his arms and simply held her. "I missed you very much. And Jeremy. It's been a long time, Sophie." He lifted her face, his palm beneath her chin. He kissed her, his mouth warm and firm. She remained passive.

"Kiss me the way I know you can," he said against her lips.

"I can't," she said and tried to press her face against his neck.

"I am close to consummating our marriage right here, Sophie. It wouldn't be all that comfortable. Come, kiss me, you really must, you know, to hold me over until I can take you in our own bed tonight."

And it would happen, she knew. There was nothing she could do about it. She kissed him, kissed him with all the expertise she had garnered over the past two years. It didn't content him though. It aroused him until she thought he would fling up her skirts and press her against one of the boulders. He was breathing hard, his hands on her back, down to her hips, lifting her, and then she pushed at him. He stopped instantly.

He slowly lifted his head. He looked down at her, no expression on his face. "You are a tease. You are behaving just as you did on Jamaica. You have just spent several minutes making me wild. You have held back from me, controlled me. I had forgotten during the past eight weeks how very good you were at manipulation. I suppose I had rearranged my memories, had come to believe that since you were my wife, you would welcome me, you would treat me with some honor, some sign that you had come to accept me, even perhaps like me. But nothing has changed, has it, Sophie?"

"You took me by surprise."

He said something very crude and she flinched. "Don't tell me that shocks you? Dear God, you could probably outcurse me — no, no, this is absurd. I have just come home. I saw my brother and he told me that you were here, in his thinking place, that you came here quite a lot. And I saw Sinjun with Jeremy and he seemed very glad to see me. I suppose I was a fool to think you would extend the same courtesy to me. Look, it doesn't matter now. I won't annul our marriage. I'm an honorable man. I consented to wed you despite the fact that in the end, there was no reason for me to have to. Do you understand, Sophie? Your precious uncle wasn't shot or stabbed. Someone, Thomas probably, had garroted the bastard. I didn't have to marry you to keep you from the gallows."

"Garroted? I don't understand."

"Yes, he was. I made a grave mistake. If only I had paid more attention, but you see, his body wasn't a pleasant sight. I just assumed that you had shot him, but you hadn't. And I lied to save you, said that he'd been stabbed. The jest was on me, it certainly was. Garroted, the bastard was garroted."

"Is Thomas still free?"

"No. No, he's snug in that small dwelling Cole had planned on keeping you in. I didn't leave Jamaica until he'd been captured."

She turned away from him then and stared out over the sea. It wasn't the soft turquoise she was used to, it was savage and cold and very gray. "I thank you, Ryder. Your family has been quite nice to me and Jeremy. Now, though, since there is no reason for me not to return to Jamaica, I can. I will be responsible for Camille Hall and the plantation until Jeremy comes of age, I will —"

"Shut up, damn you!"

"You don't like me, Ryder. You can't possibly want to be my husband. I know about you now. You see, no one believed me to be your wife because everyone swore you would never wed. There were too many women hereabouts you enjoyed. It is odd. For the first time since Jamaica, I have been cut, not because I'm a tart, but because you are. I have found it vastly amusing save when Sir Robert tried to coerce me. If I could merely borrow some money from you, Jeremy and I could be on our way. Your life could return to what it was, to what you obviously enjoyed."

"I told you to shut up. You will go nowhere with Jeremy, my dear."

"Why? What do you mean?"

"I mean that I am his guardian. His legal guardian. You are nothing more than a female, his sister. I am responsible for the running of Camille Hall and the plantation. Emile is managing Camille Hall for me and Jeremy. Now, I should like to return to the hall and speak to my family. I wish to see if Douglas has accepted Alex as his wife."

"He has."

One of Ryder's eyebrows shot up. "Really? I understand that you were ever scarce there. You must be terribly observant to know my brother's feelings and be absent at the same time."

There was a distance between them that was growing even though they stood not two feet from each other. She couldn't blame him; but she couldn't blame herself either.

"Why?" she said at last. "Why, Ryder?"

"Why what?"

"Why don't you just let me go? Let me return to my home, resume my life."

"Ah, and what a life it would be. Even though your pretty neck would stay intact on your shoulders, you don't believe that all would be forgiven and forgotten, do you? You are the whore of Jamaica, my dear, and nothing will ever change that, even marriage to me. It's true. Everyone feels very sorry for me. You took advantage of my honorable nature and manipulated me into giving you my name. No, there is no going back for you, Sophie. There is only the present and that becomes the future soon enough. Now, I wish to return to the hall. Are you coming?"

He mounted his stallion, a magnificent barb she'd admired and fed whenever she'd been in the stables. His name was Genesis and she'd somehow known even before she'd been told that this was Ryder's horse. He looked down at her, arrogant, cold, aloof, and she hated it and accepted it.

"Tonight, as soon as it is politely possible to leave my family, you and I will adjourn to my bedchamber and I will take you and you will try your damnedest, Sophie, to act like a reasonable woman."

He said nothing more, merely gave her a small salute, wheeled Genesis around, and galloped away from her. She walked slowly to Lilah, climbed into the saddle, and rode after him.

CHAPTER 14

"My mother still resists believing me, but it is perversity on her part, no real conviction that you aren't actually my legal wife," Ryder said to Sophie as he tugged off his cravat. "She will get over it and treat you at least as nicely as she does Alex, which isn't very nice at all, but it will do for the present. You appear to get along well with Douglas and Alex. Of course you would like Sinjun. She's a nosy brat — Lord knows I'm the brunt of her nosiness — but all in all, she's an incredible girl."

Ryder turned to face her as he unbuttoned his white shirt. "Jeremy appears pleased to be here. I will decide soon if he will have a tutor or go to Eton for the fall term. Incidentally, I'm delighted Alex put you in my bedchamber. I've never shared it before. It's strange to see your gowns next to my shirts and britches in the armoire."

Sophie was standing by the front windows. She was doing her best to affect a casual pose. The evening hadn't been all that long for Ryder wanted her very badly. She knew that. Even as she'd walked beside him up the wide staircase, she'd known that if she looked at him, she would have seen the desire in his eyes. She knew well what desire looked like, both on a man's face and between his legs. What she didn't know was what to do about it. She felt incredibly weary, incredibly experienced and jaded. She didn't know what to do about that either.

He said again, "Don't misunderstand me, Sophie. It pleases me to see your gowns beside my clothes. Yes, Alex did well."

"Douglas put me in here. Alex was ill and in bed with a cold."

"Smart man, my brother. I also like the gowns Alex gave you. The pink is very pretty with your coloring. We'll see to some more new gowns for you soon enough."

She wanted to yell at him that she didn't want him to buy her gowns or anything else for that matter, but she remained still and silent.

Ryder sat down in what he had told her was his favorite wing chair. He tugged off his boots as he said, "My mother isn't always amiable, as I'm sure you've learned since you've been here. I had hoped she might change her colors just a bit, and perhaps she will. I don't want you to feel hurt. You should have seen what she did to Alex upon her arrival."

He flicked his wrists and both boots flew toward the huge bed in the center of the bedchamber, sliding smoothly underneath. Only one heel stuck out from beneath the duster cover. Sophie stared at that heel. He grinned at the boots. "I'm a bit off. I've been doing that since I was a boy. I always beat Douglas. It's in the wrist, you know."

He stood, his hands going to the buttons of his britches. She watched his long brown fingers on the buttons as he said, "How does it feel to be back in England?"

"It's cold," she said, still staring at his fingers. "I'd forgotten. Also, living in Jamaica for four years thinned my blood."

He smiled at her and pulled down his pants.

She closed her eyes, which was absurd really because she'd seen him naked, seen his sex swelled, seen him sprawled on the cottage bed with Dahlia over him. She swallowed.

"Sophie."

His voice was quiet, very warm and intimate. She opened her eyes. He was standing not three feet from her, quite naked and quite relaxed. He was smiling at her, his hand held to her. "You are my wife. Come here."

She didn't move.

"Should you like me to undress you? Is that why you've waited?"

"I should like a bath."

He blinked at her. "Very well. Let me ring."

He strode away from her and pulled on the silver-tasseled bellcord. He turned, then said as he climbed into the huge bed, "It is just as well. I have much more to say to you and we can have a pleasant chat while you bathe. If I touched you right now, I suspect we wouldn't say much until morning."

He wouldn't leave. She hadn't expected him to. He was behaving quite nicely, really, not lashing out at her, not condemning her, or calling her horrible names like her uncle had when she'd gone against his wishes.

It was another thirty minutes before Sophie was seated in front of the fireplace in the deep copper bathtub. She'd undressed in the shadows by the window and slipped on a dressing gown. However, to step into the tub, she'd had to take the damned thing off and she knew he was watching her. And she thought, I must accustom myself. He will do whatever he wishes to do to me for as long as I live. Then she shook her head at her thoughts, for nothing was right, nothing was as she'd expected it to be. He was acting so normal, so relaxed, as if they'd been here, in this bedchamber, chatting about everything and nothing for the past ten years.

He said nothing until she was soaping herself. "I like your hair wet around your shoulders and streaming over your breasts. I'm smiling, if you would but look at me once. I am happy to see you. I can't wait to get my hands on you, but I'm sure you recognize all the male signs — the lust-glazed eyes, the erratic speech, nonsense, most of it. I even like the way your legs are sticking up. The flesh behind your knees is very tender, by the by, and I will show you how much you will enjoy me touching and kissing you there.

I must remember to kiss that small birthmark of yours too."

She lathered her hair with a vengeance. It would take a good hour to dry it.

"I can't wait to kiss you silly. Perhaps I can convince you to return my kiss. I will try my best." He sounded so sure of himself, so completely confident. She rubbed her scalp until it hurt. He also sounded amused.

"Shall I come and rub your back for you?"

"I wish you would go away," Sophie said, opening her eyes through a haze of soap. It stung and she gasped, ducking her head under the water.

"Very well," he said agreeably. "I will doze here in bed and wait for you. I really forgot everything I wanted to say to you. Why, I won't even think of you — my wife — all naked and wet and soft. You have five more minutes, Sophie, not a second more." He consulted the clock on the mantel as he spoke. Then he leaned his head back against the pillow and closed his eyes. He crossed his arms over his bare chest.

When he opened his eyes she was standing swathed in a voluminous white nightgown. Her hair was matted and tangled wet down her back. If she got any closer to the fireplace, she'd be standing atop the flames.

She was trying to dry her hair.

"Hold still," he said and rose. Ryder wasn't a randy boy. He was a man and he'd proved not only to himself but to her that he could be patient. He would continue to be patient. He took another towel from the chair beside the copper tub and pointed to his wing chair. "Sit down."

She sat like a prim schoolgirl on the edge of the chair, her hands in her lap. "Now, where are your comb and brush?"

He spent another fifteen minutes brushing her thick hair. He set the brush aside. He smiled down at her. "You look like a Madonna. You are quite lovely, Sophie. You please me. Your hair has so many varied shades in it. Yes, you're lovely. You would please me even more if you opened your eyes. I'm naked, 'tis true, but you've seen me on several occasions. Surely I don't displease you?"

She opened her eyes then and looked him straight in the face. "Please tell me the truth, Ryder. Did you truly believe I was pregnant?"

Their wedding and the subsequent damnable night were stark in his mind, but he managed an indifferent shrug. "I had no idea. You refused to tell me the course of your monthly flow. It was possible you were pregnant, based upon my knowing nothing." He wondered if and when he would tell her the truth. Ah, soon, he knew, for he hated lies. They were always lying in wait to trip a man up. And Sophie was fast-witted. If he didn't tell her, she would catch him and he didn't want the consequences of that. Actually, though, she would know it was a lie soon enough.

Always his wit, she thought numbly. He drowned her in his damnable wit, in the easy flow of his speech. Had she used to be like that? Had she mocked him and teased him as he now did her? Memories flooded through her. Ah yes, she'd done it with great skill, even to touching him just so to make him mad with lust for her. But now she was a silent fool, dull-tongued and stupid. Why couldn't she treat him as she had Sir Robert? She sometimes wished she had herself back again but then she'd realize she wasn't exactly certain who that self really was.

She felt his hands on her wrists. He pulled her upright and against him. He said, his breath warm against her damp hair, "Now let me tell you how we're going to spend the greater part of this wonderful evening. I will not rush you. We must take time to learn each other. I will kiss you and —"

He paused, kissed her lightly on her mouth, then said, "No, let me just show you. Do me a favor, Sophie. Forget all those damned men. Just forget them. They have nothing to do with us, with this. This is private, this is us alone, a man and his wife together."

But she couldn't. She also knew she couldn't refuse him. He was her husband; he had full and complete control over her, more control, in fact, than her uncle had exercised, which had been unbearable. If he wanted to strip her naked and tie her to the bed, why he could do it. She tried to be calm. After all, she'd had weeks and weeks to come to grips with it. She'd learned that much, surely she had. She wouldn't start screaming or become hysterical. She wasn't that way, and even if she had ever been that way, her uncle Theo would have beaten it all out of her long ago.

When Ryder pulled her nightgown over her head, leaving her as naked as he was, she drew back, hunching over, unable to stop herself. He lightly touched his fingertips to her ribs. "No more bruises. Have you had any more pain?"

She shook her head. "Good," he said and brought her against him again.

For the first time he held her naked against him. His heart was pounding in deep, fast strokes. He wanted to come inside her this very instant and bury himself in her, his wife. He wanted to hold very still, to feel her around his sex, to feel the gentle tensing movements of her inner muscles. But he wasn't stupid. She needed every bit of his expertise. Ah, that was the rub. She was making it a damned serious business. Ryder had always laughed before, for to him making love was a grand pastime filled with mirth and smacking kisses and shared moans and sighs. He wasn't laughing now; he didn't have a single jest in his head. It was going to be a grim business.

It would be enough, this expertise of his. He'd never failed with a woman before, never. He caressed her mouth, nibbled on her ear, found that very sensitive place in the hollow of her throat that made every woman he'd ever known squirm and moan when he'd caressed there with his tongue.

He told her how beautiful she was as he stroked

his hands over her breasts, told her how much she pleased him, how much he wanted to touch her everywhere, with his hands and with his mouth. Her nipples were a dark pink and when he took one in his mouth he thought he'd spill his seed. The taste of her, her texture, were nothing he'd ever experienced before, which was surely false, but it seemed true to him now. He frowned even as he let the feelings settle deep within him.

He clasped his hands beneath her hips and lifted her onto her back on the bed. He came down over her, kissing her breasts, caressing and lifting them, wanting her desperately, more and more as each instant passed.

He slid his left hand over her belly, stilling a moment when he remembered the ugly bruises. God, he'd never forget them or the soul-deep rage he'd felt. She'd been hurt so badly. He slowed his hand, easing his fingers lower, until he was cupping her and he felt the stiffness of her body, despite her softness, and he pressed his fingers between her thighs. He found her woman's flesh and gently probed. He wanted to come into her now, this moment, for his need for her was so great that he trembled with it. Unlike the Ryder Sherbrooke before he'd met Sophie, he didn't want to lose his control. But it had been so very long that he'd wanted her, so very long that he'd been celibate, that he simply didn't know if he could hold himself under control.

Perhaps, he thought, staring down at her, just

perhaps this was why he'd wanted to marry her. Perhaps he'd known that she would do this to him, that she would be like no other woman in his life. He closed his eyes as he eased his middle finger inside her. His breath hitched with the effort to keep control of himself. The feel of her around his finger, the softness of her, the heat of her, made him grit his teeth. She made a soft keening sound and he took it for burgeoning passion. It had to be. Sweet God, it had to be passion. How could she not want him when he was edging toward madness with need for her?

She was tight, her muscles squeezing his finger. He knew it would be over for him soon. He eased deeper until he touched her maidenhead. He smiled; he realized now he'd known he would find it. He widened her as best he could for he didn't want to hurt her too much.

He pulled her thighs wide and came down between them. He looked at her face. "Sophie, I'm coming inside you now. No, open your eyes. Remember, there's no reason for you to be embarrassed. We've already done this. There is nothing new here. Believe me. If you could try to relax, you just might enjoy it."

She looked at him as if he were mad. She closed her eyes against the urgency of his expression, then opened them again. No, she would bear all that he did to her. It wouldn't be bad. It would be over soon enough.

That damnable lie. He had believed it would help her to relax with him. It hadn't appeared to do anything of the sort. He knew he couldn't wait. He guided himself slowly inside her. He promised himself he would only come into her for a very short time and then he would ease out of her and give her his mouth. Yes, just a bit more, just until he knew she accepted him, for he wanted her to experience having him inside her before he brought her to pleasure. He said as he came deeper, "You are my wife," and there was wonder and satisfaction in his voice. "It is very odd for me, you know. I've never had a wife before, never thought to have one, but you are here with me and we are in my bed and I'm coming inside you. Please accept me, Sophie."

Accept him, she thought, holding herself as still as possible. She had no choice but to accept him. She waited, afraid, willing it to be over, willing him to make those ugly grunting noises the men made, the noises that soon meant they would be through, their sex shriveled, and shortly asleep and snoring.

She was a virgin and she was his wife and she would be his now. When his sex butted her maidenhead, he pushed forward as gently as he could. It held. He cursed, knowing he should withdraw from her. He tried, he really did, but he couldn't make himself pull out of her. He looked down at himself inside her. He shook and tried to pull away again. He couldn't. He leaned down and kissed her instead. His tongue was deep in her mouth when he groaned and thrust deep, tearing through her maidenhead until he was touching her womb and then it was simply too much. Even as he became aware that she was struggling against him, even as he tasted her tears in his mouth, he groaned again, feeling such swirling, utterly wild feelings, that he jerked frantically at the intensity of his release.

He stilled. She lay quiet beneath him. He was heavy on top of her, his breath still deep and fast, his body damp with sweat, his face on the pillow beside hers.

She hadn't expected the pain. Dahlia had never complained of pain, not that Sophie had ever asked her, but, on the other hand, Dahlia gave her opinions on everything with lazy abandon, comparing the men down to such details as the noises they made during their release. Sophie couldn't imagine that Dahlia would suffer pain willingly or in silence. Thus, this pain did surprise her and she burned deep inside with the stinging of it, and the alien fullness of him. She knew about a man's seed and knew it was in her as was the pain he'd inflicted upon her. How could a woman possibly enjoy this if it hurt so badly?

She'd known all about intimacies, known all about six men and their bodies and their needs, but she'd never realized that his sex entering her joined them in such a way. He was deep inside her still and she could feel him, feel every slick bit of him. It was as if he were trying to be a part of her but she wouldn't allow it. No, he was the different one and soon he would separate himself from her. She pressed her hips deeper into the mattress. She sucked in her breath, wishing he would just be done with her and leave her.

Ryder managed to balance himself on his elbows above her. He was actually smiling, a tender smile that confused her. "I'm sorry I hurt you. I won't hurt you ever again."

"Why did you hurt me this time?"

No more lies or evasions, he thought, and said simply, "This was your first time. You were a virgin just as I finally realized you would be. I had to get through your maidenhead. That's what hurt you."

She stared up at him, her eyes darkening as she finally understood. A lie, it had all been a lie, him taking her at the cottage, her possible pregnancy. "You bastard!" She heaved upward, trying to buck him off her.

"I know. I'm sorry for it." He clasped her wrists and pulled her arms over her head. He was heavy on top of her and she felt him growing inside her. It couldn't be, not this soon, no, she wouldn't allow it. She wanted, quite simply, to kill him.

"I am sorry I lied to you, Sophie. At first I meant it as simple punishment for what you'd done to me. Not very nice of me, I'll admit, but then again, what you and your uncle did to me wasn't any better. It gave me a power over you to have matched you at your same game. After, when I decided I would marry you, I used it against you. And I won."

"How can you believe that marrying me is winning? That is errant nonsense. I am nothing, less than nothing. I have no dowry, no reputation, no —"

"Damn you, you will be quiet."

Her eyes went a very dark gray at the anger in his voice; her face was as pale as the white sheets. "No matter your anger, you can't change what I have been, what I am. You haven't won a thing, Ryder."

"I will always win with you, Sophie. It's best you remember that."

Without warning, without any sound at all, she jerked her right arm free of his hold, and smashed her fist into his jaw. He saw the flash of movement but he wasn't fast enough, simply because he'd been laughing and bragging and telling her how omnipotent he was, in short, her master, the one man who would handle her always to his satisfaction.

Her fist hit him hard and he jerked back with the surprise and the flash of pain. She shoved at him, her legs striking him hard on his back, and he went over the side of the bed and landed with a loud thud on the wooden floor.

She lurched up and stared down at him.

He was laughing, lying there on his back, rubbing his jaw, and laughing. At her.

She scrambled off the other side of the bed, grabbed her nightgown and pulled it over her head. She was panting with fury, with fear, because she'd seen the blood on herself, but she knew it couldn't be her monthly flow. He'd hurt her, all right, hurt her so badly she was bleeding.

God, she hated him, hated herself, wished she could topple the bed over on top of him. It was rosewood and very heavy. She tried, but she couldn't lift it.

He stopped laughing, rose and shook his head. He stood on the other side of the bed now, just looking across at her. She couldn't help herself. She looked at his groin, at his flat belly and the thick mat of hair that surrounded his sex, at his legs that had pressed against hers. He wasn't fully aroused now and he was wet with her and with himself and there was blood too and she gasped.

Ryder looked down at himself then back at her face. He pulled back the covers and looked at the stains of blood on the sheet. "I won't seek retribution for that blow until after I've got you cleaned up."

"You come near me and I will break your back. You've hurt me quite enough, Ryder. No more. If I die from what you've done to me, so be it. I deserve it for being such a colossal fool, but you will stay away from me."

"I told you that the hurt is because this was your first time. As for the blood, that won't happen again either. Good God, if a woman bled every time she had a man, the species would cease to exist in a very short time. I'm not lying to you, Sophie. I do find it passing strange that you are ignorant of this. The bleeding signifies your passage into womanhood."

"That is sheer nonsense and you know it. I am nineteen years old, Ryder, very much a woman."

"Oh, I do agree, my dear wife, indeed I do. But my rending of your maidenhead now means you can bear a child. There will be some stretching for a while yet until you become used to me, but it won't hurt. Indeed, I've been told it's a very nice feeling."

"Yes," she said, "told by doubtless two dozen women!"

Acrimony? He wasn't certain. He prayed it was acrimony, a goodly dose of it. He walked around the end of the bed. She didn't back away from him as he'd imagined she would, instead, she flung herself at him and punched her fists into his belly, against his chest, tried to hit his face.

It was a silent battle and he became aware of that silence and wondered at it. Fighting was a loud business, at least in his experience — cursing, grunting, yelling. But she didn't make a bloody sound save for her harsh breathing. And he realized then, and said aloud, "You learned how to fight, to struggle, without a sound, didn't you? You knew that any sound could have awakened Jeremy and you couldn't allow that. Damn you, Sophie, it's different now. That mangy old bastard is well and truly dead. Damn you, yell at me when you fight me!"

She tried to kick him in the groin instead and

he simply turned quickly to the side and her blow landed on his upper thigh. He ripped her nightgown off her and threw her onto her back. He brought his full weight over her.

She was heaving and jerking against him and he simply let her, holding her hands over her head. He didn't look at her heaving breasts, tried to ignore her legs thrashing against his, her belly tensing against his.

When she finally quieted, he said, "You didn't enjoy me touching you or kissing you at all, did you?"

She looked at him as if he'd lost his mind.

"No, that was a rather stupid question, wasn't it? We will change all that, Sophie. You are remembering the past year, aren't you? Those men, and what your uncle made you do. Dismiss it, Sophie, relegate it to a time that no longer matters, a time well gone, and forget it."

She realized then, in a flash of understanding, that she didn't doubt for an instant that he wouldn't hurt her no matter how much she tried to hurt him. Never would he raise his hand to her, never would he smash his fists into her ribs. She could probably shoot him and he wouldn't hurt her. She lay there simply looking up at him. Those blue eyes of his were blazing, brilliant as sunlight against a clear sky, yet somehow deep and calm. She said slowly, "You were a part of it. You were the biggest part of it. I knew everything would fail once you came, but my uncle wouldn't believe me. I tried to tell him you were different, because I knew, somehow I knew what you were, but he wouldn't listen. I didn't want to get near you but I did, and look what happened. How can I forget it?"

"In what way did you believe me different from the other men?"

She wished she hadn't said it but she had. "The others were so pleased with themselves, so filled with their pride and conceit, for they had gotten me, just a simple woman really, nothing more, but I was a prize, a possession, no matter how temporary, and it gave them stature and prestige in other men's eyes. You don't care what others think of you or what you do. You see things differently; you react differently."

He looked thoughtful. "Oh, don't get me wrong, Sophie. I wanted you, don't ever mistake that, but it was a game to me. I wanted to best you, to conquer you. Perhaps I wished to teach you a lesson, as I said, but things changed. I married you. Surely that isn't such a bad thing. You are safe with me, as is Jeremy. You are secure, you will never know fear again in your life. Now, you will forget the past. I am your present and your future. Can you feel me? I want you again but I will bathe you first and give you a while to ease. Will you continue to fight me?"

"Yes."

He sighed and rolled off her. He walked to a long, low dresser and pulled two cravats from a drawer. "I regret doing this for it will probably make you so angry you won't speak to me for a week, no matter that I'm your husband and you vowed to obey me."

She jerked off the bed and ran naked to the bedchamber door. His hand slammed against the door above her head. "Are you quite witless, Sophie? You are splendidly naked, my dear. It is doubtful that any of my siblings or any of the servants are wandering the halls, but who knows? I prefer to keep all your female endowments just for my eyes. You are quite beautiful. Your legs are long and firm. You run well."

He took her hand and began to pull her back to the bed. She kicked him hard in the back of his leg and he felt the pain spurt through him and his grip loosened. She jerked away from him, and this time, she was at the door and through it before he could stop her. She ran down the long corridor, unaware really that she was naked and out of control. She simply ran until, quite suddenly, there was a shadow in front of her and she ran full tilt into it and it wasn't a shadow but a man and he was in a dressing gown. It was the earl, her brother-in-law, and his hands were wrapped about her bare upper arms and he was holding her gently yet firmly.

"Let me go!"

"You need some clothes," Douglas said, so stunned at the appearance of his new sister-in-law completely nude that he was surprised there were any words at all in his mouth.

"Please," she began, trying yet again to jerk

away from his hold, looking back over her shoulder even as she struggled. Ryder was striding toward them, wearing a dressing gown, carrying another dressing gown over his arm. He looked furious.

Douglas saw the look on his brother's face in the dim light. He had no idea what was going on, but he felt the fear coming from her, and he felt a protectiveness that wasn't unlike what he felt toward his wife.

He eased his grip on her arms but didn't release her. He said quietly, "Your wife appears a bit distraught, Ryder."

"Yes," Ryder said when he reached them. He was dizzy with anger at her. And here was his brother, holding his wife, and she was naked. "Give her to me, Douglas."

Douglas knew there was no choice. He also knew Ryder wasn't a cruel man. He wouldn't hurt her, but he would give her a good dose of speech that could shrivel the stoutest of hearts.

He said quietly, "I trust everything will soon be all right?"

"Yes," Ryder said again. "Sophie, put this on. My brother doesn't need to see my wife."

Douglas released her. She was still, not moving when Ryder wrapped her in the dressing gown. It was soft, very soft from many washings; it smelled of him. She shuddered, but didn't move, didn't say anything. Everything had gone awry.

"Sleep well," Douglas said, his eyes resting a moment on his brother's face.

"Yes," Ryder said, took Sophie's hand, and led her back down the corridor.

Douglas stood there many minutes until they went into Ryder's bedchamber. What the devil was going on here?

Ryder didn't say a word. He just pulled her back to the bed. He took her squirming body and eased her down on her back. He pulled away the dressing gown. He reached for the cravats. He was over her again, straddling her, and he wrapped the cravats around her wrists, and secured them to the headboard.

"Now," he said, and moved off her again. He stood by the bed and looked down at her. She was pale and furious and still she made no sound.

"There is a lot of blood," he said and frowned. "I am sorry I hurt you, Sophie. Now hold still and let me bathe you."

She held still because she was too tired to fight him further. She tugged once at her wrists but his knots were secure. Why hadn't he said anything yet about her flight and capture by his brother? She felt him hold her legs apart and closed her eyes tightly. He was looking at her and she felt the wet cloth stroke over her. She hated it, this knowing he had of her, this power he had over her. He looked at her and he saw a woman's body that belonged to him.

When he was done he was silent for a moment, then, "Sophie, look at me."

She opened her eyes. He didn't like the message in them.

"What you did was foolish. I do not appreciate your showing my brother your body. I don't understand why — but it doesn't matter right now. You're tired; you're not yourself. Would you like to sleep now?"

"Yes."

He untied her wrists but didn't release them. He massaged them gently and thoroughly. And when he saw her looking about, he said, "No, no nightgown. Just the two of us together."

The bed could hold six people side by side and still he held her tightly against him. The strong beat of his heart sounded beneath her palm, the prickle of hair against her legs.

As for Ryder, he closed his eyes and sighed. "I like the feel of you against me. You're warm and soft. I locked the door. I do hope you don't snore too loudly."

"I do. I sound like a pig."

"How would you know? I know that I'm the first man ever to have you, the first man to hold you naked against him. If you are not delicate and soft in your sleep, I shan't tell you. I don't want to hurt your feelings."

She snorted and he kissed her hair.

He lay back and closed his eyes. Damnation. He hadn't given her any pleasure, not a dollop, not a blessed whit. He hadn't done anything particularly well with her, and that was unusual for him because he was well used to giving as much pleasure as he got. He hadn't with her. He would have to teach her to forget all the ugliness of the past months, including his own part in it, which could prove a formidable task. But he had to. He had to teach her how to love and how to make love. He felt her breasts against his chest, very soft breasts. He saw also in his mind's eye the look on Douglas's face. He must have heard them arguing and he'd come to investigate. Still, he'd held his tongue. He'd been gentle with Sophie.

Damnation.

He slept.

CHAPTER 15

Ryder awoke in the middle of the night. Sophie was warm and soft against him. He was hard. He hurt and he wanted her, then, at that very instant. It seemed he'd wanted her forever. He wasn't completely full-witted and thus rolled her over onto her back, kissing her mouth even as he arranged her for himself, and came fully into her, hard and deep.

She cried out.

Ryder froze, but the madness prodded at him, and all his fine and honorable vows about her pleasure escaped his brain from one instant to the next. He was more awake than before but it made no difference. It was intense and power-ful, this lust of his, and he thrust deeply into her, then pulled nearly out of her, heaving with the strain of it, the savage pleasure, again and again until suddenly he stilled. Then it dug at him again, this urgency for her, this frenzy to have her, to make her a part of him, to bind her to him. But he wanted to slow down, to make it last beyond the moment he knew was left to him. He held her tightly to him and rolled over, pulling her on top of him. He forced her upright and pulled her knees under her and against his flanks. She was riding him now, and she splayed her fingers over his chest to hold herself up. He thrust upward, holding her waist, then sliding his hands to her hips to lift her and bring her down on him, to show her what to do. All women enjoyed riding the man once in a while; they could set their own rhythm. They drove him mad with lust and they laughed as they did it, until like him, they moaned and flung their heads back. But Sophie wasn't moving; nor was she moaning. She held him deep inside her and he was forcing her to hold him, more deeply than the first time. Her breasts were thrust forward, beautiful and white and he gasped and pressed her further down on him. He couldn't see her face clearly in the dim light. And he wanted to. Then he heard her sob. He twisted about until he could see her face more clearly. Her eyes were closed and tears were rolling down her cheeks.

Sweet Lord, was he hurting her? He hadn't thought, hadn't realized, that this way of making love was deep, very deep and she was unused to a man, not just a man, but to him, her husband. Quickly, he lifted her off him and onto her back once again. When he rolled over onto her, he came into her again, not so deeply this time.

He wanted to pull out of her, to kiss her and soothe her, to tell her that he hadn't meant to go so strongly into her before she was ready to take him, but suddenly she moved, twisting to the side, and it sent him right over the edge.

It was a repetition of the first time, and he was furious with himself once he'd regained his wits. Again, he was balancing on his elbows over her and he felt the force of her sobs against his body, felt her heart against his, and he didn't like what he'd done.

"Go to sleep," he said and rolled off her.

She did eventually, but he listened to those soft, gasping cries of hers for more minutes than he could bear.

He awoke the following morning at the streaming of sunlight through the front windows. He felt her weight against him and smiled until he remembered the fiasco of the previous night. He'd been a clod, not once but twice, a selfish clod, a fool, a half-wit. He didn't understand it, and he didn't like himself for it.

Well, it was done. He would make it up to her. He would exercise more patience than he ever had in his life. On the other hand, he hadn't ever needed patience with a woman; a smile, a jest, a caress, and most had come to him. He knew the experiences in his life hadn't demanded much of anything that he couldn't readily and willingly give. Ah, his life had been filled with laughter and hour upon hour of pleasure and reckless freedom — the pounding strength of his stallion beneath him and the utter yielding of all the women he'd known and loved and held. His life had held no responsibilities he hadn't asked for. And that included his children, all seven of them. No, they were a joy, not a responsibility. It was true. His life had been fashioned by a benign deity. Now everything had changed. The woman he'd brought into his life, the woman he'd chosen for himself, didn't want him. There didn't seem to be laughter in her, no spontaneous joy, no wildness that came from deep within, and burst forth freely and gladly.

There was darkness in her. He understood at least some of this darkness for he'd seen it himself, he'd seen the results of it. Hell, he was the victim of it as well as she was. As for himself, the patches of pain and uncertainty that had come as they must to every man had been few. He'd been lucky and he knew it and he thought about it now, starkly. Everything was different and he perforce must also be different because of what he had done and of what she was and what he wanted her to become and be to him.

She still slept. He eased up until he was on his elbow and could look down at her. Her hair was tangled about her head, wild on the pillow, her face blotchy from her crying and she looked beautiful to him. This girl who wasn't really a beauty, not like some of the ladies he'd known so well, no she wasn't a diamond like Alex's in-credibly lovely sister, Melissande, but she was impossibly beautiful to him, impossibly and in-explicably dear. He lightly ran a fingertip over her eyebrow. Slowly, she opened her eyes. She didn't move, didn't make a sound, merely looked up at him. He felt the tension building in her but ignored it.

"Good morning," he said and kissed her mouth.

She froze. He watched her eyes darken, then become carefully blank. He wouldn't tolerate it, this withdrawal from him. "Stop that, damn you. I won't hurt you again, I swear it."

"Men always hurt women."

"I admit that your experience hasn't shown you much of the other side of things. Men included."

"You hurt me two times last night. And you will do it again and again because you are the man and stronger than I am and you have the control and power and you can force me to do anything you wish to do."

"All that? Perhaps I should consider announcing my godhood." The studied lightness gave him a moment to think. The good Lord knew he needed many such moments now, with her, with this wife of his.

She shoved at him but couldn't budge him. She was panting now, and he could practically feel her urgency to get away from him. It was unnerving. It was frightening. "No, Ryder, I don't believe you. You will force me whenever you want a woman. You are lying to me. All men lie to get what they want."

He let her go and rose to stand by the bed. "You will learn to believe me, to trust me."

She was now on the far side of the bed. She

simply stared at him and he saw all her fear of him in her eyes, a damned irrational fear, and in that moment he wanted to throw her out of the window.

The irony of it didn't escape him. He wondered what the hell he was going to do now. He rang for bathwater. Once he'd dressed, he left the bedchamber, left her alone and silent, lying in bed, the covers drawn to her chin.

Sinjun said to the breakfast table at large, "I saw the Virgin Bride last night. She probably came to visit Sophie and got the wrong bedchamber. Just think," she added, turning toward her sister-in-law, "you just might get a visit from the family ghost too. She won't hurt you. She just wants to welcome you to the Sherbrooke family. She's been around for ever so long and all the past earls have written about her."

"Be quiet about that damned ghost," this earl said. "There is no ghost, Sophie. The brat has a very active imagination. Ignore her."

"A real ghost? You're not jesting?" Jeremy whispered so that just Sinjun heard him. He wasn't about to disagree with the Earl of Northcliffe.

"Yes, I'll tell you all about her. Later, when we go riding."

"I've never seen her," Ryder said, setting down his coffee cup. He took a bite of egg, looked at his wife, and winked at her. "Perhaps she'll visit us. Would you like that?"

"A ghost. Yes, I would. Who is she?"

"A young lady whose husband was killed before they could consummate their marriage," Ryder said. "Sixteenth century, I believe. She has long, very blond hair and all the filmy trappings, so Sinjun tells us. Evidently she appears only to the women of the family."

Alex opened her mouth then shut it.

"The Earls of Northcliffe write about her, as I said," Sinjun said. "It is too bad of Douglas — he refuses to hear about her, and more than that, he swears he won't pen a word about her."

The earl harrumphed and gave a stern look to his wife, who was now studiously separating the kippers on her plate. He said to the table at large, "We must have a ball or something equally formal so that Sophie can be introduced to the neighborhood. In the meanwhile Alex will take you about, Sophie, to meet our more illustrious neighbors."

"Will Tony and Melissande come?"

"Doubtless they will, Sinjun," Alex said. She continued to Sophie, "Melissande is my sister. She's incredibly beautiful and she married Tony Parrish, Viscount Rathmore. He is Douglas and Ryder's first cousin. You will enjoy both of them. Perhaps Tysen can come from Oxford as well. He is the youngest of the brothers and plans to be a vicar."

The dowager countess said sharply, "She cannot go to a ball dressed in Alex's castoffs, Douglas."

"No, I quite agree. We will have that seamstress

in from Rye. You know, Alex, the one who fitted you up."

Lady Lydia said to no one in particular, "Ah, dear Melissande. How I wanted her for my daughter, but Douglas wouldn't oblige me. I did have hope for you, Ryder, but Tony was impossible about the entire matter."

"Tony is married to her, ma'am," Alexandra said easily. "Besides, Tony is always impossible. It's part of his charm. You will like him immensely, Sophie, as he will you. As for Melissande, well, she is also many times vastly amusing."

Sophie stared down at the congealed eggs on her plate. All these people she didn't know and didn't care about, no more than they cared about her. Like all the men on Jamaica, Tony would probably look at her and decide she was a loose tart. She picked up a scone and nibbled on it. Conversation flowed around her. She vaguely heard more insults tossed in her general direction from her mother-in-law.

She suddenly felt him looking at her. She raised her head to see Ryder simply staring at her, his fork halfway to his mouth. What was wrong? Was there butter on her chin?

He grinned. "You look beautiful this morning, Sophie, but a bit pale. I want color in my wife's cheeks. After breakfast, change into your riding habit and I will show you this favorite place of mine. Unlike Douglas, I don't spend a lot of time striding over cliffs that could crumble beneath me. No, this is another sort of place. You will like it."

Sophie didn't imagine that she would like it at all. He likely wanted to take her to a private place and come inside her again. She hurt inside. The muscles in her thighs pulled and ached. She didn't want him near her. She said nothing.

She wanted to spend some time with Jeremy, but before she could open her mouth, Sinjun and Jeremy had risen together from the table. Sophie watched her little brother place his hand in Sinjun's and smile up at her. The two of them left the room together.

Ryder said very gently, "Sinjun is a new treat. You, my dear, are an old tale. I am pleased they do well together. You and I will fascinate Jeremy later."

She disliked his knowing what was in her mind; she disliked his logic, his reasonableness. Few men she'd ever known had been very reasonable. Ryder hadn't been reasonable either on Jamaica. He'd been cynical, utterly ruthless, and calculating as the devil. This was another side of him she didn't like, didn't want to see or to recognize.

Ryder said to his brother, "While Sophie changes into her riding clothes, would you like to join me in the estate room? I need to speak with you."

Lady Lydia took only one parting shot. "I say, my dear boy, should you like to invite the Harvestons to your ball?"

Since neither dear boy knew who it was their

mother was addressing, both merely nodded, Douglas wincing and Ryder wanting to curse.

"The Harvestons, of course, have three beautiful daughters," Lady Lydia said. "They are just returned from a visit to American relatives in Boston." She added, a sapient eye on Sophie, "I don't like this at all."

"I don't either, ma'am," Sophie said, tossed her napkin on her plate, and pushed back her chair before Jamieson, a footman, could assist her. What her mother-in-law had meant, of course, was that she didn't like Sophie, who was a nobody, in her mind.

"Take your time changing, Sophie," Alex called after her. "Douglas and Ryder probably have a lot to discuss. It's been a long time and they're very close, you know."

In the estate room, Douglas was sitting behind his desk, watching his brother pace the length of the room. They were silent for moments.

"She's a charming girl," Douglas said.

"Yes, she is."

"She doesn't behave at all like a bride. She spent most of her time before you arrived alone. She is also unhappy."

Ryder paused in his pacing long enough to curse.

"I had believed her homesick at first, but that isn't it at all."

"No."

"Last night — it surprised me. Quite took me aback. I was on my way to the kitchen to fetch Alex some milk when I saw her flying down the corridor, her face pale as her skin. You don't have to tell me anything, Ryder. But I would help if I could. Is it because of something you've done that she is unhappy? Did she find out about all of your women? Did you hurt her? Is she jealous?"

"It is because of a lot of things. Thank you for taking such good care of her until I came home. I do wish Mother would control what comes out of her mouth, but I suppose it isn't to be expected."

"No. She will come around eventually. If she becomes too outrageous I will simply threaten to move her to the dower house."

"An excellent threat."

"Exactly."

The brothers grinned at each other. Douglas said, "I was vastly surprised when your wife and her brother arrived on the doorstep. Hollis knew immediately, curse his damned hide, knew the very instant he saw her that she was quality and that she belonged here. There is another thing. At first she avoided me. I couldn't figure out why. I was polite, I was solicitous, I tried to make her welcome. Then I realized she didn't trust me. She didn't trust me as a man. That I found very curious, inexplicable really. Why is she unhappy, Ryder?"

"She's afraid of me. She was probably afraid of you too."

There was utter silence. Douglas said, clearly disbelieving, "That's utterly absurd. Why would your wife be afraid of me? I did nothing unto-ward. Nor have I ever known a woman to be remotely afraid of you. Why, they pursue you, they won't let you alone. All of them want to get you out of your britches."

"Things change."

"Would you like to tell me what happened in Jamaica? No, no, not about Uncle Brandon leaving you Kimberly Hall and the fiasco surrounding all that, but why exactly Sophie Stanton-Greville doesn't want to be here with you as your wife, why she ran out of your bedchamber, seemingly terrified."

"It isn't a very uplifting story, Douglas. There have been many men in her life and none of them were nice." God, he thought, what an as-inine thing to say. "That is," he amended care-fully, "the circumstances of Sophie and all these men weren't very nice."

"I understand perfectly. No, no, you don't have to strain yourself to be more equivocal. If you need me, Ryder, I'm here."

"Thank you, Douglas."

"The boy is delightful. Was he born with the clubfoot?"

"Yes, he was. He rides very well. Do you think he would survive at Eton?"

"Let's give him a while longer to adjust, I think."

"She hates sex. She hates me touching her."

Douglas simply looked at his brother.

"Damnation, but it's very complicated," Ryder

said, and plowed his fingers through his hair, making it stand on end. "I shouldn't speak so personally about my wife. The thing is she doesn't want me, never did want me. I manipulated her into marrying me. Can you imagine that? Me being the one to want to marry? Me, forcing a woman to marry me? But I did it and I'm not sorry for it. She didn't want to marry any man."

Douglas waited, saying nothing, until finally, "This is passing strange. If you wish to speak more about it, I'm always here. Now, I must tell you — Emily had twins. Unfortunately neither of them survived. She is looking forward to seeing you. She said something Hollis didn't completely understand, something about it being better this way because it wasn't fair, that she hadn't wanted to do this to you."

"I will see her as soon as I can."

"Do you understand what she meant?"

Ryder simply shrugged and looked out the window.

Douglas picked up a singularly beautiful black onyx paperweight and tossed it from one hand to the other. "I suppose you've decided what to do about all your women and your children."

"Yes, I've given it a lot of thought. There wasn't much else to do coming home."

"What, no available ladies on board ship?"

Ryder gave him an austere look.

"Just remember, Ryder, your life before you married Sophie was yours and you were free to do whatever pleased you. As was mine."

Ryder gave his brother a crooked smile. "I doubt she'd even care if I paraded a hundred women in front of her nose. She'd probably beg them to keep me away from her."

"One never knows about a wife, even one who appears to want to slit one's throat. Sophie just might surprise you, that is, if she does find out about all the other women."

"Ha."

Douglas pulled a sheet of foolscap out of the drawer of his desk. "Your most recent tally is seven children." He stopped, and stared at his brother. "You know all that. You've evidently decided what you will do about it."

"Yes, I have. I'm a married man now. There will be no other women."

The earl sat back in his chair. "I'm pleased you've decided to be faithful to your wife. Keeping a herd this size content would tax even the strongest man. Fidelity does have its advantages."

"I agree," Ryder said, then appeared startled at what he'd said. "I can't believe that I agree, but I do. Wanting only one woman is a startling revelation. But I want Sophie and only Sophie. Good Lord, it's rather unbelievable, I know, but there it is."

"For what it's worth, I've also discovered that a wife is very precious. A wife is beyond anything I had ever imagined in my life."

"Alex is a good sort. I'm relieved you worked things out."

"Oh, we did and therein lies a tale. Some long night this winter I'll tell you about it. It certainly would be more enlivening than writing about that damned ghost, the Virgin Bride." The earl rose. "I would say, old man, that you have quite a task ahead of you. On the other hand, nothing of true importance should come easily."

"I already appreciate her, if that's what you're getting at. It's odd but I truly do. She's important to me, more important than you can begin to imagine. You told me once that I thrived on challenges, the higher the stakes, the better I did. I won't lose this one, Douglas. I can't."

"You love her, then."

"You spout nonsense, Douglas. Love — a notion that makes me want to puke. No, pray don't go on and on about how much you adore and worship Alex — I see quite clearly that you're besotted with her. But love? Don't get me wrong. I like Sophie, certainly. I want her and she makes me feel things I've never felt before. I want her to be happy. I want her to realize that for whatever reason, she is important to me. There's nothing more to it than that and, indeed, that's quite enough. She's got me for life."

Douglas simply looked at his brother, a very black eyebrow arched upward a good inch.

"You haven't seen her as I did on Jamaica. You think her unhappy, a quiet mouse, no doubt. She's a hellion, Douglas. I wanted to tame her, wanted to make her submit to me." He shook his head and began pacing again. "I wish the hellion would come back." He grinned. "She was a handful and a more mouthy chit you'd never meet."

Douglas still just looked at his brother.

Sophie was smiling like an idiot, she couldn't help it. Her own mare, Opal, was here at Northcliffe, brought back from Jamaica by Ryder. She leaned over and patted her mare's long neck.

"Ah, I have missed you," she said, and threw back her head, letting her mare gallop ahead. She'd thanked Ryder, too shocked at what he'd done to really show him how much she appreciated it. He wasn't acting like himself again. It was disturbing, this kindness of his, this seemingly endless understanding and gentleness.

Ryder had shrugged and said only, "She would have eaten her head off if I'd left her at Camille Hall. She was fat and lazy and gave me these woeful looks every time I saw her. She neighed all the time I was around and soon it sounded remarkably like your name. What was I to do?"

And she'd said only, once again, "Thank you."

Ryder rode beside her, pleased at her pleasure, knowing that he'd surprised her but good. She owed him. He wondered how she would proceed to repay him, for repay him she would. He knew her well enough to know that she'd see this as a debt.

When she sent her mare into a gallop, he let her go ahead of him down the narrow country lane that bordered the northern boundaries of Northcliffe land. He slowed his own stallion, Genesis, a raw-boned barb who was black as sin and had the endurance of twenty Portuguese mules.

He began whistling. He was home, the day was glorious, warm, the sun bright overhead, and he'd pleased his wife. Things were looking up. He knew what he was going to do about his women and the solution was sound. As for his children, it was simply a matter of telling Sophie about them at the right time. He missed them. He would go see them all tomorrow. He'd brought back gifts for all of them.

Sophie rounded a narrow bend in the road and pulled over under the shade of an immense oak tree, old as the chalk cliffs just some miles to the south. She drew in a deep breath and realized she felt good. Ryder was behaving in a very civilized manner. Except for the previous night. That was reminiscent of the arrogant, utterly ruthless man she'd known on Jamaica. Perhaps today he'd realize that she didn't want him to touch her again, perhaps he'd simply be nice to her and remain civilized. She frowned.

She waited for him for some ten minutes, then turned to see if he were coming around the curve. There was no sign of him.

She fidgeted a moment longer, then wheeled Opal around and urged her back down the road. She felt a spurt of alarm. Could he have been hurt?

She saw Ryder. He wasn't at all hurt. There was a woman on a bay mare pulled to a halt next to him. They were in the middle of the road and they looked to be in intimate conversation. She saw the woman stretch out her hand and lightly touch Ryder's sleeve. She saw Ryder smile, even from here, she saw his white teeth in that utterly devastating smile of his. He then leaned closer to the woman.

Something in her moved and twisted. Something in her rebelled and boiled. Her jaw clenched. Her gloved hands fisted on Opal's reins.

Without thought, she jabbed her boots into Opal's fat sides and sent her straight toward her husband and the hussy who looked ready to leap onto his horse's back and onto his lap.

Ryder looked up and saw Sophie galloping *ventre à terre* straight at him. The look on her face was grim and pale. Jesus, she looked fit to kill. He grinned like a fool. He'd at first been uneasy when Sara had flagged him down. Now, seeing his wife ride toward him angry as a wasp, he was glad Sara had come. Anger bespoke feelings other than indifference.

Sara was speaking to him. She hadn't yet seen the madwoman bearing down on them. She was asking in that soft, gentle way of hers if he wouldn't like to kiss her. She leaned toward him and he felt her sweet mouth on his cheek, her gloved hand on his chin, trying to turn him toward her. He opened his mouth to tell her to stop, then shut it again. No, let Sophie see another lady kissing him. Her mouth was smooth and fresh but he felt nothing but anticipation to see what Sophie would do. His wife was on them then, and he had to jerk his stallion back so she wouldn't slam into them. As for Sara, she looked at the woman and actually paled.

"Just who the devil are you?"

It was Sophie's voice and Ryder hadn't heard that tone for more than two months. It was cold and angry and arrogant and he loved it. There was fire in her eyes.

"Damn you, keep away from my husband!"

"Your *what?*" Poor Sara was trying to make her mare back up but the beast was eyeing Opal with fascination and refused to move.

"You heard me! What are you saying to him? Why did you touch him? How dare you kiss him! Keep your blasted fingers and hands to yourself — and your miserable hussy mouth!"

Sara blinked. She turned from the woman to Ryder, who was lazily sitting his stallion, his eyes on the woman's face. He was smiling. His eyes were gleaming. He looked arrogant, naturally, Ryder was the most arrogant beast she'd ever known, but there was no cynical glimmer in his blue eyes, no, just pleasure and she didn't understand it. Goodness, if his eyes had been dark, they would have looked wicked. "She is your wife, Ryder?"

He turned to Sara then and nodded. "I was about to tell you but she rode down on us like one of the damned Greek Furies. Sophie, draw in your claws. This is Sara Clockwell and she is a friend of mine. Sara, my wife, Sophie."

It was at that instant that Sophie realized what she'd done. She'd acted like a shrew, a jealous, possessive termagant. She'd yelled and cursed and insulted this woman. And Ryder loved it. He looked very smug and satisfied and she'd just given him more fodder than a five-acre wheatfield needed. She felt humiliated; she felt exposed and very uncertain of herself and what she was and why she'd behaved as she had.

She nodded to the woman, silent as the grave now, a very lovely young woman with large breasts and an uncertain smile on a wide mouth. She said to her husband, her voice stiff as a fence post, "I am sorry to disturb your conversation with your *friend*. Since you haven't seen each other for quite a few months, I will leave you alone to renew yourselves." She wheeled Opal around and rode away fast as the wind.

Ryder merely smiled after her, the wickedness alive and thriving in his eyes. Douglas had been right about Sophie surprising him. It was beyond wonderful. Sweet heavens, he felt a surge of hope.

"Your wife, Ryder?"

He didn't hear hurt in her voice, just utter disbelief. He turned to look at Sara's bewildered face. "Yes, she is. I met her on Jamaica and wed her there. We have been separated until just yesterday. She's a hellion, isn't she? She speaks her mind openly. Forgive her but she is possessive of me. I like that, you know." He rubbed his hands together in pleasure.

"You . . . you like that?" Sara managed, still trying to grasp this beyond-odd situation. "You have never wanted a woman to be possessive.

Why, Beatrice told me that —" Her voice broke off and she blushed.

Ryder's left eyebrow shot up. "You and Bea? Come, tell me the truth, Sara."

"Bea told me that you hated any sort of clinging or orders or demands from a woman. She said you hated for a woman to be serious, to bedevil you, to . . . well, she did also say that you were honorable and a woman could trust you. She said you were lighthearted and fun, that you only enjoyed women in your bed. She said you were always generous with pleasure and I told her I knew that for a fact."

Ryder was silent for a long moment. So his mistresses discussed him, did they? It made him feel rather strange. Of course men discussed their mistresses, but that was the way of things. But women discussing him? He said finally, his voice very quiet, "Bea was wrong. Sophie is strong-willed and I fancy my days of freedom with other ladies are well over."

"You don't mind, truly?"

He grinned at her.

"But I wanted to see you, to tell you that —"

"That what, Sara?"

She said on a rush, "That I am going to marry David Dabbs. He's a farmer near Swinley."

"Congratulations. Then, I take it, you have no more use for me?"

She shook her head uncertainly, and decided it was her best course to essay a laugh. Sara had never been able to laugh when she was supposed to. But it hadn't seemed to bother Ryder. He'd always adored her breasts and her ears, he'd tell her in the next breath, even as he pumped into her, soft little ears that tasted like plums and peaches. She hadn't understood him, but she'd had more pleasure with him than she expected to share with the dour David. But a husband was a husband, and they lasted until they died, they had no choice in the matter, and now even Ryder was one. It was amazing; it was unbelievable, but he looked quite pleased about it. And this wife of his was possessive.

Only now he was frowning.

"You must go after her, Ryder. She is angry that she saw us together. She is angry that I was kissing you and that you were, well — there it is."

Ryder turned to grin at her. She sounded pleased that his wife was jealous of her. He enjoyed her show of vanity. Perhaps one day, Sophie would be just a bit transparent so that he wouldn't have to flay his mind to constantly outguess her. He leaned over and kissed Sara's cheek. "I wish you luck with your David, Sara. Good-bye."

Ryder didn't ride after his wife. He turned Genesis back toward Northcliffe. A wife should have to stew in her jealous juices once in a while. He certainly had no intention of apologizing to her for Sara or any of the others. Ah, what was she doing now?

He was whistling as he dug his heels into his stallion's sides.

CHAPTER 16

Sophie returned to the hall an hour later. She felt like a fool. She wanted to kick herself. She didn't, quite simply, understand why she'd done it. She left Opal with a huge bucket of oats in the stable, spoke with the head stable lad, McCallum, a man who was crusty and likable and looked at her just like he would a horse, then walked toward the mansion. She stopped suddenly, disbelieving, shading her eyes from the bright sun. No, it couldn't be true. Not again. There, standing on the deep-set front steps, was a young woman, a very pretty young woman with very black hair. Ryder was standing on the step above her. She was leaning into him and her hand was on his right arm. He was speaking quietly to her and she was nodding. Sophie's stomach churned and her jaw locked for the second time that afternoon. All rational thought fled her brain.

She shrieked, waving her fist at her husband, "You damnable rotter!" She picked up her skirts and ran toward them, unable to stop either her feet or the words that flew out of her mouth.

"How dare you! Get away from my husband. If you try to kiss him, I'll break your arm!"

Tess Stockley froze. Then, because she wasn't stupid, she took a quick step back. "My God, who is she, Ryder? She looks like a madwoman. I don't understand . . . is she another one of your women? This is very strange, Ryder. Why is she so angry? Surely she knows she's just one of your women."

Ryder didn't reply. He was watching Sophie dash toward them, her hands holding up her skirts so that she could run without fear of tripping. He was enjoying the view of her ankles and the look of utter outrage on her face. Her hair was coming loose from its thick bun and thick tendrils were straggling down about her face. Her charming borrowed riding hat fell to the dirt.

A madwoman indeed — his madwoman. What marvelous timing. His Sherbrooke luck had returned. He crossed his arms over his chest, his heart speeding up in anticipation. Normally his women didn't come to Northcliffe Hall, but Tess had worried because he'd been so long in coming home. Bea had told her to stop her fretting because Ryder was like a cat, he always landed on his feet. But she'd come anyway, and she'd been near to tears when she'd seen him safe, and she was so happy to see him . . . then this strange girl was screaming at them.

Ryder's jaws ached from smiling so widely. He yelled out, "Hello, Sophie. Did you stable Opal? Did you feed her? You wish to say something to Tess? She's a friend of mine, you know. Do come and meet her. We were just talking of Jamaica and sea travel and —"

"You miserable bounder! Another one? How many women do you have? Are they all young and beautiful? By all that's sinful, you should be hung and shot and disemboweled! Why, I should —" Her voice swallowed itself. She paled. She shook her head and the bun fell to thick strands of hair, tangling down her back. "Oh no," she said, unable to believe herself. "I didn't just say that, did I?" She picked up her skirts again and ran away from the mansion toward the Greek statue–infested gardens. She just might enjoy those nude statues, Ryder thought, staring after her. Had she already seen them? He must remember to ask her. He thought of making love to her beneath a woefully bad marble rendition of Zeus seducing some swan or other.

He turned back to Tess, who was gazing with incredulous astonishment upon the fleeing Sophie. He said, smiling like a besotted fool, "She's my wife. Her name is Sophie Sherbrooke, and she's very possessive of me. You must keep your distance from her."

"Your *what?*"

Ryder knew a moment of irritation. Was his marrying such a bloody shock? Such a cause for disbelief?

"My wife, dammit. Now, Tess, since I am a married man, I must tell you that I cannot see you again. However . . ." He paused then smiled.

"We have had much enjoyment together, you and I. But now it must stop. Do you think perhaps you would like to wed in the near future?"

She stared at him as if he had two heads. "But you love women, Bea says you need a variety, and —"

"What is Bea, your mother superior? Does she invite all of you over for tea parties to pour advice down your gullets? No, don't answer that. Sophie is my wife. Now, my dear, if you should perhaps like to consider getting yourself leg-shackled soon, why then, let me tell you about this very nice man in Southampton. He is the first mate on a barkentine, a solid man, quite admirable, really. Quite a manly man I should say, arms thick as an oak trunk."

Tess looked at him for a very long time. She said finally, "A girl should marry, I suppose. Sara says that husbands can belch and snore, but they'll stay because they have to. What is his name?"

Ryder told her. She was interested.

He felt very good as he walked into the huge entrance hall. He would have given a great deal of guineas to have been present at one of his mistresses' tea parties.

It was nearly midnight. Ryder rubbed the grit in his eyes with the heel of his hand and reviewed yet again the list he'd compiled during the voyage home. He was pleased. He leaned back in his chair and closed his eyes for a moment.

He pictured Sophie in their bed, probably still awake, probably afraid that he'd come to her and force her again and she'd be more vulnerable if she were asleep. But he hadn't gone to her and he wouldn't for a while yet. He'd keep her guessing. He had her there for he was as unpredictable as she was, his dear heart, and he knew it drove her quite mad. He'd said not a word about her behavior earlier in the afternoon. Not a single word. If there had been a knowing gleam in his eyes whenever he looked at her, well, that couldn't be helped. He'd been exquisitely polite. She'd gotten herself all puffed up, he recognized the signs, and for once she was completely transparent to him, and he'd simply sidestepped her with the ease of long and successful practice. He was well versed in the ways of women. And even Sophie, hide it as best she could, was still a woman. The presence of his talkative family was an unquestioned aid. He'd sent her to bed with a nod and a pat on the cheek. She'd looked three parts furious with him and another three parts bewildered. It was promising.

He shook himself and penned down another name on the foolscap. Joseph Beefly. Miserable last name, but the man was nice and steady, and a girl could do much worse for a husband. He did have a bit of a paunch, but on the other hand he didn't drink too much and he didn't abuse women. His breath wasn't offensive and he bathed often enough. He rather thought that Emily would do well with Joseph. As Sara had said, Tess her echo, a husband, after all, was a husband, and had to, perforce, stay put. Ryder paused for a moment to stare pensively into the wispy flame cast out by the single candle at his left elbow.

The list he'd compiled was impressive and he'd managed to add a couple more names. Alongside each woman's name he listed at least four men's names. It was a good thing he'd lived here all his life. He knew nearly everyone within a fifty-mile radius. So many men, thank the good Lord. Choice was important. The good Lord knew, too, that not all the women would want husbands. But he wanted to be certain each of them was well taken care of. He would naturally provide them all with dowries if they wished to wed. Those who didn't — well, they would get dowries too. He wondered if he should also compile a list of possible protectors to be found in London. No, it was too crass, far too crude for a polished sort like him.

He thought of his children then and smiled. They were a constant in his life and would always remain so. He didn't doubt for a moment that there would be more. Lord, he missed them. He anticipated the following day with pleasure.

Finally, having tired of his list and of making Sophie writhe in uncertainty, he rose and stretched. He blew out the candle. He knew every inch of Northcliffe and had no need to light his way.

Sophie wasn't asleep. She was sitting up in bed, staring toward the far corner of the bedchamber.

Ryder quickly lit a candle and quietly approached the bed. At first she didn't pay him any heed. Then she turned and he saw that her face was pale, her eyes dilated, and she blinked into the candlelight.

He frowned down at her. "What's the matter? Did you have a nightmare?"

She shook her head. He stared a moment at all that tousled thick hair that fell onto her face and over her shoulders. She ran her tongue over her lips. Her hands fisted at the covers at her waist. "I think I just met your Virgin Bride."

"Excuse me?"

"The Virgin Bride — the Sherbrooke ghost. I guess Sinjun was right, she wanted to welcome me to your blasted family. Maybe."

"Bosh. You had a strange dream, nothing more."

Sophie just shook her head. She'd been afraid at first, very afraid, but then the young woman, a ghost presumably, had merely looked at her, and she would have sworn that she spoke, but she knew she hadn't because she'd been looking at her face and her lips hadn't moved. But she knew she heard her soft voice clearly saying softly, but with absolute conviction, "Don't worry. Even when they come it will be all right."

"Who?" Sophie had said aloud. "Please, what do you mean?" The young woman had shimmered in the dim light that hadn't really been there, just shimmered and retreated, quickly, yet there hadn't been any real movement, nothing jerky,

349

just the quiet grace of the still air. She'd seen her clearly yet the bedchamber was dark, too dark to make out the details she knew she'd seen. Then she was simply gone, her hand stretched out toward Sophie, just as Ryder had come into the room.

"Sophie, there's no such thing as the damned Virgin Bride. It's a simple legend. Sinjun is a fanciful girl — it wouldn't surprise me if she occasionally plays the blighted young lady just to tease us. No, you dreamed her up."

"No I didn't. She spoke to me, Ryder, only she didn't, not really, but I heard her, and the words were very clear."

He was caught, he couldn't deny it. He set the candle on the tabletop beside the bed and sat down beside her, not touching her. "What were the words she didn't really say?"

"She said that I wasn't to worry, that even when they come it will be all right."

He frowned at that. Such a message was unexpected. He'd rather thought the words would hark to some sort of secret treasure or some such. Perhaps that Sophie would bear twins and they would grow up to wed English royalty.

"What the hell does that mean? Who are 'they,' for God's sake?"

"I asked her but she just disappeared. Then you came in. I think you chased her away."

"Nonsense."

Sophie turned to him, frowning, then realized that she was in her nightgown and he was sitting next to her, fully dressed, thank God, but still. He was here, sitting on the bed, and he was her husband. She forgot the ghost and the message. She forgot her lamentable behavior of the afternoon. She even forgot, for the moment, those two very lovely young women. She very slowly began to move away from him until she was on the edge of the other side of the bed.

Ryder pretended not to notice. He rose, stretched, and began to take off his clothes.

She wouldn't watch him this time, she wouldn't. She said, "What have you been doing? It's quite late."

"Ah, just a bit of this and that."

"You were with one of your legion of women, weren't you?"

"Legion? No more than a small battalion. I'm only one man, Sophie, no matter how much you stand in awe of my strength and vigor."

"I don't care. Your claims to such prowess is absurd. You are jesting with me, mocking me, and I don't like it. Keep a hundred women, nay, five hundred. It matters not to me."

"Are you certain about that, Sophie? You saw only two today and you went really quite charmingly mad."

She looked at him. He was naked. He was just standing there on the other side of the bed, quite without a stitch of clothing on. He was tall and lean and very nicely formed, she would give him that. She looked furtively toward the bedchamber door.

"No, no more races down the corridor. I prefer to be the only man to see you wearing only your beautiful hide."

"It was very embarrassing. It was difficult to face your brother today."

"I imagine that it was. However, perhaps Douglas is excessively myopic. Now, just to clear the air between us, I know that you've wanted to box my ears all evening. Please feel free to box metaphorically, to express your heartfelt rage, to expound freely on your woman's ire."

"You would like that, wouldn't you? You would enjoy me squawking like a fool so it would make you feel important. Men like to have women fighting over them, they like to be the center of everything. Well, I will tell you, Ryder Sherbrooke, I felt nothing! Absolutely nothing, less than nothing. It was merely that I felt angry for your brother. It must be beyond embarrassing for the earl to have all these women hanging about Northcliffe Hall, hanging on your arm and whispering nonsense into your ears and kissing you."

"Really? That sounds very rehearsed to me. Not bad, don't misunderstand me. Just practiced, perhaps a dozen times." He scratched his belly and her eyes followed every movement of his long fingers. He wasn't all that hairy, but the thick light brown hair at his groin . . . she managed to look back to his face. He knew she'd been looking at him, he knew, but he said only, "Goodness, so you wish me to believe that all your curses at me were in defense of my poor beleaguered brother's sensibilities?"

Sophie knew she was digging a hole that would eventually reach to China if she didn't stop now. She tightened her lips until it hurt. She just shook her head.

"It pleases me that you've found a bit of control. But, my dear wife, if you wish to continue to rant, please do, I don't mind."

"Go to the devil," she said, then concentrated on keeping her mouth shut.

Ryder raised his arms and stretched. She was looking at him again and he knew it, and his sex swelled quite predictably, there was nothing he could do about it. She stared at him for a very long time, then jerked, as if finally realizing what she was doing. She looked away, toward the windows.

"You quite terrified both Sara and Tess," he said, dumping a bit of oil into the fire. "They couldn't accept at first that I would enjoy a possessive, quite jealous wife."

She managed not to take the bait.

He smiled at the back of her head as he stepped to the bed. He pulled back the covers and climbed in.

She felt the bed give and knew if she were going to run it had to be now.

"Don't, Sophie."

"Don't what, you wretched bounder?"

"Try to run again. I locked the bedchamber door."

This was ridiculous. She knew it and so did

he. She closed her eyes a moment, then slowly she turned to face him. "Ryder," she said, "I don't want you to force me again. Please don't shame me or make me beg you."

"Lie down, Sophie. On your back."

She shook her head.

"Now, if you please. If you're good to me, I will tell you a story. Would you like that?"

"No," she said, but she lay down.

"Good." He leaned over her, looking down, studying her face. A beautiful face to him. He touched his fingertip to the tip of her nose. "I'm very glad you're here," he said.

"Why?"

"Because you're you and I managed quite by a wonderful stroke of luck to find you and I even had the good sense to marry you."

"That's absurd. I'm nothing, when will you admit it? You were simply caught up in a series of very strange happenings. You felt sorry for me, finally, nothing more. Your mother despises me. I don't belong here. Please, Ryder —"

"I was thinking about that," he said slowly, and his fingers continued to lightly touch her jaw, her nose, her mouth. "About not belonging here. You're right."

She froze, a blaze of unexpected pain going through her.

"No, no, you misunderstand. This isn't your home. Alex is the mistress here, though I imagine she must fight my mother to gain what she wishes, the poor girl. No, this isn't your home. I have a home, Sophie, in the Cotswolds, not far from Strawberry Hill. That's where my cousin, Tony Parrish, and his wife, Melissande, live."

"You have a home?"

"I've never lived there. It's called Chadwyck House. I visit it three or four times a year. There is a good deal of farm acreage and there are some twenty tenant families living there. I have a steward — a fellow named Allen Dubust — who deals with the daily affairs." He paused, frowning a moment. "I'm beginning to believe that a man should deal with his own affairs. What do you say, Sophie? Shall we go to Chadwyck House? Would you like to be the mistress of your own home?"

Her eyes had lightened. He wasn't mistaken about that. There was pleasure there that temporarily had tamped down her fear of him.

"Yes," she said only. She opened her mouth but he lightly touched his fingers over her lips.

"No, my dear, I know you would like to ask me all sorts of questions to keep me from making love to you. We will speak more of Chadwyck House afterward."

"I want you to stop reading my mind before I have a chance to do it properly for myself."

"I have this affinity for you. I can't seem to help myself. Now, Sophie, I want you to do me a favor."

She stared up at him, frozen and wary.

"I am your husband. I won't ever hurt you. I have your best interests at heart. Nod your head if you at least understand what I've said."

She nodded.

"Good, a healthy start. I want to make something else very clear to you. I will make love to you every night. I want you to become used to me, to trust me. I want to erase all the other men, I want you to simply dismiss all the meanness and violence of your uncle from your mind. I want you to think only of me, of us."

"It is very difficult."

"I know, but today you were a hellion again, a possessive wench, the savage Amazon who saved my hide in Jamaica from Thomas's knife. So I have hope. Now, let's get that nightgown off you. I want no clothes between us, Sophie, not at night, not when we're alone. I want to look at you. I want to feel your breasts in my hands."

"Ryder, I really don't want —"

"I don't give a good damn, Sophie, so stop your bleating. Tonight, perhaps you will allow yourself to have some pleasure. I'm going to kiss you, every sweet inch of you. I will never give up on you, so you might as well accustom yourself to coming about to meet me halfway."

He kept talking, nonsense really, some of it quite amusing, and he would have given anything for a simple smile from her. But she just lay there, silent and withdrawn. She didn't fight him, but she held herself stiff, her hands fisted at her sides. Ryder wanted to nibble on her toes, he wanted to taste the soft flesh between her thighs, but the woman who lay on her back beneath him wasn't about to give an inch. Oddly enough, he wasn't unduly disturbed: he hadn't lied to her. He would never give up. She didn't realize it yet but they would be together until they shucked off their mortal coils. "I see I will have to wait a while longer to kiss every white inch of you." He did kiss her breasts, enjoying the taste of her, the texture of her flesh, and his hands were on her belly, and then lower, his fingers finding her and lightly stroking her. She tried to pull away. He stopped. It was a beginning.

Ryder wasn't about to enter her until she could take him without pain. He'd promised her and he wouldn't break his promise. No more savaging her as he'd done the previous night. He simply drew away from her, patted her cheek, and told her to stay put. He fetched a jar of cream from the night table beside the bed.

"What is that?" Her eyes never left his fingers, which were dipping into that jar.

"You will see. Hush."

He pushed her back down onto her back and held her there, his hand on her belly, pressing her thighs open with his legs, while he eased his slick finger inside her. He closed his eyes a moment at the feel of her. Dear God, he wanted her. He smoothed in the cream slowly and gently, his finger going more deeply into her, and then he inserted a second finger to widen her. It was almost more than he could bear. She was trembling and trying to pull away from him, but he held her still.

"Stop, damn you!" She tried to bring her legs together, but succeeded only in pushing his finger deeper inside her.

"Shush, sweetheart. No, I will use cream on you until you let me love you properly. Don't you like my finger sliding inside you, Sophie?"

"No."

"I like it very much. I will do it every time we make love. Get used to it. Ah, you're more yielding, Sophie. Can you feel it? You're softening for me though your active brain doesn't like it."

When he'd widened her, when he had made her soft and ready, he came over her. Very slowly, he came into her, controlling his entry, watching her face in the candlelight. There was no pain, he knew it, and he knew that she wouldn't ever be able to throw that up at him again. He also knew that he wouldn't be able to bring her to pleasure this time either. What was important was that her body begin to recognize him, that when he touched her, she would eventually respond without her mind trying to dismiss him.

He would have her yet. Patience was all he needed. He stroked deeply into her now, then pulled nearly out of her. He continued slowly, every feeling in him attuned to her. It suddenly occurred to him that he was behaving quite differently with Sophie than he had with every other woman in his male life. Before, when he'd come into a woman, he'd known almost instant irreversible lust. He couldn't have stopped if a tidal wave had swamped him. But not with Sophie. She was at the center of all his feelings. His body, his mind, both were focused entirely on her. He would do anything to bring her around and he didn't care how long it took him to succeed. He would win. His own body would wait. Another novel occurrence, and one Douglas would doubtless disbelieve.

He remembered his brother's joke about having his valet sew his britches shut because Ryder couldn't stop once he'd begun, he couldn't make himself withdraw from a woman. With Sophie it was different, simply because he was different.

He wished he could make her laugh. He lightly caressed his fingers over her belly, down, to find her again. He teased her soft woman's flesh, nothing more, just teased and stroked. Soon she would respond to him. And he kissed her and didn't stop kissing her.

He found his release eventually, but he didn't yell like a wild man. He moaned his pleasure into her mouth, holding her close to him, letting her feel the movement of his sex deep inside her, letting her feel the heat of his body.

He was amazed at himself and pleased. It was a start. She was lying there, but this time there were no tears. If he wasn't mistaken, she looked surprised. Exactly about what, he wasn't sure. He continued kissing her until he eased off her. Then he pulled her against him, stroked her hair, massaged her scalp, and said quietly, "Now I will keep my promise. Remember? I said I would tell you a story if you were good to me. You did well, Sophie. You will do better the next time and the next time after that. Now, this story is about a one-legged pirate who found himself marooned with three lusty women. The first woman's name was Belle and she was a strapping girl, all breasts and wide hips. Well, she fell instantly in love with him — of course he was the only man she'd seen in a good three months. She flung him onto the beach and ripped off his clothes. But then the second woman came along — her name was Goosie — and she saw that wooden leg and knew this was the man for her. Her favorite hobby was carving wood into ships and such. She'd carved up a good dozen palm trees during those long three months. So the two women were arguing and shouting at each other and the pirate was lying there quite naked and grinning like an ape at his good fortune, when the other woman — her name was Brassy — came along. You wouldn't believe what she did."

Sophie gave out a loud snort, then settled into snoring.

"Very well, you don't as yet appreciate my stories. Tomorrow night I'll continue with my tale, and you'll learn what Belle and Goosie and Brassy all did to this poor one-legged pirate."

He kissed her forehead, and whispered against her damp flesh, "Perhaps tomorrow night you might like to put the cream on your hand and slick it over me. What do you think?"

She said quite clearly, "No. I would rather cosh your thick head and heave you and all your damned women into the sea."

"On the other hand," he continued, pleased as a rooster turned free in the hen yard, "perhaps tomorrow night we won't need the cream. I'm an optimist, and I'm your husband."

"How many women do you have? How many mistresses?"

"More than three, at least I did. They're all in the past now."

She stiffened.

"That was the first thing I heard when I arrived in Montego Bay. You had three lovers. Well, I have known more women than you were reputed to have known men. I won't lie about that. It was before I'd met you and wanted you and married you."

"I don't care if you keep them all."

It was such an obvious lie that he merely leaned down and kissed the tip of her nose.

"You're beautiful," he said.

"You're the one who is myopic, not your damned brother."

"Ah, a bit of vinegar, a dab of testiness. Let's get some sleep. I fancy that I will wake you up early in the morning. You'll be all sweet and warm with sleep, Sophie, and I'll come inside you, and it will be slow and gentle and you will enjoy it. At least a bit."

She said not a word. Ryder didn't despair.

When he awoke the next morning and reached for her, she was gone. Well, hell, he thought. He wouldn't tell her of his fond plans again.

"Alex," Ryder said to his sister-in-law the following morning at the breakfast table. "I would appreciate you taking Sophie around to meet our neighbors. As for a ball, let's wait a while for that."

"Ah, so you realize this girl won't do well with all our illustrious friends."

Ryder merely smiled at his mother. She had come armed to the breakfast table, and she'd fired her opening salvo immediately. "No, not at all," Ryder said easily. "On Friday, Sophie and I are going to our own home, to Chadwyck House."

There was instant pandemonium at the table. "You can't mean it!"

"Goodness, Ryder, you just got home! This is your home!"

And from Douglas, nothing, merely a smile, nearly hidden as he slowly sipped his coffee.

Alex said slowly, her voice instantly quieting the voices, "That gives us two days, Sophie. There is also the matter of clothes for you. We don't have much time."

It was at that instant that Sophie realized Jeremy wasn't smiling. He was staring down at his plate.

Again, Ryder, the bounder, seemed to know exactly what was going on. He knew exactly what to do. He said easily, "Well, Jeremy, I hope you don't mind staying for a couple of weeks here at Northcliffe Hall. I know Sinjun can be the very devil, a veritable nodcock, but if you think you can abide her for a while, then you may remain here."

Jeremy shot a guilty look at his sister. Sophie forced a smile. "It's up to you, Jeremy."

"Sinjun's going to take me to Branderleigh Farm to buy a pony," he burst out, half guilt, half unmistakable excitement.

And that was that. Sophie found out from Sinjun that Ryder was paying for the pony.

During that day and the next two days, while Sophie was meeting all their neighbors, and being fitted for new clothes, Ryder was visiting his former lovers. Of course they all already knew he was married. Bea had called a meeting. Three of the five women were interested in marrying. He presented the names on his list and left them each to ponder the good points of each man. Emily was still in bed, recovering from childbirth, but she would mend and he even made her smile twice. The other two wanted to go try their luck in London. He gave them money and wished them luck. As for Bea, he simply shook his head when she opened the door of her cottage to him just after luncheon.

"Busy Bea," he said, and hugged her. "I swear you would do me in if you weren't so fond of me."

"Good thing for you that I am, Master Ryder!"

She loved to call him master, it was one of her favorite fantasies. Bea had great common sense and the most unusual preferences of any woman he'd ever known.

"I hear you've visited all your women and presented them with possible husbands."

Ryder rolled his eyes as he followed her into her small pristine drawing room. "Would you care to peruse the list for yourself?"

"Oh, not me, sir. I'm off to London to make my fortune, just like Laura and Molly. Actually, I think I'll ask Emily to come with me. The last thing she needs to do is fall into a decline. That's when a female is most vulnerable. I'll make certain she doesn't fall into the clutches of another despotic man. It's a boardinghouse I'm thinking about, Master Ryder, all my own. I've saved enough money, you know. You're a generous man, but still a man. I will remain my own woman and I will find another lover as polished as you are."

She ground to a halt and he picked up her hand and brought it to his lips. "There are no other men to be found who are as polished as I am."

She laughed and punched his arm.

"Now, my dear, I don't want you owning just any boardinghouse, no, I want you to buy a property in a very good section of London. I will give you the name of the Sherbrooke solicitor in London and he will see to it for you. Also, you will get a boardinghouse dowry from me."

"You will miss me, Ryder."

"Oh yes. I most certainly will. Wish me luck

with my new wife, Bea."

"You need luck with a woman?"

"More than you know. I've met my match."

As Ryder rode away from Bea's cottage, he wondered if perhaps Sophie would enjoy playing slave girl to his master. Perhaps he could bring her around to it by November. Yes, the days would be shorter then and it would be chilly outside. It would mean long hours in front of the fireplace. He pictured her wearing soft veils, her hair long down her back, teasing him, and he would have her dance for him, like Salome. It would lead to laughter, this kind of play, and to passion. Then he wondered what the ghost had meant by "when they come . . ."

CHAPTER 17

Ryder's last stop of the afternoon was at Jane Jasper's spacious three-story house just outside of the small village of Hadleigh Dale that lay seven miles east of Northcliffe Hall. The house and drive were surrounded by oak and lime trees, thick and green now. He heard his children yelling and laughing before he saw them. He smiled in anticipation as he turned Genesis onto the short drive and dug his heels into his stallion's sides.

Jane and her three helpers, all young women with immense energy and goodwill, all of whom he'd selected himself, were standing in the front yard watching the children play. There were four boys and three girls, all between the ages of four and ten. They were well clothed, clean, loud, and Ryder felt such pleasure at the sight of them that he wanted to shout.

He saw Oliver standing a bit off to the side, a tall, thin boy of ten, leaning on his crutches, but there was a grin on his face as he shouted advice to Jaime, all of six years old and full of male bravado, on how to smash the grit out of

Tom, a cherub-faced little boy who could curse more fluently than a Southampton sailor. John, the peacemaker at only eight, a barking spaniel nipping at his heels, was trying to keep them from coming to blows.

Jaime spotted Ryder first and let out a yell. The instant Ryder dropped Genesis's reins and turned, he was nearly brought to the ground by flying arms and legs, and three dogs all leaping and barking madly.

They were all shouting, laughing, all of them talking at once, telling him what they'd done during his absence, all except Jenny, of course, who hung back, her thumb in her mouth. Her mop of dark brown curls shadowing her small face, her ribbon long gone. Ryder gave his full attention to the children, trying to answer all of them at once. He grinned at Jane over Melissa's small head as the little girl took her turn and hugged her skinny arms around his neck until he yelled with imagined pain, making all the children shout with laughter. He was listening to Jaime's near brush with a sunken log while learning how to swim when Jane and her helpers brought out glasses of lemonade and plates of cakes and scones. He sat in their midst, drinking his lemonade, tossing bits of scone to the dogs, listening to their stories, their arguments, all in all, enjoying himself immensely. Jenny sat quietly, two children away from him, slowly and methodically eating a small lemon cake.

After Ryder had distributed all their presents

and stepped back to witness them attack the wrapped packages with ill-disguised greed, he walked over to Jenny. She raised her small face, and her blue eyes — Sherbrooke blue eyes, light as the blue of a summer day — were wide and not quite so blank as he remembered. She smiled and he saw joy in her expression, he knew he wasn't mistaken.

"My little love," he said and kneeled down in front of her. He pulled her thumb from her mouth, ran his fingers through her soft hair, and then, very gently, brought her against his chest. The little girl sighed softly, and her arms crept around his neck. He kissed her hair, then closed his eyes, breathing in the sweet child scent of her. God, he loved her, this child of his loins and of his heart.

"She does better, Ryder. She is learning. She is more a part of things, she is more aware."

He didn't release his daughter as he looked up to see Jane standing just behind her.

"She misses you dreadfully whenever you're gone for any length of time, even more this time, which is a very good sign. She asked about you every single day."

"Papa."

Ryder froze. Jane smiled. "That is her surprise for you. She's been practicing. She has said 'papa' for the past two weeks, each time I've showed her that small painting of you."

"Papa."

For a moment, he felt his throat close. Then

he buried his face against her neck and felt her soft mouth against his face and she said again in a very satisfied voice, "Papa."

"I've brought you a present, pumpkin."

Her eyes lit up when he pulled the brightly wrapped package from his coat pocket.

Inside was a gold locket. Ryder showed her how to open the locket. On one side was a miniature painting of her and on the other a painting of her mother, who had died birthing her. Ryder remembered the birth, remembered his fear and the endless pain. He also remembered his joy when the small girl child finally came from her dead mother's body, and she was alive. Not completely whole, but alive, and that was all that had mattered to him.

Jane fastened the locket around Jenny's neck and immediately Jenny ran off to show her prize to Amy, a little girl of six who smiled a lot more now than she had five months ago. He heard Jenny yell, "Papa give! Papa give!"

"You're doing very well with her, Jane. You're doing well with all the children. God, I've missed them. I see Oliver's leg is much better. What does Dr. Simons say?"

"The bone is mending and he doubts Ollie will have a limp. He's a very lucky little boy. As for Jaime, the burn marks on his legs and back are completely healed. He's a smart one, Ryder. He reads every book you send over. He spends every shilling of his allowance on even more books. He is well known to Mr. Meyers, who

369

owns the bookshop in the village. As for Melissa, she's got quite a talent with watercolors. Amy wants to be an Italian soprano, God forbid."

Ryder nodded and smiled. He followed Jane to the wide porch and the two of them sat down, watching the children. He listened carefully as she told him of each child's progress, of each child's needs.

He couldn't seem to take his eyes off Jenny, who was now proudly displaying her locket to Melissa, who'd gotten a French doll and wasn't in the least jealous. Ryder knew the children understood that Jenny was his real child, but he doubted it meant much to them, even to Oliver, who sometimes seemed to Ryder to be older than he was.

"I hear you married," Jane said abruptly, her eyes searching his face, and he knew she hoped it was a false rumor.

He smiled. "Yes, I did. Her name is Sophie."

"It's a surprise. To me. To your other women as well, I imagine."

"You're wrong about that. Bea has a very busy tongue. I have visited with all of them."

She arched a thick black brow.

"I'm married now, Jane." His voice was austere as a vicar's and she marveled at it.

"And the children?"

"What do you mean?"

She looked off toward a small knot of boys, craned her neck and her ears, then shouted, "Tom, stop saying that horrible word! Oh Lord,

370

where do they hear such things? Don't curse! Particularly at John — you know he hates it."

Ryder, who knew Jane's worth, wasn't at all surprised when Tom shut his mouth, shrugged with a show of sublime indifference to keep his male pride intact, then turned to throw a ball to Oliver, who hit it expertly with one of his crutches. John, yelling, ran after the ball.

"What does your new wife think about the children?"

"I haven't told her."

"I don't suppose you've told your brother or your family yet either."

Her voice was tart but he just grinned at her. "It's none of their business," he said easily. "My sister knows, has known for a long time now. She keeps quiet though, for the most part. She refers to the children as my Beloved Ones."

"How did she find out?"

"The brat followed me here once, well over a year ago, and watched from the branches of that oak tree over there. Sinjun's smart. She will also keep her mouth shut." Ryder shrugged. "But as for the others, I've always felt that it's my business and mine alone, and that's how I will continue to feel. There is no reason for them to know. At least now since I'm married and made it clear to my brother that I will be the most faithful of husbands, I won't have to endure any more of his quarterly bastard meetings."

"Are you really certain about all this, Ryder? Fidelity just because you're married? It's not the way of your class, I understand."

"Perhaps that is true for many, but not for me. Ah, Jane, the earl has more faith in me than you appear to. He knows I will be faithful to my wife because he is besotted with his own and is firmly in the constancy corner. Thus, no more children, at least the way he looks at things. Poor fellow."

"At last you can quit your damned playacting."

"Now, Jane, not all of it is playacting."

"Ha, do I ever know that. Sara told me about a woman she'd met in the village. The woman knew who she was, asked how you were, and then proceeded to tell Sara that she'd first met you when you were sixteen. Then she gave Sara this vacuous smile. Just when did you begin, Ryder?"

Ryder frowned. "You will find no pot filled with gold at the end of that rainbow, Jane. Forget her, forget all of them. As for my wife, she will come around to believing me a faithful hound soon enough, I daresay. But not just yet. Actually, she's already met Sara and Tess, quite by accident." Ryder looked off toward the very green rolling hills in the distance, smiling. "She stews quite nicely. Sharp tongue in her mouth that I quite like. A wealth of curses that even Tom would appreciate. Hopefully I'll hear more out of her in the near future."

Jane gave him an odd look, saying slowly, "So, you don't see any reason for your family to change their opinion of you?"

"No reason at all. Why should I? They are all quite fond of me."

"You are purposely being perverse, Ryder. I don't understand you. You enjoy the reputation of a Lothario? You like being known as a womanizer, a satyr?"

"Haven't I earned it?"

"Yes, but that's not what I mean."

"I enjoy women, I always have. It's no secret. I know women, how they think, how they tend to feel about things. Ah, yes, Jane, even you. No, no, don't call me cynical again. But the children, well, that's quite different, as you well know. I have a feeling that what you really want to ask me is if I will forget about them now that I have my own family."

"You wouldn't do that precisely, but perhaps you wouldn't come to see them as much as you do now, which would be understandable, of course. It's just that I would hate to see them hurt."

"The children are my responsibility, and I love them. Nothing will change. I am taking my wife to the Cotswolds to my house there on the morrow. If there is any emergency, simply send a messenger to me there. It's quite near to Lower Slaughter, and only a day and a half away. Oh, incidentally, my wife has a little brother who's lame. Isn't that rather an odd coincidence?"

Jane just shook her head at him. If she were ten years younger, she herself would have very much enjoyed frolicking in Ryder Sherbrooke's bed. He had a way about him that drew women, a manner that had nothing to do with his good looks and well-formed body, a way that assured a woman he wouldn't ever be selfish or unheeding of her needs or of her wishes. As it was, they'd been friends since he was twenty years old, a young man wild as a storm wind, a young man who hated cruelty toward children even more than he loved making a woman scream with delight. Jane had been thirty at the time, filled with sorrow at the death of both her children in a fire, and frankly uncaring about her future. Ryder had, quite simply, saved her. He'd given her a year-old baby — Jaime — to care for. A baby, he'd told her in an unemotional voice, he'd happened to find dumped in a pile of garbage in an alley. He'd just chanced to hear a mewling sound and found him. A year later, he'd brought her Jenny, his own child. It was the first time she'd seen a sorrow to match her own.

She watched him as he rose, dusted off his britches, and went off to play with the children. She wanted to meet this wife of his.

Sophie was standing straight and still while Mrs. Plack, the seamstress from Rye, fitted a riding habit to her. It was a pale green wool with gold braid on the shoulders and Sophie agreed with Alex that it was very smart indeed.

But she couldn't help but fret about the cost of all the gowns and underthings and bonnets and slippers and now three — goodness, *three!* — riding habits. She fretted out loud. Alex merely shook her head and said, "Your husband's orders, my dear Sophie. Stop worrying. When I was first married to Douglas, he didn't want to buy me even a handkerchief. No, no more out of you. I have a feeling that all this largesse frightens you, that it represents something of a debt you will owe to Ryder, and that debt is growing with each article of clothing. Am I right?"

Sophie said not another word.

"Are you getting tired, Sophie?" Alex asked after another hour had passed.

Sophie shook her head for Mrs. Plack was working so hard, trying so much to please.

"Well, I am. Mrs. Plack is very nearly through with you. The clothes that aren't finished by the time you and Ryder leave for Chadwyck House I will have sent immediately to you."

"It is absurd," the Dowager Countess of Northcliffe said from the doorway.

Alex winked at Sophie. "What, ma'am?"

"That Ryder is taking this girl to Chadwyck House."

"This girl is his wife, ma'am."

"Just look at that shade of green. It makes her look quite bilious. Just how much of my son's money are you spending? I will have to tell him that you are greedy and that is why you married him."

Sophie said not a word, but she did close her eyes. She thought she heard Mrs. Plack snort.

"I think it goes charmingly with her complexion," said Alex.

"Ha," the dowager said. "You have no taste in colors either. 'Tis Douglas who selects all your clothes."

"You're right," Alex said easily. "I'm very lucky that Douglas is so splendid."

"Humph," the dowager said. "You don't fool me, miss, you weren't speaking about clothes."

"Well, Douglas is splendid when it comes to clothes as well. Except that he wants my necklines to touch my chin. He accuses me of flaunting if I can't touch my tongue to the top of my collar."

Sophie giggled.

The dowager looked aghast; she opened her mouth, then closed it again. However, she was made of stern stuff, and said after only four more seconds had passed, "I wonder why Ryder isn't here. Doesn't this girl consider him splendid?"

"Oh yes," Alex said quickly. "It's just there is so much to be done before they leave for Chadwyck House. Ah, ma'am, her name is Sophie, you know."

It was another five minutes before the dowager took herself off with nary a conciliatory word out of her mouth.

Alex rolled her eyes yet again, then rubbed her fingertips over her temples. "I never had a headache in my life until I met my mother-in-law."

It was another half hour before Mrs. Plack was

finished. She was quite pleased with the sum of money Master Ryder was paying her and was effusive in her thanks to Sophie.

Once they were alone, Alex jumped to her feet and rubbed her hands together. "Now, Sophie, why don't we go to the estate room and steal some of Douglas's brandy?"

Sophie stared at her sister-in-law. "Every time I think I'm beginning to know you, you say something I don't expect."

"That's what Douglas says."

"He's right," Sophie said. "Let's go."

It was the earl who found two giggling ladies sprawled out on the Aubusson carpet in the middle of the estate room an hour later, a depleted bottle of his prized French brandy on the floor between them. Alex was lying on her back, hugging her sides, laughing her head off. Sophie was on her stomach, twirling her hair around a finger, saying, "No, no, Alex, it's quite true. I'm not lying. The pirate really had only one leg and all three of the women wanted him, each for her own reason."

"But Goosie? You're making that name up, Sophie! You say she wanted to carve his wooden leg into a ship? That she'd already carved up a dozen palm trees?"

"Ah," the earl said, coming down to his haunches, "so Ryder told you about the one-legged pirate and his adventure on the island, hmmm?"

Sophie was drunk. If she hadn't been, she would have been so embarrassed she wouldn't have been able to face him for a good year. As it was, both she and Alex burst into fresh laughter, Sophie saying on a strangled breath, "So you know the story, do you? Tell us the ending, Douglas. Ryder didn't tell me yet and Alex really wants to know."

"Do you want to know?" Douglas asked his wife, who was now lying flat on her back, grinning up at him like a fool.

"Ryder made up those names — Goosie, indeed! And Brassy — 'tis too ridiculous."

Douglas raised his hand. "No, it's true, I promise." Douglas eyed the brandy bottle, then grinned down at his wife, leaning down to kiss her mouth. "No hope for it, I guess." He picked up Alex's snifter, filled it with brandy, and downed it. He set the bottle down, arranged himself cross-legged, and said, "Now, as to the story — Goosie was a very popular lady. Actually, she was the first one to escape off the island. She'd only begun to carve up the pirate's wooden leg. All she managed to carve was what looked like a keel. She went to St. Thomas with a crew of Dutchmen who were all blond and couldn't understand a word she said. But the captain, ah, he wasn't Dutch, he was a Dane and, of course, blond, but he understood the universal language, and that is one language that Goosie spoke quite fluently." He leaned down and kissed his wife again.

"You mean French, Douglas?"

"No, no, Alex," Ryder said from the doorway, "my brother is talking about love."

Sophie stared at her husband, stared at the

brandy bottle, then flopped over on her back, and closed her eyes. She moaned.

"May I join the party?" Ryder asked.

"You said you'd be busy all day," Sophie said, her eyes still tightly closed.

"I was. It's after five o'clock now."

"Here," Douglas said, and handed his brother the nearly empty brandy bottle.

But Ryder had no intention of getting drunk. Therein lay disaster for a randy man. He'd watched and listened from the doorway for a good ten minutes and had been charmed. Sophie was drunk. He'd heard her laugh, a sweet, merry sound that warmed him to his very toes. Hell, all of them were going to feel vile tomorrow, but that was many hours away. The hours Ryder wanted were those just ahead. He tilted up the bottle and pretended to drink the rest of the brandy, then carried the bottle over to the sideboard and fetched another.

"Tell us what happened to the one-legged pirate," Alex said. "Douglas doesn't know, I'm sure of it. I want to know about Brassy. Douglas keeps avoiding it and going on to other stories."

"Actually, Brassy's story is shown in the gardens."

"What are you talking about?" Sophie said, still not looking at him.

"There are statues hidden deep in the garden. Haven't you yet seen them, Sophie? They were brought over by our very own uncle Brandon — you know, the fellow who left me Kimberly

Hall. Let's go and I'll show you. Then you can come back and tell Alex."

"An excellent idea," the earl said, coming up on one elbow. Ryder saw that his brother wasn't at all drunk. What he was, the fraud, was enjoying himself immensely. He was running his fingers lightly over his wife's arm, then up her shoulder. He watched his brother's fingers lightly caress Alex's ear. Douglas was a cunning bastard, no doubt about it. Ryder grinned at him, then reached out his hand to take Sophie's. He pulled her to her feet, jerking hard at the last minute, and she came flying against him and he held her against his chest for a moment, before touching his fingertips to her chin, kissing her, then releasing her.

Sophie looked profoundly worried, and said even as she was weaving slightly, "Statues, Ryder? A statue of Brassy? How is that possible? Why Brassy and not Goosie?"

"You will see," Ryder said. "Douglas, take good care of your wife," he added, and led Sophie from the estate room. As he closed the door, he heard Alex giggle.

"I suppose this drinking orgy was brought on by something awesomely miserable?"

"Your mother," Sophie said.

"I quite understand."

"You will really show me Brassy?"

"I will show you whatever you want to see," he said.

When he led her onto the narrow paths of the

garden, trees planted so closely together that there was a thick green canopy over their heads, she said, "This is beautiful. I didn't know about that turn back there. Why is this hidden?"

"You'll see," Ryder said.

He watched her look at the first statue — entwined statues, actually. The woman was sitting on the man's thighs, her back arched, her marble hair hanging loose, and his hands were on her hips, frozen in place, half lifting her off his sex.

Sophie gasped. "This is just awful."

But she didn't sound as if she thought it awful. She sounded very interested. She was weaving a bit again and he put his arm around her and brought her close to his side. "He's inside her, Sophie, as you can see. Not a bad life for a statue. Frozen for all eternity in the throes of pleasure."

"That looks difficult."

"Nonsense. Would you like to try that or see some other statues? There's a good deal of variety."

She nodded, looked surprised that she'd nodded, then slipped her hand in his. Ryder felt a surge of lust that was wonderfully familiar, but he also felt a deep tenderness that made him frown. What he was doing was dishonest. He was taking advantage of her drunken state. Who cared?

He led her to the next exhibition, this one very nearly hidden behind a half-dozen yew bushes. Sophie gasped but she never looked away.

"You would prefer this way, Sophie? It's a bit

381

difficult for a woman to find pleasure in this position, but I think I could manage it. Also, with a woman on her hands and knees, the man is very deep inside her. Ah, but his hands are free to roam, it's just that —" He broke off. "Let me show you."

She looked up at him, her eyes blurry, her voice sounding uncertain. "I don't think so, Ryder. I should like to see more. I would like to make my own selection, if you don't mind."

"No," he said, awed by his discovery of a very different wife, "I don't mind a bit."

He showed her all the other groupings. When they came to the one with the man between the woman's raised thighs, his head thrown back, his mouth yelling his release, she stopped cold and simply stared, saying nothing.

"You are a traditionalist then?"

She thought about that for a moment, then suddenly, she paled and swallowed convulsively. "Ryder," she said, "this isn't good." She pulled away from him, fell to her knees, and vomited.

"Well, hell," Ryder said.

Sophie wanted to die. Her mouth felt as if it were filled with foul-tasting cotton, her head pounded, and even the beating of her heart made her shudder.

Ryder had carried her back to the house and put her to bed. He met his brother in the upstairs corridor, and the two of them had laughed then sobered quickly.

"Is Alex in as bad shape as my wife?"

"Probably worse. I have the remedy. My only problem is getting Alex to drink it."

"We could trade wives if you liked just long enough to get the potion down their respective throats."

So it was that Ryder found Alex lying on her back, her arm over her eyes, not moving at all.

"Don't worry, Alex, it's just me, Ryder. Now, I'm going to raise your head and you're going to down every bit of this potion. You will feel like trouncing Douglas within the hour, I promise you."

Alex looked at her brother-in-law, so surprised that it wasn't her husband that she opened her mouth and drank.

It wasn't quite so simple for Douglas, but Sophie was very nearly beyond embarrassment with him, and thus only moaned once before drinking the vile potion.

The brothers met in the corridor. Douglas said, "Sophie's asleep now and will probably stay that way until tomorrow. Sorry, Ryder, you will just have to contain your lust tonight. Now, tell me how you're going to travel to Chadwyck House and what I can do to help you."

On a very foggy Friday morning, the Sherbrooke family was gathered outside the mansion to see off Ryder and Sophie. Ryder moved away from his wife when she held Jeremy against her.

"I will miss you, love," she said for the first

383

time. "Be a good boy, won't you? Your pony is wonderful and you must remember to take good care of him."

"His name is George, Sophie." Jeremy suffered all her advice because she was his sister, and he loved her, but at the end of it, he was beginning to squirm. Ryder saved him by lifting him up and saying, "Cosh Sinjun over the head every once in a while. She needs it. We will see you soon, Jeremy." He lowered the boy, shook his hand, and then assisted his wife into the carriage.

Three carriages bowled down the long drive. The second one held Tinker, Ryder's dour valet, and a young girl he'd insisted Sophie hire to train as her maid. She was painfully shy and her name was Cory.

The third carriage held mountains of luggage, most of it Ryder's.

"This is very difficult," Douglas said, staring after the carriages. He turned to smile at Jeremy, who had surreptitiously wiped a tear from his eye. "Ryder will take very good care of your sister, my boy. Don't worry. We'll all be together again soon."

As for Sophie, she didn't want Ryder near her, much less taking care of her. All she could think about were those utterly dreadful statues and staring at them and wanting Ryder to do all those things to her. It was beyond embarrassing and he knew exactly what she was thinking and how she was feeling.

"You're a bounder," she said aloud.

"And you are a traditionalist," he said, "despite everything you know about men. But you will want eventually to experiment with my poor man's body. You needn't worry that I'll forget any of the interesting positions of the statues in the garden."

"I wasn't thinking about those horrible statues. I hate it when you know what I'm thinking."

"Ah, perversity. Thank God I'm your husband. Otherwise you would spend all your time with me in the agony of mortification."

"I'm no more with child than I was in Jamaica."

Ryder wanted to cry, but he didn't. He grinned at her, patted her gloved hand, and said, "Perhaps there is something to having a harem. No need to have to put things off, you know."

Chadwyck House lay only five miles to the east of Strawberry Hill, the seat of the Viscount Rathmore, and very nearly in the middle between Lower Slaughter and Mortimer Coombe. Ryder had no idea if Tony Parrish and his beyond beautiful bride, Melissande, were still at Strawberry Hill or if Tony had taken Melissande to London. He really didn't care. They reached the Chadwyck House grounds by late afternoon.

"Have you ever before been to the Cotswolds, Sophie?"

"No. It's very beautiful."

"You're in for a treat. Just wait until October. The leaves are brilliant, the air crisp, and you want to cry it is so lovely."

But all thoughts of crying for loveliness fled Ryder's mind when the carriages bowled to a stop in front of Chadwyck House. He hadn't been here in close to a year he realized with a start. Eleven and a half months. And this had happened in that short period of time?

The graceful Tudor manor house with its diamond-paned windows, several of them broken, looked as if it had been left to molder. Ivy climbed to the second story of the house; the grass and weeds covered everything, even sprouting through the cracked stone front steps. The stables looked deserted, field implements lay rusted and unused next to the stable.

Sophie frowned. "I don't understand," she said finally.

"Nor do I."

He jumped from the carriage, then assisted her down.

He heard Tinker say, "Good Gawd, what the hell happened here?"

"I'll find Allen Dubust and find out," Ryder said. Sophie looked at him. She realized in that moment that she hadn't seen him this angry since Jamaica, since he'd found her beaten.

"Stay here," he said shortly, and strode up the cracked front steps. He pounded on the oak double front doors.

He pounded again.

Finally, very slowly, one of the doors opened just a crack and an old wizened face peered out.

"Master Ryder! Lawdie, Lawdie! The good Lord finally answered my prayers!"

"Mrs. Smithers, what's happened here? Where is Allen Dubust? What the devil is going on?"

"Lawdie, Lawdie," Mrs. Smithers said, then pulled both doors open wide.

"Sophie, come on in. Tinker, bring Cory, and oversee the luggage. I don't think there's much help coming out of here."

The interior of the house was a mess. Ryder started to curse, then noticed that Mrs. Smithers was leaning on two broomsticks roughly fashioned as crutches.

"Tell me what's happened," he said. He saw Sophie from the corner of his eye and added, "This is my wife, Mrs. Sherbrooke. Sophie, this is Mrs. Smithers. She's been here forever. She will tell us what happened."

What happened was that Allen Dubust had thrown Mrs. Smithers down the stairs after dismissing all the other servants because she'd refused to believe him and threatened him with the local magistrate. "I told him he were a rotten sort and I always knew it and I wouldn't leave and he couldn't make me. I told him I'd tell everyone what he did. He didn't like that. He picked me up and threw me down the stairs." He'd stripped the house, taken all the money, sold off land he had no authority to sell, and left the district. "He told me, he did, that he'd been telling everyone that you had sold Chadwyck House." Unfortunately, Mrs. Smithers hadn't seen a blessed soul, because, after all, the house was vacant, and since she couldn't walk, there was no way she could get to the village to tell anyone what had happened. She'd barely managed to get to the front doors.

Sophie said, "I will have Tinker ride immediately back to Lower Slaughter and fetch a doctor for you, Mrs. Smithers."

"But the house!" Mrs. Smithers wailed and looked for the world as though she would burst into tears.

Sophie patted her bent old shoulder and said gently, "It's just a house. We'll fix it up again. You'll see. It's you we're worried about. You've done very well. Don't you agree, Ryder?"

He looked at his wife. Jesus, he thought, she'd certainly changed from the frightened, wary girl who'd lived in his brother's house. He cleared his throat and said, "Everything will be put to rights. You first of all, Mrs. Smithers. I'm proud of you and I thank you."

Two hours later, Mrs. Smithers was tucked into bed, heavily dosed with laudanum, her broken leg properly set by an aghast Dr. Pringle, who just kept shaking his head. "I just don't believe she managed to survive," he said over and over again. "That old woman just wouldn't give up."

Once the doctor had left, Ryder and Sophie stood facing each other in the filthy entrance hall.

"I couldn't have manufactured a more excellent nightmare," he said. "I'm sorry, Sophie."

To his surprise, Sophie grinned. "Let's go to

the kitchen and see if there's anything to eat."

There wasn't, not a scrap. But there were rats, big ones, who had enjoyed themselves for the past three weeks.

Sophie frowned, and said to a shrieking Cory, "Do be quiet. You're hurting the master's ears. Now, I want you to go stay with Mrs. Smithers. Mr. Sherbrooke and I are going to Lower Slaughter and hire help, and buy food."

"Yes," Ryder said, staring at his wife. "Ah, Tinker, please help the coachman with the horses and the luggage."

He rubbed his hands together. "Nothing like a challenge, is there?"

CHAPTER 18

There was no bed.

Ryder just stood in the doorway of the great master bedchamber and stared blankly about the bare room. He'd avoided looking into the bedchamber earlier because he'd always hated this room. Damned dark and the ceilings were too low. The thick dark gold draperies still covered the long windows, draperies so ugly and shiny with age that Ryder wished Dubust had taken them as well, curse his hide.

No damned bed. It was too much. Sophie was exhausted, he was still so furious he hadn't allowed himself to feel weariness, and Mrs. Smithers was sound asleep, snoring loudly, after consuming a feast of food. She was in the sewing room, which had been quickly converted for her. Cory would sleep in the room with her. Dubust, the discriminating bastard, hadn't touched any of the servants' furniture.

He turned to see Sophie standing right behind him, linens on her arms. She said as she gazed about the room, "Oh dear. I'm so sorry, Ryder."

"According to the good doctor, Dubust simply told everyone that all furnishings were being sent to Northcliffe Hall. I still can't believe it. Damnation, Sophie, it's all my fault." She shifted the linens and he quickly took them from her.

"We will have to sleep on blankets, I suppose. You're so tired, sweetheart, I'll stop my ranting until morning. All right?"

"I don't particularly like this bedchamber, Ryder."

"I don't either, never have, for that matter. Let's go downstairs. Mrs. Smithers said Dubust slept in here, acted as though he were the prince of the castle. Damn, how could I have been such an irresponsible idiot?"

"If I didn't know firsthand just how awful the consequences, I'd suggest that we try to find a bottle of brandy."

He was forced to smile down at her. "You don't have to down an entire bottle, you know. There is a concept known as moderation."

"Ah, the concept of moderation — as in you and the very modest number of women you have in your herd?"

Was that acrimony he heard? He grinned down at her like a fool. "Herd? Did you hear Douglas say something? No? Well, let me tell you that I have only one mare now and she appears a real goer, glossy coat, good shoulders and flanks, lots of endurance, thank God. She'll need all the strength she can get with an idiot for a husband and an empty house. Come, Sophie, before you fall on your face, let's build ourselves a nest. Thank God, Dubust didn't take all the blankets and pillows."

"No, he just wanted all the furniture. So many beautiful things, Mrs. Smithers kept telling me over and over, most of it from that damned second George, she said, not the crazy third George."

Ryder burst into laughter. "She's right. Let's go find a place to stretch out our exhausted bones."

It wasn't long before they were lying side by side, as comfortable as three blankets could make them. "Well, at least we've gotten things started," Sophie said. Without thought, she reached out her left hand and found Ryder's. For an instant, he stilled, then brought her hand to his lips and lightly kissed her wrist and palm.

"Yes," he said. "But it won't be easy, sweetheart. Damnation, I should be whipped."

"I have to admit it has in the past seemed to me to be an excellent thing to do to you, but not for this. This isn't your fault."

"And just whose fault is it? Mrs. Smithers's? Dr. Pringle's?"

"All right, so your judgment of Mr. Dubust wasn't correct. I wish you would stop flailing yourself, Ryder."

But he couldn't, at least not to himself. Irresponsible fool, that's what he was, and he knew it and despised himself for it. He'd already planned to change things, had already thought about it a good deal because he was now married and a husband, for God's sake, but he'd been too late.

Sophie was right. Flailing himself didn't help a thing at the moment. They'd at least gotten things started. Whilst they'd been in Lower Slaughter, they'd managed to find two women who had worked before at Chadwyck House who were perfectly willing to come back on the morrow. But for now, there was merely filth and more filth. They slept in the Blue Salon, on the floor near the floor-to-ceiling windows — "Hell," Ryder said, "we can call this the Black Salon if we want to. The good Lord knows there isn't a patch of blue left."

He cursed luridly.

"So much for your first night at my wonderful house," he said, and punched his pillow. He then pulled her closer to his side. "I'm sorry, Sophie. This is all a damned bloody mess and I've dropped you right in the middle of it."

She didn't answer. Not that he expected her to, because he was so furious, so ashamed that he'd let himself be such a lazy, worthless clod that such a thing could happen, that he wanted to rant, and so he did. "I'll find the fellow. It shouldn't be difficult. All the furnishings were catalogued, a fact I doubt our Mr. Dubust knew about. But Uncle Brandon was a great one for detail, indeed so much detail, I think he died finally from choking on it. In any case, we'll track all the things down, then I'll find Dubust and cut off his . . . well, the fellow will end up in a bad way, I swear it."

Ryder paused a moment, then realized that his bride was fast asleep. He kissed her forehead.

Life, he thought as he eased into sleep himself, was occasionally irritating and made one face up to what one was. On the other hand, life did bring some pleasant surprises, like the wonderful soft one who was nestled in the crook of his arm. Her palm was lying over his heart.

The next few days were beyond anything Sophie had ever experienced. She felt like a general directing her troops, that is, when she wasn't spending her time on the front line side by side with them. She spent her days immersed in dirt, bone tired by mid-afternoon, and having more fun than she could ever remember. What she was doing meant something. She felt wonderful. She felt worthy for the first time in a very long while.

Her hair was bound up in a dirty bandanna, smudges on her face, her gown too short and just as dirty as her bandanna, when Doris, a very fat good-natured woman, yelled from the front entrance hall, "Mrs. Sherbrooke! There's a gentleman here."

Sophie barely had time to set her broom aside when she came face to face with a very handsome man who had something of the look of the Sherbrookes. She said, her hand thrust out, "You must be Tony Parrish."

"Guilty, ma'am. And you are my cousin's new wife." He turned then and called out, "Come in, love, and dredge up all your wondrous charm.

394

Our new cousin doubtless needs it."

When Melissande Parrish, Lady Rathmore, floated on fairy-slippered feet into the entrance hall looking like a princess stepping into a slum, Sophie could do nothing but stare at the incredible vision. She had never seen a more beautiful woman in her life.

"You're Alex's sister?"

"Oh yes. I'm Melissande, you know, and you must be Sophie. You're a surprise to every Sherbrooke in England, so Tony tells me. No one ever thought that Ryder would . . . that is, Ryder is so very much in demand with the ladies, but Tony believes he won't see his other mistresses now and —"

"I believe that's enough abuse of the topic, love," Tony Parrish said, and leaned down and kissed his wife full on the mouth, much to Sophie's astonishment.

Melissande blushed and said, "You shouldn't have begun that in the carriage, my lord, and now you will —" She broke off, shook herself, and said to Sophie, "My husband is a dreadful tease, you know. Now, I see no place to sit. It is very strange. Whatever shall we do?"

Sophie was stymied. In that moment, Ryder strode into the house, looking so beautiful in black Hessians, buckskins, and white shirt open at his throat and wild and male that she wanted, in that brief instant, to hurl herself into his arms. He'd changed so very much in the past three days. Or, she thought, her brow puckering, perhaps it was she who had changed, but just a bit, just a tiny little bit. No, he was just Ryder and she didn't feel a blessed thing toward him. He had a very nice smile, his teeth white, his face so very expressive, his light blue eyes crinkling at the corners with pleasure. There was something different about him. It took another moment for Sophie to figure out what it was. He was clearly in charge here. It hadn't been that he'd lived in his brother's shadow, no, not that, but here, at Chadwyck House, he was the master and he fitted the role very well. And I, Sophie thought, am the mistress.

The cousins shook hands, slapped each other on the back, and insulted each other's manhood in high good humor. Sophie felt herself stiffening as she waited for Ryder to turn to the beautiful woman at Tony's side. She was waiting for him to metaphorically fall at the fairy slippers of the gloriously beautiful Melissande.

He didn't.

He smiled down at her, a social, quite impersonal smile, and said, "Welcome to Chadwyck House, cousin. I told Tony to keep his distance else I'd put him to work."

"I'm not such a sluggard," Tony said. "Behold two willing slaves to do your bidding."

"We're not going to London until next week," Melissande said, looking around her and shuddering. "Until then Tony insists that we help out. However, it is much worse than I'd imagined. I've never been dirty before and I think that grime beneath one's fingernails is quite disgusting."

Artless, Sophie thought, achingly beautiful and artless. She tucked her fingers into a fist because her fingernails were black with blackening from the grate.

"You won't do a thing," she said to Melissande. "At least not in that gown." Sophie looked at her husband, a question in her eyes, but Ryder was looking at Tony, who, in turn, was grinning at his wife, saying, "You've been sweaty, very sweaty. Ah, I do remember a time in the Northcliffe gardens — you remember, don't you, sweetheart? — beneath that statue of Venus trying to cover her bosom with a very small hand — that you got really quite grimy and you didn't give a good damn."

Melissande punched him in the arm.

"Some things never change," Ryder said, shaking his head at his cousin. "Then again, some things change so much that it leaves a poor mortal nearly speechless."

"Ah," said Tony, "that is a state my dear wife hasn't yet quite achieved. But she draws ever nearer."

Melissande said, puzzlement in her voice, "You appear pretty, Sophie, even though you are wearing that horrid thing around your head and your gown is beyond awful. But you're not beautiful. It is all very odd, you know. I simply don't understand it."

Sophie blinked.

"There is simply no accounting for a man's

preferences," Ryder said easily. "I daresay it is a lack in my man's character. She means," Ryder said in his wife's ear, "that it's incomprehensible to her that I, a manly man by all accounts, would prefer you to her."

"I can see why she would feel that way," Sophie said. She smiled at the vision. "You are very beautiful."

"Yes, I know, but Tony prefers that I try to turn aside such compliments, that I treat them as if they were as insubstantial as snowflakes, that is his metaphor, you know. That is the correct term, I believe. But I have no doubt at all that your compliment is terribly sincere and, after all, you're not a gentleman, thus it can be accepted gracefully, don't you agree, Tony?"

Tony Parrish, Viscount Rathmore, looked perfectly serious. "Such logic is irrefutable, my love." He said to Ryder, "All right, tell me what I can do. Incidentally, I brought six men over to help and four women."

Sophie felt like hugging her new cousin. More help, bless his kind heart. She gave him a dazzling smile that made him cock his head at her. "I see," he said slowly. "Yes, Ryder, perhaps I do see."

Four days later, Chadwyck House was spotlessly clean, and completely empty save for a big bed in the salon and the furnishings in the servants' quarters. Mrs. Smithers was cackling with pleasure, still eating like a stoat. She was delighted that the master had come home to stay and was cursing Allen Dubust for a bounder.

As for Allen Dubust, he'd been caught in a pub in Bristol, his pockets lined with the sale of all Chadwyck House furnishings, all ready to board a ship bound for America in a matter of hours. He had rent money as well from all the farming tenants. It was actually Uncle Albert Sherbrooke who saw him first and Aunt Mildred who screamed him down, offering three guineas to a group of young toughs to bring the lout down and hold him on the ground.

The furnishings were coming home. The rent money was coming home. Dubust was going to spend many years in Newgate, rotting. Mrs. Smithers cackled endlessly with that news. All would be well. Ryder felt profoundly lucky. He'd been stupid and irresponsible and he'd been saved despite it all. The wondrous Sherbrooke luck was with him still.

All the tenant farmers made their appearance and it was quite a surprise to Ryder that he actually enjoyed spending time with each of them, speaking of their needs, their profits, their willingness to set everything to rights again.

He realized with something of a start that he was a happy man, despite the havoc he himself had brought about because he'd been an absent landlord. He was setting everything to rights. He wrote his brother, detailing all that had happened, and Sophie's first bout with Melissande, who was, truth be told, developing into a quite acceptable female. She had even offered to oversee the polishing of some new silverware that Tony had presented to them from Mr. Millsom's warehouse in Liverpool.

It was a Tuesday afternoon, the sky overcast, the air chill. The gently rolling hills were serene and so lovely that Sophie wished she had more time simply to ride about and look. As it was, she had to ride into Lower Slaughter to the draperers. There was so much still to do and she loved it. She was humming to herself, thinking about Jeremy and wondering when he could come to live with them.

There, in the middle of the road, she came face to face with Lord David Lochridge. They stared at each other.

"Good God," he said. "It is you, Sophia Stanton-Greville. No, no, you married that Sherbrooke fellow, didn't you?"

Sophie felt sick to her stomach. She could only nod at him.

Lord David's eyes narrowed. "You did marry him, didn't you? Or are you his current mistress?"

"No," she said.

He laughed, and it was a nasty sound. "Would you like to know something else, my dear Sophia? Charles Grammond lives very near to Upper Slaughter. He'd gone to the colonies, to Virginia, I was told, but he hated it and moved here. He has a great-aunt who helps support him and that prune-faced wife of his and those four wretched children who are of no account at all. He's very much on the straight and narrow now, else the great-aunt will cut him out of her will. Isn't that a pleasant surprise for you? Two of your former lovers here, your neighbors."

"I must go," Sophie said, tightening her fists on Opal's reins.

"But not too far. We have much to discuss, don't we, Sophie? I will, of course, speak to Charles. I do wonder what he'll have to say. You see, I'm engaged to marry a local girl who's so rich it will take even me a good ten years to go through her fortune. Ah, yes, we must talk and make decisions. I do expect you to keep your mouth shut in the meanwhile, my girl, else you will be very sorry, both you and that husband of yours."

It was in that instant that Sophie remembered what the ghost had said — not really said, but told her so clearly in her mind — something about when they came it would be all right. Was this what the ghost meant? If so, how could it be all right? Nothing could ever again be all right.

She'd left the West Indies and come to a new life, a new life that had such promise until now.

She silently watched David Lochridge ride away from her. She did her errands. The draperer, Mr. Mulligan, shook his head when she left his shop. Poor Mr. Sherbrooke had wed himself to a half-witted female. It was a pity.

When she returned to Chadwyck House, she

went upstairs to the master bedchamber that she and Ryder had changed completely. The walls were painted a soft pale yellow. There was a lovely pale cream and blue Aubusson carpet on the floor. She went to the now sparkling-clean window and stared out over the newly scythed east lawn. So beautiful. It looked like a Garden of Eden. It was her home. But not for much longer. Slowly, very slowly, she eased down to her knees. She bent over, her face in her hands, and she sobbed.

Mrs. Chivers, the newly installed housekeeper, saw her, managed to keep her mouth shut, and searched out the master. Ryder, not knowing what to expect, and firmly believing that Mrs. Chivers had misinterpreted Sophie's actions, still came to her immediately. He stopped cold in the doorway, staring at his wife. He felt a coursing of sheer fear.

He strode to her, nearly yelling, "Sophie, what the hell is wrong with you?"

She whipped about, staring at him. Oh God, what to tell him? That everything was over now? That the Sherbrooke name was on the verge of being ruined and that she was responsible? Oh God, Ryder had temporarily lost his furniture but she had brought utter devastation on his family.

She tried to get a hold of herself. He dropped to his haunches beside her and she felt his hands close over her upper arms. Slowly and very gently, he turned her to face him. Her face was without color, her eyes swollen from crying.

"No, no, don't cry," he said and pressed her cheek against his shoulder. "There is one very good thing about marriage, Sophie. You're not alone. There's another person to help you, no matter what the problem, no matter what the hurt. Talk to me, sweetheart, please."

She shook her head against his chest.

Ryder frowned over her head. It was she who had kept his spirits buoyed since they'd arrived here. It was she who'd directed the servants, who had overseen the meals, who had herself swept and cleaned and dusted and smiled through it all. She'd been happy, dammit. He knew it. What the hell had happened?

Her crying stopped. She hiccuped. He felt the soft movement of her breasts against his chest and felt instant and overwhelming lust. Her monthly flow had ended several days before but she'd been so tired, so utterly exhausted at the end of each day, that he'd simply held her at night.

But now, he wanted her. Very much.

"Talk to me, Sophie," he said again.

She straightened and leaned back, still held in the loose circle of his arms. "My knees hurt."

"We have a bed. Come, let's sit down."

She eyed that bed, knew that he wanted her, she wasn't blind. His sex was swelled against his trousers. She saw Lord David naked and stroking his sex, she felt again how he'd kissed her, stabbing his tongue into her mouth before she'd managed to distract him, and how he always stripped off his clothes at the cottage and showed her his body and his sex and how big he was and how he was going to take her.

And Charles Grammond, middle-aged, his belly sagging, not a bad man really, pathetically grateful when she'd first told him she would take him as her lover, and then how he'd changed, catching her in the middle of the day to force her against a tree and she'd had to hit him with her riding crop and he'd only laughed and pulled his sex from his britches and told her he wanted his sex in her mouth and she could do it now. And, dear God, she'd helped to ruin him even as she'd told him what a wonderful lover he was. And he pranced about, so pleased with himself, bragging about his virility — didn't he have four living children to prove it?

Now both of them were here. Both of them believed her a whore. Both of them would take great delight in ruining her. She clearly remembered the looks both men would give her whenever they saw her, and what they said to her in their lewd whispers, how they spoke about the nights they'd spent with her and what they'd done to her and she'd done to them. . . .

She jerked away from Ryder. He stared at her, his head cocked to one side in question.

She bounded to her feet, turned, grabbed up her skirts, and ran from the bedchamber.

He stared after her. He'd seen the blankness on her face when she'd looked at the bed, followed by the myriad facial expressions he knew were from her damned memories of Jamaica, and all when she'd seen his sex swelled against his britches.

He had hoped, prayed, that she was coming around to trusting him. His jaw tightened. He wouldn't let this continue, he couldn't.

He bided his time for the remainder of the day. There was always so much to be done that there wasn't any particular discomfort between them, even during dinner when they were alone. That night, at ten o'clock, Ryder stepped into their bedchamber, and saw that Sophie wasn't in bed. She was seated in a wing chair in front of the fireplace, her legs tucked beneath her, a book in her lap.

"I finished my work," he said.

The book, a collection of essays by John Locke, slipped off her lap. She made no move to retrieve it.

Ryder leaned down and picked it up. "Where the devil did you find this?"

"Your Mr. Dubust left it."

"I don't blame him. Listen to this: 'Latin I look upon as absolutely necessary to a gentleman.' What an appalling notion. I imagine that my youngest brother, Tysen — the future cleric — is now quite fluent in Latin. He says that his congregation will glean his meaning from his intonation, that the words aren't important, that God didn't mean for common folk to really understand in any case, only to gain the holy essence — whatever that may be — which will come from him, naturally."

"Your brother really said that?"

"He tried, but he hasn't the facility to be as fluent as I am."

"Nor has he your modesty, I doubt."

"Good," Ryder said, tossing the book back into her lap, "a bit of vinegar. Now, Sophie, it's time for you to come with me over to that bed. I know you had a bath earlier so that excuse went out with the bathwater."

"I don't want to, Ryder."

She was twisting her hands. It was amazing, his strong Sophie, the woman who had directed a score of servants during the past week, humming while she worked, was wringing her hands like a helpless twit.

"Nor do you want to tell me why you were crying this afternoon?"

"No. It isn't important, truly. It was just that . . . I lost some silverware."

Ryder only shook his head at her. He stripped off his clothes then came back to stand in front of the drowsing fire, naked, to gaze down at the orange embers.

She stared at him, she couldn't help it. He stretched out his hand to her. "Come along now, sweetheart. I'm going to try my damnedest to give you some pleasure tonight. And if I fail you tonight, why then, there will be tomorrow night and the night after that."

She shook her head even as he was jerking her to her feet. He picked her up in his arms, carried her to the bed, and gently laid her on her back. He quickly unfastened the sash on her dressing gown.

He ignored the stiffness of her body, the pallor of her face, the damned wariness he saw in her eyes. He stripped off her nightgown, then straightened and stared down at her.

"No, don't cover yourself."

She turned her face away from him, and fisted her hands at her sides.

"You're beautiful, Sophie, not a dream princess like Melissande, certainly, but as she pointed out, you're pretty nonetheless. I'll keep you. Now I'm going to . . . no, let me just show you."

He came down beside her, lying on his side, and very gently he stroked his fingertips over her jaw, her lips, her nose, then smoothed her eyebrows. He simply looked at her and touched her face.

She looked up at him then.

"Ryder," she said, "I know that you want to take me. You don't have to play about with me as you're doing now. Please, just get it over with. I won't fight you. I know that it will do no good. I'm tired and want it over with."

He laughed.

"Ah, all those other damned men. 'Take you' . . . what a wonderful way to say 'making love.' Well, let me tell you something, Mrs. Sherbrooke, you're my wife. I want to play with you until you're yelling with pleasure. I want you to enjoy yourself. I want you to laugh and kiss me back and play with me. No, you can't begin to understand that, can you? But you will come to understand."

He leaned down and kissed her mouth, very gently, his own mouth light as moth's wings. He continued kissing her until he finally felt her ease beneath him. "Do you know how wonderful you taste to me? How much I enjoy kissing you?"

"It isn't bad," she admitted, sounding a bit worried. Even as she parted her lips to speak, he gently slipped his tongue inside her mouth and touched hers.

She started, becoming stiff as a bed slat.

Ryder was again in firm control of himself, just as he'd been before. Everything in him was focused on her, on her reactions, her shifts of expressions, the lightness or darkness of her gray eyes. All that he wanted was for her to become one with him, to replace all her memories with him — his laughter, his sheer joy in life, his pleasure in her.

He simply continued what he was doing. There was all the time in the world. The night was long. He figured she didn't have a chance.

He talked to her, distracting her from the memories he knew crept into her mind whilst he touched her. He told her how much he admired her breasts, that they were as white as fresh snow and as round as her belly would be when she was carrying his child. Ah, and her belly, he spanned his fingers to her pelvic bones and told her she should easily carry their children, as many as she wished to bear, and then he began to caress her, his fingers light and caressing her warm belly. When his fingers lightly touched her woman's soft flesh, she lurched up in bed and scrambled away from him.

He was so startled that she escaped him. He watched her blankly dash naked across the bare floor to the windows on the eastern side of the bedchamber. She stood there, her back to him, her head bowed.

He went to her, frowning, but said nothing, merely placed his hands on her shoulders and pulled her gently back against him.

"Now, what is all this about?"

"I feel so dirty."

Good Lord, he thought, staring at the back of her head, the dam had finally burst. About time too. He said slowly, "Finally you tell me the truth. It's about time, Sophie. Now we will deal with it."

She was silent.

"Somehow I don't believe it was my fingers between your thighs that brought this on, but it helped, didn't it? It made you remember — did you see one of the men doing that to Dahlia? Did one of the men force himself on you in that way?" He waited, but she said nothing. "All right then. You're not built as I am, Sophie. For you to reach a woman's pleasure, you must know caresses there between your thighs. There is no reason for you to feel dirty or ashamed or anything else except excitement and anticipation."

"It's not that entirely."

"Ah," he said, and felt a wrenching in his gut. As for his sex, all desire was long gone. "So some of those men touched you there? Fondled you there? Is that what this is all about? You would still have me battle memories, bloody ghosts?"

Ghosts, ha! she thought, shaking unconsciously.

"Sophie, talk to me."

"I'm sorry, Ryder."

He shook her then. "Damn you, woman, stop bleating like a twit sheep! You were a hellion when I met you and now you become a pathetic scrap on me. Stop it, dammit!"

She screamed at him, "All right, damn you, all right!" She jerked away, looked frantically around the bedchamber for something to hit him with, didn't see anything, and dashed from the bedchamber.

"You're naked!"

"Go to the devil!"

He was grabbing for his dressing gown when she ran back into the bedchamber. She was carrying a broom. She rushed at him, like a horseless knight in a joust, and he couldn't help himself, he laughed. He hugged his belly he laughed so hard, at least until she hit him on the head. Then hit him again and again, cursing at him all the while.

The pain of the sharp bristles finally got through to him as well as the sharp throbbing over his left temple, and he grabbed the broom handle.

But she was strong, bloody strong with determination and rage.

It took a good deal of strength on his part to get it away from her without hurting her.

He tossed it aside, and grabbed her, pulling her roughly up against him. He kissed her hard. His hands were on her buttocks, bringing her up to fit intimately against him. She arched her back and tried to bite him.

"The good Lord knows I'm glad you're back," he said, and kissed her hard again. He threw her over his shoulder and carried her to the bed.

"You feel dirty, do you? Well, my dear wife, let's just see how you will feel when I get done with you."

CHAPTER 19

She fought him, kicking, twisting, panting with effort. She shrieked at him, called him every name she'd ever heard hurled at another in Jamaica.

He only laughed and held her down.

When he was kissing her belly, she yanked viciously at his hair. It was then that Ryder just sighed, stripped off one of the pillowcases, and tied her hands above her head to one of the huge carved bedposts.

She could still hurt him with her legs but he could bear that. He went back to his pleasurable task. He kissed her white belly, slipping his tongue into her navel while his hands were stroking her inner thighs. He paused then, and looked at her. "You will like this, Sophie." He dipped down, suddenly, and lifted her hips. He covered her with his mouth and she screamed, a high wailing sound that moved him not one whit.

He gently eased his middle finger inside her. Ah, he thought, she was damp. But still so very small. Well, it wouldn't matter once she'd come to pleasure.

And she was loosening and opening, feeling something near to pain deep inside her, low in her belly, and it held her, made her want, and despite herself, despite her screaming curses at him, she was raising her hips to bring herself closer to him. His finger was deep inside her, moving in and out, and his mouth found a rhythm that drove her wild.

She knew something was coming, she wanted it desperately, and she still wanted to curse him for what he was doing to her. Then she moaned, jerking so violently he nearly dropped her, and she froze, but just for an instant.

Ryder raised his head from her for just a moment. "Still feel dirty, Sophie?"

She yelled at him even as her hips jerked and heaved, "You damned bounder, you bastard, you —"

"Just another moment, sweetheart, and you'll understand. Keep cursing, it makes me want you to scream with pleasure all the more."

She was crying now, her breath short and gasping, and he knew she didn't understand that she was close, very close, and in the next instant, he pushed her, his finger deep, his mouth just as deep. He felt her legs stiffen, then felt the heaving contractions, the spasms that lifted her back off the bed.

He kept her there, locked into the climax, forcing the pleasure to continue, not to stop, but to go on and on until she was crying from the power of it, the finality of it, her acceptance of it. When finally she grew soft and yielding in his hands, he pulled her thighs wide apart and came into her, deep and hard.

He felt the sweet aftershocks of her climax and it was more than enough. He found his own release in the very next instant and he yelled his pleasure, not at his own climax, which was incredibly powerful, but at hers, at what he had finally given her.

She was slick with sweat, her breath deep and fast, and he lay on top of her, his sex still deep inside her, and he gently laid his palm on her heart.

He kissed her slack mouth. He simply looked down at her until she finally opened her eyes.

Shock, dazed shock.

He kissed her again, and she tasted herself and she simply couldn't believe what had happened, couldn't believe that she'd lost herself so completely, that even as she'd hated him and cursed him and wanted to kill him, her body had exploded into ferocious pleasure, and she'd wanted it, oh yes, she'd wanted it more than anything. And he'd watched her, and felt the wild spasms and known, known what he was doing to her, known how he was controlling her, known exactly what she was feeling. He kissed her again, then came up on his elbows.

"Your heart is finally slowing."

She looked at his chin but felt the warmth of his chest against her breast, against her heart. He would mock her now, she thought, he would blare his triumph over her, he would grind her under and proclaim his mastery. She stiffened, waiting, knowing what would come.

He gently pushed the hair off her forehead, hair damp with the wildness of her pleasure, and he said very slowly, his voice deep and rough, "I love you, Sophie Sherbrooke. I never thought such a thing existed, but evidently it does. I love you and I will love you until I cock up my toes and pass to the hereafter and I will still love you even as I float about in eternity. And I will continue to force you to pleasure until you accept my love and take me into your heart as well as into your body."

He suddenly looked startled. She felt him hard within her once again and, to her horror, she squirmed.

He didn't laugh, didn't mock her. He threw back his head, closed his eyes, and groaned. "Do you have any idea how you feel to me? Come with me again, Sophie, all right? Just let yourself go, forget all the past, those damned ghosts, just think of me and how I feel deep inside you. Just think about what my fingers are going to do to you, and my tongue —"

She didn't want to fall apart again, but there didn't seem to be much choice. In but an instant of time, she forgot about choice anyway. When he told her to wrap her legs around his flanks, she did so willingly and quickly, hugging him hard, lifting her hips to bring him deeper, and he groaned and she felt a burgeoning of those same feelings, those frantic barbaric feelings that stripped off everything except that wrenching pleasure that was so great it was nearly pain, but it wasn't, it was within her and within him and somehow it made them as one. His hand was between their bodies, stroking her, caressing her, and then his mouth was against hers, his tongue deep inside her mouth just as his sex was inside her body. And she was howling and bucking in her frenzy, and he encouraged her, telling her what to do, telling her what she made him feel. Then, just as he plunged so deep he touched her womb, she convulsed with pleasure and screamed.

Ryder was with her, holding her tightly against him, kissing her nose, her cheek, her eyebrows, her ears. He told her again and again that he loved her.

"Am I too heavy?"

He wasn't, not really, but her wrists were cramping, not because of how tightly he'd fastened the pillowcases, but because she'd jerked and twisted so violently, wanting more of him, more of herself.

"Can you untie my hands?"

He raised himself with effort, ducked his head down again and kissed her, grinning as he did so. "I can't get enough of you, Sophie."

"I don't mind kissing you," she said as he untied her wrists. He pulled out of her and came down onto his side. He rubbed her wrists, frowning at the redness. "I didn't mean to tie them so tightly. I'm sorry."

"It wasn't that," she said, not looking at him. "It was the other."

"What other?"

She looked at him straight in his blue eyes. "How you made me feel. I was an animal."

"Ah, another condemnation perhaps? Based on your wonderful objective experience? I hate to tell you this, Sophia, but we are both animals, carnal as hell, and so wonderful that I pray you'll go wild and ferocious on me every night." He paused, frowning. "Perhaps every morning as well. Ah, and there's the hour just after luncheon, you know, when you're just a bit tired and —"

She laughed.

Ryder was so surprised that he simply stared down at her. He kissed her again and six more times.

She kissed him back, but her body felt so languid she doubted she could have roused herself even if Mrs. Chivers had shouted fire. She felt beyond herself; she didn't understand. She didn't know what to think. And she had laughed.

She said, "Do you really love me?"

"Yes."

"You didn't just say it because you were inside me and your lust . . . well, you know what I mean."

"Yes, I know what you mean. Now, I'm not inside you. You've exhausted me twice. I'm limp and nearly expired. My wits have gone begging. I have no sensation below my heart. And I love you."

"You never said that before."

"I didn't realize I loved you before. Things have changed and I don't mind telling you that I'm quite pleased about it. No, Sophie, don't feel that you have to fill in the silence."

"You're the master here."

He said easily, accepting her words, understanding them, "Yes, I am. You want to know something? It feels good, damned good. I never felt I was needed at Northcliffe Hall and of course I wasn't. It was and is Douglas's home and his responsibility as the Earl of Northcliffe. But Chadwyck House, it's mine, Sophie, it's ours, and our children will grow up here, and this will be their home and, why, I might even wear a smock and become a farmer on Wednesdays and Fridays. What do you think?"

"I think you would look beautiful in a smock and hobnail boots."

"Ah," he said, and kissed her mouth. "Dear God, but I love kissing you."

Tell him, she thought, tell him, but she was afraid to, afraid he would search out both Lord David and Charles Grammond and threaten them or kill them, she didn't know which. But she knew there would be an awful scandal and she couldn't do it to him, to the Sherbrooke family, to Jeremy, to herself.

She kissed him back, urgently, wanting only to bury her misery, to forget it for just another instant, just one more moment, and she succeeded. He caressed her, and when he came into her again, she cried out in her climax, and Ryder thought he would die from the pleasure of it. When they slept, Ryder dreamed of his children and knew, even in his dream, that he would have to tell her about them very soon now and pray that she would understand.

Ryder didn't tell Sophie anything; he had no chance to. She was still sound asleep when he left the house the following morning, from exhaustion, from his exhausting her.

The following afternoon, when he was in the north field with three of his tenant farmers, a carriage pulled up in front of Chadwyck House. The Earl of Northcliffe, Alex, Jeremy, and Sinjun spilled out.

The earl simply stood there, his wife's hand in his, and stared at the house and grounds.

"You've done very well," he said to Sophie, who didn't look like a waif today but was actually wearing a gown that Mrs. Plack had made for her. Her hair was a bit mussed because she'd been polishing the crystals on a chandelier in what she now thought of as her own room, which was set at the back of the house, its doors giving onto the garden.

"Hello," she said, then turned to Jeremy, holding open her arms. He limped to her and hugged her, saying as fast as he could talk, "It's wonderful, Sophie! Oh goodness, I've missed you. Look, Sinjun, just look at the stables, certainly big enough for George and —"

"Who's George?"

"My pony, he's a barb and all black with two white socks and fast as the wind, Sophie."

"As in the second George or the crazy third George?"

Douglas laughed. "Actually, this George is a tradesman in Hadleigh who bears a remarkable resemblance to Jeremy's pony."

Alex said, "You've done marvels. We were so shocked to hear about what that wretched Dubust had done."

"The furniture will be back in the next few days. Alas, I have only three chairs and one table downstairs."

"Perfectly adequate," the earl said, then frowned as he looked around. "Where's Ryder?"

"He's with some of the tenant farmers."

Douglas stared at her. "Tenant farmers," he repeated blankly. "What is he doing?"

"I think they're talking about crop rotation. Evidently Mr. Dubust was more than just a criminal. He wouldn't allow the farmers new implements and discouraged letting fields lie fallow as they must, you know."

"Yes," Douglas said slowly, "yes, I know. And Ryder is dealing with this?"

"Not only is he dealing with it, he quite likes it."

Sinjun said to her brother, "Can Jeremy and I go find Ryder? It is late, Douglas, and he should be finished with all his rotations soon now. Please?"

"Go along, brat."

"Walk north," Sophie called after them. "See

420

the trail just by the stables?"

An hour later, Ryder, Jeremy, and Sinjun strolled into the drawing room that held only three chairs. Ryder walked over to his wife and kissed her. "Look who found me. And I wasn't even wearing my hobnails or my smock."

Sophie felt a deep surge of pleasure at the sight of him and could only nod.

Ryder grinned at her, and lightly caressed his knuckles over her cheek. "No, Douglas, don't say anything, if you please. Things change, all right? To show me proper respect, call me Master Ryder or Farmer Ryder. I begin to think that I must design a new plow, one with style, one that will be made by an artisan as famous as Hoby or Weston. What do you think?"

"I think you're mad, Ryder, utterly mad and very happy."

"And what do you think of our home?"

"That it is a home and you've made it thus in a very short time."

"I must give Sophie credit for accomplishing a bit, a very little bit, but I don't wish to make her feel useless."

Sophie squawked and flew at him. Ryder, laughing, his blue eyes as light as the afternoon sky, gathered her against him and held her and then swung her about.

The earl looked at his wife, who was smiling at them.

The Earl and Countess of Northcliffe didn't

mind at all sleeping on piles of blankets in a guest room. Indeed, if Ryder were any expert on the matter, and he most assuredly was, he knew that his brother and sister-in-law quite enjoyed themselves. His brother was a man of a creative nature.

The earl and countess remained for only a day and a half, for they were on a visit to the Duke and Duchess of Portsmouth. As for Sinjun and Jeremy, they were to stay for a long visit. Sinjun's goal, she said, giggling, was to see Ryder in his farmer's smock.

Not an hour after the earl and countess had left, Sinjun found her brother in a rather ardent embrace with his wife. She cleared her throat. Ryder looked up and frowned at her. "Go away, Sinjun. You're only fifteen and you shouldn't be witnessing all this excess of affection."

"Ha," Sinjun said. "You should see Douglas and Alex when they think no one's looking. You wouldn't believe what I've seen him doing, and Alex always throws her head back and makes these funny little noises and —"

"Be quiet, brat. Now, this had better be urgent or I'll tan your backside."

"I've got to speak to you, Ryder. Alone."

This was a very serious Sinjun, and Sophie, having regained her equilibrium, merely nodded, and took herself off.

Ryder crossed his arms over his chest and leaned against the mantel.

"I'm too late."

"Too late for what?"

Sinjun, to her brother's absolute astonishment, turned red and wrung her hands. "They're nearly here. I rode as fast as I could back here to warn you. Oh, Ryder, I'm sorry, but there was nothing I could do. I know how you feel about Douglas or any of the rest of the family knowing how wonderful you are, but —"

Ryder had a peculiar feeling in the pit of his stomach. "What are you talking about?"

"The children should be here in no more than two minutes from now."

"You have two minutes, then, to explain all this to me."

"I took Jeremy over to Hadleigh to meet Jane and the children. All right, you can tan my bottom later for that, but Ryder, he fit right in and much enjoyed himself. He and Oliver are the best of friends. Oh dear, there's only one minute left. Jane came down with the measles. She immediately sent me a message saying the children had to leave so they wouldn't become ill; then Laura, one of her helpers, sent me a message at Northcliffe and she didn't know what to do. So I told her and Jane to send all the children here. What else should I have done, Ryder? Told Douglas?"

Ryder looked off into the distance. "Well, that solves one problem, doesn't it? Is that the sound of carriage wheels I hear? Probably. Who paid for all this, Sinjun?"

"I did. It took nearly all my savings, but I managed. I didn't want the children to travel by stage, so I hired four carriages, three for them and one for all the luggage, and I managed to secure four rooms at the Golden Calf Inn in Reading."

Ryder grinned at his sister. He patted her cheek. "You did well. Let's go meet all my brood. Good God, I hope none of them have come down with the measles. It can be quite nasty."

"What about Sophie?"

"Sophie isn't a fool," he said, but to Sinjun's fond and alert ears, his voice sounded very odd.

When he and Sinjun arrived on the front steps of Chadwyck House, there were Sophie and Jeremy assisting child after child from the carriages. Only Laura Bracken had come with them because the other two helpers had come down with the measles along with Jane. Laura, bless her heart, was exhausted. The children, luckily, were all well.

It was Jaime who first spotted Ryder. He let out a yell and rushed at him. Ryder swung the boy up in his arms and tossed him into the air, then hugged him tightly against his chest. The other children were on him in the next moment, and there was pandemonium for the next five minutes.

Sophie saw the little girl standing off to one side, her thumb in her mouth. She didn't understand any of this but, oddly enough, she was content to wait and see. It wasn't perhaps so strange with the children hanging on to his arms, legs, and neck that he wouldn't look at her.

Sinjun grabbed her arm. "I swear this isn't what you think, Sophie."

Sophie said easily, "No, I doubt it is. That boy over there must be all of eleven or twelve years old. Surely Ryder couldn't have fathered him. No, I'm learning that with Ryder nothing is as it appears to be."

"They are his children, his Beloved Ones," Sinjun said, desperate now, "but not really, all except for Jenny. Ryder saved each of them at different times, you know. He loves children and hates cruelty toward them, and —"

Ryder, dragging four children and holding two others, came down the steps, grinning hugely, but not at Sophie. He looked over her left shoulder as he said simply, "These are my children." He introduced all of them to his wife. Sophie smiled and spoke to each of them. A moment later, she realized with a shock that Ryder was embarrassed.

Then he got a huge smile on his face as he looked over at the little girl who was standing alone, watching silently.

"Now, all you wild savages, I want you to go with Jeremy and Sinjun to the kitchen. We don't have any furniture yet, but you can sit on the kitchen floor and Mrs. Chivers and Cook will make sure you have scones and biscuits and lemonade. Go now, and later I'll tell you all about my adventures and why the house doesn't have any beds for you."

"And I'll tell you more stories about the Virgin

Bride," Sinjun said. "Who knows, maybe she's followed Ryder and Sophie here."

Amy shrieked with excited terror.

Ryder simply took Sophie's hand and led her over to the little girl. Sophie stood still, watching her husband go down on his knees. He opened his arms and the little girl came to him. He held her close, kissing her hair, stroking her back, and she heard him saying over and over, "Ah, Jenny, I've missed you, little love. Now, would you like to meet Sophie? She's not as pretty as you, but she is nice and she makes me smile. Just maybe she'll make you smile as well."

He looked up at his wife and she knew that this was his child, and that the little girl wasn't like the other children. There was a look of near desperation on his face and she realized that he was worried that she would snub the little girl.

"You should have some faith in me," she said as she came down to her knees beside her husband and held out her hand, making no move toward the little girl, who was huddled against her father's chest. "Hello, Jenny. That's a lovely dress you're wearing, much nicer than mine. I'm very glad to meet you and I'm very glad you're here. Your father has missed you very much. How old are you?"

Ryder raised her right hand, folded down her thumb and said very slowly, "One."

Jenny said, "One."

Ryder folded down the next finger and said, "Two."

When he reached her little finger, he only bent it in half and said, "There now, I'm four and a half years old."

"Yes, Papa."

There was such pride and love on his face. Another Ryder, no, another side to him. She said now, "Such a big girl you are and just look at that lovely locket. May I see it?"

Jenny very slowly stretched out her hand, and her fingertips lightly, tentatively touched Sophie's palm. She held out the locket and Sophie opened it. "Ah, what lovely paintings. You and your mama? Yes, I can see that you're as pretty as she is. You have your father's beautiful eyes though."

"Papa," Jenny said, and threw her arms around Ryder's neck again and buried her face in his neck.

"It's her new word," Ryder said, immensely pleased.

"Now, little love, my old bones are creaking. Let me heave you up — you're such a great big girl, Sophie's right about that — and let's go into the house. You'd like some lemonade, wouldn't you?"

Pandemonium reigned in the kitchen. Mrs. Chivers looked as if she'd just been dumped willy-nilly into Bedlam, but she was smiling, thank the good Lord. Cook, a Mrs. Bedlock, was running to and fro from the pantry. It was Sinjun, though, who was in charge of the brood. Each child was finally seated on the floor with a plate filled with goodies.

"There won't be anything left to eat," Mrs. Chivers said, staring from one child to the other. "I have three grandchildren and they all eat like it's their last meal."

"Then we'd best send Mrs. Bedlock to Lower Slaughter to buy out the town," Sophie said. Ryder looked at his wife, still didn't meet her eyes, and she would have sworn that he blushed.

He neatly managed to avoid her for the next several hours. It wasn't difficult because each of the children wanted his attention. He showed them the east wing, told them about Mr. Dubust, making the man a villain fit to rule the world, but his aunt, dear Mildred, had shrieked him down and now he would pay for his crimes.

Sophie merely bided her time and made decisions as to where the children would sleep.

At last she managed to corner him as he tried to slip past her out of the house. "Oh no you don't, Ryder. I want to talk to you and it's now or I will make you very sorry."

That ruffled his manly feathers and he said sharply, "Oh, and just how do you plan to do that? Tie me down and have your way with my body?"

She grinned at him. "Come along. We're going for a walk."

Sophie walked beside her husband in the apple orchard just behind the house. It was private, with not a single child hiding behind a tree. Sinjun was with the children, playing mediator, mother, and nursemaid. Ryder was silent. Sophie started humming.

Suddenly she laughed. "You're embarrassed! I couldn't believe it, you were actually embarrassed. You couldn't meet my eyes. Is it because I never, even for one instant, believed all those children to be yours! Ah, if that is it, why then, what a blow to your manhood."

"Go to the devil, Sophie."

"No, that isn't it at all. I had hoped to enrage you out of your damned silence. No, you were and are embarrassed because you don't want anyone to know that you're not a care-for-nothing rakehell. You enjoy being the *homme terrible* and this, my dear, truly ruins that devil-may-care image."

"Maybe it doesn't. What the hell do you know? Did that wretched Sinjun speak to you?"

"Yes, at first she was desperate because she was afraid I'd get a gun and shoot you. Then later I pinned her against the wall and forced her to spill out the truth — you know, during all those hours when you assiduously avoided me. She told me she'd hoped you would have spoken to me before this, but that you were very reticent about your Beloved Ones, that you didn't consider the children to be anyone's business, even your family's. That it was your damned money and you could do whatever you wanted to do with it. Sinjun also said that Uncle Brandon probably was whirling about in his grave at your philanthropy, but that maybe he wouldn't spend so much time in hell because of the good cause you were putting his money to."

"She appears to have spilled her innards. I'll wager she even sang out about the quarterly bastard meetings, didn't she, curse her eyes?"

Sophie looked perfectly blank.

"Then forget it. God, the chit finally kept her mouth shut about something that is none of her business."

"Not on your benighted life will I forget it. Bastard meetings? What's that? Tell me this instant."

Ryder cursed and Sophie just laughed. "That won't get you out of it. Now, what's a bastard meeting?"

"Oh hell. Douglas and I had a meeting every quarter to count up bastards, so as not to lose any by accident, you know. He believed all the children were my bastards."

"I do wonder what he will say when he finds out the truth."

"He won't," Ryder said, his voice sharp. "It's not any of his damned business."

She arched an eyebrow at him. "You are so good, so kind, so wondrously chivalrous, why, I think I will cry."

"You could better consider keeping your mouth closed. It's not as if I don't much enjoy women," he said now, clearly irritated with her calm acceptance. "Dammit, Sophie, I have given five — five! — women their congé! I even made up a list of possible husbands for each of them. I will provide dowries for the three who wish to wed, and the other two are going to London and I am providing for them too. I am a lover in demand, and they are all saddened unto profound depression that I will no longer pleasure them."

She laughed. "Ah, Ryder, you are amazing, you know that? Truly amazing. You brag about your women and keep mum about your children. You know, I would never expect a man of your character to not take care when you climbed into a woman's bed. I'm very surprised that your brother knows you so little."

He sobered. "Don't blame Douglas. He only came home from the army less than a year ago. He believed what I told him, and as I told you, I am known for my prowess with women, far and wide, so my promised fidelity to you shakes him profoundly. He believes in true love because of it. Before, he merely accepted that lust ruled my head. As for him, he has a little girl nearly Jenny's age."

"Well, he is sure to suspect something is amiss with his opinions of you when he and Alex return to find a houseful of children."

Ryder cursed. "Damn Jane and her cursed measles!"

"It is fortunate that Chadwyck House is so very large. I fancy the east wing will accommodate all of them quite nicely. Indeed, I've already seen to their rooms — while you were ignoring me. Now, tell me about Jane. Do you think she would like to live here?"

"I don't know. Jane much enjoys her independence."

"Well, it's early yet. We will see. Doubtless she and I can work out something."

His face grew tight. A frown gathered on his brow. His lips thinned. Sophia looked on, fascinated. He kicked a pebble from his path. "You know, damn your so agreeable little hide, you could show a bit of jealousy. As my wife it would be thoroughly appropriate. I dislike your cursed understanding, your damned unctuous acceptance. It is fine, in its place, but its place isn't here, it isn't now. Damn you, Sophie, stop being so bloody tolerant."

"I've already attacked you with a broom. I am unable to jerk up one of the apple trees and cosh you with the trunk. However, if you insist on punishment, upon vituperation from a jealous wife, well then, you will have it."

She threw herself at him, hooking her foot behind his calf, and he went down, Sophie sprawled on top of him. She grabbed his hair to hold him still, then kissed him, every bit of his face, from his hairline to his earlobes.

"You sweetheart," she said, and kept kissing him. She pressed her belly against his and he moaned. She raised her head, looked at an apple tree just to her left and said, "Goodness, do you think we have enough bedding for all the children?"

"I am going to beat you, Sophie Sherbrooke."

"I hope you didn't give so much money to

all your former mistresses that we won't have enough to buy food for all those little mouths. Goodness, did you go into debt with all the gowns Mrs. Plack made for me? Three riding habits, Ryder, three! How is it possible for there to be a more generous, a more giving, a more magnanimous man in the whole world? Or at least in the whole Cotswolds?"

He grabbed his arms around her back and rolled over on top of her. "Now you listen to me, you damned thorn in my flesh. I refuse to accept your sweet kisses just because you've decided I'm not the scoundrel you believed me to be. Ha! Half of what you say is sarcasm and you don't cloak it well. You don't even try. You rub my nose in it. Now you think I'm this benevolent philanthropist, this saintly creature, and even said so in that mocking voice of yours. The whole idea makes me want to puke. Damn you, I'm barely a nice man; I am barely to be tolerated. Don't you dare continue your kisses and your good humor just because now you think I'm different and bloody worthy."

"All right," she said easily, and clasped her arms around his back. "You're still the same. I think you're a bastard, a bounder, a man without conscience, a clothhead who has no caring for anyone save himself and his own pleasures and —"

"Damn you, I'm not a bad man either. Ah, that's it, Sophie. No more of your agile tongue, that I — fool that I am — called forth myself. To think I begged you to give me back the hellion

433

I married. No more. I will not let you have the upper hand any longer. You do too well when I deign to let you have it. No, now I'm going to take the reins back and you're going to moan, not speak your damned banalities that enrage me."

"But, Ryder, you were embarrassed because your good deeds literally came home to haunt you."

He jerked up her gown, tore her shift, unfastened his britches, and plunged into her.

She couldn't believe that her body was warm and more than ready, truth be told, and she accepted him, craved him, the full length of him, and she lifted her hips to take more of him.

"Now do you feel dirty, damn you?"

She bit his shoulder, then licked the spot and moaned into his neck. He felt her hands pressing against his lower back, then against his buttocks, lifting her own hips even as she did so and he said again, "Do you feel dirty?"

"No." Then she cried out, and he took her cries into his warm mouth and took his own release.

"Do you still feel embarrassed?" she whispered against his throat.

"You're lucky I am an understanding and giving man," Ryder said.

"Yes, even to me, your wife."

"You will cease your taunts, Sophie."

"All right," she said, and kissed him full on his mouth.

It was at that moment, just when Ryder was ever so willing to resume their lovemaking, that Jeremy's voice came loud and clear. "Ryder! Sophie! Where are you? Melissa cut her hand and is yelling for you."

"What can one do?" Ryder laughed and rose, hauling Sophie up with him.

CHAPTER 20

Mrs. Chivers brought Sophie the plain envelope with only her name in straight block letters printed on the outside.

"The Meyers boy delivered it, ma'am," Mrs. Chivers said in a matter-of-fact voice. "Quite plain he is, looks just like his father."

"Thank you." Sophie's hand was shaking as she took the envelope, but Mrs. Chivers didn't notice. She walked quickly into the small back parlor that she'd appropriated for her own use, shut the door, and leaned back against it, just staring down at that envelope.

The contents weren't all that disturbing on the surface. She read:

> *You will meet me this afternoon at three o'clock beneath the old elm tree at the fork of the road that divides Lower Slaughter from Upper Slaughter. Don't be late and it would be wise not to tell your husband anything. I wouldn't want to have to kill him.*

It was signed with a simple "DL."

David Lochridge. Lord David.

Sophie walked away from the door and to her small desk. She sat down and placed the letter in the middle of the desktop and continued to stare at it. She didn't move, just stared and wondered what the devil she was going to do.

She had only two hours to decide.

"Sophie! Are you in here?"

The door was flung open and there was Sinjun, looking as beautiful and windblown as Ryder did when he galloped in from the fields. Her blue eyes sparkled, just as did Ryder's, with the simple pleasure of being alive.

Her expression stiffened in an instant.

"What's the matter? What happened?"

She was also as perceptive as her brother. "Nothing is the matter, Sinjun." Sophie rose. Slowly, very slowly, she folded the letter and slipped it into the envelope. What to do with it?

"I came to fetch you to luncheon. Unless, of course, you don't want to be part of the madhouse, which it will doubtless be. Ryder claimed he had a headache and was going to muck out stalls in the stable. I think Jane is probably right. She always says that adults should only dine with adults. Children only with children and guards."

Sophie smiled brightly. "Then we should continue with Jane's procedure. Have Mrs. Chivers tell Cook that the children will luncheon in the breakfast room. How many guards did Jane have?"

Sinjun laughed. "At least five."

"Good. See to it, please. Also, call in Ryder from the stables." And she laughed, she actually could laugh.

Sinjun left the room without demur and Sophie quickly put the envelope into the top drawer of her desk, way in the back, beneath some other papers.

Ryder returned quickly enough when he heard of the new arrangement from his sister. He and Sophie and Sinjun were the only ones who sat down to luncheon in the huge dining room. It was blessedly calm.

"This room is far too dark," Sinjun said as she forked a healthy bite of ham into her mouth.

"Yes," Sophie said, not raising her head. She made small piles of her food on her plate and proceeded to push the piles around.

"If you're sickening of something you'd best speak up," Ryder said sharply.

She dredged up a smile for her husband. "I'm fine, just a bit tired. Jenny had a nightmare last night, as you know. I had a difficult time going back to sleep."

Ryder frowned at her but held his peace. Actually, she'd fallen back to sleep instantly. It had been he who had worried about the nightmare for a good hour.

What the devil was wrong with her? Was she regretting welcoming the children here? Were they tormenting her? She wasn't used to bedlam and that's what seven children were. Or maybe

438

she was backsliding again. She'd made love to him sweetly the previous night, but who knew?

Sinjun, bless her oblivious heart, continued with her monologue about the refurbishing of the dining room.

Ryder took his leave after luncheon. He kissed Sophie lightly on her mouth, ran his fingertips over her eyebrows, studied her face, but saw nothing he could interpret. There was so much to be done, so many decisions to be made. He had to see Tom Lynch in ten minutes, a farmer of intelligence and sound common sense. Ryder sighed and took his leave and hoped doing nothing was what she needed right now.

As for Sinjun, she was quick to absent herself, saying only that she was going to play with the children.

At precisely three o'clock, Sophie pulled Opal to a halt beneath the elm tree, whose trunk was so thick and gnarly that it looked far older than the surrounding hills, probably older than all the goblins that supposedly lived burrowed under those hills.

She hadn't long to wait. Lord David rode up looking as arrogant and self-assured as he always had. An angel's face with a devil's heart.

She didn't say anything, merely waited.

"You lied to me," he said in a very pleasant voice.

"What a novel thing to say, considering the man who's saying it."

"You told me you had the pox. You said you

wouldn't be my mistress anymore because you didn't want to infect me. You lied. You don't have the pox else you wouldn't have married Ryder Sherbrooke. You just wanted to be rid of me."

"That's true."

"But that's absurd! Truly ridiculous. *You* not want *me* anymore?"

"It's true nonetheless."

"Ah, so you wanted Ryder Sherbrooke, and you knew you had to get rid of me else he could have found out about me, and if he had, why then, he would never have believed that you preferred him over me. Yes, if he'd known about me, he would have realized that you knew what a real man was like and wouldn't be taken in by the likes of him."

Sophie stared at him, wondering silently at the workings of his mind. "You think like no one I know," she said finally. "Besides, why do you care now? You told me you were going to wed an heiress. I can't imagine that you would want your betrothed to know about what you believe happened between us on Jamaica. Surely you cannot believe that I would say anything. You want this marriage to go forth, do you not?"

"I spoke to Charles Grammond. We've come to a decision."

She felt a frisson of uncertainty for the first time. Lord David was possessed of a mind that ran in only one direction; it was probably the key to his success at gambling. He couldn't be diverted or sidetracked or brought about to see another point of view. His voice had lowered, deepened, and in that instant, she saw him naked, standing in front of her, and he was laughing and drinking the rum punch, becoming sodden, becoming ready for Dahlia, thank God.

"What do you want, David?"

His back straightened and he threw back his head like a little king. "I am Lord David to a whore like you."

"What you are is a pathetic, corrupt, filthy-minded little bastard."

He raised his arm then lowered it. "No, I wouldn't want to bruise that lovely face of yours. Your husband would surely notice and Ryder Sherbrooke is a man I won't wish to have as an enemy."

Sophie supposed that she, as a woman, would never be accounted as an enemy worthy of notice. Well, she would tell him the truth and let him stew on it.

"I will tell you something else, *Lord* David. I never slept with you. Such a thought frankly turns my stomach. I never slept with any of the men. It was Dahlia, a girl you perhaps met in Montego Bay, always Dahlia at the cottage who came to see to you after you'd drunk yourself silly."

He looked startled, then laughed. "Don't tell me that is the tale you tried to pass off on Ryder Sherbrooke."

"It was all my uncle's idea. He forced me to

pretend to take you all for lovers so he could gain what he wanted for himself. The rum punch all of you drank with great enthusiasm was, quite simply, drugged. You being the way you are, most men being the way they are, why, it was very easy."

"Oh? And what did your uncle want from me?"

"He wanted you to ruin Charles Grammond so he would have to sell his plantation, which he did, to my uncle. Then, after you'd done what he wished you to do, he told me to dismiss you. The pox infection was his idea and it worked quite well. I remember you turned positively white with fear."

"You're lying. You will tell me no more lies. Your uncle was a gentleman who was distraught over your whoring ways. No one believed that you didn't murder him, even when Cole had it said about that your uncle was garroted by Thomas. And that damned Sherbrooke helped you escape Jamaica and punishment. Now you're blaming him! Jesus, a lady wouldn't even know what the pox is. You're no lady. You're nothing but a cheap little whore and both Charles and I have decided that we enjoyed you enough so that we'll continue our little trysts."

"As I said, you're pathetic and if you think I would ever allow you near me —"

"I'm near you now and I fully plan to get nearer."

"Ah, rape?"

He merely shrugged. "Your husband isn't a

442

stupid man, but just maybe he is where women are concerned. I don't pretend to fathom why the hell he married you when he could have simply taken you until he was bored with you. Oh no, Sophia, if you screamed rape to him, he would probably kill you, because once a whore always a whore."

"You make no sense, *Lord* David. You said you didn't want my husband for an enemy. He married me. He loves me. He wouldn't kill me, he would believe me, not you. He would kill you."

"Are you so ignorant of your husband's nature? Of his reputation? Like you, he must have a great deal of variety. You loved sex, God, you started on your career when you were barely eighteen. You want sex still, I doubt it not. You can't stay faithful to one man, even to Ryder Sherbrooke, who, I've heard, has bedded every woman who resides in Kent. Now he's in the Cotswolds and no woman will be safe from him. You'll see. He'll parade his mistresses under your nose and laugh. Well, my dear, Charles and I are going to allow you to continue with your ways just as he will with his."

He dug his heels into his stallion's sides, and came up close to her. He reached out his arms to her. Sophie raised her riding crop and brought it down hard on his arm. He yowled, jerking back.

"You're utterly mad!"

His face flushed with rage, but before he could

do anything, the silence was broken by what sounded like a pack of wild dogs, all howling in anger, growling deeply and viciously, bounding ready to attack, and to kill. Wild dogs in the Cotswolds?

"What the bloody hell!"

Sophie pulled Opal back from him. An arrow came flying through the air to land in Lord David's upper arm, just nicking it actually, but certainly ruining his superfine riding jacket. He screamed more in anger than in pain. He had no weapon. He had no way to defend himself against an unseen enemy.

"You brought someone, you perfidious bitch! This isn't over, you'll see!"

He wheeled his stallion about and was soon lost to her sight. Sophie just sat there, trying to breathe deeply. It was no surprise to her when the underbrush surrounding the road spilled out seven children, Jeremy, and Sinjun, all of them oddly silent after their sterling performance. Sinjun carried the bow. It had been she who had shot Lord David. Sophie climbed down from Opal's broad back.

Jeremy came to her and enfolded her in his arms.

"He's a bad man from Jamaica," the boy said. "I told Sinjun who he was."

"You did well." She raised her head. All the children, from four-year-old Jenny to ten-year-old Oliver, stood silent, all in a line, watching her. She wondered how they had known, then

444

decided she didn't want to know. She tried to smile but it was difficult. She said finally, "I was in trouble. Thank you all for your help. I truly believed a pack of wild dogs had somehow come along. You were splendid. I'm very proud of all of you."

Sinjun said quietly, "I didn't think you wanted Ryder to know just yet. We will figure out what to do, Sophie. You're not alone anymore. But Jeremy doesn't understand everything that happened on Jamaica. You need to tell me more."

"Yes, I will. Now, listen to me, all of you. I know that you all dearly love Ryder. But I beg you not to tell him of this. The bad man is as mean as a snake, he isn't honorable or good like Ryder. He wouldn't fight him fairly. I don't want Ryder hurt. Please don't say anything to him. All right?"

Amy said, "What's a hore?"

Tom slapped his hand over the little girl's mouth. "That's not a nice word. Don't say it again."

Amy, affronted, yelled back at Tom, "You say horrible words to Jaime all because Ollie said you grew up on the docks. You —"

Oliver got into the argument, waving one of his crutches about, and then Jenny said in a very carrying voice, "I want to go pull up my dress and visit Mrs. Nature."

Sophie felt something loosen inside her. She laughed, really laughed, and soon the children joined her, and it was Sinjun who carried Jenny off into the underbrush to visit Mrs. Nature.

Sophie realized on the way back to Chadwyck House that none of the children had promised her not to tell Ryder.

Jane and her two helpers were nearly recovered and would come to Chadwyck House within the next two weeks.

Sophie, who knew all about Jane now, realized that the woman wouldn't be happy living in another woman's household. There would be no problem. They would simply build another house in the small knoll that stood not one hundred yards from the main house. Ryder agreed and work would begin soon.

To Sophie's astonishment, Melissande decided after only one visit to Bedlam House, as Ryder had christened it, that perhaps having a child wasn't such a bad idea after all. All the children, even Jenny, told her over and over again how very beautiful she was. They were afraid to touch her for fear of somehow hurting her perfection. As for Melissande's husband, Tony, he groaned and said there was no hope for it. He was immediately taking her to London. "I can tolerate — just barely — some nodcock fool young man telling her that her eyebrows are like an artist's brush strokes, but all this nonsense from a pack of children? No, Sophie, it is too much. I will go into a decline if I have to hear much more."

Tony sighed deeply. Ryder laughed. Melissande beamed at all the children, patting every single head. She promised each of them a special sweet-meat on her next visit.

Ryder strode toward the house one afternoon, tired from a long day in the fields, speaking to many of his farmers. He'd also met with architects and arranged for artisans and workers for the new house. He'd also heard gossip about his gaggle of "bastards," and he'd gotten a good laugh from that. Just wait, he thought, just wait until there were a good fifteen children. Then what would the busybodies say? He wasn't at all surprised to realize that eventually, there would very probably be at least fifteen children, perhaps more.

It was a hot day, far too hot for this time of year, nearly Michaelmas now. He heard the children before he saw them. Always, they were ready for him. They had set up some kind of signal system. In another minute, many of them were there, escorting him to the house, all of them talking at once, even Jenny. She was talking like a magpie now and he realized it was his influence that had brought the rapid progress. He wouldn't let her out of his sight after this. He quickly forgot his fatigue; he laughed and listened to each of them and all of them at once, and silently thanked the good Lord yet again that none of them had come down with the measles.

And each night there was Sophie beside him, accepting him now, and he knew she enjoyed his body, knew that she looked forward to their time alone so she could touch him as much as she wished to, and accept his touches. Only last night, he had actually made her laugh when he was deep inside her. He felt good. He couldn't imagine the stars aligning themselves in a more propitious stance.

He was whistling until he found two letters in the top drawer of her desk. Sophie was in Lower Slaughter, three children and Laura and Sophie's maid, Cory, with her, buying cloth to make clothing. The seamstresses of Lower Slaughter — all three of them — were in alt because of the sudden manna from business heaven that showed no sign of ever diminishing. It was during Sophie's jaunt that Mrs. Chivers had complained to Ryder that the butcher was cheating them royally, and here they were, not royalty at all, and he really should do something about it and not spend all his time with those dirty farmers. And so he was looking in Sophie's desk for the butcher bills. And he found the letters from David Lochridge.

The second letter was even dated and the date was yesterday. He read:

I have made up my mind. You will become my mistress again. Charles Grammond will deal with you himself. I intend to enjoy myself again as I did on Jamaica. Come to the old Tolliver shack on the north side of your husband's property at three o'clock Thursday or you will regret it.

Signed merely "DL."

The damned bastard.

And damn Sophie's beautiful gray eyes. She'd said nothing; he'd known something was wrong. Indeed the previous evening, she'd wanted him urgently, too urgently, as if she wanted to keep something unpleasant at bay. But he hadn't questioned her; he'd merely given her what she'd wanted, what she'd appeared to need; he'd allowed her to escape this for the time she'd exploded into her climax.

She'd unmanned him with her silence.

He crumpled the letter in his fist, unaware that he'd even done it.

"Papa."

He looked up blankly. There was Jenny, standing in the doorway, looking from his face to the wad of paper fisted tightly in his hand.

Ryder forced himself to toss the crumpled paper back onto Sophie's desk. "Hello, pumpkin. Come here and let me hug you. It's been more than an hour since I've seen you — far too long."

Jenny raced to him and he raised her high in his arms and kissed her nose. "What is it you wish, little love?"

"Can you teach me to shoot a bow and arrow like Sinjun so I can shoot that bad man?"

He froze tighter than a spigot in January. "Certainly," he said. "Tell me about it, all right?" And she did. He would have laughed at all the children playing at being wolves if he hadn't been so angry. God, but they'd done well. Routed the bastard. And Sinjun, shooting him through the upper arm. Well done of her.

He'd strangle his sister once he got his hands on her.

Then he'd strangle his wife.

"Jenny! Where are you, pumpkin? Jenn—" Sinjun came through the doorway, stopped short, and immediately said, "Oh dear. Hello, Ryder. Whatever are you doing here? This is Sophie's room and —"

Ryder merely stared at his sister, words, for the moment, failing him.

Sinjun sighed. "I suppose Jenny said something?"

"You're not stupid, Sinjun. You are very quick to perceive when your perfidy has been discovered. It's a relief. I detest boring explanations. Yes. Jenny wants me to teach her how to shoot a bow and arrow so that she can shoot the bad man."

"Oh dear. I'm sorry, Ryder, but —"

He was controlled now. He said to Jenny as he disengaged her thin arms from about his neck, "Now, love, I want you to go with Sinjun. She's going to give you a biscuit and some lemonade. Papa must do some work now. All right?"

"Papa," Jenny said, and went immediately to Sinjun.

"Go," Ryder said to his sister. "This time, you will keep your mouth shut — to my wife."

"All right," Sinjun said, and her voice was very small, so small in fact, so diffident and timorous, that Ryder nearly smiled.

At two-thirty on Thursday, Ryder calmly pulled his horse to a halt some thirty yards away from the Tolliver shack. He tethered him next to some goat weed to keep him quiet.

He felt a mix of anticipation, rage, and excitement all coming together inside him. He wanted to see David Lochridge. He wanted, quite simply, to pound him into the ground.

He waited in the thick elm trees that bordered the shack, whistling behind his teeth, his excitement building and building. He wondered when Sophie would arrive. He wondered when Lochridge would get here.

However, it simply never occurred to him that another person would put in an appearance here, of all places. He was frozen in silent shock when an older woman pulled an old-fashioned gig to a halt in front of the shack not five minutes later. She was plump, wearing a stylish gown, a bonnet far too young for her, for she was in her mid-forties, he guessed, and she looked somewhat familiar, but that couldn't be. Good God, was she here for some sort of tryst? Was this shack used for illicit affairs?

He didn't move. He watched the woman climb down from the gig, and lead the old cob around to the back of the cottage, out of sight.

What the devil was going on?

Sophie and Lord David Lochridge arrived at the same time, from different directions. Both Ryder and the other woman were well out of sight.

Ryder watched as Sophie dismounted Opal, turned and said very clearly, her voice as calm as the eye of a storm, "I am here to tell you one last time, *Lord* David, that I will have nothing to do with you."

"Ah, you're still being the tease," he said, but Ryder saw him looking around. For more wolves? His eyes fell on the riding crop she held in her right hand.

"No, I'm not teasing you. When I saw you last I told you the truth. All that happened on Jamaica was my uncle's doing and I was never with you intimately at the cottage, with you or with any of the other men. Now, if you don't choose to believe me, why then, I guess I will just have to shoot you."

Ryder's eyes widened. She drew a small derringer from her pocket and pointed it at his chest.

Lord David laughed. "Ah, a lady with a little gun. Come, my dear, we both know you haven't the nerve to do anything with that toy, much less pull the trigger."

"I thought you said I murdered my uncle. If you believe that then how can you possibly believe that I wouldn't or couldn't pull the trigger on you?"

Lord David was in a quandary. He eyed her closely. He fidgeted; he cursed. Finally, he said, "Come, let's talk about this. There's no reason for violence. I'm merely offering you my body. It is for your pleasure, just as I pleasured you on Jamaica. Why are you being so unreasonable?"

"Unreasonable, am I? And what about dear Charles Grammond? Does he wish to continue your silly fictions as well? Will I have to face him down as I am you?"

"Charles isn't my problem. He will do what he wishes to do."

Sophie was now the one who looked thoughtful. "It would seem to me," she said at last, "that we are at something of an impasse. You wish to wed an heiress; Charles Grammond must be discreet or his aunt will kick him out and leave him no money in her will. That is what you told me, isn't it? All right, then, I won't kill you if you will cease all this damnable nonsense. Go away, David. Just go away and marry your poor heiress. I wish I could warn her about you but I realize that I can't, not without hurting my husband and his family. There will be no scandal for either of us. Do you agree?"

In that moment, Lord David raised his chin and whistled. In the next instant, an older man came up behind Sophie, grabbed her arms, and wrested the derringer from her.

"Ah, Charles, your timing is of the best, as usual."

"Yes," said Charles. "I've got you, Sophie. You're beautiful. I'd forgotten, but now that I've got you again, why David and I will share you, just as before."

Sophie turned and screamed in his face, "You

fool! You idiot! Don't believe David, he's a fraud, a bounder, he fleeced you out of all your money so that you lost your plantation on Jamaica!"

Good Lord, Ryder thought, staring at the man. It was Charles Grammond, one of Sophie's other lovers. Still he didn't move. He would have time to act. Besides, Sophie deserved to be frightened, just for a bit, for her perfidy.

But he realized he couldn't let her be frightened, not for an instant, not if he were there and could put an end to all of it. He stepped forward, but was forestalled by that other woman.

She came stomping forward around the side of the shack, there was no other way to describe it. Her cheeks were red, her bosom heaving. She was very angry.

"You let her go, Charles!"

The man stared at the vision coming toward him. He said in the most pitiful voice Ryder had ever heard, "Ah, Almeria. How come you to be here?"

"Let her go, you old fool. Are you all right, Sophia?"

"Yes, ma'am," Sophie said, staring at Almeria Grammond. Charles released her and she took two quick steps away from him. She was rubbing her arms.

Lord David looked flummoxed when Almeria Grammond turned on him. "As for you, you wretched cheat, I personally will see to it that this poor girl you intend to marry cries off. I will not have you for a neighbor!"

Ryder laughed, he couldn't help it. His excitement, his anticipation of at the very least breaking David Lochridge's face, had degenerated into farce, worthy of Nell Gwen and the Restoration stage.

He stepped forward. All eyes turned toward him. "A full complement now," he said, his voice as bland as the goat weed his stallion was reluctantly chewing. "Save, perhaps, for Lord David's betrothed."

"This is impossible," Lord David said. He was markedly pale and his long thin fingers were clenching and unclenching. "This should not be happening."

"One would think so," Ryder agreed easily. "You are Mrs. Grammond, I take it. I'm Ryder Sherbrooke, Sophia's husband. How do you do, ma'am?"

She gave him a slight curtsy, then looked at him more closely. Sophie watched, fascinated, as Mrs. Grammond's color rose again, only this time it was from the pleasure of Ryder's attention. Goodness, it appeared that a woman had to be on death's door before she was immune to him. Then she actually stammered. "A — a pleasure, Mr. Sherbrooke. Do forgive my husband. He is a nodcock. He has never had much sense, else Lord David wouldn't have ruined him. He won't bother your poor wife further."

"But how did you know?" Charles Grammond finally said, staring in utter horror at his wife.

She bestowed upon him a look of tolerant scorn.

"I always read any letters you receive. Most of them are from tradesmen and you have no notion of how to deal with tradesmen. I do. Your aunt and I have discussed this in great detail and have come to an understanding. However, when I found this letter from the little lordling here, the cheating weasel who ruined us, I realized what had happened. Naturally, he couldn't prevent telling you all about the supposedly nonsensical tale Sophia had told him about her innocence and her uncle's guilt.

"I knew Theo Burgess when he was young. Even as a young man, he was a pious little fake. He was the kind of man who preaches goodness to all mankind on Sunday and cheats his book-keeper out of a groat on Monday. Goodness, it was all very clear to me. In addition, of course, I followed you one night to that cottage and saw this other girl. You are such a fool, Charles. I won't allow your stupidity to prevent me and the children from living as we ought. You will now apologize to Mrs. Sherbrooke and to Mr. Sherbrooke and take yourself home. I will deal fully with you later."

Charles Grammond said, "I apologize, Sophia, Mr. Sherbrooke." He then looked at Lord David and frowned. "Surely you will no longer insist that she's a whore."

"She is, damn her!"

Ah, at last, Ryder thought, rubbed his hands together, and strode to Lord David, who had put up his hands in the stance of a prizefighter.

Ryder laughed for the sheer joy of it, and knocked him flat.

Mrs. Grammond clapped her plump hands together.

Sophie, still stunned, simply stood there like a mute idiot.

Lord David came up on his elbows and shook his head. "I'm quite good at fighting. You knocked me down. It shouldn't have happened. Who taught you?"

"Stand up and we'll see if you can't improve," Ryder said and offered him a hand.

Lord David wasn't, however, a complete fool. He stayed on the ground. He said to Charles Grammond even as he was turning to leave as his wife had told him to, "You can't allow your wife to tell Agnes — the heiress's bloody name is Agnes! — about all this! Her father would ruin me. He would see that I was run out of the county."

Charles Grammond never slowed. He disappeared into the elm trees. His wife, however, turned to the felled Lord David.

"You're a poltroon, sir. However, I will make you a bargain. I won't say a word to your betrothed's father if you return all the money you cheated my husband out of on Jamaica."

Lord David turned white. "Madam, I haven't a sou. Why do you think I'm marrying this awful female named Agnes?"

"That, my lord, is your affair," said Mrs. Grammond, and she actually sniffed. "I expect to hear from you within three days, no more, else you will surely regret it. And don't think you can threaten to ruin the Sherbrookes with your nasty little stories. Both my husband and I will make certain everyone knows you're a liar.

"Now, Mr. Sherbrooke, Mrs. Sherbrooke, I do hope these two fools haven't overly upset you. There will be no more threats or problems from either of them. Good day to you both." She gave Ryder the sweetest smile imaginable, nodded briskly to Sophie, kicked dust in Lord David's face, and marched around the shack to where her gig was stationed like a waiting army.

Ryder laughed. He couldn't help it.

Sophia said in a wondering voice, "The Virgin Bride was right. She said when they came it would work out all right."

"There is no bloody ghost," Ryder said. "Just stop it. It was a lurid excuse for a nightmare that you hadn't yet had." He turned to Lord David, who was now sitting cross-legged in the dirt, shaking his head as he stared at his dusty boots. "As for you, you will keep your mouth shut. Unlike Mrs. Grammond, I won't content myself with ruining you. I'll kill you. Do you understand me?"

Lord David sighed deeply, and nodded. He was clearly distracted. He said on another deep sigh, "I wonder if I can convince the chit to elope with me. It's the only way I can get the money in three days."

Sophie and Ryder just looked at each other.

EPILOGUE

Ryder leaned down and kissed the nape of her neck, her flesh warm and soft against his mouth. She sighed and said nothing, merely leaned her head back against his belly. He kissed her forehead, then moved to her ears, his hands lightly encircling her throat, caressing her jawline with his thumbs. She sighed again and tried to turn to face him, but he held her still.

"You taste so bloody good," he said, and kissed her neck one more time. He ran his hands down her arms, then sighed himself, and released her. "No time, dammit, to show you what other uses one can make of a desktop." He eyed the very feminine writing desk, adding, "We will take great care if ever we make use of this feeble-looking thing. Perhaps I could simply have you lean against it —"

"Ryder!"

He gave another long-suffering sigh and came over to repose himself against the writing table, crossing his arms over his chest. "I'm testing its strength," he said. "For future reference." He looked down at the list of numbers. "What are you doing?"

"Adding up the accounts for Brandon House. Soon, my dear, next week, I think, we will have an exodus. Jane and I are planning a party. Jane's impatient."

"It's not that Jane complains, exactly," he said. "But she is looking forward to moving into her new house. The children as well."

"I will miss them."

"The little heathens will be only a hundred yards distant. Whenever you want madness, it's just a short walk away."

"How is little Garrick?"

Ryder immediately sobered. His eyes narrowed and his jaw tightened. Sophie patted his fisted hand. "He's safe now."

"Yes, he is. Dammit, Sophie, how could that bastard treat a four-year-old child like that?"

"There are many more like him, more's the pity, children sold as apprentices to such brutes as that chimney cleaner, Mr. Ducking. But you saved Garrick, and now he will learn that life can be more than pain and tears. He smiled at me this morning. He and Jenny are becoming great friends. I love you, Ryder."

His jaw loosened, and he smiled. "Yes, and well you should love me very much, woman, since I give you my poor man's body every night for your diversions."

"You make me sound unnatural in my appetites."

"Your appetites are wonderful. Have you yet started your monthly flow?"

His bald speech still could disconcert her, leaving her tongue-tied. She gave him a bemused smile and shook her head.

He leaned forward and caressed her belly with the palm of his hand. "Perhaps our son or daughter is beginning?"

"Perhaps," she said, and she stared at his mouth. He'd taught her over the months to enjoy kissing as much as he did.

"Stop that, Sophie. There is no time, unfortunately." Still, he leaned over and quickly kissed her soft mouth. He would never forget the night when he was nipping at her bottom lip as he was telling her the story of the farmer who fell in love with his prize pig, when all of a sudden, she giggled, and bit his chin, and said she fancied a prize bull.

It was the first time their lovemaking had been filled with laughter and silliness and nonsense. He looked fondly at her mouth, shrugged, and kissed her again.

"My brother, Alex, and Sinjun will be here very soon now."

"Yes," she said, breathless now.

"Damn him."

She blinked. "Ah, this dog-in-the-manger attitude of yours, Ryder, you really must stop it. Allow poor Douglas to enjoy himself, to feel useful."

461

"He doesn't have to take my children away."

"He has given Oliver a tremendous opportunity, admit it. Someday he will be the earl's assistant steward, perhaps eventually even his steward or his secretary. Oliver will make something of himself. He will be properly educated. Douglas is very fond of him."

"Damn him."

Sophie just grinned at her husband. "I shall never forget when Douglas and Alex walked in, completely unexpected, and all the children were shrieking and playing and eating and yelling in the entrance hall because it was raining outside, and Douglas just stood there as calm as a preacher, and said, 'I have surely come to the wrong house.'"

Ryder remained stubbornly silent. He tapped his fingertips on the desktop.

"Douglas did take your revelations well, Ryder. He accepted what he saw as your lack of confidence in him, though I know it hurt him. He didn't yell at you, as I know he wanted to."

"That was because Amy had climbed up his leg and he was forced to pick her up and she was telling him that he was pretty."

"Your family is very proud of you."

"I never wanted their pride. Don't you understand? It's something I just do because it's important to me, it means something, and there's nothing saintly about it, Sophie. It costs me nothing, really. I would that every Sherbrooke would shut his and her respective mouth. It becomes excessive, and downright embarrassing."

"Your mother doesn't embarrass you."

"No, she refuses to speak to me for dirtying my hands with slum brats. It's a refreshing attitude from a family member, and so I've told her. She didn't laugh when I encouraged her to maintain her censure. Now, who is that letter from over there?"

"From Jeremy. It just arrived an hour ago. He is well and enjoying his studies." She picked up the two pages to look at them again.

Ryder grabbed them and began to read. Soon he was nodding and smiling. "Good. He thrashed that wretched little bully, old Tommy Mullard's son. Tommy was always a coward, big mouth and all threats, until one simply slammed one's fist into his lard belly. You see, Sophie, I was right to teach Jeremy how to fight mean and dirty. I even taught him how to kick with his lame foot. Lord, did he ever become good. Sinjun even played his adversary, poor girl. She had many bruises on her shins before he left for school. And don't be fooled, boys at school can be cruel. It's encouraged, unfortunately, you know, the old theory of toughening up our young aristocrats, making real little stiff-lipped soldiers out of them. But Jeremy is holding his own. It helps that he's the best rider at Eton." Ryder rubbed his hands together, such was his pleasure.

Sophie thought she would burst with love for him at that moment. He was a remarkable man, but the hint of someone actually saying it, giving him even a modicum of praise, made him turn red with embarrassment, and defensive to the point of yelling. She said only, "It also helps that he's part of the Sherbrooke family."

"Of course," Ryder said, and continued reading.

He had barely finished the letter when the door burst open and Sinjun came dashing in. The room seemed to lighten with her presence.

"My dear," Sophie said and quickly rose to give her sister-in-law a hug.

"Ah, Douglas and Alex are right behind me. I raced ahead so I could see you first. You both look wonderful. Is that a letter from Jeremy? I got one three days ago. He told me all about how he beat the stuffing out of this dolt bully, and —"

"Enough, brat! Hello, you two."

The Earl of Northcliffe strode into the room, his wife on his arm. "You won't believe what I have to tell you, Ryder. Oliver has quite impressed my steward and all my tenants. I took him around and introduced him to everyone, and you wouldn't believe his questions — intelligent and thoughtful, all of them. Jesus, I was so proud of him. And now he has no limp at all. Oh, hello, Sophie. You look well. Here's Alex."

Sophie could only laugh as she watched the shifting and myriad expressions on her husband's face.

"Oh, another thing," Douglas said before Ryder could vent his spleen, if venting were indeed what he had in mind, "Alex is pregnant. We will have a babe in May. What do you think about that?"

No one had time to think about anything. Alex turned suddenly very white, gasped, and looked helplessly up at her husband. "I can't believe you did this to me. I'm going to be sick."

She ran from the room. Douglas shook his head. "I hope she misses that beautiful Aubusson carpet," he said, and turned to run after her.

Ryder and Sophie looked at each other. Sinjun stared after her departed brother and sister-in-law. "Goodness, I don't know if I wish to ever have a babe. Alex is always being sick at the most inopportune times. I think I would prefer having another Bedlam House, like yours and Sophie's, Ryder."

"It's Brandon House," Ryder said. "After dear departed Uncle Brandon. Sophie says that it will speed his way from the depths of hell. She thinks he might even gain purgatory, but only if we use his money and not the money we earn ourselves."

"Alex is pregnant," Sophie said, bemused. "Just fancy that."

"It happens, you know, particularly when one and one's wife perform all the proper rituals. Oh yes, Sophie might be pregnant too," Ryder said, turning to his sister.

"That leaves only Tysen," Sinjun said. "Oh dear, he plans to marry that girl you can't stand, Ryder, you know, the one with two names — Melinda Beatrice — and no bosom. Then there's only me left."

"You have all the time in the world, brat."

They heard the unmistakable sounds of someone being vilely ill. "Yes," Sinjun said fervently, "I do have all the time in the world, thank God. Do you know that just last week Alex got ill right in front of Hollis. He never turned a hair. He said in that royal way of his, 'My lady, I do believe you should carry a handkerchief in the future.' He gave her his. Then he instructed that a covered chamber pot be placed in every room. He conducted Alex on a tour to show her where each one was located. Oh, congratulations, Sophie. You feel all right, don't you?"

"Of course. I won't get sick on your slippers. Thank you, Sinjun. But we don't know yet if it's true or not. Ryder is just being optimistic."

"Not optimistic. Her monthly flow is late, by four whole days."

"Ryder! Sinjun isn't yet sixteen!"

Sinjun only shrugged and looked very world-weary. "I have three brothers, Sophie, and two of them are outrageous. I can't be shocked, I don't think."

"As for you," Sophie said, turning back to face her husband, "you will mind your tongue in front of your sister."

"But I was going to tell her the story about the eccentric Mr. Hootle of Bristol who wed every woman who would have him. He had this compulsion, you see, and every time a woman smiled at him, he lost all judgment, and dropped down to his knees to propose."

"That," Sophie said with approval, "is quite a proper tale. You may continue. One hopes it becomes more edifying."

"Then one day when he was on his knees, one of his other wives came upon him and his soon-to-be-betrothed. The two women compared what they knew and were not pleased. They took him away to a small room, took all his clothes and locked him in. Then they sent in all these other women, two at a time, all naked as sin, to prance and parade in front of him, and the poor man was tied down so he couldn't fall to his knees and propose or do anything else —"

"Enough! You are dreadful." Sophie fell against him, laughing and kissing his chin.

Ryder looked fondly at the writing desk behind him. Sinjun sighed. "Well, I see I shan't get any more sensible conversation from either of you. I shall go see Jane and the children."

When the door closed, Ryder said to his wife, "I saw the Virgin Bride last night."

Sophie stared at him. "You saw the ghost? Truly? But gentlemen don't believe in her, that's what Douglas and you are always saying."

"I was wrong," Ryder said. "She floated in our bedchamber last night, visiting, I imagine, for she supposedly never strays from Northcliffe Hall. Anyway, she smiled down at me, and said something, but not really, you know, but I heard her words clear and calm in my mind."

"Yes, that was exactly how it was with me. What did she tell you?"

"She said, even as she glittered and shimmered all over me, that we had the possibility of having fourteen children. She said it was all a matter of me stiffening my resolve if we were to have these children in this lifetime."

"You are going to suffer for that, Ryder, you surely are."

"You promise?" He kissed his wife, and knew such pleasure that he wanted to yell with it. He released her, and locked the door. He methodically stoked the fire, then turned back to his wife. "The Virgin Bride must know what she's about. The good Lord knows you women believe every supposed word she doesn't say. Very well then. Let's get to it, madam."

The employees of G.K. HALL hope you have enjoyed this Large Print book. All our Large Print titles are designed for easy reading, and all our books are made to last. Other G.K. Hall Large Print books are available at your library, through selected bookstores, or directly from us. For more information about current and upcoming titles, please call or mail your name and address to:

G.K. HALL
PO Box 159
Thorndike, Maine 04986
800/223-6121
207/948-2962